THE DAEDAL PIT

SISTER SEEKERS BOOK 3

BY
A.S. ETASKI

Published by Corpus Nexus Press
ISBN: 978-1-949552-05-8

etaski.com
etaski.com/sister-seekers
miurag.etaski.com
www.patreon.com/etaski
www.goodreads.com/etaski
www.bookbub.com/authors/a-s-etaski
www.facebook.com/asetaski
mastodon.online/@etaski

Cover Design by Eris Adderly
Book layout by DocKangey

Dedicated to the unwaveringly curious, in delight and delirium.

CHAPTER 1

MY NAKED BODY STREAKED ACROSS A LOW, DAMP BASIN SOME DISTANCE OUT-
side of the guarded boundary of Sivaraus. Leaping over the odd puddle
without a speck of light to go by, breathing in the cool vapor drifting
off the weeping stone, I climbed farther up and then down again into a
smaller, drier cavern, searching for the path that might lead me home.

I had been allowed one blade, like the first time, to defend myself
should I run into a threat other than the one I expected. The largest
creature I had encountered so far was a juvenile lizard escaped from a pen
or one of the rarer, wild ones. I had paused, decided she was too small to
ride, and left.

My time was spent in near-constant motion, traveling upon silent,
tough feet. I could have tried for a defensible place to hide, but that
would neither get me closer to my challenge line and victory nor did I
want to be cornered and dragged out of a hole by my ankle like some
furry yuru. Again.

She loves to play when there's time for it.

It *was* possible to evade her, to make it back to Sivaraus if I kept
moving. If I managed it, it would be another notch upon my novice's
belt.

Inevitably, I became winded and slowed to a walk. The tunnel was too broad and high for comfort once I heard something far off behind me. I scanned the stone, and the flow of Radiants revealed a smaller offshoot, a tunnel just large enough to walk upright if I hunched over.

I listened outside it, my keen hearing in full service as my heart slowed to normal, subtle drips and scurries of small creatures confirmed it wasn't a dead-end or a den. It may be rather short, at the same time turning me back in the direction I wished to go.

I climbed in, inhaled to gain a sense of what lay ahead. Nothing too different from the moist pathways and tiny caverns I'd been exploring thus far, although I was careful where I placed my feet.

The right environment for pincerworms.

Making it to the end of the passage, I slowly extended my leg down, one long step into the next cavern. Another pause and I spotted an exit tunnel on the other side leading in the right direction.

I smiled in total darkness. *Another step closer to home.*

Clearing the ceiling and the open floor first, I chose a direction and followed the cave's perimeter, fingertips lightly touching the wall now and then. My scalp and nipples inexplicably tightened, then the rest of my naked skin followed as a shuddering frisson gripped me. I stopped in front of an oddly placed boulder streaked with exposed quartz, ragged as scars.

I could not fail to recognize the spell laid upon that quartz.

Danger. Threat. Leave.

A direct message. I'd be a fool to discard it.

But it's a Davrin ward.

Way out here?

Caught in place, I weighed my choices. The Noble I'd been would wisely walk away. That Third Daughter wouldn't even be out here in the first place. Yet, the Red Sister I was now would be expected to take advantage of an opportunity, *any* opportunity, and especially those from other Davrin which may threaten the Valsharess.

This is why the Sisterhood exists.

Another Dark Elf had placed this warning here, and I had no way of knowing if my Elder, Varessa D'Shea, knew about it. If she didn't, she needed a report from me more useful than my saying it was here. She had always expected me to investigate further, to follow my instincts.

She always will.

As a novice starting out, I'd been issued bracers which helped me overcome magical wards. I was trained to break those spells typical of the average Noble and merchant talent should I need to enter where they did not wish me to go.

On the stronger ones set by the Priestesses and a few "top tier" Sorceresses, I'd made progress but disrupting them still came at too high a cost for me. I had passed out and woke later with a crippling headache for the rest of the wake cycle.

No bracers to protect my mind and body or to help me focus, and only a handful of Red Sisters I knew could take on a Priestess ward with their bare hands and naked will. The Lead Sisters, Jaunda and Qivni, were two of those, and my Elders seemed confident that, soon enough, I may become another one.

They think so because of my abnormality.

I was the only Elf in Sivaraus sensitive to the mind mages of the Deepearth, our psionic enemies: the Tragar Dwarves and the Ornilleth thought flayers. I could sense their presence, and I could do a few of the simpler mental tricks: link minds, share memories, detect "loud" thoughts nearby.

One reason I hadn't run into any problems out here so far.

My Elders kept this warped trait of mine a secret for now, as did I, for I would surely be executed or imprisoned, given to the Priesthood to study. D'Shea and Rausery would protect me from the Prime's distrust or the Priesthood's clutches in exchange for new discoveries for use as a defense against these enemies, or for the revival of those minds struck down by them.

I had achieved that second goal by accident. My Sister Reishel had been struck down in the last battle with the Ornilleth. She had come out of her coma and was back with us.

My Elders wanted this, wanted more of it, and I wanted it, too. But eventually, they would also want me pitching stones through the air without hands like a Tragar or searing a mind to incapacitate the body with pain, like an Ornilleth.

In time, they might want me to bend the will of another and command them. To make my own thrall army or control a politically advantageous Davrin like a puppet.

If we went *that* far, I didn't see myself having a place in Davrin society ever again, no matter who controlled me: Sisterhood, Priesthood, or the Queen of Sivaraus. But I didn't see a lot of other options.

I swallowed my apprehension once again.

One cycle at a time. Let's see what the strength of this ward is. Start there.

Touching the quartz stone with my bare hand hurt, sudden and sharp, but I applied what I knew about magical pain being transient, how it did not damage the body unless one believed it would and held on to it. Any ward like this began as a trick; the magic tried its hardest to convince you the pain was real harm. If you believed this, it became harmful in truth.

~*Do not believe it.*~

I bit the inside of my cheek to keep from making any noise, the surge of magic enfolding my body. A sensation like a thousand moths beating their wings rippled against my thoughts.

~*Let the pain pass through. Yes.*~

My bare feet grounded me. I could see the flow begin at my hands only to seek a useless mark within the stone beneath me, the power dissipating.

~*Perfect. Good. Move the rock. Discover what the Priestesses are hiding.*~

My Elders needed to know.

I had managed to get past the first trick of pain; my control was the best it had ever been, with or without the bracers. But the moment I tried to push the stone without breaking the ward, the second stage of the spell arose, and it was far more powerful than the first.

A massive shadow-fear swept over me like a rancid flood, disrupting my calm breath, barreling into my thoughts like a stampede of demons, turning my knees to water as I stumbled.

Leave! Threat! Run. RUN.

~*Pain! Fear! Release, release now!*~

My mouth opened, though the scream erupted from my mind. I did not know how long I was stuck there, but the boulder had not shifted before I surged to my feet and sprinted several long strides away.

When I stopped, quivering, I fell to my knees and gasped harder than I had in my jog getting here. I came back to myself eventually, I recognized my surroundings and hadn't pissed myself.

That's something, at least.

I was still inside the small cavern, and this ward was Priestess level for certain. The compulsion of that spell was to run and *not* stop, to keep going until my body was unable to take another step, possibly a cycle from now.

I had resisted that punishment somehow, had stopped before I ran blindly into danger I didn't see coming. I was learning, my will and understanding growing stronger.

But I can't try again. Can't risk it.

I kneeled behind a different large stone now, one where I could still see the quartz, and I remained in place for much longer than I should have. I stared at the shock of white crystal in the dark, trying to glean anything more about it as if my Dark Sight could pierce right through to whatever hole it was hiding. I assumed it was a passageway; otherwise, why place a ward there?

Still, I knew no more after the fear and shaking subsided than I had when I first touched it; D'Shea would be disappointed.

I heard a subtle scrape in the dark. Then it went still.

I looked up first. In the wilderness, one should *always* look up. My eyes adjusted, spotting movement beyond the camouflage.

Spider leg —

I gasped.

The Dread Spider shrieked as if nine voices of the Abyss sang in disharmony.

Fuck!!

I ran full out then because freezing in place was instant death. Running wasn't much better — Driders were predators and loved pursuit — but I *had* to move if I had a prayer of thinking! I ran toward a lower tunnel opposite from where I'd climbed in. My mind flew with my feet, body and will, working in tandem.

She was guarding the ward.

If that was true, there must be set points the monster couldn't pass, having been placed here by Auranka the Keeper. This, of course, meant the Valsharess had ordered that ward to be set by someone. Probably the Priesthood.

Shit. What did I stumble into?

The creature behind me embodied the clash of Braqth's Curse and the Goddess's Blessing, an affliction sometimes viewed as a reward but more often feared as punishment.

Although a Davrin became one of the most potent guardians in Sivaraus, an avatar of our Goddess, and would never age, the Dark Elf's mind was stripped away by the transformation, reduced to the fundamental instincts of hunting and killing. No self-awareness, no memories, no true will.

A beast of empty thought.

The whispers of Sivaraus said a Dread Spider bore only the lingering sense that it never wanted to be aware of what it had become.

I'd never spoken this blasphemy aloud but had thought for many turns that only a Queen of the Void would try to convince us this was, in any way, a desirable reward for an Elf.

The Drider screeched again, and I shuddered as distilled hunger and rage washed over my senses. I gave in to the urge to glance behind. I was sorry I did, even if the terror helped me gain distance in a surge of speed.

The lower part of the twisted hybrid was the abdomen of an enormous spider; the upper half was mostly that of the Davrin torso, nude from the waist up. Her face was somewhat recognizable as an Elf, except for the glossy mandibles warping the mouth, the extra set of empty eyes, and the deformed hands with fingers that had fused together to form pincers.

Some hair on the head remained, but it was matted, unkempt, coming out in patches while growing back randomly. Veins of tainted Radiants pulsed through both the neck and the malformed waist where it met the hard, bulbous part — a detail which hadn't been in Headmaster Phaelous's Drider constructs outside the Wizard's Tower.

Nor had they that sick, fetid smell.

I didn't know how far she might follow me out of the cavern, but I repeated to myself — prayed — that she *had* to stop somewhere! The next scream almost made my ears bleed as I beat her to the next tunnel by several, precious ticks, but soon I heard her squatting down and scrambling in after me.

She had slowed down but wasn't stopping, and some piss finally dribbled out of my bladder. Maybe I'd only live if I found a small tunnel too small for her to fit before she caught up with me—

Coming around a curve, Jaunda and I slammed into each other. Expelling a lurid curse, she caught her feet while I fell flat on my back. My dagger was still in my grip.

"Lead!" I cried, so glad to see a fully equipped Sister, even as Jaunda roughly hauled me to my feet, cuffed my ear hard, and shoved me forward.

"Move, cait!" she bellowed, spinning around to stand between me and the Drider.

She was already in motion for what happened next; something had been in her hand even before we'd collided. Recognizing the sturdy bottle of alchemist's fire along with the igniting pouch, I launched into a sprint as she snapped the round top off the bottle and poured the last component into it.

The Drider skittered toward her, and Jaunda pitched it before running to catch me.

Shutting my eyes against the bright flare of light, I heard the whoosh and the shriek simultaneously, the scent of magical fire and a wave of scalding air rushing at my back. The fire would burn upon the rocks for some time and drain the tunnel of breathable air fast. Even if the Drider might approach the light — I wasn't sure but didn't dare look this time, only to be blinded — she *must* retreat to her cavern or suffocate.

Blessed or cursed, she still breathes air like the rest of us.

I coughed more than Jaunda when we reached a larger cavern with more air, my lungs burning. I thought that now the Hunt must have ended.

She caught me.

Well, I'd run right into her.

Regardless, I didn't make it to the border. I was leaning over, hands on my knees and trying not to puke in a rock-hole somewhere far from victory. Jaunda could do what she wanted with my naked ass, that was the deal.

Even as I thought this, my Lead strode up to me. I expected her to grab my hair — kept longer than hers for a reason — and maybe pull out her Feldeu to force my mouth down onto it. I wished my head wasn't swimming so I might enjoy it.

But then Jaunda passed by me, left me unmolested for the moment, and reached behind a rock to haul out another Davrin whose hands were bound behind her with a choke rope around her neck.

I stared at the other naked Red Sister.

Reishel.

My peer in the Hunt hadn't made it, either. In fact, by the looks of her knees, she had been caught a while ago and dragged along while Jaunda next hunted for me.

Part of me waited — *hoped?* — for our Lead to pull the two of us somewhere safe to receive our comeuppance at the tip of her magic staff, but I got my first hint that I should take the near miss with the Drider more seriously when Jaunda cut Reishel free, both wrists and neck.

Move, caits, she signed with her red-glove hand, her strong face hard set. *We return now. Hustle.*

We did, although the fatigue of the long hike started to show.

If Jaunda felt cranky for not getting her playtime, with our twin dirt stars and drooling slits presented before her before going back on duty, she wasn't letting us see. Reishel and I shared a look, knowing better than to voice any disappointment or apology.

Playtime was over. The Game in Sivaraus continued.

CHAPTER 2

LEAD QIVNI MET US IN THE LIZARD STABLES OF THE CLOISTER. A SCOWL LASTing more than a tick was rare with Jaunda. The Sisterhood's Warrior Lead, with her short-cropped hair and tall lift to her ears, appeared relaxed when we made it back. Reishel and I were still naked, our uniforms left here.

In contrast, a frown was the resting expression for the Mage Lead, and while the muscular power of Jaunda suited her frame and attitude, I thought Qivni would look better in silk robes of some office like Elder D'Shea.

That wasn't to say Qivni hadn't molded her own body to hold her own in combat, but I'd also heard her banish a demonblood back to the Sanctuary with a complicated Abyssal snarl. I wasn't sure anyone else could do that.

Jaunda and Qivni didn't even have to hand sign; the latter led us silently to a room where we wouldn't be observed. My Lead pulled out the black bag she used for captives and put it over Reishel's head, instructing her to kneel off to the side and wait. She obeyed, and my skin prickled as both Leads looked at me.

What the fuck had I done now?

I intercepted a message from the Sanctuary, Qivni signed, her reddish-brown eyes flicking to me. ★I am to see the Prime receives it. Sirana needs to stay in the Cloister until then.★ Her usual frown deepened in concentration. ★Did you discover a lair?★

★Yes,★ Jaunda replied. ★An accident. We weren't looking for it.★

★I understood you did some damage.★

★Wasn't going to let her eat us.★

Qivni nodded, and my stomach tightened up a little more as undefined fears crept into clarity. The Sisterhood had to answer to the Priesthood for the clash with the Drider. Not good for me. I should have left, but maybe it had been too late even before I discovered the ward.

Both Leads appeared as though they had questions for me but refrained. Among Nobles, I'd have assumed this was to prevent juicy details being heard by the other as they vied to get me alone later. Here, it was more mutual discipline respecting the same Elders, adding a touch of self-preservation.

Jaunda slapped me on the back, and I caught myself, wincing at the sting between my shoulder blades.

"You and Reishel, go wait. Don't talk."

She pulled Reishel free of the black bag, who took it as a sign to stand, and my Sister and I left with a double, "Yes, Lead."

Sweaty, dirty, and tired, we stopped by the sluicers for a quick, cold wash and left as soon as possible, drying off with small, thin towels as we walked the curving, strangely lit halls of the Cloister. There was a kit to help the scrapes without wasting healing potions along with our red leathers and equipment locked away in Gaelan's room.

Once again, I forcibly suspended her ward before jiggering the lock to let us inside.

"You're getting good at that," Reishel commented.

"Need to try other rooms or mages," I remarked. "Nice of her to switch up the effect as she does."

"Lets you practice without getting your ass beaten."

I grinned, opening the door to let us in.

I had been a Red Sister for just over a turn now, and I had seniority over two in the Sisterhood: Reishel and Jael, the latter being the true youngest, initiated only in the last turn.

Reishel was technically under me in rank yet had been in the Sister-hood much longer. She had returned first from a coma after a psionic attack and survived both the wilderness and the Prime.

The First Sister had satisfied her own doubts about the youth's will-power, though Reishel had been tested to within a finger-width of her life. If not for Elder D'Shea and me, she would be dead.

As it was, the Sisterhood had the first Red Sister in our history to come back after being struck down by an Ornilleth. Reishel had dropped down to the bottom rung in exchange for being given a second chance.

Given access to our uniforms, we didn't put them on yet but tended to superficial wounds from the chase. We relaxed and, having been forbidden to talk about what I had found, soon put our mouths to some other use.

~Suck me ... ~

Resting belly-to-belly, our heads between each other's thighs, we licked to release the tension built up but never satisfied. Our noses nuz-zled fur and folds; tongues tasted our scents and juices as we distracted ourselves from the waiting.

I floated in leisured pleasure, stroking and squeezing Reishel's but-tocks above my forehead, tugging her clit with my lips and prodding her pucker with a thumb. Gasping, she served me earnestly in return. A rush of concern accompanied her efforts.

~Are you alright? What happened? What did you find?~

These weren't words of any spoken language; it was not even a distinct voice. Just a skimming thought or sense of emotion; a hint of her state of being, her current mind. This sometimes happened when we had sex, ever since D'Shea had brought the revived Red Sister back from the brink. The Sorceress had used a mindlink spell with me, my own willpower entwining with Reishel's, preserving a starving mind while her body struggled to heal.

It was better for both my Sister and me, less frightening, if we let it lie. Allow it to come and pass through.

My crotch was good and hot; I pressed it harder against her sliding mouth. I added a second, lubricated finger to her netherhole, spread them to stretch her ring and make her squeak against my mound. ~*I'm alright. I found ...* ~

What had I found? Something to do with the Sanctuary and my Elder would want to know if she didn't already.

Threat and opportunity. Never anything else in Sivaraus. Otherwise, the Spider Queen might get bored.

Reishel felt my fear, and she sucked me harder; I felt my intrigue and sucked her right back. The both of us so aroused, we whimpered and writhed in a sloppy, mutual release. Waves of warmth and satisfaction hidden from the other Sisters.

Mostly.

My face sticky from cheeks to chin, I fell back from her humid treasure and drew in a fresh, cool breath. A pair of red leather boots stood on either side of my head, and my gaze followed the long pair of red-clad legs up to the armored bust and smirking expression of D'Shea's favorite conduit mage.

"Void take me, Gaelan," I uttered in surprise. "How did you get in so quietly?"

"It's my room. You're welcome." She set down a supply satchel, released her cloak like she intended to rest. "What are you doing back? I assumed Jaunda would still be reaming you two by turns in a stock-lock somewhere. She doesn't get much time off. Wrings it for all it is worth."

I grimaced as Reishel climbed off me and we sat up, mirroring expressions of guilt. She spoke first. "Can't talk about it."

"Uh-oh." Gaelan didn't ask more, deftly changing the subject. "Elder Rausery is out in a 'no magic' training exercise with the Prime."

"Again?" Reishel griped. "Third group this quarter."

"She's rotating." Gaelan sat down in uniform at her workbench, unpacking her satchel. It was all spell components. "I can hardly keep up with the potion demand when they come back, though. Their mock weapons aren't blunted enough."

"I heard they're all pitched skirmishes against each other," I said. "What does the Prime expect? A bunch of House Guard will turn guerrilla against the Valsharess's Army?"

"Always possible, I suppose," Gaelan said, maroon eyes fixed on sorting first, then prepping measurements. "But I don't see it any time soon."

"Prime would say we should be 'ready for anything,'" Reishel said, but I shook my head.

"Only if it suits her taste to be ready for it."

"Sirana," Gaelan said, though she did not look over, her face kept placid. "Be careful."

I exhaled; glad I'd at least hidden my sneer aimed at our absent First Sister. "We use a lot of sweat, blood, and components on exercises better suited to invading and taking over a Noble House, but the Sisterhood has never been for that."

"Nor do most of us wish it," Reishel assured.

"Think that's going to change?" I asked ominously.

"We probably won't know about it until after it's decided," Gaelan said, setting out five empty vials in their tray, methodical enough to remind me of the buas in the Wizard's Tower. "But if you two can't say what went down to cut a Lead's break in half, go somewhere else. I have a lot of work to do."

"You sound more like a wizard each time, Gaelan," I teased.

She snorted. "You never knew my Mother. But you didn't have many mages at home, either."

We fell into an awkward silence, and I glanced at Reishel, who shrugged and signed for me to get dressed. After wiping down our faces and donning our uniforms, we left the barracks of our ranking Sister, thinking to go to the mess hall.

Gaelan had been a merchant making potions for the Nobles when the Sisterhood grabbed her, yet I knew far less where Reishel came from. It was another aspect of the Sisterhood no one told me, but I'd begun to figure out.

First, the longer a Red Sister survived, the less she spoke of any blood family to those caits beneath her rank; this was expected and enforced to an extent.

So, theoretically, the Elders knew the origins for all but the Prime, but the knowledge did not flow downstream to the rest of us. The more Sisters died, the faster old connections were forgotten; with every new Sister we initiated, that was one more who never told a story.

Reishel was older than both of us and didn't speak about her family. I hadn't learned she had some link to the farm and food supply until we were searching for an abducted healer.

Gaelan lay between her and me in age but had only been in the Sisterhood five turns compared to Reishel's score; the mage seemed to volunteer to me whatever bits she could get away with outside of D'Shea's hearing.

In contrast, I had studied Jael's origins firsthand, witnessed her collection and testing, had welcomed her in. I would always remember her roots as the lowest-born Noble, but although she knew which House I came from, I hadn't been keen to tell her details about my abusive sisters and negligent Matron, or my lonely turns at Court when she had never even been to the Palace.

Jael and I learned about each other by action, and this seemed to suit us, making our early bonds stronger without the fetter of our former Noble ranking.

Letting the past fade held a certain wisdom if one intended to be a true Red Sister, yet I had learned swiftly that this pillar of our foundation clashed harshly with those of the Priesthood, as was revealed in my recent meeting of the Conceiver, Wilsira Tachnathon, Mother of the Sathoet Kerse from my trials.

"It is a false shield the Red Sisters hide behind," she'd said. "A gap between them and Braqth. It is impossible to erase the first century of upbringing, and, for certain, one can *never* erase shared blood."

Perhaps that last part was true, but at the time, I hadn't dared convey the foul taste in my mouth at her speech.

The Conceiver lusted for her own son and was jealous of his seeming regard for me. Possibly without knowing it — or maybe she did — Wilsira had suggested to me a "divine right" in a would-be Priestess doing what my sister Jilrina had done to me. To explore power and

18

blood and heritage, supposedly, to know what all Nobles were up to.

Davrin 'passions' better served to Braqth? Fuck you.

If the Sisterhood was here to forget such rotting blood bonds as a defense against manipulation from the Priesthood, then it was a balance of powers I could live with being where I was. At the same time, part of me did worry at there being pitfalls I couldn't see just from ignorance.

Maybe I would let go of the bonds but never forget them entirely lest they were used to trap me. I wondered how well that worked for Elder D'Shea, since our Sanctuary Liaison, Tarra Lelinahdara, worked directly with us at times.

Well. You've seen her under Priestess-related stress, Sirana. She fucked the Abyss out of you like she believed we were both about to die.

I touched the sapphire pendant I regularly wore beneath my armor. Then, with a requisitioned "gift" from a wizard who hated my guts, I'd proven I could withstand will-bending tactics from one of the highest Priestesses, the Conceiver herself.

"So, your affliction isn't revealed immediately," the Elder Sorceress had said, relieved though not entirely on my account. "And the challenge is just beginning."

My affliction. Indeed.

Threat and opportunity. I had seen this truth gleam in my Elder's eyes more than once since then when I caught her in deep thought.

What are you planning?

Much as Gaelan had said of the Prime, I wouldn't find out until the Sorceress had already decided.

"Novice in the hall!"

Mela and Graer launched themselves up from their bench near the door and grabbed Reishel and me, forcibly shoving us toward the storerooms and heating stones to the hoots of four other Sisters, all about equal rank.

"Let me guess," I groused, "you were still arguing who was going to cook when you heard us."

"Make enough for second helpings," Graer chortled, nearly lifting me on my toes to move forward.

"Funny you'd rather eat stock from someone who barely cooked for herself a cycle since birth."

"You're a fast learner, Sirana, and Reishel knows a thing or two. So, learn. And you'll know about it if we all get gut trouble."

We would be stuck in the mess hall heating up pots of seasoned mash and scooping it on shroom cups for marks. Before Mela, Graer, and the others were finished with huge, double helpings, Rausery's teams of skirmish fighters stumbled in, the first wave still smelling of blood, sweat, and the deep caverns.

The noise swelled to a startling level across the fiberstalk benches and tables like they all had a lot of thoughts to unload.

Our youngest, Sister Jael, was among them but not part of a group, and she quickly saw refuge joining Reishel and me in the prep of more food. We could use the hands anyway, and she ate bite-by-bite as she hustled between tasks and serving, something which didn't seem foreign to her as it had been with me early on.

I was impressed by how fast the feisty initiate slipped out of attempts to grab her as she set down large bowls for her superiors, Thena and Suna, of course, with Moria making a weaker attempt. Panagan ignored them and ate first.

"Sack-sucking, festering cunt pockets don't touch me," Jael hissed as she returned, and as always, I couldn't help but smile at the lurid cursing. "My ass is still sore."

"Victory pile-on?" I murmured.

"Yeah. And not just me. But *they* didn't get a turn on me."

I nodded. "Been there. And you don't have to go with them. You can say no."

Jael snorted. "They won't listen any more than they did when I first got here. I won't get out of here without bending over."

"I'll help you."

"Me, too," Reishel whispered. "You'll leave with us."

"Three against four," the youngest said, her hateful snarl far too familiar. "We might put up a show, but we'd all get dragged off, and the others will help."

"I don't think so," I said.

"You got lucky last time," Jael challenged. "You said so."

"Call Gaelan," Reishel suggested to me. "Then it will be even, and we'll have a mage. They don't."

"She's busy making potions," I said, trying to think of something else.

"She'll answer!"

She might.

"Hey!" bellowed Lunent Taney. "Where's the next pitcher?!"

"Coming!" Reishel leaped in, grabbing two pitchers of untainted water before Jael could reach them.

Glancing out the doorway, I had to admit that Reishel and Jael were right; the ones getting worked up for a post-meal fuck were Thena and her crew, maybe a few others if they could decide who was on the bottom. I caught the sneer as the Corpora leaned to see Jael in the prep space with me then peered after Graer and Mela as they left satiated by the bounty.

Thena is glad.

I frowned in thought. She was still furious with me for humiliating her in front of Graer and her constant partner, for the word of it spread from them. I took it as a sign that Thena preferring they leave might mean another challenge with her was winnable. Even if I didn't understand the preference, she wasn't assured of the outcome. Suna and Moria would follow hot on her heels. Panagan didn't seem as interested.

Three against four.

I used a message pellet for something wasteful. I'd report it to D'Shea later. I could send the message, know she received it, but she'd have to use another pellet to reply. She didn't.

"Well?" Reishel asked, catching me in a blink a few moments later. Her ruby-red eyes stared into mine.

"We'll see," I said, taking out the next round so Jael could hang back, right as some freshly sluiced Sisters entered.

I brought sustenance to a grateful, clean set of five, one of them pulled me down into a kiss, gripping my ass before letting me go with a pat on the rump; then she dug in with the rest. They were far too hungry and glad for the ready meal to be interested in a fight.

By Jael's count, these would be the last team from the Prime's exercises as well. There were no Elders or Leads in the room. Lunent Taney was the ranking Sister, and she looked too full and drowsy to care about organizing a mess fight if Corpora Thena started one.

So, when Gaelan entered, only Thena cooed a familiar, contemptuous, "Hai, Gae!"

Suna and Moria snickered, and Panagan smiled as my close Sister came right to me at the washbasin to clean the pots and scraped platters and bowls. No one protested.

★No Jaunda this time?★ the mage signed, our bodies blocking others' view.

I shook my head. Jael was watching as she cleaned up and reset the heat on the stones to dormancy.

★Could get messy.★ Gaelan looked behind her again. ★A lot of witnesses if we lose.★

★A lot of witnesses if we win,★ I corrected, ★and they're full and tired. Panagan's cock isn't in it, either. It's just us and the three.★

The former merchant smiled; I could see the decision made on her face. ★Been waiting five turns for this.★

"Alright, good," I said aloud, loud enough for the diners to hear us as I wrapped up some mash in a mushroom pounded flat and dried. "Think we're done! Let's go."

We exited, and Thena and Suna got up immediately to block the door. I stood in front with Gaelan; Reishel and Jael were behind me. Moria and Panagan stood behind our group.

"Look at all the other bowls and spoons," the Corpora said with a sweep of her hands across the benches. "They're not done. You're not finished cleaning."

I smiled coyly, lifting my wrap. "You can finish up while we go eat. We got the pots for you."

"Cute, Blue Eyes." Her deep red gaze locked with mine, and she took her superior's stance. "You don't give me orders."

"Correct, Corpora. I'm aware of precedent."

"If you cook," Reishel said, "cleaning goes to the ones who ate."

I grinned. "Unless they are as fast as Graer and Mela getting back out."

A few in my periphery nodded as they shoveled more food in their mouths, some chuckling. None of them stood up from their bench, but one did call out.

"Ai! Thena's team got here first and loitered longest, they can clean."

There were a couple woofs and huffs of agreement, and Suna scowled at the one who called. "They have to get past us, first," she began, but Thena lifted a hand.

"This is really about the recruit, isn't it, novice?" she said. "You blocking her pucker like you think you're Jaunda?"

"Learn from the best, they say," I replied. "Never learned much from you."

We heard a couple of hisses and coos to the side. The Corpora and I were still staring at each other's eyes. Her frown didn't match the sadistic sneer I remembered from my initiation and gave me confidence that I could push us farther away from where we began.

A couple more moments and something shifted inside my mind. It wasn't a blink or a glance.

It was a shove.

~Remember how it ended last time?~

Thena blinked. Her pupils contracted like a void shrinking in a pool of lava. She took a step to the side. Stopped herself. Suna was uncertain what her superior was doing. Someone behind us moved closer.

"Hey," Jael said. "Back off!"

Gaelan whirled and pitched her meal-to-go, a thick and harmless paste, to splatter someone's face — Moria, from the position and bark of annoyance — and I moved in front of my mage Sister so that Thena and I were still eye-locked. Reishel moved up to face off with Suna.

~Fight. Or don't. But know that we always will.~

Something at my chest felt like it burned a hole in my flesh. Gaelan prepared a spell with more consequence than pasty hair, but no one had yet drawn weapons. The mess hall was silent; even the ranking Lunent was waiting to see what happened next.

My three allies and I had recognized escapes from Corpora Thena's team among the Red Sisters but plenty more submissions. However, Moria and Panagan had a different view of me after we fought for the Prime's amusement, the archer even more after she and I went after Jael and the Tragar in the wilderness. The perception wasn't unified as it had been before I had joined.

My Lead had promised me that things would change.

"Stuff your slits full of egg sacs," Suna growled, scooting forward and giving her Corpora the opening she always seemed to need.

Thena raised a fist, signaling with reasonable dignity as she wrenched her gaze from me. "Stop, Sister." Then she looked at Gaelan and Reishel, not me. "Fine, you troop of shit-green 'cruits. I guess you stone heads are *finally* learning something."

The other three backed off with little pressure; I could imagine one or two might have been relieved. There was space for us to leave, but Gaelan and I both knew better than to expose Jael's back as the last one out.

"Come on," I said, taking the youngest's arm and pushing her forward and out first, followed by Reishel and then Gaelan and me, together.

Thena's group let us go, but we watched our backs just the same. As distance and relative safety grew together, our mage looked like she wanted to flex her arm while Reishel looked proudly at me. Jael was cautious and slow to believe that she had walked away with me twice when Thena wanted her instead.

But it worked.

I'd never known strength in numbers before. *Never like this.*

My chest felt sore and yet filled with something lighter than air. I rubbed at the blue pendant beneath my leathers and realized this was the source of the burning sensation earlier. While I surreptitiously peeked down looking for blisters, seeing none, Gaelan leaned over and sniffed at Jael.

"Mm. You stink, cait."

"Fuck you," she growled.

"Sure, if someone else wears the Feldeu."

"I will!" Reishel volunteered.

"Great! But I'm not eating those holes if they're gummed up with dirt and cunt juice. Let's get Jael sluiced."

"Yes!"

Our youngest looked at me, and I grinned at her, winking.

Still distracted that there might be a burn mark when I stripped down.

CHAPTER 3

"WELL," THE PRIME SAID, HER ANCIENT FACE TWISTED IN A SMIRK, "THAT DID it."

Elder Rausery had made it back in time to invite herself into the briefing as Qivni had been required to peel me away from my bundle of Sisters to stand before the Prime.

Lead Jaunda was there, ready and calm with one of her more placid expressions, and I mimicked her. The Prime was the only one relaxing in a chair. We waited for Elder D'Shea, some of us more anxiously than others.

"Did what, Prime?" Rausery asked.

The Elder General's short, white hair was brushed back in clipped waves, lightly touched by gold strands at her temples. The Prime's hair was close-cropped and almost entirely gold with age; a light mix of white and silver remained, not unlike Headmaster Phaelous, whose hair was much longer and white at the end. The only venerable Davrin I had seen with all-gold hair were the Valsharess.

"Reminded the Conceiver that our novice exists. She must be bored."

Both superiors knew why the Drider guard and ward had been there, but neither Jaunda nor Qivni did. My stomach trembled as I wondered if this was a true disadvantage or was there opportunity in it somewhere?

There's always opportunity in Braqth's Game.

A favorite saying of the Sanctuary, but many said it was a weighted game, favoring only a few at the top. I couldn't disagree. My job as a Queen's Enforcer was to maintain that playground while the city continued as it had for millennia. I stood somewhere above the baseline but, Rausery had made clear, I could easily slide into the Drider Pit or the dungeon if Wilsira Tachnathon or another caught knowledge of my psionic "affliction."

"What I don't get," the Prime said like I couldn't hear her, "is why this cait didn't just pass out and end up in the Drider's web. She ran far enough for Jaunda to hear and come save her lowbie backside?"

"Sirana has talent resisting the effects of wards, Prime," Elder Rausery explained with confidence. "You heard the Priestess at her trials, she was never easy to wrap around magic fingers. We've been testing her since then, D'Shea and I, and Sirana is progressing faster than most her age."

"Useful," the Prime granted, glancing at me briefly. She wasn't impressed but perhaps was glad that a first-turn Sister and former Noble was "tough" at something. "Guess it makes sense, given why the Conceiver noticed her in the first place."

My cheeks warmed. I wasn't sure if the Prime knew how it happened inside the Sathoet chamber where I first met Priestess Wilsira, but I recalled it ending with my leathers down, legs apart, being double-tongued by two demonbloods front and back.

Three had ejaculated all over my legs and boots when I'd come. From what I'd heard later, the Conceiver had been trying to probe my mind while I was distracted. She'd failed.

The Elder Sorceress joined us a few moments later, sweeping in wearing a mask of elegant calm which fooled the Prime, yet I could feel her underlying fear still weighing whether the best defense may be an offense. A breath after she was caught up on Lead Jaunda's report, she had decided.

Not yet.

D'Shea said, "I understand, Prime. I shall prepare my subordinate and send her forward without delay, per the Conceiver's request. Give us three cycles."

"Hold on, D'Shea," the eldest Sister growled, finally rolling up out of her creaking, fiberstalk chair, displaying her full height. "The Priestess specifically requested Qivni as the escort. The Conceiver's entourage — including Sirana — leaves *this* cycle."

"What? That's —"

"Her due, given the circumstances. No prep, Sorceress, the novice leaves in the next mark on her mission."

"Understood, Prime, I'll see it done," Rausery volunteered and received a curt nod of acceptance.

D'Shea's pursed mouth failed to reflect her true frustration. I knew my Elder, knew how she hated being made powerless and how her superior delighted in the use of authority like a blunt club. Although, the Prime didn't know about what Elder D'Shea had done before to prepare me, and I was careful not to tip her off by appearing anything but nervous.

Which is true enough.

"Dismissed," said the Prime.

LEAD QIVNI LED ME THROUGH WITHOUT PAUSE OR DISTRACTION. WE TRAVELED a combination of under-rock passageways, inner hallways, and above-head spyways to the Sanctuary. Her hair was tied back in its usual severe bun at the nape, every white strand in place, and her intense, brown-red eyes kept forward on her task.

Calling the attention of a powerful Priestess on account of how I'd interacted with her demonblood son was exactly what the Lead had warned me about when Kerse had stalked me in the halls during the last Worship Ball. She neither said nor signed, "I told you so."

Instead, it was: *Expect more bad dreams.*

My brows lifted in silent comment, inviting her to go on. She looked at me, her frown deepening.

★You touched that Consort after being on the altar,★ she reminded me, ★and you screamed yourself awake in my room.★

I nodded that I remembered, although I didn't conflate the two because she didn't know about the Tragar I'd killed.

★You touched that ward guarded by a Dread Spider,★ the Lead continued with confidence, ★and you'll be near those who set it. Expect restless Reverie. My advice? Don't fight it. Don't embarrass the Sisterhood by shrieking and sniveling like you did before.★

I acknowledged Qivni's instruction and opinion by sign, even granted in my head that she had a point, but still turned so she wouldn't see my eyeroll. Making the Red Sisters look weak was what worried Qivni verbally, perhaps, but I wagered there was more beneath the surface. I looked forward to watching her in the Sanctuary.

Qivni had once said I could ask her no questions about her past or preferences. I figured the Elders and Jaunda respected this because I had heard no gossip about the mage Lead. I had been given no foreknowledge of previous connections, even with this new game arising.

However, I could observe the free tells in a place I bet she knew well. There was a reason the Conceiver had asked for this Lead. There was a reason the Prime kept the Elder Sorceress out of my transfer. I didn't even expect to see the Liaison.

The Conceiver was setting her pieces into place for some entertainment. Wilsira was old enough to anticipate familiar peers like the Prime and believe a youth like me hadn't the experience or power to spar with her. Where it came to putting sadistic pressure on younger caits, the two powerful Davrin were farther on the side of allies than not. This was apparent even without hints I'd noticed, such as the open-ended use of the Conceiver's Sathoet during my trial in exchange for a vague favor later.

"There were many times before as well," my Elder confirmed.

"Why? Humiliation or temporary control of a new Red Sister?"

"Personal pleasure is always part of it. Before I became an Elder, she often tricked a young Red Sister into pregnancy by a bua in the Sanctuary, to steal our Sisters from us and control them, compromising their long-term loyalty afterward.

I put a stop to that. The Prime refused to see it as a pattern. She only saw 'caits being stupid about poles' and deserving of punishment if she took seed in the wrong hole."

Finally. D'Shea had told me. This had been the threat of which Rausery had warned me when I was brand-new in the Cloister.

"Did many come back?" I asked.

"No. Or, not for long." The Sorceress paused. "A few who could prove themselves again. By then, the Priestesses had a greater number of children by our Sisters than those we got back to stay."

"The Valsharess has no objection to such use?"

D'Shea shook her head, seeming weary. "All part of the Game. How we beget is not important, so long as we do and earn Braqth's continued favor —"

Did she really believe that?

" — which the Priestesses do very well."

I kept my mouth shut. Then, "How did you put a stop to the trickery, Elder?"

"I ..." she began, her dark crimson gaze losing focus a moment. Then she sighed. "I cannot say, lest she hears of it." My Elder met my eyes. "Be ever wary, my clever novice."

Qivni and I wound our way through the Sanctuary unescorted by initiate or page. We passed the main purple floor, then the gold one on the second floor. Those present and working fell silent and shrank back to hide from the color of our leathers. My ears automatically strained for sounds of children when we passed the third, blue floor.

We skipped the next two floors through a spyway ladder and exited to the sixth floor filled with extravagant painting and weaving decorations, though fewer marble statues or metal sculptures. The walls were warm to the eyes, white tinted with yellow. The sconces held heatless torches glowing a vibrant blue; a few held ember-tipped rods whose only purpose seemed to be to release curls of scented smoke.

Although I enjoyed the scent, I wondered how soon one might become dizzy or drowsy breathing in here.

The doors were far apart compared to other residence floors; only one ornate, double door per Priestess, and their spacing suggested spacious chambers beyond. We walked farther to the Conceiver's quarters. Her door was recognizable, being the only one with a stylized cluster of beautiful, kneeling Consorts worshipping her wide-hipped grandeur.

Qivni touched the inlaid pebble of jade, announcing our presence to those within. I heard nothing until the left door opened, and I was met with the large, limpid eyes of a bua pretty enough to be a Royal Consort. If that was true, however, he wasn't ready for the Nobles; he hadn't been given away at the last Worship Ball.

The servant wore only a wrap around his waist and had a pearl sheen to his simply braided hair when he looked down and wordlessly stepped aside. We entered.

"Goddess Blessing, Red Sisters."

Wilsira's voice drifted to us, low and throaty, accompanied by the rustle of silk robes and jingle of jewelry. There she stood with all regalities in the doorway of a private suite.

Now that I wasn't in an ill-lit prison chamber surrounded by demonic sons, I could see the Conceiver's curves were more pronounced than most Davrin, her breasts fuller and hips and backside broader. She still wasn't any taller than me, but I better grasped the sense of her presence, even if I couldn't see her mage's aura as my one-time collector could.

"Goddess Blessing, Conceiver," Qivni said, bowing her head very low at the waist. I followed suit, choosing to stay silent over echoing in a half-voice mutter. "The Red Sister Prime sends me with her regards and your new escort for your journey."

Journey?

Wilsira waited until we straightened, and her mature face bloomed into a captivating smile I hadn't thought her capable of. "The novice Sirana. A delight to see you again."

Uh-oh.

I smiled. "The same, great Priestess."

"And Lead Qivni. It's been a long time. I'm glad the Prime granted you as well, albeit only a short time." The Lead bowed again, not as low and a bit stiff, adding nothing before Wilsira continued as if missing the sound of her own voice. "I still owe a reward earned, and I am content to repay the debt."

"Priestess?" Qivni asked, her brow furrowed in confusion.

Any kind smile on a matron figure's face was to be seen with suspicion, yet Wilsira didn't seem to care as she held that expression without a twitch of a laugh. She nodded toward the Consort-in-training, where he stood with his back to an elaborate tapestry a few steps from the door.

"Take him, Sister," Wilsira said with a flutter of her dark hand. Fine, silver chains threaded together shifting in delicate song. "He could use the experience. You'd be doing us a service. He'll lead you to a spare room."

The youth moved forward without explicit command and sidled up to the Lead Sister, bowing his head to her and displaying willingness without eye contact.

"Uh," Qivni began. "A generous offer, Priestess."

My ears felt huge. How eager I was for any hint as to why Wilsira offered this "reward."

The Conceiver's gaze remained fixed on Qivni despite the tilt of leisured pleasure and generosity to her lips. Did Wilsira expect a Red Sister would fuck upon any opportunity? Or would it be an insult to the Priestess? Perhaps a bruise to Qivni's pride, to refuse whether she was in the mood or not?

The best hints would be in the tics on my collector's face as she made her decision. At first, there were none I could read, but then the Conceiver stepped closer, extending her arm and two fingers straight out, tucking them beneath the bua's chin to lift his eyes from the floor.

Qivni met his eyes, scanned his face, and swallowed.

She wants him.

I could tell that was genuine, but this wasn't just her being enamored of an attractive face. This was a test, a temptation, or a reminder. Certainly a taunt. Neither of them gave me anything more, however, before Qivni bowed thanks and motioned for the sensual, barely dressed servant to lead her to another room and close the door.

"There," the Conceiver said, keeping her voice low and peaceful. "We have a bit of time now."

"Indeed, Priestess." I smiled. "Do you require assistance packing?"

Ah-ha. I spotted a touch of annoyance behind the mask.

"I have servants for that. Or I do it myself if such handling is not meant for the Unanointed."

"Very good, Priestess. What sort of threat do you expect on this trip? Of what should I be most aware?"

"You're getting ahead of yourself, novice."

"Apologies, Priestess. My training. The Prime always presented a briefing of the mission." I paused. "Will your son be with you or staying in the Sathoet chamber with his brothers?"

Something flickered in her maroon eyes. "He shall be attending us. Now, come."

She spun around as if to free her face from my scrutiny, motioning for me to follow her to the largest suite spilling out into four joined rooms at the back of the short hall. A trunk was open along with a wardrobe, and nearby items lined up upon standing chests and vanities.

I did not know how many cycles' worth of "supplies" she planned to bring, but all in my sight was ten times the weight that a Red Sister would carry and, on the surface, none of it useful in a fight.

The obvious kind which might shed blood, anyway.

Perhaps much, or all, of the jewelry was magic-imbued and intended for "softer" effects like persuading, spying, and sending one to sleep. Maybe there were sharp tacks hidden in the fabrics and accents which delivered poison of varying levels in a struggle. Priestesses strictly controlled how they were touched.

Inhaling the ritual incense could cause hallucinations and relax inhibition. I'd learned it hadn't been *solely* the contents of a small, pink vial I'd drunk which had led to me, as a young Noble, sprawled upon the floor in a mass congregation and mounted by three buas at once. D'Shea had said the air I'd been breathing had mixed with the drug I'd quaffed.

★"★★One component may be resisted with your training. Far more difficult are two or three such exposures together. Half of the Sanctuary is illusion as compared to what is real, Sirana. The Priestesses would have you believe standing in their mere presence places you upon the edge of the Abyss, that this power presses the walls, aching for the invitation to be controlled. The realm of the Spider Queen is neither as simple nor as obedient as that."*

My Elder had been earnest and convincing, and I believed her. Yet Kerse, the Conceiver's elder Sathoet son, was supposed to be just that: well-heeled and simple-minded. D'Shea had shown her skepticism when I suggested he had acted without Wilsira's knowledge at the last Worship Ball. I had asked about that well before this sudden change in my fortune.

"Threat outweighed opportunity if you spoke too soon around the wrong ears," she had said. "So I discouraged you. I've not seen those signs yet, but he *is* the eldest living son. If you cannot avoid being near him and his Mother again, Sirana, try to discover who made the choice to stalk you without making a stupid accusation to the enemy."

I supposed I was grateful the Priestess and I would be leaving her personal quarters soon. I wouldn't be kept in these chambers over the next ten or so cycles I could expect to be in service on behalf of the Prime. I still didn't know what the Conceiver planned, but I *did* know how long. I always thought better outside on my feet than inside upon my back.

Wilsira began a tedious show of packing her trunk on her own. I looked around for a cait or bua suite keeper; beyond new polish of the surfaces, there were no signs of them. Likely a deliberate choice.

"I am traveling by coach to three Noble Houses and will be checking on my Consorts," the Conceiver told me as she folded a smooth, shining sash into a perfect square before laying it gently in the trunk. "A surprise inspection for a Matron gifted with a Sanctuary breeder. The newest Houses sometimes need guidance on how one should be treated."

Good opportunity to snoop around and enjoy some theater outside of Court.

I nodded. "Yes, Priestess. If I may beg your pardon, I've heard no stories of a Priestess showing up with her Sathoet at a Matron's Gate."

"Then you must have had your ears stuffed with spider silk, infant." She shook out a kerchief before folding a piece of multi-gem jewelry inside.

"With her Sathoet," I repeated. "I've heard of the visits, of course. Always an excellent opportunity for a Matron to brag if the visit goes well."

"Hmph," Wilsira huffed with a smile, glancing at me before slipping the wrapped valuable in a side pocket of the trunk. "Still too young to know what you say, child."

"Not so. I did not say it was never done, Priestess, only that I have no stories to draw upon. How might I expect the plantations to behave with a Sanctuary Son upon their grounds?"

Hands now empty, Wilsira turned to face me, her hands relaxed upon her hips. Her tits looked heavy inside her robe, especially when she inhaled deeply, letting it out slow with a single eyebrow raised. "With respect. With fear and awe of the direct touch of our Goddess. What else?"

"Perhaps their presence explains the Houses that do not brag after a visit?"

Eyes narrowed. "Are you insulting our divine conceptions, Sirana?"

Both brows lifted high on my forehead. "Of course not, Conceiver! I've met yours, and I've said your son is smart and well-endowed. That's genuine."

My ears picked up a subtle shift somewhere behind me. I paused. Only now did I think that Kerse could be eavesdropping, if not outright spying with the candlelight bent around him like a cloak. Wilsira could see it on my face; she smiled.

You're quick, Sirana.

At the snap of his Mother's fingers, I covered my surprise as Kerse seemed to step out of the busy, gilded wall.

Vaporous colors stretched as if to hold him before losing cohesion and vanishing. Taller than either of us with too many features from his demonic sire, the half-Elf crouched down to be shorter than the females in the room, his knuckles lightly touching the colorful rug, white-tufted elbows resting on muscled thighs.

The Sathoet watched me with blank, yellow eyes, keeping his sharp teeth behind his muzzle lips for now. The coarse white hair following his spine seemed puffed up a bit at his thick neck and the back of his bestial head. Like the pretty bua who'd met Qivni and me at the door, Kerse only had a dark green wrap covering his genitals and buttocks. The rest of him was all bulges, sinew, and tough, black skin with a set of white claws on hands and feet.

I couldn't read his face.

"Well met," I said, undecided on a name or honorific. I grinned at Wilsira, instead. "And well-fed. I think he's grown since last I saw him."

"Interesting that you would notice," the Priestess said, though she was not displeased.

Her son turned his head from both of us, toward the front of the chambers. Kerse's nose was more sensitive than a pureblood Davrin, but I wondered about his ears. Mostly Elven — long and pointed and a little ragged along the edges — but were they keener as well?

Then I heard it.

I moved fast, and the demonblood's entire body flinched as if he would leap in pursuit.

"Red Sister!" Wilsira barked. "Kerse, stay!"

Before she had a chance to utter any such order to me, I was out in the front rooms again, lunging for the door through which Qivni had gone. Inside, I heard her wailing, and I couldn't tell if she needed help. I'd never heard the sound before.

It wasn't locked; I went in.

Completely unprepared for what I'd see.

"*Aaaa,* oh Goddess, *no!*" the Lead cried, burying her flushed, sweaty face into the bedding. "I can't — ah!"

Qivni was bent over the bed, kneeling on the floor; cloak and belt off, uniform still on complete with gloves, but bared from hips to knees, pants crammed down to bunching leather. The meek little bua I'd seen before was nude, crouched with a two-hand hold on her wrists crossed behind her at the small of her back.

What the — ?

The bua's cock was wedged deep and tight in her netherhole, abnormally thick for the youth's size, and straining it as he humped her backside in short, vicious strokes. The Consort panted and grunted like a rutting animal, quivering, barely in control, his face turned away as he fucked her.

Another male Davrin was in the room, fully dressed, wearing deep blue robes.

Goddess fuck me, I *knew* him!

The wizard kneeled by the bed, his fingers buried deep in Qivni's cunt and stroking as roughly as the slender one abused her ass, though in longer, experienced strokes. Tiny arcs of blue light jumped over his knuckles and across her netherlips, and the Red Sister arched her back, lifted her head from the mattress.

"Oh, Braqth, *yes!*" Qivni cried then. "Aaaa, yes, I'm gonna — !"

I'd never seen this Lead climax before; it'd been hearsay that she even could. Now, I had no doubt.

Her peak set off that of the Consort, who screamed in pleasure as his spear spurted in her rippling anus. The surly wizard from my trials concentrated on enhancing and elongating the Lead's ride back down, a skill I hadn't realized he had.

Her climax was more powerful because of him. I was envious, hearing the unfettered moaning, watching her drool onto the blankets from one set of lips and down her naked thighs from the other. In that moment, she did not know where she was.

I had never ... *never* heard of Rausery's Lead letting go like this!

"*Shyntre!*" Wilsira bellowed, louder than she had yelled at me.

He and I jumped and spun to face the Priestess. I backed up to gain space, and the wizard pulled his fingers from the Lead's body, scrambling to his feet.

"What in the Abyss are you doing?" demanded Braqth's Priestess.

"What she *asked*, Conceiver," Shyntre panted, his scowl like Qivni's, although he kept his eyes on Wilsira's middle. Not the floor, not her face.

Kerse stood at the doorway behind us, peeking in. I grew a little concerned that Qivni hadn't lifted her face off the mattress; she seemed too lax. Her cumming like that hadn't made her pass out, had it?

Even weirder, the Consort still crouched above her ass, gripping her wrists like reins. The bua caught his breath, resting his weight on her, in no hurry to pull out.

"I told you to wait until I summoned you," Wilsira hissed to the wizard. "Leave this room. You, too, Sirana. Let Qivni be alone with her bua."

The son of Headmaster Phaelous obeyed readily enough, but I read resistance and hesitation. I didn't understand why; I only knew I felt the same.

"Lead?" I asked her directly. "Can you hear me?"

Qivni mumbled something but didn't lift her head.

She's confused, and the fucking Consort still won't get off her.

"Sirana. Out!"

The Conceiver seemed about to send Kerse in to drag us out. Reluctantly, I left with the wizard and watched the Priestess firmly shut the door behind us.

Calmly, Wilsira folded her arms, lifting her chin to look down her nose, disapproving of the young wizard. I wagered that he didn't give two dung-squats about that, but she waited still, and Shyntre was smart.

He took to one knee by her skirts, head down and waiting in silence. Unlike many males, Shyntre kept his hair cut very short, so I could see the back of his neck as he showed Wilsira supplication. The whole of it, including his naked nape, was unusual enough in my experience to seem sexy.

"Your pardon, Priestess," I asked, wondering if I'd regret it, "but what is he doing here?"

Wilsira exhaled, clearly disappointed with her spoiled surprise. "I always take a Red Sister and a wizard from the Tower with me on my trips. Shyntre is my choice this time. He is coming with us."

Fuck Braqth's Tits … Someone had been doing her research.

Through the door, I could hear Qivni griping, first in a familiar tone but then it grew more desperate. "Get it … out. Just … p-pull it— …*aaa!*"

I winced. *That really hurt her.*

"Seems it's been some time since our Lead practiced with that orifice," Wilsira chuckled, motioning for us to take a few more steps with her away from the door. "A shame."

"Well, he loo —" I began.

The sharp look from Shyntre brought me up short. Irritated as I wanted to feel at his attitude, I knew he was right.

Quiet, Sirana.

Since when did I need to blare out everything that I *thought* I knew, anyway? That had never been the way to survive at Court.

Shyntre held his wet hand curled and slightly away from his body; the Priestess motioned for him to lift it, which he did. I watched as the Conceiver took firm hold of his wrist and studied the cunt juice up close, sniffing lightly, perhaps tempted to take a lick?

"Baby?" Wilsira said, pulling the wizard closer to offer his hand to Kerse. "Would you like a taste of this Sister's cunt?"

Shyntre tensed and leaned back, his eyes widening like he thought that the Sathoet would chomp off a finger.

"Relax, he won't bite," the Priestess teased, missing the nose wrinkle on the demon son's snout as he had an impulse to refuse.

As if he had a mind of his own.

"Come, spread those precious fingers, mage."

I acted upon my own impulse, then.

"Wait, allow me," I said, stepping around Wilsira's back to the wizard's outstretched and imprisoned hand. "She's my Sister." I winked at him. "I clean up after them all the time."

Wilsira saw Kerse's expression and did not protest before I extended my tongue, caught one dark finger lengthwise and drew it in, closing my lips around it in a sensual suck. All three of them watched, saying nothing.

I cleaned that finger most of the way and captured the second, cleaning that before following the musky flavor smeared across his knuckles and palm. I wasn't intimately familiar with it but had been there once before. Plus, I knew the tang of feminine nethers when I tasted it.

And something else. The Consort's spending?

But he came in her ass. Was that the first time or the second? Surely there hadn't been enough time for a rebound, unless Consorts were just *that* magical.

Might explain why it tingles.

Shyntre pulled his arm back as soon as I'd finished, and Wilsira loosened her grip on him. He stared between us, looking as though he might try to run. He didn't appear so eager for sex that he lacked the willpower not to invite himself into an impromptu session. Even if Qivni had asked, which I didn't see happening.

What the fuck are you up to, wizard? Why are you here?

Qivni cursed then, stumbling behind the door as she sounded like she was righting her uniform. Clumsily.

"Priestess?" The Consort's voice, sounding oddly scared.

"Ah, go wait in the dining space," Wilsira said to us, stepping forward to take the door handle. "Get something to eat and let me see Qivni out, now that she's had her reward. I'd like to leave the Sanctuary within the next mark."

The next mark? The Conceiver was moving fast. Barely enough time to see what was happening and react to it with so much undercurrent I was missing, like my first few times at the Wizard's Tower.

I hoped I would have time to think about this later.

CHAPTER 4

THE CARRIAGE WAS LOADED AND STOCKED FOR A SPAN-LONG JOURNEY. THE spidery black metal of the wheels was well-formed with suspension capable of absorbing shocks on the rocky road. There was a decorated enclosure with padded cushions for the Priestess and up to three more to sit in comfort, the carriage's rear and underside balanced with what she carried with her.

The four beasts pulling this load weren't our quiet riding lizards, who didn't have the back muscles for this. We used a species of rare omnivores in the Deepearth, Uroans — rare because of the expense needed to keep them fed.

So, of course she would be taking four of the suckers.

Four-legged with wide, clawed feet, capable of keeping a gallop for brief periods and maintaining a brisk walk for eternity, they possessed broad shoulders, short necks and faces, and a soft, moisture-sloughing brown coat we rarely needed to trim.

The snouts were barely long enough to root in collected mud and silt for additional nibbles, and the eyes were small and mostly useless. They guided themselves by smell and possessed excellent balance, and our harnesses gave them direction.

"Come, buas," Wilsira commanded when she grew tired of the Palace slaves loading and properly balancing the carriage. "Inside."

Kerse and Shyntre climbed in first, eyeing each other with dislike. Once they'd each taken a seat, across and diagonal, I watched the Conceiver climb in without assistance, without touching anything. She took her seat next to her half-blood son with a sigh.

The Davrin driver climbed atop the carriage to guide the beasts, a contingent of eight Palace Guards signaled they were ready, and I mounted a lizard to ride alongside the carriage. Red Sister escorts — even single ones — were usually displayed publicly like this; there were enough sources of light along the streets to assure the color of my uniform would work as intimidation or potential draw as a target over the divine mage of the Sanctuary.

Although standard procedure, I imagined that Wilsira only wanted the entertainment of being escorted by both me and the wizard on this tour. Our respective functions were merely convenient, and she wasn't expecting any sort of trouble or danger that she couldn't handle.

Or one would hope she'd have mentioned it by now.

Regardless, I would be a fool and a failure as a Red Sister to think I could let down my guard. A bored and jealous Priestess with no outside danger to distract her? More than enough reason to be on high alert.

I was not yet used to being so visible as we moved down from the Rulers' Rise and into the winding streets of Sivaraus itself; every passerby noticed me riding alongside the coach. Some stopped in their tracks; some slowly retreated, trying, and often failing to be discrete. Others watched warily as they moved on with their business. Only the very young pointed at me, often the instant before an adult slapped their hand.

"Do not gesture in such a manner," I heard one mother hiss, shaking the youth's arm. "They kill disobedient children like you!"

I raised my brow, though the Mother didn't see. A bit more thought went into something like that, and child deaths were far rarer than those of the adults, who usually earned it. But who was I to interfere in some traditional passing on of legend when it maintained my Sisterhood's reputation?

I noticed much more than I had as a Noble how many non-Davrin slaves, servants, and independents were present as well, and what kind. The quick, squat Pytes were common and worked with a variety of small beasts. There were a few, rare Tragar, hard-earned slaves from the look of it and no possibility of being psionic. We had many more of their lesser, furrier relatives, the Ketro, who were generally stronger and more enduring than the Pytes.

Different from all of them and far fewer in number were the amphibious Yutogul, a slime-skinned race that worked hard to maintain mutually beneficial relations with us by trading deep water resources for those of agriculture and mining.

Davrin outnumbered any single race on the streets, at perhaps five out of ten, and the Valsharess maintained a significant Palace Guard to keep order in the streets. Still, there were the others who were integrated and useful in Sivaraus. They were the reason Wilsira could lounge so pleasantly in an elegant carriage pulled by four hungry Uroans in the first place.

"S-Speed for a cliff and d-die, Monstress!"

Calm settled upon me. I looked toward the stuttering shout, pegged its owner, and evaluated quickly: a mature, female Davrin in a thin, dirty gown. Hair shorn very messily, and no weapons but for a tired, old eating knife in her right hand. Her gait was unhealthy and her gestures unfocused.

No threat.

Wilsira leaned cautiously out her window as the driver slowed the carriage. I looked up and around in case this was a distraction for something bigger.

"B-Braqth's Whore in that carriage, h-hear! M-May you rot in the bellies of the Driders!"

The Priestess frowned and said to me, "Silence her."

I drew my hand crossbow and aimed it without reply. Those on the street moved fast, darting to get out of my way, and the crazy Davrin was within range. The point of the bolt aimed at her feet, and once released, the packet of sneeze powder attached burst open, quickly enveloping her.

The commoner's breathing was so starkly disrupted, alternating choking, sneezing, and coughing to create a great racket, that she had either inhaled badly or was truly in bad condition.

She dropped her dull knife to the ground.

"Kill her, Red Sister!" Wilsira demanded, being clearer as our backup guard surrounded the carriage and the choking cloud dissipated.

With no other threat choosing to act and the Priestess protected, I spurred the lizard forward, ready for its customary burst of speed, bearing down on the dissenter and plucking her up by the hair. She shrieked as I folded her over my saddle and kept moving into the inky shadow of an alley.

Once out of sight, I directed the lizard up, selecting an easy path for it to climb as I held my prisoner tightly.

Kill her.

She smelled as though she hadn't bathed in a long time. The "threat" was weak as well, barely struggling. I stuffed a cloth into the older Davrin's mouth, which at least muffled her unintelligible ranting as we climbed.

Soon I had enough height to be able to see the Priestess's carriage while fewer on the street could see me even if they knew where I'd gone, and none could interfere. The driver had moved forward without me. I had maybe half a tick before I'd jump across smooth and curved rooftops to keep them in sight.

"Prsh-shesh *cugh!*" the squirming female said through her gag. It sounded focused as a curse.

"What?" I chuckled, pulling the soggy cloth out and stuffing it beneath the collar of her dress in case I needed it again.

"P-Priestess cur!" she spat again.

She sobbed, her jaw quivering as she struggled to breathe over the saddle. She tried to straighten up and slide off, but I pressed my hand to her back. It took little effort on my part to control her. The constant stuttering, the way she trembled, and the fever coming off her body all implied she may have been poisoned. I hadn't done it.

"C-cunt f-fed my child to the Abyss …" she wheezed. "She didn't d-do anything wrong. My d-daughter ..."

"And you are?"

"N-no matter ... only n-need my ears a-as p-proof ..."

I glanced at where the carriage and guards moved down the street. No troublesome figures followed them, and only now individuals cautiously crept out from where they'd hidden when I charged forward to snatch my prisoner.

"Give me your name, and the name of your enemy," I said.

She wept as I'd only seen Kaltra weep before, and I could see badly healed lash marks peeking out from her neckline. I hooked one finger to lift it up so I could see farther down her back.

Scar tissue marred her flesh and obstructed the normal flow of Radiants I could see. It would have taken spans to form those while healing draughts had to have been kept out of her reach. Only one place where this happened so deliberately.

The dungeon beneath the Palace.

When did you get out? How?

"Answer me," I repeated. "Your name."

"Daleina ... M-merchant."

"And the cunt in the carriage you want to see die?"

My writhing prisoner growled. "T-Tachnathon."

I was curious how she knew. But first, "What did she do to your daughter?"

"Ab-abducted! Know it was h-her ..."

"How so?"

"Th-they say ... sh-shadows ... speak ..."

"And they released you, Daleina?"

"N-no ... escaped ..."

"How?"

"Y-you know! S-sent ... only m-marks ago ... P-poisoned my l-last meal, assumed I'd die of it in p-prison ... you were w-wrong! I w-want them to know! I w-want them —"

This was followed by an incoherent wail, and she shook her head as if trying to dislodge a spider that had crawled in her ear.

"Know what, Daleina?" I said, taking her hair to force her face to look toward me.

Her eyes and cheeks were sunken, her eyes dull and flicking unfocused at all points around her. "Th-they're breeding ... and f-feeding them ... ch-children ... to ... d-demons ..."

I was hesitant to take her description literally; she was out of her mind and probably hallucinating from the poison and abuse. "How old was your daughter, Daleina?"

"S-she just ch-chose a sire ... wanted ... b-baby ... her own ..."

Grown, then.

I urged the lizard to turn then, navigating over the rooftops; I'd lost sight of Wilsira and that wasn't good. The older, dying Davrin continued mumbling but she grew less and less coherent. Something about swapping unborn children, abominations, more eating, birthing, and eating again. It weaved a gruesome tapestry, but I didn't know what to make of it.

Daleina weakened, the slow poison catching up to her as I caught up to the carriage. Her ranting had stopped, and it was only a matter of time before her breathing did as well. I didn't really have to do anything to "kill" her, and I didn't care to bring Wilsira any body parts when I could bring her the whole corpse.

Wilsira leaned to see out of the carriage when she heard me come alongside her. She had been smiling, chatting, but blinked at the body slung over my mount. She frowned. When I came closer still, she leaned back, wrinkling her nose.

"What are you doing?"

"She's silenced, Priestess," I said. "I gathered you didn't want me to leave her body smelling up Sivaraus streets for enemies to find?"

"And what are *we* going to do with it, Sister?"

I shrugged. "Identify it? Report it?"

"No reason. An annoyance, nothing more."

I smiled. "Aren't there others searching for a prisoner escaped?"

The Priestess shook her head, bringing a scented cloth to cover her nose and mouth. "I'll send a message once we reach our first destination.

We don't have time now. Drop that diseased thing somewhere else and dispose of it, Red Sister. Perhaps your resistance to filth is heightened by crawling in and sucking on shit, but your mount isn't, and neither is mine."

I chuckled and turned the lizard away, Daleina's head lolling and her body unmoving.

The population crunch loosened as we left the center of Sivaraus, and I remained farther from the carriage while keeping it in sight. My mount had to deal with the scent of death a little longer. A few times, he tried to turn his head back and nibble on a leg, but I struck his nose with the crop each time.

I held on to the body much longer than the Priestess preferred, but that was only part of why I'd done it. The meat was not good for scavenging, so I needed a place that wouldn't poison viable soil or a water source or sicken kept beasts. It was more difficult than I thought, finding such a place.

At least it gave me some time to think.

If the rants held any truth — if I discovered whether Wilsira knew about this prisoner — then why steal a merchant and her grown daughter by force? Not beyond the Priestesses' resources but seemed clumsy compared to how they manipulated the Nobles.

Could they not have convinced the mother and daughter to come along willingly? Did they not want to? It made little sense to me.

Perhaps the old Davrin was insane for another reason, pushed to create a personal cause for her grief, an enemy on which to focus her rage — all in the delirium of mistreatment and toxic blood.

The symptoms of the poison indicated a rough distilling of a mushroom that Red Sisters rarely had cause to use in our tasks. It worked slowly, was cheaply made, and sometimes the victim didn't even die because it required multiple doses. I knew the Priestesses had much better resources than to resort to what had been done to this Davrin.

I stopped at an outcropping of bare rock as we crested a small hill and checked for a pulse one last time. *None.*

I dismounted before pulling the dead weight off to lay it on the ground. I checked her body for any unique marks or items but saw only the scars and found no possessions. Plucking out a small bottle of alkaline, I dribbled it over her to accelerate the decay of meat and bone while dissuading any creature keen on survival from touching the body.

The lizard hissed when it smelled the first wafts of my handiwork, and I remounted, setting out to catch up again to the carriage.

We were headed to visit three different Houses to check on three Consorts. We would pay respects to the Matrons, and Wilsira would discuss whatever business she had with them, spending a cycle or two in each place. Passing from one to the next would take only part of the next cycle.

I learned the specific House Names only as we approached the first.

"Protecting your body is more difficult when I don't know where it is going earlier than this, Priestess," I'd commented at her window, riding alongside.

Wilsira chuckled, and I could see Kerse's yellow eyes glowing from the deeper shadows next to her. "You failed to ask earlier, Red Sister."

True, I'd been prodding her about bringing the demonblood. "Would you have answered then, Priestess?"

She gave me a sardonic grin. "If I choose. It depends. You responded most creatively to that threat back in the streets, Sirana. I don't wager planning helps you much. But I have faith in the Red Sisters' training."

Undoubtedly.

"She was no threat, Priestess," I said. "Just loud."

"Well, our ears enjoy quiet, don't they?"

"So, who was she?"

Wilsira sniffed. "Why would I know?"

"You said she was an annoyance, Priestess."

"That's what all prisoners are."

"You ordered me to kill her. Because she was loud? Not for how she got out?"

Finally, she dropped whatever attitude she'd been trying for and narrowed her eyes at me. "Not for discussion, Red Sister. Mind your tongue and your duties."

Shyntre stared at us from deeper inside the coach, and even Kerse glanced over, yellow eyes curious. Although I had enough questions from Daleina's own mouth to annoy the Conceiver to no end, my Elder had warned caution. I took the message and dropped it.

Our first stop that eve was House D'Verin, the Fourth House. At such status, the Matron's lands were in a better location to reach the center of Sivaraus, the roads maintained and patrolled more often.

This Matron had previously been gifted with Auslan back when I'd found him in solitude on that tiny farm. Since then, he had been returned and regifted to House Itlaun, the Tenth, and D'Verin had been awarded a different Consort from the most recent Worship Ball.

A younger one.

This gave me ample warning that we may be heading to House Itlaun on this tour to check on the same Consort who, unbeknownst to the Conceiver, I had molested before D'Verin returned him to the Sanctuary.

Won't that be a balancing act?

Curgia and Auslan each knew my face from separate visits; they might give me away to the Priestess. The Noble Daughter was still pregnant with Kerse's offspring, last I knew, and D'Shea wanted to keep our knowledge of the sire secret for as long as possible, not to mention keep our informant Consort in his role longer than half a turn.

I must also consider Shyntre's potential to distract me with the stubborn line of his back, with his knowledge of the blue stone around my neck shielding my thoughts from the Priestess, and the mental image of his fingers deep in Qivni's quim ... which refreshed in my mind's eye at unexpected times.

All of us in the same spot. No way to play it cautious if we go there.

Given how clearly and deliberately the Priestess had chosen this one wizard I couldn't ignore to attend her, I fretted that she might also know about my spying on her and Kerse as they'd dominated and impregnated

Curgia. If Wilsira knew *that*, perhaps she even knew of my connection with the Consort, and she had done *all* of this on purpose.

Don't panic.

I must discover if Wilsira knew about my second run-in with Kerse at the Ball. If she didn't, she might not know that I'd watched him breed Curgia.

Because Kerse didn't tell her. Something concerning on its own.

I also wanted to think there was no way Wilsira could know about Auslan. She wouldn't unless he betrayed his agreement with the Sisterhood. He threatened his own life by telling her. He wouldn't do that; he had said as much.

It's just coincidence.

Granted, not a coincidence helping my situation, but I could not become paranoid before I had more evidence that I should worry in truth. Shyntre was the only one the Priestess knew with whom she could taunt me; I must go forward with this. Perhaps I would get lucky, and Curgia and Auslan may not see me with Wilsira, so they would have no chance to suggest to the Priestess that they knew me.

"I can appreciate keeping me on display in grand gesture, Priestess," I said through the window as we rolled along the road. "But may I suggest I do what I do best and watch from shadows while you deal?"

"Nonsense," she replied. "How would you guard my body being in another room spying from a peephole? You are a far greater deterrent where they can see the reds, my cait, and far more effective at your function if you can cover me in an instant."

She made my argument look as weak as it truly was. Perhaps there was no way to avoid being seen by those at House Itlaun if we were going there. In truth, it wasn't really Auslan I worried would give me away, it was Curgia.

The Second Daughter wasn't a quick study in the first place, and unlike the Consort, she did not come with the benefit of knowing the political background and having much to lose. If her first sight of me made it clear that she'd seen me before, Wilsira wouldn't let it go until she knew why.

That would be messy.

"As you wish, Priestess."

"Not thrilled, I see," she said. "Am I that distasteful? Or too old for your taste, perhaps?"

I gave her an odd look then smiled. "Not at all, Priestess. I'm sure even Shyntre would agree you carry your wisdom well. Do you dance?"

She laughed, and for an instant I wondered whether it had been genuine. "Every cycle."

We approached the main gate, and I pulled up the cowl on my cloak, to establish a pattern if for no other reason.

"Ah, adding mystery," she said from the coach. "I approve. I hadn't realized you were so shy after your stunt in Sivaraus, Sirana."

I chuckled. Part of my periphery blocked by the cowl. "You tease, Priestess. I consider my own Elders' wisdom."

"Indeed. What wisdom is that?"

"Always leave the Nobles wondering who is watching."

"Ah-ha. We agree on this, young novice."

The Priestess nodded to her Sathoet son, and Kerse champed his teeth and bowed his head, vanishing before my eyes. He had cloaked himself before we reached the gate.

I DISCOVERED THAT I ENJOYED BEING EXEMPT FROM ALL SOCIAL EXPECTATIONS.

Wilsira and Shyntre did all the bowing and gestures and traditional words at House D'Verin, and I stood and watched. I wasn't sure where Kerse had gone off to after the carriage stopped in the courtyard; I only knew that he wasn't standing at Wilsira's elbow as an invisible wall.

Meanwhile, I was not introduced, and no one asked my name. Furthermore, few spent more than a moment looking at me before their eyes drifted somewhere else. Most of my weapons were covered by my cloak, my hands out of view as I stood near to Wilsira — but not too near.

I was the Dragon in the room, and everyone ignored it.

The downside was that no one behaved naturally, taking care with their words and gestures. The chances of me learning anything truly secret were nil, and I needed to work harder to occupy my mind and keep from becoming bored or complacent. Amusing at first to watch them sift, sort, and turn over every word leaving their mouth for possible offense, but it grew wearisome soon enough.

The Priestess was invited in, and soon we stood inside the Matron's mansion, in a room with an unusually high ceiling and broad enough to hold a party, with a grand staircase leading to the second level.

"Will you call your Royal Consort down, please, Matron?" Wilsira asked.

The travel trunks were barely off the carriage and being lugged up by the servants, and I spotted a flitting expression or two of surprise among the young Nobles, but the mature Matron — older than my own Mother — bowed to perfection.

"Immediately, Conceiver."

The young beauty was escorted down the main stairs promptly, fast enough to know that he had been waiting for the summons. The Consort stood before the Priestess, eyelashes down but chin still up, so Wilsira could see his flawless face and that he was in excellent health. He could have been Auslan's cousin, although his eyes tilted differently, the nose a different shape, the mouth not quite as enticing for my tastes.

The Matron D'Verin had caught from her new bua quickly; the bump at her middle was only a little smaller than Curgia's the last I'd seen. Neither of her present Daughters visibly carried, and from the covetous looks on their faces, I guessed the Matron was keeping the Consort to herself for now. From the others standing present, Matron D'Verin had a very large family compared to mine.

Wilsira lightly touched the youth's face, and I saw a brief tremor in his mostly naked form. "Wonderful. A primary concern of my visit, as you know, but I'm swiftly reassured of the good order of your House, Matron."

"Thank you, Conceiver."

"I believe I will take a brief respite before we dine. It was a tiring ride here."

Pfft. Tiring ride ... I kept my face still.

"Certainly, Priestess. We look forward to the grace of your company. Please allow our serving bua to show you to your quarters. They are even more comfortable than last time." Our hostess paused. "Are you sure you would not prefer separate quarters for your wizard? I can provide them."

Wilsira's mouth twitched. "I am sure. He will stay with me. Goddess blessing, Matron."

As we were led down the spacious and decorative hallways of House D'Verin, I proved to be more distraction than our poor serving bua could handle. Perhaps my own age, he kept looking at me in brief, darting glances, trying to see farther into my cowl, even to the point of nearly leading us down the wrong path.

"This way, bua," the Priestess said irritably. "I know where I rested last time."

"Y-yes, Priestess." When he finally found the correct door, he went inside to make sure no one else was there and returned out with the keystone to hand to the Priestess. "Your trunks are inside. The call gem is by the bed ... um ... should you need anything else ... uh ... Priestess."

He'd looked twice at me and forgotten his speech. I supposed it didn't reflect well on the Matron and her selections on who would serve whom. I wondered if the Priestess would complain just to cause trouble for him.

Wilsira looked at me with amusement that barely covered her irritation. "Perhaps you should simply strip him now, Red Sister, and satiate his curiosity. The bed is over there."

Fear flashed across wide, red eyes as the young Davrin swallowed, and his face became heated. He stuttered something when Wilsira cut him off.

"About your duties. Before you irritate me further."

"Yes, Priestess!" He bowed and left quickly.

Only after I'd swept the room a second time and called the two of them in, only after Wilsira had closed and locked the door did she laugh out loud.

"Oh, my," she chortled. "Bravo for staying so silent and still, Sirana. Intimidation and beauty clashing together. So amusing."

"He's never been so close to a Red Sister?" I guessed.

"I wager it's the blue eyes on top of the red leather," Shyntre muttered, kneeling to check that the wards placed upon the trunk locks were still intact.

"Indeed, my clever wizard," Wilsira agreed. "And the similar youth between them. He is flushed and ripe for the taking, but with less experience of powerful females given their wealth of beautiful Consorts. He's had other servants."

"You can tell all that about him from looking, Priestess?" I asked skeptically.

"Well." She winked. "His thoughts about you were at the very fore of his mind. You meet up with his dreams far more than the rest of us."

She exhaled a performative sigh of regret and moved to her trunks as Shyntre slid smoothly out of her way and I stayed quiet. She murmured a command word, and I heard something click on one before she lifted the top. She removed her jewelry first, placing her things gently inside the trunk, then began to undress in front of us as she lifted out other items: soap, towels, a silver brush.

"I shall bathe now," she announced, locking her trunk again. "I'd like some privacy. You two will remain here."

I wasn't against this idea, but I was beginning to wonder where Kerse was and whether he would join his Mother at any point.

"Don't lock the door," I said. "Watch for spiders in the tub."

She gave me a look. "You sound like my Mother."

I grinned. "Old advice is still sound advice, Conceiver."

She harrumphed and led herself to the bathroom, closing the door. I did not hear a click, but once I heard water running, I stepped over to test the handle anyway. It turned fully and was unlocked. I let it go without opening the door.

When I turned around, Shyntre had his arms crossed, dark red eyes watching me as boldly as any cait. The sapphire blue pendant underneath my armor felt like a suddenly heavy lump.

His thoughts about you were at the very fore of his mind ...

Wilsira's tease about "skimming" the servant was likely deliberate. I knew now that she had tried to read my mind the first time we met, as she distracted me, surrounding me with three horny Sathoet. It hadn't worked, thanks to this mystifying stone around my neck, a piece of jewelry given to me by this same, damned wizard, the last I'd seen him.

I had no idea if this young mage had made it or if it had been his sire, Headmaster Phaelous. Either way, I figured it had been neither Shyntre's idea nor preference to run after me outside the Wizard's Tower, making sure he placed it directly in my palm.

"Why were you fing — ?"

"You're being too inform —"

We stopped talking, staring at each other. Shyntre sighed.

Why was I fingering your Lead? he guessed by hand-sign.

I shrugged and replied. *Yes.*

I already said. She asked.

You weren't in there when she walked in with the Consort.

How do you know?

Fine, I don't. But you weren't offered as part of the reward, I witnessed it.

Shyntre shrugged, both his fine hands fluid in a longer response. *The Priestess also kept Kerse in her suites where you couldn't see. Wagering she had a proper reveal with him? Got a better reaction?*

I narrowed my eyes, one hand on my hip. *For a wizard's opinion unasked, you're too informal.*

The wizard's mouth tightened at one side. *That happens when you've served the Sisterhood and Priesthood more than once and haven't been laid open on the altar.*

Yet.

He seemed to want to smile but quashed it.

I considered. *And the soldier who 'served' with you in my trial?*

Didn't survive your trial.

How do you know?

That was my other assignment after rutting all you could take.

I wanted to scoff aloud. ★I could take more. And I don't believe you."

★Why not? I was there, forcing you, wasn't I?★

★Then executing an obedient bua we shared? Seems more a punishment, not a reward.★

He narrowed his intense eyes, looking sly. ★My apologies if I poached your quarry before you could find him. Hope you didn't waste much time searching.★

How could he even *tell?*

We glared at each other a few ticks, then I smiled a little. ★How did you kill him?★

He dared to look disgusted. ★Fast. He never did anything to me.★

I nodded. ★And kill slow if they did. I can appreciate that, wizard. I've done the same.★

Shyntre raised a brow but let that go. ★I tried to say before, you're being lax with the Priestess. Letting your guard down. You seem to think she can't make you do anything you don't want to do.★

★Incorrect, wizard. Regardless, how is that a concern of yours?★

His nostril raised in an annoyed snarl. ★It isn't. Never mind, novice.★

★Oh, I think it is. Somehow.★

I stepped closer, within distance to touch him. Shyntre never blinked once, and I couldn't tell if he was about to fight or flee. Those intense eyes watched my hand as I lifted it to rest on the chest piece covering my heart.

"Guess what I brought," I whispered.

Suddenly, the wizard looked afraid, but not of me. As his gold-flecked eyes flicked into a darkened corner of the room, I heard the quiet shuffle of clawed feet coupled with the deep breath of a chest much broader than a Davrin. It sounded exactly like noises inside the Abyssal chamber at the Sanctuary. The next moment, when the air finally moved, I recognized the musk of scent and a surreal bend of the candlelight.

Shit!

I'd damned near revealed my secret to withstanding Wilsira's mind-sweeping spells! How long had Kerse been watching our hands while his

Mother bathed?

Being lax, indeed.

How did he get here? He must have been the whole time, could have slipped into the chambers before we arrived and avoided my own sweep. He and his Priestess had stayed here before, after all.

Shyntre backed away from me when Kerse showed his full, hideous face and strong, bestial body. Although the wizard got no closer to the Sathoet, his focus seemed to be on putting space between myself and him, while looking at the demonblood. I narrowed my eyes at him.

What do you know about all this, wizard?

The bathroom door opened, a moist cloud of fragrant steam flowing in.

"Ah, that's better," said the Priestess.

Kerse's timing was such that I might have thought he dropped his camouflage specifically to greet his Mother. He went to her side as she dried her gold-white hair with a soft, gray towel, crouched in quiet attention to where his head was level with her full breasts while her arms were raised. He was looking at how they moved beneath the silk of her comfort robe.

By this point, Shyntre had his back up against the far wall and was standing at calm attention. All that combative intelligence hidden again.

But not forever. He still can't pull off 'meek.'

When I looked at Wilsira, the towel came down. She draped it over a chair and crossed her arms low beneath her breasts, pushing them together, studying me. She looked clean and relaxed, her headpiece gone, and her hair down but mussed in an attractive way. I'd never seen a Priestess this dressed down. Ever.

"What do you see, Red Sister?" she asked.

"A comfortable Daughter of Braqth, Conceiver."

It was the best I could come up with, but at least she chuckled.

"Shyntre," Wilsira said, now pulling open and dropping her robe to stand nude before us all. "Help me prepare for our dining with the Matron."

"Yes, Priestess."

I knew I was caught staring when the mature Davrin planted her feet flat and apart, but I couldn't look away at first. I saw not only her pelt upon her mound, white mixed with gold, but the ritual scars, ragged and like matte amethyst, all along her inner thighs. It looked like a spider's web raked to ruin by a set of claws.

Purple and gold. Royal colors.

"Something distracts you, Red Sister?"

Her tone was defiant but not angry. Unashamed and curious.

I forewent playing dumb. "Are those Kerse's ... birthing marks, Conceiver?"

I looked up, and we met eyes. Wilsira smiled at me. Bumps erupted all along my back and up my neck at the penetrating stare.

"Indeed, Sirana. And more. Also marks from his demon sire's supplication to Braqth's Will, and, as I stand here before you this eve, my survival and proof of my divine power."

I'd never seen Abyssal scars this old, but I'd once witnessed them being created, still fresh and bleeding. Only once.

Elder Rausery once said these scars never fade.

"Guard the door, Red Sister," she commanded then, lightly touching Shyntre's back to guide him to the vanity where she could sit before the mirror.

I could only obey, standing like one of the vases at the wall, and watch from a distance as my wizard picked up a comb. Shyntre tended the Conceiver's long hair, careful in tugging out snarls to leave it damp and straight. I stared at the caster's hands as fiercely as I had Wilsira's scarred, inner thighs as he performed some complicated plaiting design, creating smooth, perfect coils to lift and pin in place atop her head.

He had styled this way *many* times before.

A wizard who demeaned and molested naked caits for the Sisterhood's entertainment also calmly beautified Priestess's hair upon demand? Phaelous's son was being given an interesting education, in addition to the spellcasting and gem working in the Tower.

A bua of many talents, and he's been alive long enough for them to notice.

Meanwhile, Kerse was given a simpler task when he began to growl, low and threatening, at the intensely focused wizard.

"Oh, come, dear one," the Priestess murmured with a throaty purr as she finished fiddling with a small, metal box with delicate, spider-shaped vents cut out of it.

She opened her legs very wide, scooted to perch near the edge of her chair, elbows braced on the arms as Shyntre continued tugging and styling her tresses for her.

"Eat a bit early, if you like. You know you make them too nervous sitting at the table, precious."

Unlike when the Sathoet had lifted his lip at the command of licking Qivni's juices off the wizard's fingers, there was no hesitation here. Kerse slid beneath the vanity and crawled between Wilsira's legs, eagerly lapping her sex, clawed hands grabbing the meat of her thighs and massaging toward her ass.

*And he's done **that** many times before.*

The Priestess moaned and writhed, cooing at her bua while gripping the chair arms. My wizard was nervous but determined to complete the styling in time for dinner. Kerse had an erection straining his waist wrap; I thought the tip of his rod would soon be poking up and out of that green cloth. And, Goddess damn it, I was horny and gawking when I should be standing guard.

I couldn't look away. I didn't think I was *this* bad at my duties.

"Ohhh, yes!" Wilsira groaned, arching her back, unmarked breasts on proud display. "Oh, baby, faster! Harder!"

I grimaced at the decadent performance, even knowing any Priestess was accustomed to being watched. Perhaps she didn't even need me here for this, but only Shyntre's anxiety and determined braiding while he stood behind her, testing the steadiness of his fine hands. But I *was* here, standing by the door and far out of reach.

I shouldn't have been aroused. I shouldn't have wanted to join in, to be having the thoughts to kneel and loosen my leathers, presenting my naked backside for their use.

Braced, with my knees apart.

I shook my head. I shouldn't be thinking that! Wilsira was like my sister, and Kerse was trained very early. It was obvious and disgusting. I should be repulsed.

Shyntre's dark blue wizard's robe had a tent as well. Tremors in his hands, a shaking in his breath; he was trying to resist. To meditate. To calm himself. I noticed the little metal box on the vanity. There was a soft glow inside and delicate threads of smoke drifting out of it.

Incense.

"Ah! Ah! *Ah!*" Wilsira cawed, her pitching climbing higher.

The Priestess climaxed, closing her scarred thighs on her son's face. Shyntre finished his last coil of her hair and then backed away, putting a stranglehold on his erection through his robe without quite falling to the carpet. The room vibrated with magic still unreleased, and D'Shea's warning returned to me again.

One component may be resisted. Far more difficult are two or three exposures together.

Was this the incense alone? It couldn't be so strong as to take an experienced mage like Shyntre, could it? Or was he vulnerable to it already? Was there a second component? What was missing to make us clamber without control on each other, thinking only to couple, as it had been when I was a young Noble?

Even though I stood trembling, aching, I could be glad my pants were still on. I was a lousy guard, but no one arrived to prove it. I heard Wilsira sigh, deeply relaxed as Kerse crawled back up to his feet.

"Mmm, perfect, my sweet. A fine way to begin the eve. Let us continue, wizard. ... Wizard? Oh, there you are. Do let go of your staff and help me dress."

"Yes, Priestess."

By happenstance, Shyntre and I exchanged a look, and I could read his face. He had known this wouldn't be easy. He'd tried to tell me.

Now, I believed him.

Effortless on her part. And this is just the first cycle.

CHAPTER 5

KERSE CROUCHED IN A DARK CORNER WHILE THE HOUSE OF FOUR DAUGHTERS and six Sons dined with their Matron and one quite young Consort. The demonblood's white mane just visible as a pale blur on the edge of the smokeless torches, though if he was still rut-ready, this wasn't obvious.

The arrival of the Sathoet made the Nobles even more nervous than the Red Sister standing behind Wilsira's chair. With him there, Wilsira didn't need me for protection inside an orderly manor like this.

After all, who would dare try to poison or stab her? For me, the challenge was keeping up my guard where I really needed it *without* making it obvious to various invested eyes that they weren't the threat to me; it was the Priestess herself.

The wizard and I are toys she brought along for her entertainment.

I hadn't truly expected more, not since forming my first idea of a Priestess. Any Priestess. This old view of mine fed my contempt into a calm and thick skin I'd learned long ago, but my ignorance remained.

I didn't know what to expect from this powerful Mother of a Sathoet I'd charmed so briefly. I only knew Shyntre must have a reason to show more wariness in front of the Conceiver than he did any of the Red Sisters so far.

Having a chance to study Shyntre sitting next to Wilsira, I thought they might share family somewhere. They did not look much alike, but they did each have the same set to their eyes and brow. The age difference was significant; equal to the Matron D'Verin and her new bua, which was enhanced whenever Wilsira reached a bejeweled hand to caress my wizard in some small way: along his ear's edge, or the exposed nape of his neck; his shoulders, and once beneath his chin.

Shyntre sat stiffer than the Consort when the Matron did something similar mirroring Wilsira, but he made no protest. He looked over toward Kerse in the corner, though. More than once.

Damn.

Although I'd spent fifteen cycles avoiding the worst of the humiliations the Court had to offer, I was now caught dead center in the middle of very old theater in Sivaraus, and Wilsira had a part she wanted me to play. What could I do about it? Resist and escalate? Dread and submit?

She's seen it all before, no doubt. Qivni was once a novice Red Sister like me, and Wilsira showed me straight away how even a Lead will bend over and take it up the ass when the Priestess wishes.

The one factor I wagered all this upon was Kerse himself and my insistence that he could act apart from Wilsira's will. Elder D'Shea could be right in saying I overestimated how far he could stretch the silk threads binding him to her side. I could also be wrong that he would do so on account of his desire for me.

Either way, my Elder insisted this was dangerous, and I had no sure way to nip it in the bud. Despite what training my Elder could give me, I had formed no plan because I hadn't yet decided how far I could be pushed.

The Conceiver wanted to find out, though.

She bends, D'Shea had said at my trials, immediately after Kerse left the chamber. *She doesn't break.*

We would see.

At the end of the meal, as if he could sense when the most nerves would fray, Shyntre dropped a utensil and looked at me out of the corner of his eye on his way down. Something well-honed in all Davrin Nobles even before Sisterhood training told me to read the flutter of his fingers the best I could.

   ★Drink now.★

THE SERVANTS HAD LEFT THE PRIESTESS'S LARGE SUITE FOLLOWING THE EVE-long dinner and subsequent show at the Nobles' tables. They had brought a sealed bottle of spiced wine and two swirled glass cups upon a silver tray, a gift of apology from the Matron. The door was closed and warded, locked and soundproofed.

"Well!" Wilsira said first, drifting over to her vanity to remove some pins and let down her coils. "That was entertaining, wasn't it, buas?"

Kerse chuffed through his nose and Shyntre pursed his mouth, re-maining silent as he went to the Priestess to assist with undressing her.

"Oh, come now, don't be sour." The Conceiver looked at me as Shyntre lowered her ornate gown and she stepped out of it. "What about you, Red Sister? Did it coax you into the mood to play? Did you wish to join in with your own weapon out and show them *both* how it's done?"

I smiled broadly, chuckling as I played being more at ease than I was. "They might have learned a thing or two if I had. The lovely one was a little awkward and clumsy on the Noble Son's back. I take it the Consorts aren't constantly mounting each other for practice in the Sanctuary before their First Gifting?"

Wilsira laughed, now nude as Shyntre folded her dress and laid it carefully back into her trunk, bringing back out her casual robe. I thought her voice was strained.

"Certainly not! *Mngh*. They're taught to worship and pleasure quims. It's the Sisterhood's duty to learn the limits of the filth pucker."

Interesting.

The beauty I'd found buried in Qivni's ass had a better idea what he was doing.

"But!" The Conceiver shrugged into her purple and black spider silk, wrapping her curves in comfort as I'd first seen D'Shea after my trials. "If the Matron wishes to remind a jealous son of her Consort's irreproachable value, it is well within her rights to demand what she did."

Indeed. It was a pity we didn't have Jaunda here to show them how it was done.

"Bathe yourself, Shyntre," Wilsira demanded next, handing him the soap and fragrance from her own cleansing earlier. "Be quick. A handful of ticks, no more."

"Yes, Conceiver."

His glance to me was so brief, I thought it was a facial tic at first. Then I noticed how hard he was squeezing the soap and fragrance — his knuckles greyed out — and I missed the moment when the Priestess lit the incense box on the edge of the vanity.

It struck me then what the second of two spell components might have been while the wizard and I had been fighting to stay on our feet before dinner. The steam coming out from the bath had been very fragrant.

And now, Shyntre was going to smell the same.

Shit.

Well, had I expected her to tease us like that and then simply go to bed after dinner? Especially after a power show provided by the Matron of the House. For all I knew, the third son hadn't really said what he had about the Consort — I sure hadn't heard it — and it was that no one dared tell the Priestess she was mistaken.

I'd taken the first of my infertility draughts about a mark ago; Shyntre's sign had been well-timed. For the next half-cycle, twenty buas could line up and fill the passage between my netherlips to a trickling puddle, and there was no chance of me catching, followed by being removed from the Sisterhood.

No chance to avoid the tests the Priestess plans for me, either. Might as well find out what I can and not waste the potion.

"What are you thinking, novice?" Wilsira asked, caressing her full breast through her thin, silk robe. "You have such an odd look on your face."

I had *no* look on my face, I had made sure.

"How relaxed you are, Priestess," I answered. "You feel safe here?"

"Hm." Her full lips lifted in practiced grace. "I do. Matron D'Verin is one of our most loyal."

"Do you need me to stay in full reds while you're in Reverie, Conceiver, or would you have me get comfortable as well?"

A glimpse of surprise. Was that two, now?

"How comfortable do you wish to get, Sirana?"

"How far may I go, Priestess?"

The mature Davrin considered Kerse, who was crouched low, exquisitely still, and studying the patterns of the carpet. He had been maintaining a plump partial erection since sniffing the lingering scent of his Mother's pleasure when we'd come back to the suites.

"Strip down, Red Sister," she commanded. "Get comfortable."

I nodded. "May I use your trunk to secure my equipment?"

"After hauling a dead body on your lap and your boots in the mud? Absolutely not."

I smiled despite the situation. I *was* more than a little grungy compared to the other three, and Shyntre smelled the finest he ever had when he exited the bathroom then. He was stark naked, carrying a lidded basket holding everything he'd been wearing.

Not unlike when my things were taken away at the start of my Sisterhood trials.

"You can add your things to mine, Red Sister," he offered.

"Warded?"

"Of course. I have objects those unfamiliar with magic don't touch, for their protection."

Wilsira lifted her eyes briefly toward the ceiling as if she thought that was cute. I wasn't sure what the wizard meant to accomplish. It might be this was another duty serving the Conceiver, an anticipation of her needs, but it was also clear he truly didn't consider me a threat. At best, I was an annoyance and complication to whatever he normally did in the Sanctuary.

This bua …

At least he wasn't squeamish.

I removed cloak, belt, and boots first, stripping down as ordered, each piece removed heightening my arousal, though I wasn't sure how much was my training as a Red Sister and how much was Wilsira's incense combined with a delectably scented wizard standing nude with an erection before me.

A surge of nebulous emotion took me as I considered how I stood once again in the presence of a mature female, knowing so little about what was to happen next. Like the orgy with the Priestesses in control of the ceremony, or when I'd been trapped in a circle of candles with Kerse.

Still, I held to one thing: I wasn't in the wilderness with Tragar and Consort, going flat mad in lust. My sex was swollen and wet, I ached to have it filled, but I still held my will for the moment.

The blue pendant slid beneath my red shirt as the darker leather armor came off after my bracers. Shyntre's basket became heavy enough that he set it on the floor and stood next to it, holding the lid. I skimmed my pants down my legs and added those, now bottomless as I considered my shirt, my final covering hiding my necklace.

Should I remove the shirt and necklace together and hide it? Reveal it but act like it meant nothing? Or was it the only obstacle between me and dropping to all fours, more helpless than Curgia … ?

I stared without blinking at Shyntre's cock for long moments as I decided, as if I'd forgotten my shirt entirely. Then I dropped onto my knees with no care for my pride as I took the wizard's naked hips in both hands and sucked down his pole as if he was my first drink of water in three cycles.

"Fuck!" Shyntre blurted, jolted off guard. "Sirana!"

I clutched him tightly, pulling the spongey head of his prick deeper into my throat, as my Sisters had taught me, and swallowed. He gripped my hair, unable to decide whether to jerk me away or cram my head closer.

"Let me go!" he hissed.

His tone was the closest to an urgent plea I'd ever heard before. It coincided with Kerse's low growl and Wilsira's rumbles of disapproval. I pulled back enough that Shyntre could free himself the rest of the way. I played up the act to hold on to him, falling to all fours with a groan as I "lost" him.

"Tastes so good," I said in a throaty, horny whisper, panting in place as I shivered, my legs open but in profile enough to hide my wet slit from Kerse and Wilsira's view. "So *good!* Goddess, I need it, wizard!"

I heard Kerse sniffing the air and whining a wordless question to his Mother. I crawled forward like a Drider about to launch out of her den, and Shyntre threw himself back, clipping and stumbling over the basket, falling on his ass. Wilsira laughed in delight.

"Stop, Sirana!" she commanded.

I obeyed, spinning to face them. I planted my ass on my heels, parting my knees wide and reaching to spread my juices over my nub and netherlips, easing a finger inside as he and the Priestess watched. My eyes were glazed over; I worked to appear confused.

"C-Conceiver?"

Exhaling slowly at the sound, Wilsira stripped the loincloth off her hybrid son with her own hands. "I have another cock you may suck instead. Blessed by Braqth Herself."

I grinned drunkenly, finger-fucking myself faster to hide my surprise at the thick, knobby shaft of his black demonic erection. It seemed different — and larger — than last time.

"Astonishin' shape, Priestess."

"Mmm," she hummed as she caressed him to full, seeping readiness. "And spicy on the tongue."

I moaned aloud as if in agreement, spread out and squatted down lower as I worked quickly toward a peak of my own. The Priestess watched a few moments as if tempted to call me closer. She may have wanted to have her son's prick in my mouth while she stood with scarred thighs so close, I would smell them. Perhaps gripping my hair, controlling everything about it.

Instead, like in the candle chamber if not the Worship Ball, she sent her son to me.

The Sathoet strutted forward, his back straight and not hunched like usual when his knuckles dragged on the ground. I had to tilt my head up to meet his yellow eyes and toothy, eager grin, but everyone had forgotten about my shirt. I straightened as well, rising on my knees to put my lips at the perfect height to receive his cock.

I loathed to stop my climb, but it had served its purpose: There remained some distance between Wilsira and me. I used my sopping fingers to reach up and caress the demonblood's hairy testicles. The delicate sack tightened up under my touch, and Kerse scented the air deeply again.

"Stay still, good bua," I whispered to him, placing hands on his muscular thighs, sliding up, opening my lips. Tilting my jaw.

His breathing became both deeper and faster, watching me. I didn't tease him much before slipping the black, pointed tip in between my lips. Kerse yelped softly and shifted his hips forward to press into my mouth; I closed lips around him and gave him focused head.

"Good cait," Wilsira cooed, stepping closer to watch my technique. I ignored her for the moment, continued sucking and touching myself.

The texture of the demonblood's member was rougher than a pure Davrin, with strange, tiny ridges hard to see but which may have contributed to my pleasure the first time we'd fucked. The bitter moisture oozing from the small, slightly flared hole tingled, and the sensation spread where it touched: the roof of my mouth, my tongue and lips, the back of my throat.

It was like a liquor intended for a potion, or an essence if one could condense and capture the otherworldly scent of a Sathoet in a bottle. The tingle slowly changed to a captivating burn, and I did not know whether or when to pull away. *Spicy, indeed.*

I felt his hands on my back and shoulders, caressing me with his claws without breaking skin. He hissed and gnarred in pleasure, stroked my skin with his palms as if in encouragement. The Priestess retired to the bed then, saying something in Abyssal which made Kerse pause very briefly before resuming his movement in tandem with my mouth.

I wrapped one hand around him as well, trying to control the depth he could go yet push him to the next level of arousal. As I increased the pace, something began to grow beneath my hand. Baffled, I lifted my mouth off to look, Kerse protesting the sudden stop.

There was a swollen bulb at the base of his erection.

"Sirranna," he hissed tensely.

I put my mouth back on, recovering from my surprise but Wilsira picked up on it anyway. She chuckled from where she lounged upon the bed.

"His breeding knot," she murmured, caressing her sex between splayed thighs in my periphery. "His sire had one."

So not all Sathoet did? None of those I'd seen thus far were smooth and pole-shaped, but I hadn't seen such a flare at the base before, either. Not even his. Kerse had been my first in the candle chamber, and I was certain he hadn't been this shape before. I'd have known if he'd lodged something like that up inside me.

"Turn around, young Sister," she commanded, her voice thick. "Present your cunt. Hold still while he pleasures you as no slim slut at Court *ever* has."

My mouth full and voice silent, my sex throbbed at her words, clenching in eager anticipation. I was shaking as I emptied my throat of demonic cock, lifted my spit-covered lips, and turned around to show him my ass. Kerse leaned down and, like the first time we'd met, swept his long, rough tongue deep into my cleft, from nub to oozing slit to twitching pucker.

"Augh!" I screamed, nearly climaxing there and then.

"Be still!" Wilsira commanded again, her voice deeper and carrying more bass.

The urge to do *exactly* as she said and think no more for the rest of the eve was powerful.

Frighteningly powerful.

We all still breathed the incense, my mouth and nose were coated with the Sathoet's leaking fluid and heavy musk, and I knew the precise moment my freshly bathed wizard eased close enough to smell his skin.

"Shyntre, strip off her shirt. I want her naked. My son shall have access to *anything* he likes on this Red Sister neophyte."

Shit …

I dropped to my elbows, my blood red shirt sliding up my back as I wiggled my hips at the demonblood, distraction, yes, but also a genuine offer. He rumbled and accepted, pinching and squeezing my buttocks as I reached back to pull both it and the black leather thong together from the nape of my back and over my head.

The pendant was off and hidden in my shirt. I fumbled to help the wizard slide off the sleeves, bunching the shirt into a crumpled pile with the blue stone wrapped inside. Shyntre gathered it carefully, picking it up off the floor.

Please don't fall out.

It was my last free thought.

Kerse reached forward to maul my naked breasts, and some woolen fog rolled over my mind as his scalding hands covered and clasped my tits. That uneven prick pressed into my backside, and I froze in place except to spread my knees a bit wider and arch my back. Presenting as ordered.

"Breed her, my bua," the Priestess whispered, sounding far away and sinister.

The Sathoet lined himself up with barely any help from me and plunged his Abyssal phallus in between my netherlips.

"Oh, sweet Web, yes," his Mother breathed.

Kerse went deep but did not yet force in the knot, although I felt the threat of it. I clung to the carpet like it was a pit trap which could fall out from beneath me at any moment as he pounded my sloppy twat hard. I held still as Wilsira breathed out, fondling herself faster as her son kept up a brutal tempo, his sword entering my sheath again and again.

"*Rath'gehenna!*" Wilsira cried, and the paralysis grew worse.

My mouth stayed open and wordless. The side of my face rubbed to a mild abrasion, and my heart raced as stunning pleasure overtook me from the points of my ears to my curling toes. I couldn't think at all as he bred me. The Conceiver didn't speak again until a rasping, huffing half-breed reached his crescendo, his thrusts stopping as he pressed very close.

Then the bulge began to enter, spreading my cunt wide, the taut folds of my sex burning. I squeaked in panic.

"Pruchizh'kigal!"

Her voice made the air shimmer as Kerse howled, and his demonic cock locked into my body. He began spurting, and something more insidious than a knot of flesh sought to enter me next, to seep in like a poison. Helpless to eject the organ which kept us coupled together, I struggled to keep the magic out instead, barely holding some intangible line by virtue of a single blurry thought.

My whole focus upon the memory of the potion my wizard had prompted me to take that eve at dinner. *Prevention.*

For a time, the Conceiver still tried. Urgent, eager power came at me from all sides, magic fluttering around me like a thousand tails of tadpoles as Kerse's spending sloshed and squished inside my stuffed channel. The exhausting climax and choking magic receded together in time, and I scrabbled to become aware again as soon as possible.

My nipples were sore from the Sathoet harshly twisting and pinching them in his excitement, my knees and elbows raw from the furious rut. Experimentally, I tugged. He was still stuck, and my sex ached and throbbed around him.

"Goddess ... oh my Glorious Braqth," Wilsira moaned, sounding about as most of us young Nobles had after the orgy, though she recovered much more quickly.

It took every effort to lift my head when I heard her roll on the bed. She had not risen to her feet but was in repose upon one elbow, having closed her marked, ragged thighs. Her perfect coils and braids of gold-white hair were now frizzed and messed up, and she was grinning at Shyntre.

"Feeling left out, *aus'bil*?"

"No, Priestess. I'm content to watch and serve."

Like the Void, you are ...

Wilsira didn't buy it, either. "Mm-hm. You've done well, Shyntre. You deserve a reward. Let the novice Sister suck and swallow her dinner from you while she waits to be released. She's not going anywhere for a bit."

Whether Shyntre truly wished to refuse or not, I couldn't tell as the stubborn male approached and kneeled in front of me. Kerse took a swipe at him, possessively holding my haunches, and I cringed as I was caught in between them. His claws dug in and his Mother admonished him.

"Stop it! Let the wizard take his reward from her mouth. Your Priestess and Mother has spoken, Kerse."

Rumbling softly, the demon-Elf grudgingly kept both hands on my ass while his knot slowly shrank as Shyntre took a firm, though not rough, hold of the hair at my nape, placing his cock at my lips with his other hand.

I looked up and into his cautious, intelligent eyes as my tongue snaked out to caress him. He sucked in a surprised breath. I paused, and he held his cock forward for me to take when I was ready rather than shoving it in as he had done when we first met.

Although it was neither the type nor circumstance of play that I had imagined when I had argued with this mage at the Wizard's Tower, I engulfed his smooth, normal rod with enthusiasm. I serviced him until his pleasure erupted in my mouth. But for his ragged breath, Shyntre was silent as his cream coated my throat.

He said nothing, and I swallowed.

The wizard smelled delicious and tasted even better, and I didn't begrudge him a good suck. I owed him something, both for the early warning and for keeping my most important secret when all else about me, especially my now-fertile womb, knelt exposed before a Priestess of Braqth.

CHAPTER 6

"HERE, SIRANA, DRINK THIS."

"I have my own, Priestess. But thank you."

"As you wish, but I wouldn't want you to go through your entire store on my account."

"That's what they're there for, Priestess. I follow my training."

Wilsira smiled slyly, her gaze one of naked lust. She tucked the vial into a hidden pocket of her luxurious gown.

"Let me finish my preparations to meet with the Matron," she said, "and I'll take the mage with me this time. I may be gone for several marks."

I nodded, standing at attention as I waited for her to leave, but she tended to take a while to get ready.

I hadn't had an easy time since that very first eve at House D'Verin. I gave thanks to Elder D'Shea for my being prepared with more infertility draughts than a typical Red Sister carried. I acknowledged the wizard with the timing of taking that first one; the "Game" would have been over so quickly otherwise.

I remembered how the Conceiver had called out my sticky thighs, a direct result of where I'd received her Sathoet's "offering."

"You *wanted* my son again, Sirana?"

Such delight. She thought she had won. She had still been coming down from her own heights.

"Unequivocally and without interruption?"

An intentionally odd question. A trap where the only way to avoid insult was to lie and be required to own it as truth going forward.

"I ... prayed, Conceiver."

Just don't ask when I last prayed, and what I hoped for.

"Was his service better than in your trial, novice, not being required to pull out?"

"It was ... far more intense, Priestess."

Kerse's Mother had looked as though she slipped real cream down her own throat. "Mmm. We can do better, young Sister. I promise. You'll never be bored on this trip. Don't forget to keep up your guard as well. As the Prime directed."

She was quite correct about that.

We had left House D'Verin early that cycle and had just arrived at House Peniel, the Sixth House and our second destination. Thus far, I'd performed my normal guard duties and performed with her son several more times for the Priestess's entertainment, with nothing I could do to protest the use of her time.

Four cycles had passed since my last Reverie. I was exhausted and using stimulants from my pouch while consuming only food and water that I collected myself. When I wore the blue Dwarf stone Shyntre had given me, I felt more alert and resistant to the incense, chants, and fragrance. When required to remove it, I struggled as much as Curgia had to resist being used, kneeling on the floor with Kerse behind her.

"*Because Wilsira is casting powerful, will-bending spells on you,*" Shyntre whispered in a rare moment alone."*This is very unusual for her. I think she likes the challenge you offer.*"

Indeed, the Conceiver hadn't needed any spells at all to break and impregnate the merchant-Noble on the first try.

A cait stupid enough to catch deserves what she gets in the Sanctuary, the Eldest Sister had threatened, *and what happens when she comes back to the Cloister.*

This wasn't stupidity. This was a lop-sided test of endurance and ingenuity, not unlike the Sisterhood trials. Like what happened with Jael and the Tragar. Instead of simple survival, however, the winning outcome was to be whether I became pregnant on my first mission for the Sanctuary and then belonged to the Conceiver's judgment over D'Shea's.

I didn't know what happened if the "catch" of a Red Sister was with a breed of hybrid that wasn't allowed to flourish under the Valsharess's law, but I didn't want to be the example where the Prime and all others found out.

"After Kerse is satisfied," the Priestess said to me now, trying for sympathy, "you *must* promise me you will rest while I'm away, Red Sister. I haven't seen you in Reverie even once since we left the Sanctuary. That's not healthy. I know they may have done some things to … alter you in the Sisterhood, but every sentient being *must* dream, eventually."

I nodded blearily; my head ached and swam at once. "Of course, Conceiver."

"Use my trunk for your equipment." She nodded toward the open one. "Once you close the lid, it shall be secure until I return."

I nodded again.

I'd been unable to rest without risking the loss or tampering of my most important tools. This was the first time Wilsira intended to leave me alone with her son and take Shyntre with her. She had allowed me to take my own draughts without verbal challenge thus far, although the wizard, for his own reasons, had helped me switch them back at least once after I'd been unable to keep eyes on my equipment.

This brought me to the other major weakness apart from sleep.

Even having a second pair of eyes to test which of the vials were D'Shea's genuine ones, I was now out of pregnancy prevention potions. Wilsira had forced me to run through them all as fast as she could, Kerse more than happy to help, and the trip was not even half over.

At long last, Wilsira had left with Shyntre, and the room was quiet in a way it never had been with her present.

Kerse and I stared at one another, and I was reminded how my cunt was rather sore. I didn't know if or how often a Sathoet needed to sleep, but I hadn't witnessed Kerse fall into Reverie as I had Shyntre and the Priestess.

The tall, muscular demonblood was crouched down at the moment, one arm resting on his thigh as his other hand balanced him as the third point of contact with the floor. His free hand moved between his legs, not lewdly but in a proper hand sign.

What?

Only when he repeated it did I straighten up off the wall and methodically checked the room, as a Red Sister should have been doing, before reaching my intended goal: the two upturned, glass lanterns in the room. I found one active bloodstone inside each.

Hmm.

Forging with magic as mages could do would never be a skill of mine, but I had used enough magical tools to know bloodstone was used for scrying spells. One could choose either visual or aural scrying, but not both. The reflection or echo of the potent life essence was absorbed to be experienced later, either for the original caster or a designated user.

Only one time, as the magic dissipated, so take notes.

Perpetual scrying stones were unheard of for the complexity in trying to read one while the spell was still active; they all had to go dormant sometime to be any use. The longer absorption bloodstones were usually fixed to a permanent set of runes and well protected, meaning everyone knew where they were.

Small, mobile pieces like these could be slipped in on the sneak, but also did not absorb information for longer than a few marks once the spell had been tapped. It was possible the Matron of the House set these in here, but much more likely that it had been Wilsira, herself. I hadn't seen her do it; was I that bad off?

He informed me without telling her.

Glancing at Kerse, trying to hide my suspicion, I took the stones into the bathing room, wrapped them up in a cloth and filled the sink with water. After submerging them and — for good measure — adding a piece of raw iron from my pouch into the water, I came back out into the bedroom suite. The Sathoet smiled a little, some of the tension easing in his shoulders.

"Anything else?" I asked.

He shook his head, though I did another sweep, anyway. He watched me without remark of any kind, and I found nothing else.

"Did you see her put those bloodstones in here?"

Kerse shook his head in the negative. "Ffeel magicks."

"Upon walking in?"

Again, he shook his head. "Affterr. Motherr's magicks."

He would know. His very existence amplified them.

I leaned against the sturdy writing desk and breathed out slowly. By the Goddess, I was tired. The quiet room wasn't helping; the air itself seemed to press on my shoulders, coaxing me to lie down.

"Neeed sslleep," he commented, gesturing at me.

"That bad, am I?" I smirked. "Had your fill of me yet, Priestess Son?"

The Sathoet must enjoy shaking his head, tossing about that white mane as he smirked. His loincloth seemed a bit heavy, fuller. "Do you dansss?"

Good memory.

"Every cycle," I muttered, repeating what Wilsira had said in the carriage.

Kerse chuckled. He got the reference.

Was this right? Was the blood of the Void, created to be a power-boosting pawn of the Daughters of Braqth, *supposed* to remember inconsequential details like that much later? I tried to remember what my Elder had said about that.

The half-breeds are creatures of appetite, Sirana, like all demons. They bear some memory like a Davrin Elf, but most easily remember what's linked to their strongest appetite or impulse at the time.

Great. I believed I had my answer, then.

"You haven't slid your prick in to stretch my back pucker yet," I said, looking at him again. "Do you want to try it?"

The Sathoet stared at me, falling perfectly still. Tensely, as if he wanted to spring at me but waited for the right instant.

Is that a yes?

Because I was out of infertility potions and had too few options, some far worse than risking that knot squeezed in where so many Sisters' Feldeus had been, anyway.

I pushed off the desk and began the familiar ritual of removing my possessions and uniform, and Kerse licked black, bestial lips, never blinking. Once nude, I wrapped up everything but the larger weapons in my cloak, preparing to place it and all else in Wilsira's trunk.

"Wearrr mage sstone," he said, motioning like there was a necklace around his neck.

I froze. *Fuck.* "Does your Mother know?"

Kerse smiled without showing teeth. He didn't have to answer; if she had, my pendant would be among her belongings now. A chill crept up my spine.

My own fault. I had practically revealed it to him as he'd spied on me and Shyntre that first time, and he'd been up close with his hands all over me multiple times, while his Mother watched from the bed.

"Why?"

"Prrotection," he murmured, tilting his gaze, studying. "Shield thoughts from magicks, yesss?"

True enough. Not even the Headmaster could easily determine the best strengths of the strange, blue sapphire around my neck, but D'Shea and I knew this one thing about it. What else could a Sathoet figure out in one fuck?

"Trying to put me at ease, demonchild?"

"Nneed sslleep, Ssiranna," he repeated. "Nno touch sstone, nno rremove sstone. Wake you when Motherr rreturrns. Hide it."

So tempting. So *fucking* tempting. Yet, I couldn't believe him. It was the height of foolishness.

"And what do you want in return?" I asked outright.

Kerse reached down, rubbing his stiffening erection through his green wrap. "Offerred puckerr. Mean it?"

"I mean it," I replied.

Reaching back, I grasped my own ass cheek, spread myself, and turned so he could see the purple crinkle in the shadow of my cleft. The Sathoet breathed harder, shivered in excitement as he jerked himself. He nodded; it seemed my netherhole was more than acceptable to him.

"And sslleep affterr?"

"That's it?"

"All, Sissterr. Deal?"

Too good to be true.

But, again, I had few options, and the continued block from Reverie would end the game that much sooner. Perhaps this was why both Mother and Son were cutting me a break.

They were having fun, and the trip wasn't over yet.

I nodded, and my hand returned to the trunk for the pendant, tugging it back out and looping it over my neck. Then, I closed the trunk, sensing the ward arise. I wouldn't be able to get dressed until the Priestess came back, but all the other pieces of my uniform would be secure without Shyntre to help.

This was the only way I might slip into any sort of restful Reverie.

Next, I stretched out on the bed, leaving it up to Kerse what he did, and rubbed my hand over my eyes and forehead. My headache had grown worse. His hot hand gently touched my ankle, and when I didn't pull away, it slid up my calf to my knee. Heavy weight settled onto the foot of the bed. Both hands caressed my thighs and nudged at them, voicelessly asking me to spread them as he loomed over me.

It occurred to me that this was the very first time we were doing this on a comfortable bed. Or while I was facing him.

Wilsira only wanted to watch him mount me like livestock, or pressed to some object, bent over it or tied to where I couldn't keep him out or away. Whatever was most demeaning for a young female Noble, she did. Any such concerns had long since been worked out of my head, however. I let her have her glee and entertainment. I was far from broken.

Drowsiness being a far greater fight now, I opened my legs for him, and Kerse quickly cupped my upper thighs and settled down to nuzzle between them. I hummed. Genuinely, I enjoyed the way his tongue felt: long, strong, and surprisingly versatile. He was unable to use any lips because of his teeth, so I could never mistake it for a Davrin's mouth.

He purred as my breathing quickened, content in my pleasure for a time. My nipples tightened. My thighs brushed his wide, hard shoulders as he slipped large hands beneath my bottom, lifting me up from the mattress and holding me in place.

Novel.

A flush crossed my chest as he licked harder and moved down to include my "filth pucker," alternating his pressure spots and catching multiple sensitive points in quick succession. I tensed, full-body, as my legs came up and wide, offering better access. My toes curled in the air when he accepted.

Braqth, he's good at this ... !

Wilsira hadn't let him try more than a cursory lick before, but now I knew something of what she had felt when the Sathoet had tucked up beneath her vanity and dove in between her marked-up thighs.

More than what she did.

His tongue swirled and coaxed my pucker open, slipping inside as his thumbs tugged and pulled at me. When he left my bunghole sopping, empty, and twitching, cords of muscle bunched in his neck and shoulders as his focus heightened on my swollen folds and the nub nestled within.

He knew right where it was, and his tongue wouldn't stop. Not until I'd climaxed.

I didn't fight him or myself. I let it come.

"Ohhh, *yes! Ah!*"

His rumbling was a constant, a happy sound, I thought, as he massaged my buttocks on my way down. As I finished gasping my ever-relaxed moans, he rose up on his knees. I braced my arms over my head as Kerse grasped my hips in both large hands and lifted them higher off the mattress, my calves framing his shoulders.

My vision swam; his eyes glowed yellow out of the shadows, looming above me.

"Nnoww?" he asked, moving his hips, the hot tip of his cock prodding between my cheeks.

Before I could reply, he poked in, perhaps without meaning to. My well-trained anus yielded with familiarity, spreading smooth and tight and easy for him. My eyes fluttered and rolled back as the triangular head popped past that sensitive ring, and he slid deeper, barely pushing while my clutching shitter hugged his rod tight.

He paused. I opened my eyes.

The half-blood looked genuinely surprised. I found a comfortable, sustainable angle, impressed how he could hold me up with less apparent effort than Jaunda.

"Now," I finally answered. "Kerse, fuck my ass."

His cock swelled and flexed inside me.

The Sathoet grunted as he pushed inside, the knot snuggling up against my hole but prevented from passing through that boundary just yet. He didn't care; he stroked himself eagerly and with surprising care as I moaned with honest pleasure. He felt *good!*

His eyes were locked on my face as that uneven, black demon's cock speared between my buttocks. His clawed hand reached forward to fondle my breasts, sharp tips brushing the blue stone settled in the hollow of my neck.

~Calm. Relax. Easy.~

With a growl and a drool, Kerse pressed forward the first time, the bulge at the thick base stretching me wider. It was partway in.

~Now out. All the way.~

He withdrew. His entire length. I scooped oozing lubricant from my sex and let it drip over my stretched hole trying to flutter its way shut.

~Again.~

Both hands on my hips, he penetrated me deeply, stroked again, spreading the new moisture around, and then pressed in hard a second time. He got a little farther in; gained more ground as my ring spread wider for him. He was halfway.

~Now out. Out.~

Once more, he withdrew to watch my slippery fingers smear more proof of my desire where the action was then circled my pearl as I nodded permission. Kerse watched my fingers, my face. My eyes.

~Again. I want it.~

My greedy ass gulped his prick down again as he slid it in. The

Sathoet huffed and thrust, fucked and rocked and teased us both. We both *knew* how close he was to that edge, to getting his knot inside me. The tension was delicious agony.

~*Yes, yes! Please!*~

I relaxed. Felt myself stretch a little more. At last, he slipped past that point of no return. I sucked in a shocked breath as my ass clamped down, locking him in complete joining.

~*Our bodies ... One!*~

Kerse threw his chin up and howled to the ceiling as his entire length flexed. Something far too hot sluiced my guts deep inside. Flooding me.

~*One!*~

I cried out as I climaxed again; blood rushed into my head as sensation began to climb. My ears seemed to develop a layer of water inside as all I heard for a moment was low rushing and a sound like the clang of a metallic heartbeat.

I shook my head to try to dislodge a different, distracting, and unsettling sound which followed: the chiming as if my blood were beginning to turn to shards of crystal bouncing off each other.

~*Free us.*~

I was sure that claws were tracing over my bare abdomen, yet I knew Kerse somehow still held my hips with both hands!

~*Free us!*~

My reaction was violent, a surge of panic. My legs snapped around his waist to counterbalance the raw strength of my core so I could pull myself up. I grabbed hold of his shoulder with one hand and had my other raised and fisted, ready to strike him or whatever with my full arm.

Heart thundering audibly, he flinched, stopping our coupling as he folded his legs down and held me tight to his broad chest in his lap.

"Ssirranna!" he hissed.

I paused as my vision cleared. Though I could not see his face, I did not see anything amiss. I was breathing too hard, trembling, and soon accepted that I couldn't go anywhere if I wanted to. My ass felt like Jaunda was making a fist inside it.

I also wasn't sure what had happened except—

Something had been touching me with all hands accounted for.

He muttered a toothy, "Ssorryy …"

I didn't hear that often. "Sorry for what?"

"Beauttiffull," he rumbled, caressing my back.

I didn't give a damn whether that was flattery or not; I focused on the problem. "What happened, Kerse?"

He adjusted his grip on me. "Sstopped magickss."

I didn't understand what he meant. Could he do that? Just "stop" magic?

He squeezed my backside and breathed raggedly, clutching me tightly to his chest as he trembled, and his cock twitched. The knot was starting to shrink but he wasn't finished yet.

I squirmed in his lap, the blue stone a hard and hot lump between us, but this only caused him to hold tighter until I could barely fill my lungs. I stopped moving so I could draw in some air.

The Sathoet shuddered every few seconds for quite a while, his warm tongue flicking out to taste the skin of my shoulder or neck. The vibrations coming from his chest were like a song that one might hear in the deepest caves, crooning and keening lower than a Davrin could hear. I felt it in my teeth and the bones before realizing it was a sound meant for my ears.

I could not remain tense this entire time; I tired even more quickly than before. His skin became superheated and moist as he held me and finished his enviably long orgasm. His breathing came in deep rows of rushing air behind my ear as he rested his chin on my shoulder. Without thought, I relaxed with him, my exhaustion setting in as heavy as marble.

My eyes fluttered shut. The blue stone cooled.

In time, the Abyssal creature leaned forward to gently lay me on my back and tugged to test the fit before taking that last, good pull to withdraw himself. His semen flooded out of my gaping mess of an orifice to soak the bedding beneath.

No lying to Mother where we fucked this time.

"Ssleep," he hissed softly, the weight of his body depressing the mattress next to me. "Nneed ssleep."

I know, I know …

I breathed out, felt myself drift, not caring that I lay in a wet spot. He nudged me and, damned if I knew why, I turned on my side. He immediately moved closer until we were sharing body heat with his chest and stomach curled protectively at my back.

Tentatively, Kerse draped a long arm over me, tucking his claws in to settle his knuckles against my stomach. Caressing.

I was too tired to protest.

I fell into Reverie the next instant, kept still and warm by a large and changing body.

CHAPTER 7

~WHAT HAVE YOU DONE TO US?~

*It wasn't just me. What have **you** done?*

~We know what we are. We know what we want.~

Then you know more than most do. It'll change.

~Accept what you have done!~

It happened. What else is there to accept?

~The merging of minds. Becoming One.~

No. Still separate. Minds are born separate.

~Fool. Not Truth. We are stronger when one embraces the Great Work.~

At the cost of something else?

~Everything costs.~

We agree. Leave me alone. I'm best on my own.

~Not anymore. It's too late. You know this. We *know* you.~

No more than I know myself.

~Heh. Knowing 'self' is the weakest of walls. It breaks often, and you rebuild often. The blind pretend it was never broken.~

Oh?

~Indeed. Consider, how does the self ever know what may cross over to stay, before the wall is rebuilt?~

How?

~Only when we face it on the other side. To see there never *was* another side.~

MY EYES FLEW OPEN.

I stood upright and barefoot on the carpeted floor before I realized that I'd heard the door unlock. Wilsira and Shyntre entered, and all four of us stared silently at each other as details became apparent.

The wizard's nostrils flared, a twitch of an expression about the strength of the scents in the room. He carried a bottle of something and two small glasses. The Priestess studied my hips and thighs and looked pleased; I had not cleaned up and the Sathoet seed was visible, sticky in some places and flakey in others.

Kerse sat up slowly on the bed and churred a greeting to his dam. His cock had been cleaned up.

"You can stand down now, Sirana," the Priestess said, soothing. "No one attacks."

My hand was fisted as if I held a non-existent dagger, my stance one ready to fight. Though, no recent attacks could be handled directly with sharp blades. Instead, a hard lump and the coil of leather filled my hand, and I noted my Dwarf stone pendant was no longer around my neck. I didn't open my hand to look as Wilsira smiled at Kerse.

"Are you feeling better, my own?"

The Sathoet nodded an affirmative and crawled off the bed to crouch submissively before the Priestess, as I'd so often seen him do when he was at her disposal.

"And did our dedicated warrior rest, at last?"

She was still talking to Kerse, not me.

Again, he nodded. "Ssleep."

"Excellent. The sharper a Sister's awareness, the better."

The Priestess looked *too* pleased. Had Kerse been instructed to do something else to me while I slept? Since his cock was clean, did he cum in my cunt while I was unconscious? It could be paranoia, except that she *really* was out to trap me.

If I didn't find anything on me and even managed to avoid detainment, D'Shea might. My crafty Elder mage wouldn't allow me back at the Cloister among my Sisters without a thorough inspection, after being alone with a Priestess for so long.

I *wanted* to go back to her, to them.

I would have to try not to sleep again on this trip.

It was late eve and the House dining had already occurred. I'd been asleep for eight marks, twice as long as I normally needed. I retrieved my belongings from Wilsira's trunk and went into the bathing room again, washed and dried myself and inspected everything thoroughly, piece by piece, as I redressed.

Nothing unusual or missing, and I didn't find obvious demon seed left in my birth canal. Sadly, I wasn't sensitive enough or knowledgeable enough about magic to do more than sense the magic in the items I used as part of the Sisterhood. I neither felt nor saw anything foreign in my skin, no marks or stains on my body, nothing in my braid as I combed it out and then plaited and secured it at my nape again.

"I am going to the kitchens, Priestess," I said on exiting, feeling a little better for being clean and having my uniform on and weapons back to hand. "I must eat."

The Priestess had reclined in a comfortable chair with a glass of whatever Shyntre had carried in. She nodded, but then Kerse growled; he was looking straight at the wizard as Shyntre shifted nervously.

Wilsira chuckled. "Why don't you take the mage with you, Sirana? I'd like to be alone. My son will protect me. Just don't roll the bua where the House can see you."

Funny.

I jerked a motion at him, and Shyntre seemed as eager to leave the room at last. He breathed out as we walked farther down the hall but said nothing directly. I let the silence remain until we'd found the kitchens.

Shyntre stood slightly behind me, allowing my uniform to get us the immediate service we could expect. Those of the House had been entirely surprised at my arrival in their servants' space, however, they had to be given time to respond. Unless I wanted to go out and hunt down my own meal.

"Y-yes, Red Sister? What do you need?"

"The stew, the bread, that fruit, that water. Lots of it."

I watched as the head Davrin instructed the little Pytes to serve up a generous helping of only the things I could see were part of a communal supply — nothing specialized, nothing that plenty of others didn't share as well. They assumed the wizard with me needed a meal, too, and handed him a platter laden with double servings to carry for both of us.

Shyntre began to protest, but I said, "Very good," and gestured for him to follow me.

We found a small patio out of doors, and I could enjoy the open air if not sit down in complete comfort, neither were my eyes still but constantly scanning the place. Shyntre set down the platter on a table and I pulled it toward me to begin eating. I was in desperate need of fuel.

"You will eat mine as well, Red Sister?" he asked wryly, though very quietly. The words didn't carry, nor were his lips easy to read.

"Yes. I presume you've eaten with the House?"

"I have."

"Good."

He studied me. "Are you eating for two, Sister?"

I kicked him under the table, and he yelped, rubbing his unprotected shin through his robe. I didn't respond further; I was too hungry. I did manage to eat most of what was on the platter, and Shyntre still regarded me with surprise.

Now I smirked back. "When a stronger body uses far more energy than it takes to study a book, wizard, that body has to eat more. Is this a difficult concept to grasp?"

He slowly shook his head. "No. I suppose, then, that most Noble Houses don't know how to feed a Red Sister."

"No, they don't. But it's rarely a requirement."

There was a pause in the quiet conversation as I observed the details around me. Not as decorative, overall, as D'Verin or even Itlaun. The materials were sturdy and as lovely as the simpler stuff could be made, but I'd often seen much better. Not quite as much wealth here at House Peniel.

"Does this House have a Consort?" I asked.

"You must have been tired indeed to wait this long to ask, Red Sister."

"Just answer the question, powder sifter."

"Yes, Sister, they do have a Consort."

I was quiet as I chewed. After I'd swallowed, "How long will we be here?"

Shyntre shrugged. "A cycle or two, like D'Verin."

"And then where?"

"Your guess is as good as mine."

"With your history, I'd say yours was probably better."

One corner of his mouth rose up. "Possible."

"So you have a guess."

"Maybe. You want to hear it?"

I gave him a sarcastic look. "Are you feeling generous?"

"Not particularly." He paused, looking rather like his Headmaster sire. "Why did you ask about a Consort?"

My sullen glower probably looked more like *him* on his best cycle. "I'm out of vials."

Shyntre frowned a little. "Since when?"

"Since we got here."

White brows lifted. "Um ..."

"I took him in my ass instead," I muttered. "Dodged the arrow for now. Can you make more?"

The wizard pursed his lips and shook his head once. "I haven't been allowed to learn, and even if I had, getting components without the Priestess knowing would be impossible. But I might have another source."

"You'd trust it?"

"Yes."

"Why?"

"Because you would, too. Think about what you saw at D'Verin."

I stared at him.

"Despite your distraction."

Finally, I shook my head.

He sighed. "Who has the most sex in the House but needs to control who become pregnant with heirs?"

Now it clicked. "There would be more vials in the Consort's bedroom?"

The mage nodded. "Matrons cannot prevent all clandestine visits from their Daughters, you realize. Best chance is she would give the bua all he needs, and his duty is to convince them it is his idea to keep their joinings secret from their Mother. No visible consequences, and covetous Noble Daughters share a Consort without spilling blood."

I sort of wondered how well that would have played out for my Mother had her first two Daughters had one around to play with?

Shyntre continued. "The Consort will tell Wilsira if either of us approach him, however."

I nodded. How well-placed the Consorts were as informants for the Priestesses.

And the Sisterhood. If only we were at House Itlaun, now, Auslan might simply hand them over without telling anyone …

Shyntre paused. "You may have to steal them."

I smirked. "You want *me* to go into a Consort's bedroom?"

"I believe your stealth exceeds mine, Red Sister."

"You can be invisible."

"But Sisters can bypass all wards."

When I didn't reply, we had both looked up again, and this time we held each other's gaze. I searched his eyes and his face for signs of treachery.

"What does she have on you?" I asked. "I thought she brought you to be an obstacle, not a help."

Shyntre was quiet as he looked around the courtyard. "That's complicated."

He wasn't going to say. Fine.

We were quiet the rest of the time. I finished up, and we were heading back where I would settle in for a long eve watching Kerse watch the Priestess and wizard sleep. I wasn't looking forward to that, unless I could get him to sign a conversation with me.

Shyntre murmured again as we re-entered the guest wing. "I asked for a separate room this time. The Priestess granted it. It's closer to the Consort, if you wanted to escort me."

I could admit I was surprised. "Granted it? Just like that?"

"Well. For a bloodstone before we got here."

I remembered the two bloodstones that should have still been sitting in the sink of water wrapped in cloth. I bit back my curse. I'd forgotten. Or rather, I'd slept through any chance to put them back in place, but they hadn't been there when I cleaned up. I might have to admit that I had swept the place and didn't appreciate being recorded having sex.

"You gave her ... ? Thanks a sack-load, wizard."

"I didn't have a chance to warn you."

I shook my head. "I found those anyway, both of them. They were absorbing water waves the whole time."

"Ah," he smiled. "Thwarting her fetish, then."

"If spying is a fetish, I think it is endemic." I paused. "Can you get it back?"

Shyntre shrugged. "Probably. Why?"

"I want to borrow it next."

We fell silent well before some servants would turn the corner. They stopped in their tracks when they saw us but only stepped aside when we didn't acknowledge them one way or another. Fortunate for them that they headed the way we'd just gone.

Shyntre led me to his temporary quarters and signed where to go to find the sleeping Consort. I nodded, noting how now he looked tired as well; the mage had been awake and tending to the Priestess the entire time I'd been in Reverie.

"Get some rest, wizard. You look like death wrapped in a spider's egg sac."

"Thank you, Sister. I shall try to recover my glowing skin and perfect hair in a single Reverie, just for you."

I grinned; somehow that familiar derision and sarcasm lifted my spirits. "I'm going to get you naked again, wizard. We'll *really* play."

He rolled eyes. "Wait until after this trip, Red Sister?"

"Consider it done. I'll anticipate your invitation to the Tower."

He glared at me, and I chuckled, choosing that moment to leave farther down the hall. Shyntre opted to let me have the last word and retreat alone into the privacy of his own guest room. I was more envious of that than I was willing to show.

Once I had managed to cross the wards surrounding the Matron's selected room for her Priestess gift, I searched around within it without setting off more wards inside. I found a healthy stash of preventative draughts — the liquid even smelled the same as what I used — and I filched eight vials of the twenty, reasonably all I could carry on my person with any subtlety.

Hopefully enough to last the trip.

Yes, the Consort would notice how many were gone, and yes, he might tell his Matron. Wilsira could hear and suspect, but she must expect things like that in this game. The Consort wouldn't know who took them and perhaps word wouldn't drift out of these lovely quarters until it was far too late.

I remembered pausing to watch the sleeping beauty before I left. He had looked so perfect, resting in his bed. I indulged in a fantasy of being able to touch him as I liked while he slept, coaxing him and then straddling him … perhaps even imagine Auslan in his place.

Not more than a moment did I spend on that, however,

I must get back to my post.

My window of opportunity was narrow enough.

KERSE HAD SAVED ME FROM EVEN EXPLAINING THE BLOODSTONE, AS IT TURNED out. While I slept, he must have taken them back out of the water, dried them, and replaced them where they'd been, spent and dormant. I witnessed the Priestess blatantly pull them back down, frowning as she gripped one in her hand before slipping it in her pocket.

She looked at me and I smiled back knowingly. She harrumphed.

The Sathoet may have acted against his dam again, but he was maddening to me in his signing after she was in Reverie that eve.

We went around and around in circles and eventually, after more than four marks and getting nowhere, I gave up. Even rested and aware, I was not able to get him to admit to any kind of plot. He even denied moving the bloodstones.

I refused to doubt the signs, though. They had been real, my mind wasn't playing tricks on me, but the Sathoet only acted as expected to act from there on.

Shyntre received his bloodstone back the next cycle — the Priestess was not impressed with his personal one, he'd said. The wizard advised me on the potency of the potions I'd claimed, but otherwise stayed in his private room. The next time the Priestess was horny, she began with watching us but then also participated in the sex.

I had no more time alone with either Kerse or Shyntre.

At last, it was time to leave the second House for the third and final one. Once on the road, the tension for me began to ramp up as the familiar shape of House Itlaun came into view.

Somehow, I'd known it would come to this. *Of course* the Conceiver would want to check on Curgia, who was perhaps still carrying her son's baby.

This would be the toughest of the tests; so many possibilities for compromising secrets, and I hadn't had a lot of time to think about plans and back-up plans.

I may have to rely as much on creative improvisation as my training, my knowledge, and observations.

Sister's Odds, don't abandon me now.

CHAPTER 8

I HAD MY COWL UP AS USUAL WHEN ATTENDING THE PRIESTESS OUTSIDE THE bedroom and was careful to avoid seeming familiar with the surroundings as we entered the plantation grounds to pass through the guarded gate.

We were expected and welcomed with show and pomp that wasn't typical for Davrins' cycle routines.

Matron Itlaun came down the steps to greet us in the courtyard, a sharp-eyed and elegant Davrin, though her body seemed wasted. The Red Sisters were probing for possible poison or spells, but all so far seemed to indicate an illness she denied publicly but only nominally kept hidden from the Court.

She was much older than my former Matron, but her current daughters were around my age. I'd read the Matron had needed to start over birthing and raising heirs when she lost her previous, fully-grown batch to a series of events that may have been more ruthless purge than straight misfortune. Not unheard of.

Matron Itlaun had also taken direct control, making sure her newest Daughters caught more heirs early with a status-laden connection to the Priesthood. The three sisters were not far behind their Matron, and I studied them while standing behind the Priestess's small entourage.

Tulia shone brightly with her pregnancy by Auslan, young and content for the moment as she did her Matron's bidding without question. At this point I wondered about First Daughter Virinay, whether she carried but was not yet showing.

No one knew yet; she had been running the plantation with her Matron during the last Worship Ball. Matron Itlaunia prioritized the focus for her First Daughter, and perhaps catching by their new Consort wasn't an immediate requirement. I could imagine why.

Pregnancy would be very distracting for an Heir budding into a Matron in her own right. It also wasn't necessary when the exact order of birthing by Virinay and her sisters wouldn't matter to inheritance.

Cousins born within the same decade of each other gained their status from their Mother regardless. Surviving half-siblings born less than five turns apart were often called "twins," sharing the same sire — like a Consort, for example — but having different Mothers.

Curgia was the middle Daughter and showed her twin pregnancy with Tulia; she had not ended it. However, I was surprised to see she chose to wear a gown cut which made it apparent as opposed to cloaking it. Her back was straight and chin up as she walked into the courtyard behind her Mother.

She allowed Wilsira to see her, her face an attempt at placid, obvious to me she tried to control her fear.

Wilsira exchanged formal greetings with the Matron, and the three Daughters stepped forward to dip their heads in welcome respect.

"Such wealth your House gains, Itlaunia," the Priestess praised the Matron, referring specifically to her stuffed Daughters. Even from where I stood, I could tell when her eyes shifted from Virinay and Tulia and landed on Curgia.

"Your very presence only enhances it, Conceiver," the Matron responded to perfection.

Kerse stood well to the back, closer to the coach, quiet and still. Even so, Curgia was aware of him and her resolve to maintain the gaze with the Priestess was tested sorely as she suppressed a shudder. She managed to keep her chin up, more impressive than I had been expecting. I made sure she didn't focus on me.

The Matron continued. "I pray our humble accommodations suit your too-brief time here."

The Priestess bowed. "It is my first visit to your homestead. I look forward to a tour."

"Anything you wish, Conceiver."

"Is your Consort available? I should like to see him with his new family."

Itlaunia had been expecting the request. The Matron bowed and turned to gesture while raising her voice. "Consort! Come greet your Sponsor from the Sanctuary."

Like the Consort at House D'Verin, Auslan would have been standing just out of sight to enter the courtyard so readily. He wore a fine, pale garment of silk, his arms still bare, his neck fully accessible and displaying his owner's circlet, smooth, dark legs visible to mid-thigh with sandals that allowed us to see his well-formed feet. His hair had been pulled up into a topknot but otherwise left flowing down his back.

Whew. Gorgeous.

I checked for a potentially stupid grin on my face, and there were too many other reactions to catch all of them, but I focused on the Consort himself and my own traveling companions, figuring pride and appreciation were the most likely to be all the Matron and her Daughters would show.

Wilsira looked the older bua over from head to toe, asking him to turn around to show his bare back, moving his hair out of the way, a cursory inspection much like the Consort at D'Verin, carried out with obedience, poise, and grace before the entire plantation. Concerning that I'd been too tired and distracted to recall something similar at House Peniel.

Auslan's face was unreadable as the Priestess reached to touch the symbol on his circlet. Wilsira trailed her nails lightly down to his collar bone and played with the edge of his garment at his chest, as if she might slip her fingers beneath the fabric to touch hidden skin. Then her fingers tightened on the silk, perhaps threatening to give it a jerk, tearing it to expose him. He remained still, without tension, watching her with a lovely, vacant expression.

The Consort at House D'Verin had betrayed nervousness and self-consciousness despite his training when Wilsira had done the same to him, and this had amused her. She did not receive the same reaction from the older and more experienced Auslan, and I felt satisfaction on this account. Even some pride.

In a different life, I may have searched for one like him to be my companion and consort if I had become Matron of House Thalluen. Coupled with the proper domestic skills, he would be quite a valuable prize to have at one's side at Court and at home.

That life was long out of reach, however, and I did not yearn for it now. The intrigue and secrets I shared with him must be enough.

The reactions of my other two traveling companions to this Consort were surprisingly similar. The Sathoet slunk back closer to the coach, looking away and setting his jaw. He was not intimidated so much as pouting.

The wizard had crossed his arms, and I knew that set look of disdain well. Even though both kept their eyes averted and did not stare with hostility, it was clear that neither of them liked the Consort. These reactions were stronger than it had been with the younger ones.

Interesting.

Was it more personal or due to unequal functions and status that each male held? I gathered that Auslan had grown up around Kerse in the Sanctuary, but what experience did Shyntre have with Consorts in general, being a Tower wizard at Priestess' and Red Sisters' beck and call?

He'd certainly known about the infertility draughts in the Consort's quarters.

Meanwhile, the challenge and distraction facing me were three males I had met individually but were all connected through this Priestess I must somehow entertain without letting her sink her claws into me, as she had Curgia.

I shifted a few steps as pleasantries started up again. The movement drew the eyes of the House; they'd known I was there but ignored me in favor of greeting rituals. Now, my movement made them nervous; it also placed my hooded face farther out of Curgia's view and closer to

Auslan's.

This was a risk, but if he had controlled his responses so well thus far, I couldn't imagine he wouldn't continue doing so.

We made eye contact. Very briefly. He looked away.

His expression did not change, and his vitals did not spike; his focus heightened but was easily explained. His hand moved to straighten his garment a bit down by his thighs, holding on to the hem a little longer than necessary, exactly where he and I had been playing tug-of-war with his modesty all that time ago, when I'd pressed him against his wardrobe with no escape.

I'd kissed him; he'd submitted to my kiss. *Answered it.*

The Consort did not look at me again while we stood in that court-yard, but I was sure that he knew it was me. He was perfect for this kind of intrigue, a potential crisis averted.

One of several.

After that, we went through a now-familiar routine to get settled into new guest rooms. I moved methodically and slowly as before, checking over the room. Wilsira ordered the wizard to retrieve food and drink. He had protested, rightly so, saying that this was the servants' job, but he'd been sent away anyway.

Because Wilsira wanted to talk to me alone.

The Priestess scratched beneath Kerse's chin, looking thoughtful. "We aren't too far from House Thalluen, are we? Tenth and Twelfth, neither having slipped or climbed much in recent centuries with their current, struggling Matrons."

"Correct, Conceiver," I said, my stomach sinking. *So much to look forward to, here.*

She smirked as if she sensed my very skin thickening. "Itlaunia tried sires of her own choosing, decent picks and alliances with Houses around her, including Thalluen, I believe. But they all died at a bad time. Now, a new, similar litter, but now leashed by the divine fertility of the Sanctuary, and thus, a better chance of survival."

I wasn't quite as good as Auslan keeping my face still. Wilsira smiled like she had been watching for it.

"You don't agree, Thalluensareci?"

I hadn't heard that name in a while.

"I've no opinion, Conceiver."

It was just as well that Wilsira cackled as heartily as she did; my own words sounded ludicrous even to me.

"Tell me. Which Red Sister executed Second Daughter Kaltra?"

Speaking that wasn't forbidden by my Elder, as far as I recalled. I could choose to try another personal lie and have her chase after it, or …

"Me, Priestess. I was sent to execute her on proof of poisoning a pregnant Matron."

Wilsira nodded; she'd known. "The second death of a Noble Daughter sired by a Consort. Matron Thalluen is not in high favor with us for this."

I didn't react.

"Of course, I understand the Sisterhood concluded the death of the first was an accident."

"At the close of investigation, Priestess."

"And you were thoroughly interrogated?"

"As a young Noble, Priestess."

Wilsira stroked Kerse's mane, watching him for a few moments as he kept his eyes on my red boots. "The heir has been born. A Fourth Daughter, and somehow the heir. Quite notable, given I have not even heard where the sire came from. I should visit again. Perhaps this trip. Rohenvi has not been seen enough at Court or ceremony."

Braqth's steaming Web of dung …

"Although," she continued, "I've no doubt the Sisterhood keeps their eyes on her. They long have, more because of the previous Matron." A slow tilt of the head. "You wouldn't have known your Grand Matron, of course. She died centuries before you were born. Your uncle passed recently as well."

I blinked, and Wilsira lifted a nostril as if recalling the Noble was distasteful.

"Faithless, that one, but a loyal adviser to your Matron. Without him, she'd have never made such an impression at Court. It's when I first took notice of her."

First, Jaunda teased me about knowing my Mother's mother — which meant D'Shea did, too — and now I had a "faithless" uncle disliked by this Priestess?

My Mother had a brother?

The Priestess was coy in her smile, eyes gleaming. "Do you not even know his name, Red Sister? Did your family not ... *talk* about certain things?"

Hysterical. Aging son-fucker.

"You are a Grandmother, too, aren't you, Conceiver?" I asked, my stomach rolling on itself.

"Oh, many, many times," she said with immense satisfaction. "Every Consort the Sanctuary has birthed is because of *me*. That is why I am called the Conceiver, below only the High Priestess and Valsharess."

I mean the reason you're here to check on Curgia. A Grandmother in blood, aren't you?

The taunt almost came out, but the reminder of status so close to the Queen made me bite my cheek to hold it back. My eyes teared up from pain, and I got control of my wits. That would have been a massive mistake to reveal to her I knew about Curgia — and thus, so did D'Shea — when I'd been instructed only to wait and watch. The Priestess was baiting me, being so close to my old family, and I'd nearly fallen for it.

Wilsira seemed able to read my body language if not my mind, seeing the shield return to both. She shrugged, standing up. "My compliments to the Prime on your training, novice. You seem to be making the transition to your new loyalties just fine."

"Thank you, Conceiver."

I wagered that meant she still wasn't bored with me.

"ALLOW ME TO GO IN FIRST, PRIESTESS," I MURMURED SOON AFTER. "I'LL MAKE sure she hasn't set any physical trap."

"Heh. She would not have the spine."

"All the same. The door is locked. Best not get complacent, Priestess. Please stand farther away, will you?"

"Very well, very well," she said impatiently as she and Kerse moved back.

I had gone in first at every door to which I'd escorted Wilsira on this trip so far. Like always having my hood up, I was glad for the habit established early so it wasn't strange now. I'd made sure to comment how strange it was that Wilsira wanted to see Curgia even before taking a tour with the Matron, while Shyntre was prepping her room alone, and Wilsira had been peaceful in her reply.

"Merely a follow up after the Worship Ball, meant just for her, as she was the one who earned that Consort for her House."

She didn't seem to care that I'd report that to D'Shea, but at least now I had my best chance at avoiding the single, largest pitfall of this challenge.

It took moments to find the right angle on my bracer to break the small ward on the door then pick the lock. This was reasonable behavior for a paranoid Noble but not enough magical resources to even make it a challenge for me.

I slipped inside the door and left it open a crack.

Curgia sat at her desk writing in a bound book by candlelight. I was in motion as she paused at the candle flickering in the light draft and the realization that the ward was broken. Her stylus fell from her hand and clattered to the floor as I grabbed her, smothering her nose and mouth with my gloved hand and holding her tight against me.

She was still sitting.

"No more noise," I whispered, and she trembled. "I've not forgotten my favor, Noble, but that's not why I've come. Right now, you'll do as I say. Do you hear me?"

The barest nod.

"She's right outside your door," I said, touching her pregnant belly lightly. "You've never seen me before, understood? If you look to me for direction even once, I'll save you the trouble of living through the next turn and cut you open right then."

Shuddering, Curgia nodded urgently, pawing at my hand to at least allow her to breathe through her nose. I obliged, and she sucked in a desperate breath through her nostrils before she moaned in muffled dread.

I repeated, "You've never seen me."

Again, she nodded, and I could see her eyes glistening, staring vacantly. I dug in my pouch for the wizard's bloodstone, the same Wilsira had tried to use against me, and placed it on the desk before covering it with the Noble's own book. I murmured the command word.

"Don't touch this, or reveal it," I said. "Talk with her. Make a deal, merchant, and you'll stay alive."

Curgia made the sign of promise, having the strength to glance at me when I released her mouth and stood up again.

"Clear, Priestess," I said, raising my voice as I glanced toward the door.

I hauled Curgia out of her chair by her hair, adding a tight grip on her upper arm as Wilsira and Kerse let themselves inside, closing the door behind them.

"Oh, Braqth," Curgia murmured, trembling visibly as she indeed recognized them both. She didn't look directly at me but lowered her head and leaned toward me. My threat notwithstanding, she felt safer next to me than she did in the middle of the room.

Wilsira cocked a white eyebrow. "Why are you holding her that way, Red Sister?"

"She tried to run when she saw me," I answered. "I scared her badly, I'm afraid. She can barely stand."

Wilsira grunted. "Well, release her. I do not think she will try again."

I did, and Curgia had to catch herself to keep from falling. After succeeding in that, she stood lost between us, not knowing what to do.

The gleam of a predator appeared in the Priestess's eyes as she looked at Curgia, but Kerse behind her seemed apathetic after a glance at the young Davrin's distended belly. He understood the concept of mating for procreation, but I could not tell whether he would be curious, hostile, or indifferent toward Curgia's infant, if it were ever born.

He won't get the chance to find out so doesn't even care.

Curgia focused on slowing her breathing, and Wilsira chose her moment to speak.

"I received your messages, child," she said. "Forgive me for the lack of reply for so long, I've been rather busy. I'm here to discuss your options."

"Pr ... Priestess," the Noble made an immense effort to collect herself and attempted a small bow. "Ah ... a surp-prise ... uhm —"

The older Davrin chuckled. "Forgive the Red Sister's overzealous actions when it comes to my safety. I apologize on her behalf if she startled you. I had thought she would announce me, but then I forget at times how ... distant ... from normal society the Enforcers actually are."

Curgia nodded. Though she wanted to look at me, she didn't. She had the perfect excuse for trembling with intense confusion now, and with my warning and the Priestess reassuring she was here to discuss a bargain, the merchant was back in more familiar territory.

First step complete.

"Sirana, please stand outside? Kerse will stay with me, I shall be safe. This is private."

Damn it.

I bowed slowly. "Of course, Priestess. Call me if you have need, or when you're ready to leave."

"Of course. Thank you, Red Sister."

I prayed for blind luck as I stepped outside. I had taken a very necessary risk with that bloodstone. Shyntre could only cast it for visual or aural, and I'd chosen aural only because I thought Curgia was not very proficient in signing complex conversations, and I'd rarely seen the Priestess do so. Both seemed to prefer to use their tongues. If they only signed, however, I was simply fucked, because I wouldn't hear a damned word from that stone.

Equally tough if I'd chosen visual, though. Them sitting and talking the entire time meant I wouldn't hear anything. I might manage at best a one-sided conversation from reading lips. And if I didn't catch the mouthed words the first time? *Gone forever.*

Bloodstones weren't foolproof; happenstance and educated gambling played so much into spying with them, more than some realized.

I stood tensely outside while servants gave me very wide berth. All I could think about was whether Curgia could follow my instructions, or whether the Priestess would intimidate her so that she would babble and give quite a lot away.

The longer I waited, the more I wasn't sure if it was a good sign or not.

What's taking so long?

I continued waiting, and when the call finally came, I was cautious stepping back inside, trying to see all details at once. The two seemed to have only just stood up from chairs set before an unlit hearth; Kerse crouched beside but slightly behind his Mother. The Priestess smiled at me, her eyes glittering with satisfaction. She certainly felt she'd gotten that for which she came, but she wasn't eying me like a Drider's imminent meal.

Did it work?

Curgia didn't look so beaten down as before; she looked hopeful. She avoided meeting eyes with Kerse, but I did see her touch the curve of her abdomen. She had the book in which she'd been writing now in her lap, and she fiddled with the pages.

Hmm.

At one point, Curgia had gone back to her desk where the bloodstone had been to retrieve her book.

Where is it now?

I approached the three of them, and the Priestess indulged in another look at the pregnant Noble while Curgia avoided my eyes. By contrast, Kerse stared intently at me. When I glanced at him, he nodded once, barely, and his arm moved a bit, enough to draw my eyes.

He palmed in his left hand.

Shit.

I'd known he could sense those stones but hadn't considered that he'd snatch it and not give it to Wilsira. Now I had to get it back.

"Are you ready, Priestess?" I asked.

"Indeed I am, Sister. I believe we are to meet the Matron for that tour before we dine."

That it was, and a long and boring thing, that tour. Curgia had excused herself, pleading belly-tiredness, so it was the Matron, Virinay, and Tulia who walked with Wilsira, Kerse, Shyntre, and me.

I pretended to listen to the drone of detail, and I certainly guarded as was my duty, but I knew the grounds well. I tried to catch Kerse's eye from time-to-time, to hint he should slip me the bloodstone, but he attended his Mother with vigilant tenacity and made no such moves.

Maybe demonbloods are less intricate plotters and far more keen opportunists.

Though I could say that about most males.

I supposed too many servants and hidden eyes were watching in any regard. Much better for Kerse to have claimed the stone over Curgia, who very well may have used it for a bargaining chip, even though she'd heard I'd kill her if she touched it.

A Noble bargaining for a Red Sister's possession? Only if she was *very* certain the Priestess could, and would, protect her from the Sister's wrath. Yet, short-sightedness and greed were all it took to do stupid things; I knew that as well as anyone.

"Ah, Consort, good to find you here," Matron Itlaun said.

We were touring the gardens now, which indeed were more impressive than the other two Houses at which we'd been, and Auslan had strolled out casually, studying a few of the sculptures and cultivated growths in perfect view. I'd eat my bracers with spider jelly if that had been sheer chance.

"Would you like to join us in our walk?"

Auslan had smiled demurely and nodded. "I would, Matron. Thank you."

Tulia smiled widely and stepped up to greet the sire of her child, caressing his face although she did not kiss him or do anything particularly sexual. "You always brighten the darkness with your presence, En — ah, Consort."

Tulia's mother had shot her an absolutely scalding look at hearing the start of Auslan's private, given name for House Itlaun. Apparently, the young cait wasn't used to many visitors. Wilsira covered her mouth to hide a laugh.

Shyntre and I hung back in the rear, and my Consort stayed dutifully close to the Matron and Tulia the entire time. Aggravatingly, he was usually directly in front of me, and my eyes were drawn to his backside on several occasions. He also did nothing to suggest he was trying to get my attention.

Perhaps he wasn't. Not directly.

Auslan could just be taunting, paying me back for past harassment. Striding ahead of me like that, so teasingly out of reach, his fingers intertwined with those of the third Itlaun daughter, who would bear his child first, as they walked side-by-side.

I was *quite* sure that if I lifted his garment this instant, the mouth-watering bua would be as nude as he had been when I'd bent him over that table with a root stuffed in his mouth.

I also knew, now, that I wouldn't have to penetrate him and stroke his nut-gland to force an erection on him. My treasure revealed would get hard for me from authentic desire.

He's said so.

"What is wrong with you?" Shyntre whispered next to my ear, and I jumped, gulping.

Damn him and his perfect ass, I signed back, motioning forward.

The wizard did a sharp double-look to Auslan then back to me. His surprise was genuine, though I couldn't figure why he was shocked as my face flushed with my own foolishness.

The Consort may not be the most threatening figure here, but he was fast approaching the strongest source of distraction, and Shyntre had realized this. My own fault if the Matron, the Priestess, or Sathoet realized the same.

I concentrated on my breath, looking around at other things. I focused on Kerse, glancing periodically to see he still palmed the wizard's bloodstone. It may contain a very interesting conversation, and I truly needed to get it back. The Sathoet had proven he was not an idiot; what would he want in exchange?

The unspoken tension within the tour group broke suddenly when a small, furry puglit exploded from the foliage. It squealed as it came from the right, bolted right beneath our feet in the middle of our group to punch out the other side. I'd already drawn a pellet and had my arm back ready to pitch it. Once thrown down, it would catch the streaking rooter in sticky webs.

I didn't have the chance.

Kerse roared and surged after it, trying to catch it.

Shyntre, Auslan, and I were all in his way.

The Sathoet shouldered into me first, his hands shoving at my middle from the side, and I used the momentum to catch hold of the wizard and Consort and get them both out of the way while trying to avoid breaking a web pellet in the process. The last thing I needed was to be wrapped up in sticky webs with the two of them.

We knocked into Tulia as well, and Shyntre somehow managed to peel her away and break her fall apart from me and the Consort. I heard Auslan grunt in pain when I landed on top of him but managed not to crush the web pellet in my palm.

"*Sathoet!*" Wilsira's voice boomed, *"Desist!"*

His snarling among the giant mushrooms and moss stopped abruptly. I heard him whine in apology. His Mother was still furious at the embarrassment.

Meanwhile, Auslan stared up at me, his face bright with warmth, his scarlet eyes wide in a fright that seemed performative. We caught each other's scents again — oh, Goddess! — and I forced myself to get off him just as his dark cock started stiffen beneath his wrap.

"Here, get up," I said, trying to make it sound like an order.

He offered his elegant hand, and I yanked him up with more force than necessary, knowing he was sturdier than spun glass. He hunched over holding his side as if he was sore, deftly hiding a partial erection.

"Consort, are you alright?!" Tulia cried, rushing from the wizard who'd gotten her to her feet and quickly checking their House stud for injuries as I stepped back.

Virinay joined her, both sisters barely willing to touch him in case that alone was too much for him to handle. Or perhaps because I was standing too close for their liking. The Nobles glanced at me, and I scoffed, daring them with a look to accuse me of mishandling the Consort.

They looked away.

"Yes, Mistress, I'm fine," Auslan gasped. "Just had … my wind knocked out —"

A loud slap sounded behind me as Wilsira struck Kerse across the face, hissing something none of us could quite hear. He nodded and whined an apology again, completely subservient. He'd caught the puglit, though. His fingers were covered in blood as he gripped it with both hands, and Mother didn't take it away.

At this point, I became aware of a source of pain in my side. A wound.

Then, an odd object prodding at it.

I turned so I had the benefit of my cloak to cover my hands and searched my right side, astonished to find the bloodstone that Kerse had been palming wedged behind my belt and, amazingly, shoved down my pants. The Sathoet had forced his way up and under the armor, and his claws had ripped my leathers and my skin. I was bleeding, though not badly enough for it to have flowed onto Auslan the brief time I'd been atop him.

Kerse had used the distraction of the puglit to give the bloodstone back to me?

Without asking anything from me first.

This solved one of my immediate problems but rose concerns of another, and now I also had to think about how to heal the claw marks well before the next time I'd be required to strip naked in front of the Priestess.

I had a healing potion, but it was intended for serious poison or major injury. I didn't want to take it for something this small, though the topical stuff I had would be too slow.

There had to be another option.

"I apologize, Priestess, I had not realized your son was so hungry," the Matron said in earnest. "We shall have the servants prepare that puglit for him, and more food, right now if needed. We are about finished with the tour, anyway."

Such tolerance and grace on behalf of her son; Wilsira was impressed, I could tell. The Conceiver nodded. "More than a bit early for your House's eve dining, I know, but my Blessing will be less distracting if he eats first, as he shall be attending me. My thanks, Matron."

"You and he are quite welcome."

Tulia was inexperienced enough to show a touch of dismay at the thought of trying to eat with the Sathoet staring at everyone at the table, but Matron Itlaun's grace made up for it as she acknowledged Kerse in her bow and nod to the Priestess. It appeased Wilsira very much.

With the bloodstone — stained with my actual blood, humorous and unsettling in a way — tucked safely in a pouch, I considered claw marks pulsing a mild but constant irritation beneath my armor. Kerse had been paying attention to how my armor was put together to have been able to dive at a chink with such precision at a moment's charge.

But then, he's had a lot of opportunity of late to observe.

It was a long meal of which I could not partake as I stood behind the Priestess, again present but tacitly ignored. I might wager that some at House Itlaun figured a Red Sister never ate at all. The one time my stomach did rumble, so did Kerse, and no one heard it over his bass.

Somehow irritating to have him helping me so much, though in truth, only because I did not know what he wanted. He must want something but had thus far refused even to admit that this something existed. I got the feeling he wanted me to believe the sex was enough, that he tried to show his gratitude for the anal rut, perhaps.

But I didn't believe it.

He's only proven he's not simple in his head.

The growing familiarity and intelligence I could see concerned me. If it didn't convince Elder D'Shea, I didn't know what would.

Once the early meal had finished, earlier patterns smoothed the eve once again.

"I will escort you back to the room, Priestess, but then I must go to the kitchens to eat as well."

"Of course, my guardian. I continue to be impressed with your vigilance and power of intimidation."

I gave her a sidelong glance but forewent commenting on generous comments.

They seem in full supply here tonight.

CHAPTER 9

AT THE KITCHENS, I GRABBED SEVERAL OF THE MUSHROOM HAND PIES INTENDED for the servants, stuffing the well-stewed and spiced treats into my mouth and chewing quickly. I would be foolish to pass up the opportunity and hurt my alibi in the process, but my purpose for leaving the Priestess's side wasn't simply to eat.

Saving the last pie for later, I slipped into the wing that held the Consort's bedroom. Unlike the previous two Houses, I knew exactly how to get inside this one unseen.

Auslan saw me emerge from the deep shadows in one corner of his room, instantly wary. He had lit a single candle by the vanity, more to my advantage, because he had been looking himself over recently though he was fully clothed now.

Quickly, he touched his ward stone near the main door and murmured the command word, affording us some privacy from any who might press their ear to the door or try to peek in through a crack.

"It is early yet, Red Sister. I could still be visited." The Consort spoke in that familiar and lovely, formal voice. "They will wonder why the ward is up."

I grinned. "We must be quick, then."

His brow lowered in confusion as I approached him, his expression slightly alarmed when I lifted my belt and tugged down one side of my pants. Once he saw the injury, he understood and even relaxed a bit.

Nodding, he turned toward his vanity without being asked.

I'd long thought that his high attention to the details of his appearance wasn't his own desire and obsession but necessary for his function, and he proved it here.

Auslan held a bottle and a cloth, gently tugging out the stopper before offering both to me.

I held my equipment out of the way, smirked and said, "You do it."

He blinked at me. "Why?"

"I know you tend those occasional fingernail scratches to keep your skin perfect. Just make it gone so I can't tell it was ever there."

Nodding, he wetted his cloth with the acrid-smelling potion inside the bottle, then slowly lowered himself onto one knee, eyes glancing up at me warily. I kept my hands where he could see them and watched as he gently wiped at the claw marks on my flank.

First, a sting, then the warmth and itching associated with the skin beginning to heal. I sighed. It felt good. Plus, wasn't this the first time he'd reached out to touch me? Of course, he had been told to, but at least I hadn't needed to grab his wrist and show him what to do.

He replaced his bottle, and I claimed the bloodied cloth for my own for I would not leave something like that here in his room. He studied me as I tucked it away.

"Why do you not have a topical healer yourself, with all those pouches on your belt?" he asked.

I arched a brow; I'd expected him to state the obvious about how the claw marks had gotten there. This question made me smile. "A mere scratch is not so important to me as it is to you. Other tools better justify the space. I cannot carry everything at once, Consort."

"But you would have a 'mere scratch' healed now?"

"Maybe I wanted an excuse to see you. Seeking healing was the reason I found you in the first place, wasn't it?"

He looked uncertain how to respond; a fact I enjoyed, given how well I knew he could hide his thoughts. I needed the distraction; we would *not* discuss that I could not have such a mark the next time the Priestess saw me naked, or why.

"Will not the Conceiver miss you?" he asked.

"You assume I'm at her leave?" I cocked a brow.

Auslan smiled a bit. "You are her bodyguard for some reason, Red Sister."

He still didn't know my name, and I could never tell him.

"I trust I am not found out?" he asked, showing that bit of fear in his eyes. "The Priestess doesn't know that you know me?"

"Give me benefit of the basics, Auslan," I chuckled, and I could see his face heat a bit on the shadowed side when I said the name aloud. It pleased me more than it should that he could react to it. I clarified. "No, she doesn't. And she won't know. There is enough time for another report for my Elder. Anything interesting happening at this House besides the new guests?"

He hesitated. "Yes, but will you give me some reason you are in your present company?"

"Why?"

"It is not usual for any Red Sister. It will help me avoid mistakes that endanger us both."

I thought about it. "Do you know my present company on a personal or functional level?"

"Both," he said. "Wilsira Tachnathon owns me. By extension, I have been near her son, as have all Consorts. Kerse is always with her and has been for centuries."

"And the wizard?"

Auslan smiled wryly. "The Headmaster's son? Yes, I know him."

You do?

That might have explained the look on Shyntre's face earlier. The Consort said nothing more, of course, but I thought over Shyntre knowing how to style a Priestess's hair, feeling annoyed that I hadn't made the connection sooner. Auslan may have read something on my face.

"Who was your Priestess when you were at House D'Verin?" I asked. "I will tell you something true about why I am here."

"Wilsira, also," he answered.

"I meant, when was it different? You said she wasn't your Mother by birth."

The bua hid his amusement as I changed my first question, but probably figuring I could look this up later. "Wilsira Tachnathon succeeded in claiming the Consorts of my first Priestess, who *was* my Mother and met with a … misfortune. I have been gifted to ten Houses, Red Sister, and only these last two by Wilsira. As you know, power and rank changes even among those in the Sanctuary. Perhaps more swiftly."

His beautiful face looked at me expectantly.

"You were correct about Curgia," I gave him without a fight. "She was forced, and Wilsira is responsible for it. The Priestess is here to check on her and her unborn."

Overt beauty notwithstanding, his eyes shone with intelligence as he worked that over in his mind. "Hm. Something has changed here, recently. Curgia has seemed to accept the pregnancy."

I nodded. "Perhaps waiting for the Priestess to come."

Or not. But he didn't need to know that. I still didn't know what was on the bloodstone, but it had seemed the two had come to an agreement.

My Consort was not satisfied. "Who is the sire, that Curgia must be forced by a Priestess? She sought an early pregnancy and may have accepted if a Priestess had simply asked."

"Any guesses?" I countered.

Auslan thought about it but ultimately shook his head. Perhaps he was not aware of Wilsira's little penchant for impregnating vulnerable targets using her own son. Perhaps he wouldn't be if his giftings among Houses were only recently given to her to decide.

"I'll tell you if you tell me what you know about the wizard," I offered.

The Consort hesitated for some reason. "First tell me what he is to you."

He had read something. Damn.

"Do you care?" I teased.

He shrugged. "I've been trained to watch who is interested in whom,

Red Sister. I can tell it is personal for you. Is that why you are here?"

I tried a useless bluff. "No, I'm on a mission that has nothing to do with him."

Until I'd walked in on him fingering my Lead to climax. I still didn't know what happened there, but Rausery and D'Shea should both know about it, if Qivni didn't confess herself.

Auslan smiled and let me see that he didn't bite full hook. However, he neither pushed harder nor demanded to know who had planted Curgia's bump.

He answered my request instead.

"Shyntre is, as I am made aware, the youngest Davrin child birthed by a Red Sister and given to the Priestesses under Valsharess law. There have been no others born in my lifetime, though there are older ones."

I was stunned, and the Consort could read that I was. He suppressed his chuckle and looked good doing it.

"The Red Sisters don't tell all their members who is of their own blood?" he asked.

No demons but us.

Blood family wasn't first anymore, but … perhaps Wilsira was right that it could never be erased completely. Not with how she'd taunted me about my Grand Matron and uncle earlier, and now this.

Shyntre, the son of a Red Sister. And son of the Headmaster …

Oh my fucking Goddess. D'Shea!

The memory returned like a club, the way my Elder Sorceress had snarled at the ancient wizard. How she had treated him, warning me how he couldn't be trusted. D'Shea had left me in the library before Shyntre ever arrived with the Dwarf stone.

And never came back.

Auslan still waited for an answer. I grappled for one.

"Um, no. Part of a challenge given me from my trials." That was utter truth, but I had to force my smile. "Nothing comes easily to the youngest. I have found the right answer to that question at last. Thank you, Auslan."

If the wizard grew up with everyone in the Sanctuary and the Wizard's Tower knowing where he came from …

And then much later, meeting the Sisters themselves, being trained to help them test recruits? To take out his aggression on them? Whose decision was that, the Prime, or D'Shea? Shyntre's temper and stubbornness, as well as his dislike for the Sisterhood, made all the sense of the world in that context.

"So he was born in the Sanctuary. Did you grow up around him?"

Auslan shrugged. "He is a little younger. I saw him on occasion but had my own training to undergo."

"And his training as a mage at the Tower? When did that begin?"

"Young. He was gifted. But he traveled back and forth between the Tower and the Palace as a child." The Consort paused, taking time to think back. "The Tower became the long-term residence shortly after he matured. He was … disruptive to the Sanctuary."

I smirked. "I can imagine."

Any son of D'Shea's would be. I hadn't guessed from looking. Shyntre didn't favor her in any obvious way, yet who else could it be?

She told me, 'If you knew what I did about the Sanctuary …'

The Consort offered a charming smile with his reminder. "So who is the sire by Curgia?"

Speaking of magical sons.

I wasn't certain I should reveal that, but Auslan was a sharp study of the Sanctuary politics; he'd heard and seen much. He might suspect, and I could likely get something in return for it that neither Wilsira nor D'Shea would tell me.

"Kerse," I told him.

Now it was my turn to stun him. I wasn't quite as good at suppressing my grin at his expression. "Disgusted?"

Auslan shifted on his feet. "Surprised. Although it *does* explain Curgia's behavior."

"Has the Priestess done this before, that you're aware?"

Auslan shook his head. "I have not witnessed it before. Is that why you are here? The Sisterhood is investigating her?"

"Yes," I answered truthfully, finally giving him a reason for my presence.

"Why would she accept your escort, then?" he asked reasonably.

"She asked for me. Made a formal request for the escort. When you talk to her, be careful. You know not to reveal that you know me."

The Consort nodded. "I will not. But why did she make a request for *you*, young Sister?"

Because she wanted to watch her son fuck the Abyss into me.

Those lovely eyes watched only for truth. Evading it entirely was impossible.

"Well. Her son has a brief infatuation with me. I think she is indulging him in having me close by."

Auslan broke the stare, blinking his eyes repeatedly. "What?"

"You heard me. Have you ever heard of her doing this before?"

"I have not. Another Priestess, possibly, but Wilsira is jealous and possessive of her Sathoet. She would never bring younger females close just to please him."

That was the firmest tone he had ever taken.

"I will not ask how it occurred," the Consort said, "but how long has he been 'infatuated' with you?"

"Since we met in my trials," I admitted.

"Which is how long?"

Damn. He would know how new I really was.

"Over a turn," I muttered.

Auslan studied my face. Perhaps he thought I wasn't worried enough, because he said, "Be careful, Red Sister. A Sathoet is very dangerous, even to their dams, if their patterns change."

"How would you know? More tales that your first Priestess told you?"

"More. What happened to my Mother. My first Priestess."

I swallowed. "Tell me what she said about patterns."

Scarlet eyes watched me, unblinking. "Tell me what you were doing out in the wilderness. When you found me."

My eyes narrowed, and I ground my teeth with impatience. I needed to know this. "Very well, but you talk first. How old was your Priestess when you knew her? A novice?"

Auslan shook his head. "A peer with Wilsira, and yes, she was wise. She liked me. The others would not have appreciated all we spoke about, but this is my first sharing since she died."

"Good. So talk."

"Abyssal blood is not stable and the demonbloods born among us need strong anchors not to —"

"Anchors?"

"Magical patterns."

"This is what you mean about Kerse's patterns changing?"

"Yes. The chaos of the Void can contribute to changes at any point in a half-breed's growth. Their Mother must be very strict with them, it helps create and hold the patterns the Sathoet follows and extends both their lives. If those patterns change and he is unpredictable, it is an indicator that the half-breed needs to be destroyed."

"But that hurts the Priestess."

"Yes, it does. She loses part of her power permanently, places a ceiling on how high she may climb in the Priesthood, if she doesn't meet her death soon after. The destruction of a Sathoet is the decision of the Valsharess alone, for that reason. Any Priestess who tries to kill the Sathoet of another as part of a rivalry is condemned to Auranka, the Drider Mistress. The half-breed first must be proven unstable and dangerous to the Sanctuary."

I hadn't known *any* of that. It was not casually spoken among Nobility or Sisterhood.

"Who destroys them?" I asked bluntly.

Auslan paused. "Usually the Sisterhood, with magical assistance from the Valsharess. It is not left in the hands of Priestesses."

D'Shea must be aware. Why couldn't she have told me all this? Her instructions to me had been clear: find out what Wilsira was up to. She needed proof that Kerse wasn't acting on his mother's orders.

And then?

Sadly, nothing. I knew I didn't have that proof even now.

The argument could be made by Wilsira herself that he was acting on her orders. I had no confession from Kerse, nothing except perhaps the bloodstone, but it could only be tapped once. If I listened to it, and it was something or nothing, it would still only be what I said it to be.

My best option was holding on to the bloodstone to give to D'Shea, let her hear whatever was on it. Shyntre would have to let me keep his stone, and hopefully D'Shea knew how to transfer the activation command from me to herself.

This grows complicated.

Not even factoring in Wilsira's own change in pattern: Leaving me alone with her son.

There were voices in the hall, and regardless, I sensed I was running out of time. I wanted to ask more, much more. All this told me was that Kerse was the oldest Sathoet only for having been one not to change much, until now.

I'd been here in this room too long. Auslan saw it in my stance.

"Hold to your agreement before you go," he said.

I pursed my lips and tried to be succinct. "You were in the path of an initiate when I found you. I was being tested to see if I was good enough for the Sisterhood. I'd been traveling that way for cycles."

Auslan stared at me intently. "Why did you attack me? Did you know what I was? If you only wanted healing, you could have simply commanded it, except you did not. You tied me up. There was no reasoning with you."

"I didn't know what you were. I didn't see the circlet around your neck. I was … not aware of a lot of things."

"Why?" he insisted, leaning forward, closer to me, as if he had a guess.

"Why is that important?"

"Am I correct that you had just been in a fertility ritual?"

"And if you fucking are?"

"I knew it. My magic made it worse for both of us, that was why I fought you. But why would the Sisterhood do this to you before abandoning you in the wilderness?"

I took a step back, feeling I had lost some ground here and couldn't afford the time necessary to direct the conversation as required.

"Sister, wait," he said. "Please, answer me. I have answered all your questions."

I shook my head, turning away. "It's not important."

"You must be among the youngest of the Sisterhood," he pressed, following me toward my escape. "I am glad they found you worthy, and that you did not catch from me. But that magic was powerful enough to have healed the harshest blight on a womb while harming a healthy one. Are the Sisters made infertile now by the Priesthood? Is that why Shyntre was the last — ?"

I spun around and caught him by his throat. His hands clapped my wrist, and his eyes went wide as he finally went silent.

"Enough," I growled. My voice shook. "The answer is no. That ... *solution* ... was individual to *me*. How I came to them."

Auslan stumbled back when I let him go, his hand covering his circlet. He nodded, swallowing, and taking the pain in stride. "That is ... what I needed to know, Red Sister. Nothing we spoke of will go past me. As always."

I scowled at him, trying to be satisfied with the reaffirmation that he would keep his mouth shut. *Save the follow-up for another time, Sirana.*

For a time after I had time to think about all the Consort had given me.

And what I had given away in order to get it.

CHAPTER 10

THE URGENT FEELING I'D HAD TO GET OUT OF AUSLAN'S ROOM AND BACK TO the guest wing was not justified when I arrived.

You were running away, Red Sister. A bold one, you are.

At Wilsira's quarters I had listened, heard nothing, and let myself in quietly, suspending the ward by habit. Neither she nor Kerse were present. Shyntre was on the wide bed, however, fully clothed and in Reverie.

I exhaled in relief yet was suspicious, wondering what else the Priestess was up to that she didn't take the wizard with her and hadn't waited for me.

Maybe she's getting as tired of us all being crammed in these guest rooms as I am.

Shyntre lay still, deeply asleep, and it was an odd time of the cycle for it. Perhaps I'd underestimated the toll this trip was taking on him as well, for him to still sleep even now without sensing me. I weighed going out as well to see if I could find the Priestess and her son — I needed to for multiple reasons, but—

Perhaps ...

Perhaps not before taking this opportunity to study D'Shea's son with his guard down.

I drifted toward the bed, lowered my weight gently so as not to jostle him. Only when I got close enough did I sense with the help of my bracers that he'd placed a "touch ward" on himself. If anyone came close enough, he'd wake up suddenly no matter how deep he'd been in dreams.

Good thing I'd stopped where I did, or his eyes would be open right now.

With his face relaxed and eyes closed, the typical hostility, stubbornness, fear, and tension were gone. I pretended for a moment that I'd not seen his face before.

Upon reflection, the dark crimson color of his eyes — without the gold flecks — *were* like my Elder's, but otherwise I did not see the Sorceress in his face. Shyntre looked too much like a youthful Phaelous, and while he had the clear, refined bone sculpture of a Noble, I did not recognize telling features from a specific family line *except* for that of the ancient Headmaster. I didn't even have a House name for the old one to ask about those family records.

I sighed softly, enjoying a rare moment of peace.

So, of course I thought on what Auslan had spoken about: fertility magic and Consorts. The argument could be made this was the entire reason I was alive and a Red Sister as well. Wilsira would like that. My own successes counted, and the events were much more than those two things, but they still mattered to my experiences in Sivaraus.

They matter a lot.

Jilrina trying and failing a fertility ritual on a barely grown cait, on me, had scarred me inside as badly as Wilsira was scarred outside. The Sisterhood had come to claim me after I'd proven some resilience, but Lelinahdara had to reverse the "blight" on my womb, as Auslan had put it.

My magic made it worse for both of us, he'd said. *That was why I fought you.*

If he hadn't, I'd be puffed with my first baby by now. I might be dead by ritual after, or I might be one of Auranka's Driders. Bumps erupted along my back and arms to think it.

Wilsira was trying to get me in that same way, if not dead, then at least ruined for the Sisterhood. Meanwhile, Kerse was changing his "patterns." Becoming dangerous or unpredictable? Not yet, perhaps. Not enough to convince the Valsharess of his destruction; I had only a vague warning from a pretty bua.

There may be a whole conversation on a bloodstone I dared not yet listen to. Or there may not.

In return, Auslan had pressed for confirmation that the Priesthood was not creating barren Red Sisters. Why? Considering what he knew, what he'd witnessed when Gaelan arrived to pull me off him, he could figure it out. He had witnessed enough.

Gaelan had demanded to know whether he'd loosed his seed inside me, even once, before she got there. He knew what happened when a Red Sister became pregnant, so he would understand why she demanded an answer — at least, in retrospect later, when I'd returned wearing a uniform.

He should have known for a fact that I'd been healed from a barren womb, not the reverse. Why had he pushed that with me so hard, then? Why think it was being used on a larger scale in reverse, somehow thinking that was why Shyntre was "the last" born by a Red Sister?

Because he doesn't know what you do. What the Elder told you. She's somehow 'seen to it,' that the Priesthood would get no more children from us.

Elder D'Shea was the last. I wondered how many enemies — or allies — that made her.

I had darker thought then, one I would never have considered before that the pretty, coveted prizes could even be involved. Say that an adept Consort like Auslan could remove the fertility from a given House rather than grant it. With the protection of the Priesthood, the Consort would not be blamed for the lack of children because he was "blessed" by Braqth, everyone knew it.

The Noble female would be the one who lacked Braqth's blessing. Such a waste. Such a shame. Such a curse deserved.

And it would be true. I'd heard, only once, a Consort stayed a decade with a family and there were no children from it. It had been the first sign of the House's final downfall: Braqth's will to grant no children.

The second death of a Noble Daughter sired by a Consort, Wilsira had taunted. *Matron Thalluen is not in high favor with us for this.*

And the Conceiver was considering a visit to my Mother after this, even though she had no real cause. A Fourth Daughter had been born, my sister, and an heir with no link to the Consorts. No link to Wilsira the Conceiver.

Except me.

Involuntarily, I shuddered. The mentions of the previous Matron Thalluen and an uncle — a brother I'd never known my Mother had. *Now* I wondered what Rohenvi knew from Court, and her motives for withdrawing before she had me by some middle House.

I wanted to know, exactly when I wasn't supposed to care anymore.

The wizard shifted and drew in a deeper breath, his eyelids fluttering at last, and I turned my head. I waited until his eyes had opened completely before, on pure impulse, I leaned down and planted my mouth on his in our first kiss.

"*Mmfgh!*"

His body jolted hard, and he tore his lips away after spluttering, rolling with too much momentum to catch himself at the edge of the bed. He landed on the floor with a thump. I laughed in a burst so hard and abrupt that my sides hurt.

"Sirana," he growled after looking around the room and seeing only the two of us. "What in Braqth's Web are you doing here?"

That was such an excellent question.

"No separate quarters this time, wizard?" I chortled. "Run out of bribery bloodstones?"

He muttered something unintelligible which still communicated his bad mood. "Maybe not, if you're finished with it."

I shook my head. "I need to keep it. Turn it over to my Elder. She should hear it."

A pause as he narrowed his eyes at me. "You owe me something for it, then."

I tapped my cheek thoughtfully. "Hm. Some rimming?"

"Ha. Funny. No."

"Smear your endowment with glaze and let me suck it off?"

He wrinkled his nose slightly. "No!"

I grinned. "I promise you'll get a taste after we're done. Please?"

He gave me the oddest look before he got it. "Wha — NO!"

I sighed dramatically, getting to my feet. "Ah well. Another time, then."

"I haven't forgotten the stone, Sirana."

"Neither have I." A beat. "If the one I'll discuss now is blue."

The sour mage rubbed his face to hide his next mutter. *"Braqth damn all Red Sisters …"*

"I heard that."

"Good, I'm gla — wait! *Oof!"*

A straight-up tackle released *so* much tension. Jaunda had that right, and there'd been so much of it lately. I grinned down from atop my wizard as we lay on the floor, then I leaned to bite and suck on his neck.

Tasty.

"Stop!" he cried. "Sirana, it's Kerse … !"

They're back?

I lifted my mouth off and glanced at the still-closed door.

Damn —

The wizard flattened his palms against my chest, barked a word, and a strong shock of energy burst out. My right shoulder went numb as my heart shuddered and skipped in my chest. I reached with my left hand to snatch hold of a nerve point in his side, pressing on it mercilessly.

"*Augh!*" he roared, his body jolting again."S-stop!"

"T-told you I'd finish it if you started up again!"

"Drider shit, you attacked me first!"

"I was playing!"

"Sure. Red Sisters *'play'*. I know what that means."

He struggled mightily but couldn't break my hold.

"Calm down, Shyntre, I don't have a Feldeu!"

"I know! I'm still not letting you fuck me just because you're bored!"

I chuckled, which sounded half-drunk as my nerves still settled, and shifted my grip to another nerve point, pressing hard and growling, "You *really* think you're going to win this one, wizard?"

He groaned through gritted teeth, "O-okay, get off ... just don't —"

"Don't what?"

"Don't touch me anymore! Let me go!"

We struggled a bit longer, and then—

"I-I apologize for th-the shock!" he gasped. "Think about it, Sirana, what would *you* have fucking thought, waking up like that?! Imagine it was Jaunda. Or Thena!"

He had a point. And how the fuck could he imagine what Thena would do, anyway?

"*Grrr.* Fine."

I released him and got to my feet, feeling ... Excited. Maybe that wasn't such a great thing. The wizard I'd once hated so much growing to be nigh irresistible? He even smelled good now.

Not as good as Auslan, but still ...

Shyntre got unsteadily to his feet. Sweat showed on his forehead as he caught his breath, stressed from the pain. He seemed a bit unsteady as he looked at me. "That spell normally paralyzes."

I cocked a brow. Now I was shocked.

"Temporarily," he added, and I smirked.

"Well, it *did* hurt, mage. Just not enough. You must have fucked up the spell somehow."

He shook his head, lips parting but no words coming out as his eyes were drawn to my chest.

"You're not ..." I paused as he kept staring. "What? What are you looking at?"

Shyntre swallowed, motioning like he had a necklace around his neck. "Will you take it out?"

I bit my lip against how I *really* wanted to answer that question and instead tugged out my shirt first, to look down between my breasts. Shyntre would be able to see the blue glow on my face, if he hadn't a moment ago, and although it was soft and iridescent, the vividness of it so close now hurt my eyes.

"Let me see," he whispered.

I pulled on the cord, lifting the sapphire blue and silver pendant out to rest on the outside of my red leathers. It still glowed.

"Is that normal?" I asked.

"As if I know what 'normal' is for this stone?"

"Your spells turned it blue in the first place."

A snort. "And you're the only one it responds to. Goddess knows why."

Our eyes were locked, though with less belligerence or challenge and more curiosity and weighing of benefits. Should I tell him I knew who had birthed him?

Probably not.

No one had confessed it, and there was no proof. It was my gut and what I'd witnessed between my Elder and the Headmaster alone telling me I had it right. But the story was based entirely on Auslan being both truthful *and* correct.

Shyntre hated the Sisterhood with no help from me. What benefit was there for me blurting it now, other than leveraging another reaction out of him? That was easy enough without pitching big secrets.

"How would you describe it 'responds' to me, wizard?" I asked.

His bright eyes narrowed. "Under what circumstances did you find it?"

Of course.

"Did it blunt your paralysis spell just now?" I asked instead, smirking. "Is that why you couldn't escape and had to apologize first?"

"Cute. And no, my spell wasn't 'blunted.' It went as expected."

"No, it didn't. The effect was reduced."

"That was you." Shyntre didn't blink. "The same as it's you when Wilsira layers the will-weakening components. You don't have the experience or knowledge I have, but that stone acts as some focus for you that counteracts at least part of the spell affecting your body."

"I thought will-weakening components affected the mind?"

He rolled his eyes. "The meat in your skull is part of your body. 'The mind' is only the outward evidence of it. The Priestess isn't attacking something nebulous; she's soaking your brain in the equivalent of a magical potion. But she must increase the potency each time. You're far more resistant wearing that pendant than when you're not but, either way, she has to try harder than she normally does."

That was interesting. I ran my glove over the smooth, polished gem. "Have you tried it?"

He lifted a nostril. "Yes, one of the times you were getting fucked by the half-breed. I feel nothing extra, just a hard, blue stone."

"Did she *see* you wearing it?"

"I had my clothes on, unlike you. And it's still around *your* neck, not hers or mine."

Feeling foolish, I looked down as if to check that he was right. The pendant had reverted to its usual appearance while we'd been talking. "So why would it glow now only to stop?"

"I have no idea, Sister. Knowing more of how you found it and why you brought it back from the Fringe might offer more insight on that."

He sounded exactly like Phaelous.

Who can't be trusted.

"I can't tell you that," I said. "By my Elders' order, I can't even bargain for it."

My continued service in the Sisterhood depends on it.

Shyntre nodded; he was unsurprised. "Which Elder?"

I smirked in good humor. "I shouldn't have told you this much, less answer you for free."

His mouth twisted. "Of course. So we're back where we stood at the Tower."

"More or less. I might have sucked your cock a few times since then."

"I'm sure that satisfied you. Both of us with the threat of spider fangs at our back."

I grinned. "You still spurted. And were nice and hard. It counts."

Shyntre shook his head. "Not to me. Do you have any idea how many buas get hard when they're afraid?" He paused. "But if you *are* surprised by this point, the Red Sisters aren't training their novices well lately."

Ouch.

I sighed; he wasn't wrong, but that wasn't what I wanted to think about right then. "Do you have *one* laughing bone in your body?"

"Possibly my tailbone."

"You have a tail?" I grinned. "Turn around and show me?"

He smiled sardonically without showing teeth. "Fuck off, Sister."

A minor burst of heat flashed through my loins. *Fucking Goddess, this wizard …*

"Teasing only makes a Sister more determined," I said.

He crossed his arms. "I've noticed. And how long I resist before I *choose* to obey determines *any* respect after. Force doesn't count in that."

"And *that* counts in your mind?"

"Correct, Sister."

I looked him over, mentally undressing him. Suddenly, I imagined him willing, undressing like Callitro, kissing me back like Auslan. Not only aroused but seemingly impossible.

Mmm. Yum.

"Has any Red Sister gotten you to *choose* to obey, bua?" I asked, my voice low.

He smiled then, fully willing to tease to me, then. "One."

"She still alive?"

"Yes."

Goddess damn him.

I looked at the door, mentally counted how long it had been since the incident in the garden. All this time spent with the Consort, and now the wizard. Uninterrupted.

"Where are Wilsira and Kerse?"

Shyntre shook his head. "I don't know. I've been in Reverie."

"She wasn't here when you lay down?"

"You think I would have slept a wink if she had been?"

"Huh." I suggested, "Shall we go find the Priestess? Do our job right, for once?"

From Shyntre's expression, this trip could not be over soon enough for him, but he nodded, nonetheless. "We should."

THE WIZARD AND I SPLIT UP IN OUR SEARCH. WE EACH HAD A METHOD TO CALL the other if needed on these grounds and having space between us helped us focus.

Rausery would kick my tailbone to hear me admit that aloud.

I had swept the areas of the House and the gardens where I most expected to find her, slowing down to avoid servants and guards who might pick up on my having lost my Priestess. I had begun to wonder if the Conceiver and her son were even still on the estate. Shyntre hadn't messaged me, and I was baffled when I confirmed she wasn't even visiting Auslan — he was entertaining Tulia this moment.

Lucky slit.

Matron Itlaun and the First Daughter were in the main office with no Priestess to entertain until the eve.

Wilsira hadn't bothered to suggest I use another prevention vial earlier when I helped to unload Kerse's balls one more time after his puglit meal from the garden. She had seemed to stop checking.

Had she given up trying to trick me, or was she distracted by the goings-on at this House more than she was the previous two?

I couldn't find Curgia, either. Perhaps this answered my question.

Would the two have acted this fast on whatever they'd discussed in private? Wilsira had taken a rest when we arrived, a private meeting right after, a leisure tour, and another "rest" before the House gathered in the main dining hall …

Shit. So, where to look next?

On the second floor, I faced the front gate of the estate; ahead of me was the nursery. In all my surveillance and sneaking around this House for the last turn, I hadn't gone in this circle of interconnected rooms built to contain and protect everything a very young Noble Davrin might need for the first turns of life.

Ideally, the young of the Nobility could be sequestered while they were most vulnerable, educated until their talents and potential became more obvious. Our learned behavior determined how soon we may be let out to wander the grounds with a governor or perhaps even our sire, if he was around. The ultimate achievement, to be allowed to meet guests while in the presence of our Matron, remained to be seen.

Otherwise, Noble youths pressed ears to the wall or sneaked about the stairs and halls like any servant.

The nursery wing had windows facing the front of the estate, its cage-like defense taking the form of beautifully wrought swirls of iron. Those inside could peer through the gaps at what went on outside in the courtyard, at the gate, and in the front fields. Only the extremely ignorant took care of discreet business in the front of any estate, where young eyes would always be alert and adult caretakers could spy.

Two good reasons the garden was in the back.

No infants yet, but soon. I'll take a listen.

The Itlaun nursery contained one older Davrin child this moment: a bua much younger than his three pregnant sisters, and perhaps the Matron's final attempt at birthing a fourth daughter without more potent, magical assistance. I'd long ago learned his name was Grelio, but because he seemed to be an ordinary and obedient Noble son, I hadn't seen much reason to watch him.

Surprised to hear a subtle shuffle, it led me to spot him now, folded into a tiny ball beneath one of the decorative tables in the hallway. His eyes grew very round when I kneeled and peered at him. He reacted at least to my weapons and uniform, even if he did not necessarily understand the significance of the color.

Or maybe he did. The stories started early sometimes.

★Outside your nursery, bua?★ I signed.

★Demon … came in,★ he answered hesitantly, one hand moving in unpracticed but understandable sign. ★Woke up. Climb out. Saw me no.★

Impressive survival instinct, avoiding the Sathoet and staying so quiet. Grelio might have a chance for adulthood.

I nodded and signed back. ★Only a demon? Anyone else?★

His young face showed an amusing honesty at what he thought about my suggesting it was "only" a demon. I smiled.

And Priestess, he answered.

Excellent. I almost stood up but paused as Grelio hesitated. *And?*

The Second.

Curgia. I nodded. *Good bua. Stay here until they leave. If a wizard comes by, hide from him as well.*

Grelio nodded, needing no further persuasion.

There were at least five different bedrooms, all on the small side but tiny Elves didn't tend to need as much space. Grelio's room — the one with the unmade bed and a warmer scent — was wide open, and I eased through to a small washroom, then another empty room being prepared for new infants, a miniature kitchen, and a third bedroom.

Then, I finally felt the itch at the edge of my senses before I even crossed it to the next door.

The fourth bedroom was warded. Powerfully so.

As I reached out carefully for the door handle, I clearly felt the discouraging magic. I wanted very much to walk away and *not* touch this door. I heard nothing inside. Nothing at all.

This fourth bedroom is without doubt empty. I am wasting my time ...

Ah, but then pain seeped through my glove as I rested my fingers on the handle. The challenge I needed. *Go away? I think not.*

My training thus far, and possibly my Dwarven stone, helped me focus and see through the glamour that would prompt my departure and suggest regrettable pain should I break the boundary. The magic of wards was illusory, fooling the senses or tricking the mind. All Davrin wards depended on overcoming the willpower of the intruder and, in many cases, succeeded.

This was where each Red Sister pushed to excel, although I was young for having both the willpower and endurance to approach a high-ranking Priestess without her permission. I wanted to enhance my resistance and focus to the point where I could get into a room warded like this stark naked. Alas, right now, I needed at least the bracers as the magic sought to overwhelm me.

This ward suggested greater pain than any other I'd run across, except for the one set upon the quartz boulder inside the Drider lair.

Prompting Wilsira to ask the Prime for me. What led me here and now.

Was there a connection? Almost certainly.

You touched that ward guarded by a Dread Spider, Qivni warned me, *and you'll be near those who set it. Expect restless Reverie.*

There had been some of that already.

When I turned the handle with intent to open the door, I began to tremble as I set my jaw and struggled to breathe slower.

No. Not real.

The pain wasn't physical, only as damaging to my mind as I let it be. Thoughts and fears *would* enter, there was no stopping it, but I need not let them stay.

I let them pass through and, the very next moment, *must* choose whether to break or bend the ward.

My eyes scanned the tiny whorls and slashes on my bracers as I searched for the right combination of runes to hold in my mind's eye. I sought to bend the magic around my own aura without dissipating it and thus warning Wilsira I was about to enter.

Six individual symbols began to glow subtly between my right and left arm, becoming intense and then fading. I memorized them in that deliberate sequence.

Claw, net, stone, void, water, arch ...

Picturing them several times through, the pain and fear withdrew, yet the spell was still in place. I turned the handle silently and pushed it open a crack.

Nothing sounded, either in my head telling me I'd broken the magic or inside as if someone were startled. No one stood in view by way of the crack, so I had no choice but to open it wider and peek around the edge.

Kerse crouched in the far corner, his elbows resting on his thighs and his fingers interlaced. He concentrated on his dam and Curgia; for the moment, he didn't notice me. He would know once I passed completely through the ward; he would watch me enter.

Yet I *must* pass all the way through. I couldn't maintain this strenuous moment of limbo, kneeling in the center of an active ward.

I went in with Wilsira unaware.

CHAPTER 11

KERSE TURNED HIS HEAD AS I QUIETLY CLOSED THE DOOR, AND HIS EYES WIDENED. I smiled and touched my index finger to my lips, standing where I was and looking around. The ward was not painful on this side of the door.

The two female Davrin I sought rested on a plush nursing couch, neatly surrounded by four candles. They were in an odd position. Curgia sat on Wilsira's lap with her back flush against the Priestess's chest, her legs open wide and feet barely touching the floor, all but her bare toes covered by the full skirt of her gown.

Wilsira sat with her back straight on the couch, her arms wrapped around the Noble and her bejeweled hands pressed flat against her rounded belly. Her own legs were hinted to be on the inside of Curgia's; I could make out the jut of her knees through Curgia's skirt, and the toes of her slippers poked out of her robes, flat on the carpet.

Both held their eyes closed, and the pregnant Davrin shivered and trembled, the rate and shudder of her breath mimicking either ecstasy or agony, I wasn't sure. Wilsira was still, her expression one of deep concentration.

The symbolism in their position struck me. Eight limbs, four eyes, swollen abdomen. Whether the spider motif was or wasn't intentional, it was appropriate.

I had walked in on a ritual. I had the chance to back out with none the wiser, but I had to choose now. *In or out?*

Stay out and let Wilsira think I could not break her wards? Go in and prove beyond doubt I could perform my function as a ranking Red Sister over a novice? Potentially force Wilsira to attack, or to lie, or something else I couldn't anticipate?

If I backed out now, waiting without rocking the boat, I could let her remain in control. Surely, the choice to take if I looked forward to kneeling on all fours as Kerse tied with me for her amusement, as at House D'Verin.

Just repeat that shit here, were Auslan might learn about it, and again later at my former Matron's House. Who knew which room would be our guest quarters?

In defiance, I stayed, and when the Sathoet realized this, he looked uncertain what to do, glancing between me and his dam. Kerse did not want to disturb her, I could see, but still thought he should.

I let him ponder this quandary on his own. Better he showed me more of his own hand, if possible.

Kerse chose a compromise: he crawled quietly across the room on feet and knuckles and moved in between me and his Mother. His body blocked easy view of the two Davrin on the nursing couch, and he was equidistant between us, neither threatening me nor interrupting the Priestess's work. He was not within physical reach of either of us.

Irritated that I couldn't see details behind him, I tried a few careful steps to one side but, as I expected, Kerse shifted with me and kept his subtly glowing gaze pinned on me. He would continue to shift until either I got close enough to touch or one of us interrupted Wilsira. I sighed inwardly.

What now?

Even unable to see, I could hear Curgia quite well when she grew distressed a short time later. She protested in a drunken murmur, gasping for more air; bodies shifted against fine cloth and upholstery, and the heat in the room picked up considerably.

"Please, please … No!" she cried, sounding like she was talking in

Reverie, confused, her mind not entirely in the waking world.

Still, Kerse didn't look away from me; he ignored the noise. An excellent guard when he cared to be. I did nothing to threaten him or his Mother, opting to take note of everything that happened instead.

Soon, I sensed the too-familiar taste of altar magic. Like an overly pungent and spicy spirit filling my nose, building pressure behind my eyes and causing me to wait in apprehension for that first clutch of pain or arousal — or both — as magical residue diffused through me.

As it always did the victims and the worshippers watching.

Over the next several moments, however, my stomach settled, and the anticipated clutch of heat in my gut didn't come. Though grateful for the reprieve, I was baffled. The Sathoet had his head tilted, curious, by the time I realized he had read my face. I could do little but smile back with more confidence than I had reason to claim.

Curgia still moaned but no longer formed actual words, and Wilsira began chanting under her breath. It wasn't in the Davrin language but Abyssal, which sounded to me like the hissing of snakes and the blackest of curses rising as harsh echoes out of a deep chasm.

An undercurrent, I realized, also in Kerse's own Davrin speech. Subtle but ever-present.

The chant crackled along my nerves and sent a shiver down my spine. I heard the Sathoet chuckle, very briefly. If he had been smiling before I looked directly at him, he'd stopped.

Breathing faster, more deeply, Kerse shifted and champed his teeth, his large body responding to the rising surge of magic in the room, shown in the fullness of his green loincloth. The hair of his mane had also stood up, and his muscles appeared pumped and heated, as if he'd been lifting heavy objects for over a mark of the candle.

Uh-oh.

A little late, I quaffed one of my prevention vials then and there.

Not an invitation — I would take great pains to avoid coupling in this nursery — but I stood in a close, warded space witnessing a ritual I didn't understand without intent to leave. I must be prepared for the possibility that the Sathoet might try to use force to couple with me.

And that he might succeed.

Kerse crouched before his dam, puffed up and huffing softly, dark pink tongue shifting out with a little drool. He flexed his hands, periodically dragging wicked claws across the carpet, his shoulders slowly weaving.

Watching intently, feeling the gathering power, I realized it must be like a loop. The chant and prayer fed to him and back to his Mother then back to him again. What Auslan had said about a Priestess losing her son to execution and what happened to her ... this supported it.

I witnessed all the signs of a symbiotic bond.

Apart from the fondling and licking.

I hadn't watched Kerse truly *fuck* Wilsira or seen her sucking his cock in return for his service, but the emotional and magical attachment was obvious. I believed how it would hurt her to lose him.

Her magic would be crippled; a part of her ripped out and gone forever. Wilsira could very well go insane from the shock, and I'd be lucky to survive another few turns if she decided the fault was all mine for "distracting" him. She wouldn't have as much to lose at that point, would she?

All the more dangerous if she remained alive as a broken Priestess.

D'Shea had seen this after my first Worship Ball as a Red Sister, and even the pretty Consort could see it looming now, enough to warn me as well.

Be careful, Red Sister.

In time, would the Sisterhood start a campaign to seek Kerse's execution to cripple the Conceiver? Was I really the catalyst for "unstable" Abyssal change? Did it even matter if I was, given how much I might not be worth in such a confrontation between Priesthood and Sisterhood?

The outcome probably depended far more on how well D'Shea knew Wilsira and Kerse, on what happened long before I was even born, if Shyntre truly was her son.

Not just hers, but also birthed him in the Sanctuary.

I stood in that nursery room, buffeted by magic but not understanding its purpose, watching for the moment Kerse changed his mind about guarding Wilsira.

As the Sathoet grew further agitated and aroused by the magic, however, I doubted it was a good idea to let him snap his web. I was too close without good retreat. He could turn on me. He had before with his Mother watching, and the potion I'd taken wouldn't have its full effect yet.

I wasn't *afraid* to direct his lust, was I? I'd done it before, had approached him first, choosing the interaction rather than reacting or having it forced upon me. Drawing this out had its benefit, but so did taking control before he acted himself and events grew even more feverish.

I had no idea what Wilsira was even doing to that poor Noble. If I were to interrupt the ritual by coaxing Kerse's release when I chose, rather than his Mother's, what then? Seemed foolish. Would I get trapped in the magic, unable to make my own choices until it was over?

Yes, I am afraid.

Too many unknowns for me to approach the Sathoet, and I could fail spectacularly from sheer lack of knowledge.

The chanting continued, as did the whispers at the edges of shadows. I suddenly felt a tight ball of vibration against my chest and reached to touch the spot, remembering the pendant. I didn't tug it out but took a quick peek down the front of my shirt.

Glowing again. Why? My first concern was that Shyntre had followed me in here.

I took my eyes from the demonblood, glancing behind me at the door

Still closed.

*Ssirrannaa ... *

Gasping in a surge of fear, I looked back. Kerse bared his sharp teeth and hissed, blazing yellow eyes peering through me. Our gazes locked, and I heard a voice.

~Free ... us!~

What in the Web — ?

~Far beyond. The proof undeniable. Know what you are and free us!~

The "voice" was disembodied, seeming to come from all around us, everywhere magic filled space and tried to drown us. It was low in volume but not in tenor, with a clarity that was hard to imagine coming from a true throat, formed with lips and mouth.

Like when Lana and I were mindlinked …

No words, but pure thought and emotion.

Although, there was very little emotion here, only something primal. *Desperation.*

"Kerse?" I forced out as a hoarse whisper. "Is that you?"

The Sathoet shook his head as if trying to clear water from his mane, his pupilless eyes closing, disappearing in that dark face. The thread that linked us snapped, and I caught myself before I could topple over.

Then Kerse opened his eyes again and looked at me as if I appeared different to him; not a threat but something welcome. He took a step forward, finally breaking his guard, lifting a large, clawed hand to reach for me.

He never looked back at Wilsira and Curgia, still in their trance.

Something had changed.

Act, or react.

I reached out to take his hand as I would a dance partner, like he *wasn't* twice as large and blunt as a club at times. I pulled myself forward and wrapped my arms tightly around his middle without hesitation. The half-breed made a surprised, inquisitive sound but took no forceful action.

He started to touch and caress my back through my cloak, pausing when I reached to touch the visible ridge beneath his loincloth. His breath hitched to a stop as I fished out his member, then he purred as I stroked him wearing my red glove. The heat of him seeped through the soft leather to my palm.

"Easy, Kerse, that's it," I cooed, alternating between longer, slower caresses and shorter, brisker tugging. "That's a good bua."

Cute the way he trembled and nodded his head with his eyes closed, occasionally sucking in breath and spit to avoid splattering me with drool. *Considerate.*

Now closer to the Priestess, I had the chance to turn us slightly as Kerse focused on the pleasure I gave him. The magic still thick around all of us, even the task of breathing seemed labored.

Curgia was writhing in Wilsira's lap, sweat sheening on her forehead and face and neck, trickling down between her breasts. Her teeth were gritted, and her hands now gripped Wilsira's wrists hard, her nails digging in and soon to draw blood. The Priestess didn't seem to notice. Whatever was happening couldn't be good for her condition. She was in unending pain.

I didn't know if I could stop it or not, or whether I should. I was supposed to learn of Wilsira's plans for Curgia and House Itlaun, not interfere with them.

Except I already had.

You have her son's cock in your hand as you watch …

Even before that, I had shown myself to Curgia in the garden, telling her what I thought I knew of the Priestess's motives. We — D'Shea and I — had been wrong this time.

Could I justify another reason why Curgia should live? Or should she simply meet her fate having made her deals with a ruthless Priestess?

"What is happening, Kerse?" I murmured.

He rumbled without opening his eyes; I still caressed him but it was more teasing, maintaining and drawing out his state as I waited for an answer. I asked again when he protested my slow pace.

"What's happening? What does she want?"

He unclenched his teeth to form a response. "Nnammess."

"Names?"

He hissed through teeth and his hips thrust at me, a demand for harder strokes. I gave it to him, then slowed down again.

"Well?"

He growled. "Outsside."

Outside what? I gave a little twist to my hand to vary the sensation; he liked it, and I kept him content while I could think. *Names. Outside.*

"Outside names?"

"Hrrrrr," he rumbled in approval, I hoped, for more than my ministrations.

Words could be magic, the will made manifest. Did he mean names from the Outside, then?

Names from the Abyss called the demon-sires to the altar in the first place, powered by a congregational orgy. Outside names, such as Kerse's *real* one, were well-guarded; only Wilsira Tachnathon knew his. The name that bound all Sathoet to their Davrin Mothers, and the true reason why a Priestess Son could never leave her.

Despite being half-demon and more magical than even his Mother.

So ... what if a Priestess has more Outside names? Say, the name of an unborn child conceived by her own son? What happens if it's never born? Why is it good for her?

"She wants a new Abyssal name?" I guessed, trying to keep it simple.

Kerse nodded once, opening his eyes halfway and lifting his upper lip slightly in a subtle snarl until I resumed pulling his black-ridged staff for him. My thoughts whirled. Is that what she wanted out of me, too? How many times had she done this to young caits?

Okay, yes.

I could justify Red Sister interference to my Elder.

I went down to one knee and began sucking as well, lavishing my lips and tongue in tandem with my gloved hand over the salty, musky erection. Kerse growled in delight and grabbed my braided hair, thrusting his hips forward, intending to sink down into my throat. I was prepared for the action, but only just.

His cock could be pointed toward the floor without damaging him. I did this now so I could rise from beneath with my chin up and throat open. I took more of him than I ever had before, letting the pointed tip squeeze its way down my windpipe, my lips impressively close to the knot that had finally formed at the base.

Kerse watched me do this, vibrating as his arousal spiked, as I coaxed him closer to the edge. When I gently applied pressure to his knot with my spit-moistened glove, it was enough for him.

He gnashed his teeth, grunted deep, and spurted once down my throat. I could have held my breath a little longer, swallowed more of his seed to hide the evidence, but the Priestess cried out, the pregnant Noble screamed shrilly, and the magic was disrupted.

Nebulous sound and sensation battered my ears and body, and Kerse had jumped back at the twin female shrieks. He didn't go far but enough to withdraw from my mouth entirely and paint my face with his semen as he continued squirting.

"Fuck!" I cursed, aiming his rod away and wiping one stinging eye.

He whimpered, closed his hand over mine to keep stroking. More semen lanced and splattered over my forearm, my thigh, my shoulder. Kerse didn't have the luxury of a long orgasm as he did when his knot locked inside my body.

With the gathered magic quickly dissipating and the two on the nursing couch coming aware, he squeezed out his ejaculate with those handful of shots before staggering back from me, crouching lower to the ground and trembling. He kept his thighs open and his hands away from a clearly sensitive penis, drooping stiffly and lolling in the air with his loincloth askew.

I licked at the salty fluid, looked over my hands and arms and chest. I might have Kerse's spunk in my hair as well. There was little chance I could prevent Wilsira from deducing exactly what had happened. She might catch me wiping to clean myself but I had to try. I grabbed the cloth I'd taken from Auslan's room and wiped the seed from my face.

The next moment I heard Curgia collapse onto the floor and Wilsira growl in frustration.

Here we go.

When I looked at her, the Priestess seemed disoriented. Such an abrupt end to that trance had left her blinking toward the ceiling and struggling to catch her breath. My hand hovered over the hilt of a dagger. It was so tempting; the first time I'd seen her weak.

Vulnerable.

Kerse shifted back into my vision and bared sharp teeth at me, warning me not to even try. Right. He still remembered which side of his meal had the glaze, never mind him leaving his glaze on my face. My eye still stung.

I sighed and moved my hand away from the dagger, tucked away the stained cloth, and looked at Curgia instead. She lay on her side, clutching her belly, her body tense with pain. I moved over to her and knelt, checking her pulse — racing — and her breathing.

She could only draw air around wet sobs of distress. She never opened her eyes but, along with the sweat on her face, tears were dripping out.

"Help," she whimpered, not even knowing who I was.

Her legs shifted, and the clear fluid mixed with blood was evident, soaking her skirts. To my right, Wilsira drew in a haggard breath. I felt her eyes land on me, and she growled again.

"Sira — ?"

"Miscarrying," I interrupted with a hard edge to my voice.

Certainly I didn't want *my* name to be given away so stupidly, but also the young Noble was now in one of those rare places within our society: no one was to take advantage of her vulnerable state while she dealt with the passing of young through her body and the immediate weakness following it. Whether or not the infant lived was beside the point.

For the next few cycles at least, a Mother must be untouchable, or our city couldn't function.

I may not be so fortunate. I hadn't realized it would be so easy to wreck Wilsira's ritual. Well, as easy as another Davrin in the Deepearth coaxing a Priestess's Sathoet to spurt in the middle of a divine ritual.

I had no idea what D'Shea would say on this outcome.

I gathered Curgia to lift her off the ground; she was my best escape right now. It was far too late for the miscarriage to be low risk, but too early for the unborn to be a viable birth. Curgia could easily die this eve. The baby would for sure.

Unless …

"Can you heal her, Priestess?"

When I spoke to her, I held the hefty, curled body of the Noble as shield between us. I thought the image worked in my favor because Wilsira, sapped of her energy and coherence, watched me warily as she shook her head.

"No. I need to … rest first."

She hadn't wanted to admit that; she might not have if I weren't carrying the Noble and had my hands full.

"Can we save the baby?" I asked pointedly.

Wilsira considered, her attention turned inward to whatever had been going on before. She shook her head slowly, sinking back in the couch. "We can't. We lost the …"

The Priestess stopped, rightfully saying no more to D'Shea's new novice. She was indeed mind-scoured and disoriented to have slipped even that much. Kerse crouched to the side as if he was blind and deaf. His loincloth had been righted.

"Release the ward on the door, Priestess," I said. "I need to take her to her Matron."

She shook her head. Her voice was raspy. "It's gone."

I moved out, thinking it possible Wilsira hadn't seen the semen on me. The door handle was more a lever that only needed to be elbowed downward to nudge the door open, and I came face-to-face with Shyntre on the other side. My heart slammed into my throat.

Fuck!

His wide, crimson eyes caught a lot of detail; I'd have to find out what later. He moved back out of my way and let me come through. "What — ?"

"Can you heal?" I asked brusquely.

The intelligent wizard didn't need further explanation as he glanced at the moaning Noble clutching my cloak in a death grip.

"Not this kind," he said. "I have gems. They're indiscriminate and heal everything. Not predictable for something like this, one damaged body inside another. You need a hands-on healer."

Great.

Weren't those all either male servants or full Priestesses? The last bua I even knew about had been stolen by another Matron, retrieved by the Sisterhood, and sent to the Sanctuary.

Where the fuck would I find one of those in time, anyway?

"Take her to her Matron," Shyntre added.

I nodded and moved past him; he did not follow me. I paused in the hall to use a non-stained part of Curgia's shirt to make sure Kerse's spending was completely wiped off my face, then ordered the House Guard to wake Matron Itlaunia.

The elder Davrin quickly met me with an attending cait and needed precious flicks to overcome the shock when I wouldn't tell her what happened. Soon enough she led me into her own quarters and motioned for me to set her Second Daughter on her own bed, seemingly uncaring of the stains it would leave.

"Go wake the Consort," the Matron told her attending cait. "Bring him here quickly."

The Consort? That was her first choice, not the Priestess?

Auslan arrived in little enough time to suggest that he might have run. He glanced at me with a bit of theatrical alarm that looked natural before answering the Matron's coaxing to come to the bed. I watched him put his hand on Curgia's hot, damp forehead like he knew what he was doing.

My mouth grew lax as I stared. *Can't be. Are you … ?*

"Shhh," the gorgeous bua soothed, now touching her round, clenching belly with a gentle palm. "You will be alright, Curgia. Stay awake if you can."

A soft moan in response, and it seemed the pain had lessened when he touched her. The blood had not slowed, ruining the expensive bedding underneath. Suspiciously, Shyntre knocked on the door the next moment and I heard him tell the answering servant that the Priestess had summoned me.

Required to leave the Matron's room, I for certain did not wish to. *Fuck.*

The Royal Consort had claimed fertility magic, no surprise, and I could see how that pertained to knowledge of pregnancies, possibly a deliverer of infants.

But is he an healer by touch?

The kind so rare among us that none of them were free and unaccounted for. Maybe that was why this older beauty was still being gifted by Wilsira more than a century later, long after a whole new selection of young faces had grown up to take his place.

You have as many surprises in your talents as the wizard, my Auslan.

WILSIRA RECOVERED FROM HER RITUAL AS KERSE KEPT AN EYE ON ME IN OUR guest quarters. She wouldn't speak to me; she just didn't want me roaming around. Following a very tense wait, she called a discussion with the Matron Itlaun, who granted it quickly.

I was ordered to guard them while standing in earshot.

In the main office, the Priestess began by blaming the miscarriage on me.

What?

I stayed quiet, standing by the door as I was bid. The Conceiver *wanted* me to hear this.

I learned that Curgia was alive but had almost bled to death trying to give birth to the stillborn.

"Only the Sanctuary's gift of the Royal Consort saved my Daughter," the Matron said, voice wavering.

I bit the inside of my cheek. *Only the Sanctuary's 'gift' of the Sathoet put her in danger in the first place.*

"She may yet heal enough to breed again, Conceiver. I am most grateful. Your breeding bua is a true treasure!"

That he is.

"Was anyone but him and you present for the birth?" the Priestess asked.

"Only your wizard."

"Good. I must say again, you shall not bray about this Consort's gift to anyone, yes? Not even your own Daughters."

"I understand, Conceiver, and of course not. He has been helping me as you promised, but I know what happens to healers like him when Nobles get greedy. I shall neither endanger him nor disappoint you, showing us favor as you have."

"Very good," Wilsira repeated. I thought she sounded tired.

There followed a pregnant pause.

"May I ask, Priestess," Matron Itlaunia began, "about the stillborn. I … it was …"

Wilsira grunted softly. "The Red Sister overheard my discussion with your Daughter when I first arrived. I had finally coaxed the youth to tell me who was the sire of her child."

Itlaunia straightened up, her thin lips pursing together. "The timing was right for the Consort, merely to satisfy rumors. I know Curgia wouldn't have hidden it from me until it became visible were that the case. I know she must have been raped at the Palace, and that twisted creature that came out of her … ! Thank the Valsharess, it didn't live. But what happened?"

Wilsira was gripping the arm of her chair a little tightly, I thought, but she tried to look appropriately sympathetic. "Curgia told me she had imbibed too many spirits at the Worship Ball after your House had been granted their Royal Gift. She had been so jealous to see Tulia mount the Consort on the altar."

"Why was it my Third?"

"That was who Braqth told me to choose."

"Ah."

"Curgia became drunk. She doesn't remember much of it, and for a long time, truly believed it to have been a horrible dream. However, I theorize she stumbled where she should not have gone, and a Sathoet must have found her. The proof was right there in her belly."

Wilsira glanced my way before continuing, "This was why the Red Sister attacked Curgia this eve, killed the unborn, and caused the miscarriage. The pregnancy had gone on long enough, our Red Sister had the means to discover the secret and deal with it accordingly."

Matron Itlaunia shuddered visibly, and I wasn't sure which of us, between me and a demonblood, she found more repugnant then. "But whose Sathoet took advantage? Not yours!"

"Absolutely not. My son is the eldest and most obedient Servant the Sanctuary has." Wilsira sat straighter, reclaiming some elegance. "I will do what I can to find out which of my sisters' half-breeds rutted your

Daughter against her will. I will try to determine whether it was a rival of mine, an intentional move against your House.

"Our Sons *all* know the punishment is dire if they are caught, whether by direction or opportunity, so he will say nothing. I shall have to perform my own investigation, and that may take time."

Itlaunia nodded. "I am grateful for your support and attention to this matter. We've worked hard to earn your matronage, Wilsira, and if this is intentional by another Priestess, then please use it as you see fit to take down your rival."

After a mutual nod and a pause, the Matron continued, "The Red Sister ... she ..." She tried very hard not to glance my way. "Why did she ... ?"

"Why did she what?"

"Why did she crush my daughter's abdomen and kill the creature growing there, only to carry her to my door for healing?"

Wilsira smiled. "Those of the Sisterhood have the dubious honor of punishing Nobles for their various trespasses before the Priesthood may seek other injustices attached. They are trained to act first, think later, and are unfeeling toward torment they cause. It was a most painful method, and the clearest message to Curgia. Wouldn't you agree?"

Itlaunia hesitated then nodded. "But ... She didn't intend to do wrong."

"Curgia kept her shameful secret and wronged you and your House in the process," Wilsira said, her voice firming up as if she grew weary of the discussion. "The Red Sister was warning you, but it seems you are being given another chance by the Sisterhood."

The Matron glanced at me. "Will we see more of them?"

"I cannot say. Only remain faithful, Matron, pay your tithes, and I shall help you from the Sanctuary."

Covering your tracks damned well, Priestess. And you know I'll be reporting to D'Shea.

It *could* be argued I'd killed the demonblood and started the Noble's hemorrhage; I had interrupted the ritual by distracting Kerse, causing the backlash of power that left all involved drained, the potential payoff unfulfilled.

But that was only the very last act.

Wilsira had coerced and blackmailed the poor fool for over a turn. She had placed the pregnant Davrin on her own lap and had been doing something to cause damage to the gravid Noble.

I had seen bloody fingernail marks in Wilsira's wrists and forearms as she'd sat there, weak and recovering on the couch. Curgia had been trying to fight her. If I hadn't interrupted, the bleeding might have happened anyway.

I didn't know exactly what Wilsira's goal this eve had been, but she hadn't achieved it. Now, she was making up new stories to exonerate herself.

And ... I was letting her.

Because making truths known to the Nobles wasn't part of my function and doing so would only take potential tools against the Priesthood out of my Elder's hands.

The Priestess and I still hadn't talked about it, and she gave me no signs what *she* thought had happened. She put on a confident mask for all to see, guiding the messy aftermath, controlling the damage to herself as best she could.

"We will still be leaving early in the waking cycle," Wilsira told Itlaunia. "I've been away from the Sanctuary long enough and have further reason not to delay."

"Of course, Priestess."

Did this mean we wouldn't be going to House Thalluen?

The relief was real, yet I was wary of it. I wanted to return to the Cloister and my Sisters. I wanted to see Gaelan, Reishel, and Jael, wanted to touch them. I craved sleep, sex, and food with far less risk assumed.

I wanted to tell what I'd seen to those with more power to do something about it. I needed answers, and a plan from my newest experiences. This was why we were loyal to each other.

More so than the Priestesses, encouraged to act alone against the whole. To kill or cripple one another. To steal their Consort sons and see another's demon-son executed.

Could I imagine Qivni and Thena doing something like that to a Sister they didn't like? Not as easily as that. Panagan had held the best opportunity against me of any Sister so far, when I suffered from the Tragar memories in the tunnels as we searched for Jael, yet she hadn't acted against me.

Conflict had been non-stop since meeting the Conceiver. The longer I was around her, the harsher time wore on me as a result. I could hope an end in sight for this, but I must prepare for the opposite.

A little longer. Then may we each return to the center of our own webs to rest.

CHAPTER 12

WHEN WE RETURNED TO OUR GUEST QUARTERS FOR THE FINAL MARKS OF OUR visit to House Itlaun, Shyntre wasn't there, and Kerse could only shrug. Wilsira had so little reserve and patience left that she snarled, "Go find him, Sirana. Bring him back immediately."

"Yes, Conceiver."

In a pouch on my belt, there was a message pellet he'd given me to call him; I hadn't used it when we split up looking for the Priestess and her son. However, this was an excuse to leave and be alone for a bit, so I conveniently forgot I had it.

I wandered the grounds efficiently, if not hurriedly, and with more servants than ever avoiding me. This wasn't bad for me, despite not being able to simply ask them if they'd seen the wizard.

In the future, if I was seen talking to Auslan or creeping around the lands, it would make sense to them and point back to Wilsira, about whom they'd been warned not to gossip. Not that I planned on being seen again, and even the Priestess hearing of my prodding the Consort wouldn't seem out of place as it would have been before now.

She should even expect it.

I entered the gardens with more care than other places, as its clusters of copses and crannies made it the most likely place to find someone on a plantation if they weren't eating, sleeping, working, or washing.

Soon enough, I heard unintelligible whispers and paused, straining my ears for the direction before I moved in to close the distance. I took my time; silence was my priority.

I spied two forms facing off in a well-concealed slant of rock and overgrown moss foliage. Given the linking threads leading to the Sanctuary that I'd uncovered on this trip, I shouldn't have been surprised when I found not only Shyntre, but also Auslan.

The pretty bua's voice returned to my mind, accompanied by that lovely, wry smile. *The Headmaster's son? Yes, I know him.*

The next instant, that look of shock on Shyntre's face when we'd first arrived, touring the grounds before Kerse charged after that puglit—

He was surprised that I was so distracted by the Consort. Did he figure it out?

I hoped not. I had far less cause to be aware of this specific breeder than the wizard; my own distracted lust had given it away. While Wilsira might attribute any future contact to this visit, Shyntre wouldn't if he suspected anything back in the garden.

D'Shea will kick my ass for slipping like that.

This moment the Consort stood straight with arms crossed and appeared the calmer of the two — no surprise — while the wizard had his hands fisted at his side, his stance hunched slightly as if he might attack the prettier bua.

The mage had his back to me in a three-quarter turn so I couldn't read his lips, and Auslan knew how to whisper while making it very difficult to read his. I could only read their body language and Auslan's expression. He looked pleased and curious, unintimidated in the face of whatever the wizard hissed at him with teeth bared.

The Consort's reply was serene.

"N- … -r business … !" Shyntre said a bit louder in his anger.

It seemed his given response to everyone. None of their business, except it always was.

Auslan still kept his lips stretched tighter with minimal movement as he replied, although now he looked more annoyed while trying his next tactic. Whatever it was, Shyntre flexed his hands as if he wanted to loose a spell on the other male yet knew he dared not.

"How … you know …"

Some demand. And he was very irritated.

Auslan shrugged and looked smug in his reply. I could read his lips then. *I'm trained to notice …*

My gut wove this mundane exchange into a thought of whether Auslan was trying to find out more about me. Or maybe more about a Red Sister's presence, an understandable curiosity, or even the wizard's connection with me.

I'd had a similar exchange with this Consort and, after a glance at the mansion, decided it was possible that Auslan had seen Shyntre enter the gardens from one of the hall windows and came down to intercept him.

He would have had to be outside his quarters. His rooms have no windows.

Should I wait and watch, or surprise them, cut off what information they might share about me? Was Shyntre likely to give anything away in a reaction in front of Auslan due to seeing me? For certain, but I didn't know if it would matter. He didn't enjoy being around me, even able to cum in my mouth on command, but I was interested in more from him.

So what? That isn't a secret. Phaelous and Callitro, D'Shea and Wilsira. They all know. The Consort can know about that.

The two Davrin even shared similar positions with a novice Red Sister, the main difference being that Auslan seemed genuinely attracted to me, despite my attack on our first meeting.

And the desire is mutual.

Would I be causing undue risk to either of them by stepping out of the shadows now and startling them? Possibly. Maybe I had to go for the long-term benefit, prevent someone *else* from witnessing that Auslan knew me, even if it meant the Consort learned more from Shyntre now than I'd like him to.

I watched more mute exchanges, frustrating for me as all I could gather was that Auslan was doing an excellent job of escalating the wizard's temper. The same as how I'd grabbed the Consort by the throat when he made me think too much about my "flaw" when joining the Sisterhood, Shyntre now shoved Auslan hard, hitting him in the chest and making him stumble backward.

The Consort caught his balance but looked surprised at the strength of the wizard's reaction. His hands came up, palms open in submission.

Another thing we have in common.

The sudden flare of my arousal caught me off guard. I knew that instant that I would *enjoy* watching my wizard and my Consort wrestle each other like Red Sisters. Neither were trained fighters with little chance of lethal tactics, so it would be high entertainment to see them rolling around on the ground, but also, it might be ...

Enticing.

If one dominated the other like a Sister, except ...

Heh, no Feldeu needed.

Divine Goddess.

The abrupt, lawless thought filled my head and my groin. Biting my lip, eyes fixed on the two buas, I squeezed my crotch through the leather to soothe the sudden ache.

Greetings, new lust-dream, come on in.

" ... hunting you, like ... done before?"

I blinked, refocusing; my ears perked up. I could finally either read or hear bits of what Auslan was saying. That outburst had loosened them both, the high tension between them seeming broken.

"What ... to catch her attention?" the Consort asked.

I could have sworn I heard Shyntre grind his teeth at the question, even with the quiet rustles and low pitch of other living things surrounding me in the garden. He whispered as well, but his more vehement gesticulations raised his words to an audible level.

"Don't be stupid, plaything. I exist! That's what I did!"

Auslan half-smiled at the insult and whispered again. " ... is not withered ... the other, Shyntre."

"No, you can't trust any Red Sister," came the bitter reply. "They're worse than Priestesses!"

We disagree, there, bua.

"You trust one."

"Only on the Surface."

My left hand unconsciously gripped the stone next to me. *What?*

Auslan looked sympathetic, once again better controlling his whispers. " ... your Headmaster at the Tower?"

The mage shook his head. "Nothing he *would* do. He *admires* her."

" ... have good reason."

Two talented Davrin, coveted by powerful females for very different reasons, watched each other for long moments. I couldn't read Auslan's face, but his eyes were oddly soft.

Shyntre tried to relax his bunched shoulders but mostly failed, rubbing a spot at the base of his neck. It made me check my own tension as I wondered at their history, both born sequestered with Braqth's Daughters and their half-breeds.

Did young buas band together to help each other survive in the Sanctuary, until they were properly trained in their function and let out among the populace? Did they then remember each other as adults if they met again, to talk and share secrets, as these two clearly had?

Or is this unusual?

I'd never heard of such a thing among young caits. I certainly didn't see how a wizard and a Consort would even have the chance to talk again beyond bua-hood, much less look at each other like this. But, then again, I hadn't been watching any until I'd gone to Court, had I? And these weren't typical Nobles with a Noble Son's upbringing.

The Consort murmured, " ... considered accepting?"

Shyntre started to shake his head. "No ... you've never ... with a Red Sister ..."

Auslan ducked his chin, leaning closer. Another exchange far too low to hear.

Then the wizard growled, "Don't tell me how to handle this. You've never been taken anywhere but silk and wool."

I witnessed a luxuriously ironic smile, yet without knowing what I did, I wouldn't have known it.

" ... Matrons and ... some rather ... odd tastes at times," he commented.

"Matrons don't practice bedroom craft with intent to terrify Nobles."

Auslan conceded the point by shrugging. "She is young, Shyntre. Do not wait … gains rank."

"No."

Such a line of pure stubbornness down that back. I rubbed myself again.

" … that was the … last time, yes?"

"You … to be known as the one … ? Especially to the youngest."

Auslan sighed. " … try, please. … the Red Sister … bore you and the Priestesses are the ones … possible for you. There is a chance."

"Not much of one."

" … so sure?"

Shyntre shook his head and folded his arms, refusing to continue a topic. The Consort gave the wizard a few quiet moments before leaning forward, and he said something else that I could not hear or read at all. I could only go off the wizard's response, which was to look down at his feet, his folded arms tightening against himself a bit more.

"I don't … to hear it …" the mage murmured, shaking his head.

" … you have to … I saw you standing … make a choice."

Shyntre trembled slightly. " … could always tell … ."

Auslan's gaze was unwavering and his body exuded confidence. "Do not … un … me torn apart … if you …"

I bit back a hiss of my own frustration. *Fucking rag-poles! Speak up!*

My sour mage lifted his head and narrowed his eyes at the more beautiful Davrin. His mouth tightened, and he shook his head. Then after another quiet moment, finally, a nod. Auslan nodded back, seeming satisfied with this wordless reply.

Damn it. What was that, buas?

If only the stupid bugs and creatures around me would stop their black noise! I wasn't sure what I'd heard but knew well that these two knew each other much better than the Consort seeing the mage "occasionally" while growing up. I didn't know how often they communicated, but they must be referencing conversations they'd had before.

Annoyed as I could choose to be that Auslan had downplayed his familiarity with Shyntre, if I were in his place, I would never volunteer that information for nothing. Auslan was also trying to counsel the mage, possibly to be more open to my advances? I wasn't sure whether I liked that or not.

At least I would know the reason in advance if Shyntre suddenly became more pliable He and I could have a very interesting conversation of our own.

Any time.

Shyntre wasn't a good pretender. He couldn't fake it like Auslan.

I smiled. *I'm not worried.*

Perhaps I was even more intrigued. Kerse and Shyntre being present at my trials and having a connection with Wilsira made sense. The Prime, Rausery, and D'Shea must have chosen my challenges, although who stood where in that debate, I wasn't sure.

Even so, I trusted my gut that D'Shea and Wilsira were serious rivals, with Shyntre in between them.

Added to that, the Sisterhood had a recently acquired Consort, a favorite of a deceased Priestess, who knew about the weakness of the Sanctuary *and* was an ally of this same wizard. I liked it.

Especially them meeting eyes. Auslan *never* watched any female so steadily or for so long.

Shyntre glanced around the garden now, trying to spy any possible watchers. I remained still, my cloak covering me. He missed me.

"Need to go," he said. "It's been too long."

Not long enough for me.

Auslan nodded acceptance, and I let Shyntre leave on his own without discovery. He was on his way to return to Wilsira's suites when I intercepted him in the halls.

"Hungry?" I asked.

"N—"

"Don't lie. I heard your stomach growling."

My wizard scowled at me, exhaled, and went to the kitchens with me to eat as we had before, and I kept it short and didn't prod him about his secret meeting just now. Shyntre also went along with my explanation to the Priestess when we returned at last, though he was rightly as suspicious as Wilsira for different reasons.

They let it be for now. We were leaving in barely five marks, and the only one seeming rested and alert was myself.

A nice change.

I meant to find out more about *all* of this. D'Shea knew much more, had kept so much so close to her chest. Know and see, but watch the webs spin wider and wrap the players tighter. Sooner or later, they'd have to cut it and start over or not be able to move.

My finding Auslan alone on a small farm of solitude, however? That had been sheer luck darting in from the fringe, from the unknowable deep shadows, where the entire game being spun was anchored.

That was Braqth Herself nudging at the game board, snickering to Herself.

AUSLAN WASN'T PRESENT WHEN WE LEFT THE TENTH HOUSE ON THE FINAL LEG of our journey. It was truly a pity; I would have liked to see his face one more time. Neither of us having been found out by the Conceiver, the sensual and intelligent prize had been my unrepentant delight on this thorny nest of a trek.

I was glad, however, to be riding a lizard alongside the carriage and having space again. Although I kept an ear out for how Shyntre managed sharing the closed space with Kerse and his Mother, I also stayed out of easy speaking distance of the carriage, glad for the lack of voices as most of what I heard was the clop-scrape of the Uroans' feet and the roll of the wheels.

I didn't know where we were going next. It would be either back to the Wizard's Tower to drop off Shyntre before heading to the Sanctuary, or it would be my former Matron's House and my childhood grounds. I rather felt that I didn't have to ask, as there was nothing more to be done preparing for either of them.

Passing through one sentry point, out of one large trade tunnel and into another, we took the left fork.

Of course.

I took a slow breath in and let it out equally so, drawing one moment out as I willed the panic and bad dreams not to come. Wilsira peeked outside her carriage and disappeared again.

We exited the tunnel on another side of the Great Cavern, an easier and better maintained path than trying to navigate the hills and ravines, the musty mushroom patches, slave fields, streams, and collections of standing ponds. I supposed the only downside was that someone in the city center always knew when one passed in and out of one's usual territory.

"It won't be much farther," the Priestess said from her window, attempting reassurance of travel soon ending.

"Yes, Priestess," I said, because I had nothing else to say.

As far as I knew, this was a complete surprise visit, and I didn't know how Matron Thalluen would respond. The Noble heir would be a newborn, tiny. Perhaps my Mother would still be abed, unable to stand, given the poison Kaltra had fed her slowly and how much strength the pregnancy seemed to sap out of her.

We had left Curgia in a similar state. I hadn't seen her with my own eyes, never had the chance to speak with her. I only took it from the Matron and Priestess that Auslan had stopped the bleeding somehow after the stillborn was out, and she had been moved to her own quarters to recover. Maybe I would have a chance to ask Shyntre. He had stayed behind while I was forced to leave the room.

Goddess, I dared not think what might happen at the Twelfth House following a Priestess visit to the Tenth. Would I be commanded to arrest someone I knew for an insult to the one I was supposed to be guarding? Would the House status fall farther in the matter of a cycle or two, or managed to stay level? I certainly didn't see us climbing on account of Wilsira visiting.

Not 'us.' Thalluen no longer. No demons but us …

Whatever I might have been expecting of my quiet, closed-off Matron upon our arrival, I could admit it wasn't what she decided to do.

Matron Rohenvi rode out to meet us long before the gate to the courtyard, having donned a fine and full, blue dress, followed by a familiar selection of House Guard at her back — and probably every lizard we'd ever had in the stables.

To my relief, she didn't bring any children with her; not my new little sister, or that orphan I'd seen on my last visit, to whom she'd spoken with familiarity. Or any buas. The contingency was all female. If I didn't know better, I would say it looked like Matron was prepared to block us.

"Oi!" the Head Guard called. "Who from On High comes from Sivaraus? Grant us announcement, Priestess!"

Confident about the status of she that rode in the wealthy carriage. My Mother and her Guard might be experienced enough with Court to know, or it could be a lucky guess.

Wilsira's chuckle drifted out the window as she leaned out toward my side. She gestured me closer and held something out. I didn't want to take it.

Announce me, Red Sister, she signed, jerking the object again.

I came closer and accepted the jewelry, a tarnished silver bracelet with small gems embedded which, by Radiants alone, looked like smoky glass. I couldn't be sure of the color until we stood in candlelight, at least. I didn't recognize it, but the Conceiver seemed to think that the Matron would.

And I am to give it to her with an announcement.

There had to be a reason for that laugh.

I rode forward to meet the Guards and my Mother. My cowl remained up, though I was tempted to take it down to give Rohenvi more warning. Wilsira would note it.

No demons but us.

I lifted my arm straight out, opened my palm to show the bracelet. Two Guards flinched as if they had expected a spell to go off. I made no other sudden moves except to ride closer and project my voice before coming upon them to offer the "gift."

"The Conceiver Wilsira Tachnathon comes to visit the Matron Thalluen of the Twelfth House."

I licked my lips to think what to say next, noting my Mother's eyes sharpen in the dark. At least she recognized my voice.

"She offers this bracelet," I finished shortly. I knew neither intent nor significance, so why say more? It would be babble.

The Matron came forward with her Head Guard beside her, a new warrior I didn't know, and extended her naked hand with more grace than I'd ever witnessed her have a care to show. My heart had picked up by the time we were close enough to make the exchange. I watched hungrily for any hint what the bracelet meant when my Mother took it from me.

She looked into my hood, at my eyes, as if to determine my health and awareness, then down again and peeled her lizard from mine, putting some distance between us to face the side of the carriage.

"Conceiver, we welcome you and your entourage to our House," Rohenvi said.

A few moments passed as I expected her to ask why we had come, to display any nervousness for this perhaps unwelcome attention.

"Follow us back to the manor for comfort," she said instead. "We offer the best we have."

"Hm," Wilsira said, leaning far enough out to be seen. "Thank you, Matron. Lead the way."

STANDING OUTSIDE THE SOCIAL RITUALS AT THE OTHER THREE HOUSES HAD been fine. Now, it was its own form of torment.

I could focus on nothing else, could not relax or let my mind wander while the Conceiver visited with my Mother. My mind seemed in a fog as I awaited something to happen but had no way to anticipate what. No way to direct what may come or how it ended.

Pleasantries.

My Mother was driving me crazy with the pleasantries. She asked Wilsira no questions, merely served as a gracious hostess for Wilsira and Shyntre while Kerse and I stood in our corners of the room. I observed those Davrin around Rohenvi supporting her every directive, hopping to a suggestion — never demanded — if not anticipated.

I had never seen my Mother this in command of her environment, effortless and at ease. I had never seen our House this collected as a whole. The Matron Thalluen did not obey in advance; she did not seem to try guessing what curried the favor of one of Braqth's elder Daughters, as it had been with Itlaunia. The House servants and Guard were tense but depended on her to run things.

Matron Thalluen anticipated nothing for the Priestess but for the required pleasantries.

When had I ever witnessed that from her?

Finally, Wilsira had to say it.

"I have come to be witness to the new heir of House Thalluen," the Conceiver said, threading her dark, bejeweled fingers and easing back in her chair with a smirk. "Will you introduce me?"

My Mother smiled. "It is a little early for her to come out to society, isn't it?"

Wilsira chuckled with seemingly genuine amusement. "Indeed, perhaps she won't even survive her first decade. Regardless, I know I'll not waste my trip."

It seemed a little colder in the room.

"Such a young Noble is worth your attention?"

"It is not unheard of. I am the Conceiver, Rohenvi. The encouragement of new infants is my duty to our Valsharess and Sivaraus." Wilsira motioned with one hand. "Have the Fourth Daughter brought here. I wish to see her. A brief look, a quick blessing, and the wet nurse may whisk her away again to fuss elsewhere."

The Matron's eyes lifted, and she straightened her back adjusting the front of her blue gown at the bust. We *all* noticed then how it strained the ties. How my former Matron managed a mature voice also somehow innocent, with just the right amount of embarrassment, was beyond me.

"I have no wet nurse at this time, Priestess, and it is time to feed her again. That she will grow strong and inherit my House."

Another distracted adjustment of her full, milk-laden breasts. I noticed the wizard looking. Kerse was, too. At the moment, my former Matron exceeded even the Conceiver's natural size. She was never that swollen before.

How recent was the birthing, anyway?

No one had told me.

"Would it be ill of me to take care of her meal as we continue our discussion," Rohenvi asked, now propped prettily on the edge of her seat, "or would you care to wait here with refreshments while I attend to a practical matter?"

No offer for us to leave this room and go to any resting quarters, I noticed.

Watch the baby suck my tit or nibble on something yourself while I leave.

Mother had grown bolder since Kaltra's execution.

Wilsira propped her head with two fingers at her temple, flicking a brief look at Shyntre. "Why don't you finish the task here, Matron? I will wait."

What's this?

My wizard was tense, keeping eyes on the floor as he sat quietly. Neither mature female blinked at this bizarre challenge, and within a few ticks, an older male servant in plain, frumpy clothing brought a grumpy, squirming infant wrapped in a fine, pale blue blanket.

She was very tiny, the youngest Davrin I had ever seen.

The servant held her very close, heavy head propped against his shoulder. When he passed the baby to her Mother, it was obvious he knew how to handle one. This one had experience tending infants, but he was far too old to have been born here. I didn't recognize him.

Another new addition to the House since I left. Where did she find this one?

It also made me wonder where the other young cait was. Natia. She wasn't here.

Rohenvi took her new Daughter and tugged the ties of her dress loose at the front, reaching in and lifting out a heavy breast with a dark purple nipple. Bringing the baby close enough, the heir lunged to attach, sucking hard and for an entirely different purpose than I did when I jumped on a tit. I also didn't anticipate the look of surprise and contentment on the

Matron's face.

"Ah! A robust feeder," Wilsira observed with a broad smile. "Indicative of strong will and health despite the difficulty bearing her. A blessing, Rohenvi."

"Thank you, Conceiver."

My Mother focused on the nursing, practically ignoring the Priestess as she kept her eyes down like Shyntre. The male servant glanced once at the high-status guests but drifted back out of the way to stand calm and still until he was called. Everyone waited in a silence I couldn't decide if it was respectful, bewildered, or embarrassing.

Rohenvi switched breasts, a drop of white lingering on the side my sister had just drained before Mother's hand tugged fabric up to cover it before exposing the other. While the infant settled into the suck, swallow, and breathe rhythm of the infant, Wilsira spoke again.

"What is her name? I shall see it added to the archives."

Rohenvi hesitated, covering it up with a cooing murmur to her Daughter. "Mm. Vekika Thallunthietti."

I thought immediately of Jael. *Aurenthietti.*

Sometimes I called her Thietti for short. She was a Fourth Daughter as well, though all three of her older sisters still lived, while Vekika had only me and may never know it.

I experienced another yearning to return to the Cloister and report to my Elder, seek release and comfort in my Sisters. It was stronger, the closer it seemed I stood to what was familiar. Wilsira must have known.

Has it truly only been ten cycles since this trip began?

"An odd name," the Conceiver said, watching the baby suckle as the center of attention. "I have never heard it before. From where did you select it, Matron?"

Rohenvi lifted her gaze at last and smiled graciously. "Invention, Priestess. My Daughter is the first in Sivaraus to be given this name. At least it will be clear in the archives where the change happened with the future of House Thalluen."

Why did that sound like an insult to my ear? And to who?

"Indeed, it shall be most clear."

Wilsira tapped her fingers, betraying the slightest impatience, yet even while breastfeeding, Rohenvi instructed the servants on keeping the guests well-tended with fragrant drinks, finger foods clearly communal and tested for poison. Only the finest dishes and utensils were used, and there were plenty of smokeless candles lit, keeping even Kerse in full view.

My Mother still asked no questions, not even who the wizard was. She offered us no Reverie rooms, no feast or impromptu gathering. It should have been a gross disrespect, taking an enormous risk against her entire House, I thought, but Rohenvi continued to talk about many useful matters going on with the area that perhaps Wilsira hadn't heard, being so far removed.

I might have expected a theatrics-stirrer like Wilsira to get bored quickly of merchant and trade talk, of the management of the estate. I know I was. A little.

Yet the Priestess listened. Seeming curious.

"There are some deep traders filtering in knowledge how to improve crop yield after long use," my Mother said, brushing her fingertip along the edge of the baby's pointed ear. "Someone is writing them down and passing them through Low Gate."

"Written. What language?"

"Davrin. It's a little strange, though."

"Like a second-user?"

"I believe so. Translated poorly."

Rohenvi paused as Vekika swallowed wrong and went into a coughing fit. She had to adjust her position, pat her little back and make sure her new heir didn't drown in her own milk. Wilsira waited through it, showing no concern but a little impatience.

I reflected that Low Gate was on the opposite side of the Great Cavern from the lowest House, Aurenthin on the Fringe, that side had the blue stone in weapons made by psionic Tragar, according to Jael. I resisted touching the pendant beneath my armor, quite glad my Mother wasn't prattling to the Priestess about the same thing, if she was indeed doing business with "deep traders" now.

Explains the new governor in her nursery. And maybe the orphan.

"It seems to be working on my land, though," my Mother resumed. "Some good, practical theory and adaptability of method. Drawn from whose library, I have no idea. Although the traders like to say someone bargained with the Great Black for a chest of scrolls of Deepearth knowledge, the last time he was awake."

"Interesting," Wilsira said, narrowing her eyes in skepticism despite giving it some thought, and it struck me that this might be linked to an old conversation, too. One from Court, or one involving my Mother's deceased brother, whom this slit still remembered.

How many places does this Priestess have her fingers inserted?

"No Noble has mentioned the Dragon to me in centuries," the Priestess remarked.

Rohenvi nodded like she wasn't surprised. "The traders are talking now. Perhaps this means something, Priestess. For certain, the knowledge they bear on scraps of fiberstalk parchment is useful, but where would it have come from, if not our own Queen's shelves? We are the only race with productive and permanent lands to use it."

"Hm." Wilsira looked to the side, considering. "Good questions, Matron. I see the isolation from the city excitement has not dulled your wit any."

Was that a compliment?

"May I have one of those 'scraps' you mentioned?"

"Of course, Conceiver."

Once again, we didn't have to leave the room or wait. The Matron was prepared and signed to another servant in the room, indicating a drawer beneath an old but fine-quality hutch. The silent Davrin retrieved what the Matron wished and brought it to her in both open hands with a bow of her head, and Rohenvi glanced at it, nodded, and motioned for her to hand it directly to the Conceiver. Wilsira eagerly took it and studied it for a time.

"Interesting," she said again but with less doubt in her tone now. "So, you might have stuffed one ear to Court speak, but you still keep another open to the echoes of the deep."

My Mother said nothing, merely rocked her Daughter slowly. Vekika had fallen asleep, it seemed, as she was detached from our Mother.

"I believe we must go now, Matron," the Priestess said, standing up.

Shyntre and Matron Thalluen each did the same. Unobtrusively, the older governor stepped forward to scoop the Thalluen heir out of Rohenvi's arms so she could tighten and tidy up the front of her dress. I stood still, blinked twice, wondering what had just happened.

"Thank you for offering us your presence, Conceiver." The Matron bowed her head.

Wilsira hummed in approval. "You should return to Court more often than every Worship Ball, Matron Thalluen, and for a single eve. I swear you travel far longer to be in the Palace than you do actually standing there."

"There has not been enough help lately to leave, but our House shall rise again."

Wilsira glanced at me and smirked. "Understandable. Perhaps you shall. Do make certain that you pray enough, Matron."

I was sure most of us in the room each had a different idea what the Conceiver meant when she used that word.

"Thank you, Conceiver," my Mother said again.

Rohenvi never once tried to guide or hurry us out the door, but Wilsira was motivated enough to do so on her own, no pushing required. We weren't staying the eve, to leave upon the next wake cycle; we would leave now and perhaps make it back to the Sanctuary very late.

What was the rush, I wondered? How much did that matter? I knew I didn't want to stay; neither did the Matron want us here around her new and vulnerable Daughter. Wilsira even seemed to forget that part about a "blessing" on the new heir.

What the fuck?

Kerse was the one who drew my attention to the orphan. He paused, sniffing the air and focusing on one of the familiar doorways to the servants' quarters. Natia was there, peeking out at us, but she gasped and withdrew the moment the Sathoet saw her.

I smirked. *Still here. Still a shrinking mushroom.*

I decided not to draw attention to her.

Outside, I mounted up, gathering my own reigns as the entourage helped the other three in the carriage. They'd stayed guard outside during the brief stay and looked to have eaten something during their wait. Nothing had been unpacked, nothing was missing. The Priestess was satisfied.

"To the Wizard's Tower," Wilsira commanded the driver from her window.

Soon after, we exited my Mother's courtyard through her gates.

This must be some sort of record for any Matron having a Priestess leave so fast without being mortally insulted.

I'd certainly learned a thing or two about my Mother I'd never known and comparing her with three other Matrons in quick succession, each in their own routines when a Priestess showed up, House Thalluen and its Matron seemed … different from those higher ones. But I could never have seen it so clearly without being away for two decades now.

I'd think about why that was for my report. And maybe ask about my Grand Matron Siranet. Even Wilsira had said there was a link to the Sisterhood.

I was named for that previous Matron. Meanwhile, "Vekika" had just been invented.

WE PASSED BY THE TOWER BEFORE CONTINUING TOWARD THE PALACE AND THE SANCTUARY. Shyntre was released from his service first.

Lucky bua.

He remembered to bow to the Priestess and me each in turn, mumbling his formal valedictions before hefting the single pack he'd brought with him from the back of the carriage and walking quickly toward the enormous front door.

He didn't look back.

I was close enough to the carriage for Wilsira to comment. She was vague in her word choice as the driver was still within earshot, but I got the message.

"Here I thought I would be doing you a favor, bringing him," she said, and sighed. "But you'd found him before that point. You two got along better than I predicted."

I gave her a look but then smiled. "If you still feel that generosity, Conceiver, you could tell me why he bothered to be unseen in the first place."

The Priestess returned my smile. "Oh, I don't know for certain, but I'd wager he asked your Elder for the right. She commanded him, of course, and he knows what usually happens next if the cait returns." She chuckled. "It did not seem to make a difference, did it? You still found him. But, you haven't claimed him. I can tell. You are enjoying the hunt, Sister?"

I shrugged. "I suppose I am."

"Poor bua," the Priestess said, the amused curve of her mouth visible even in the shadow of her carriage. She hand signed the rest of her message to me.

He can't help but resist you, though he seems to loathe you less than some. If he had taken my advice all those turns ago, it may have been that the Sisterhood would not have shown any interest in him, and he would have remained a servant to the Sanctuary. As it is now, he is more yours than mine.

"Hm," I said in as flat a tone as I could manage. Such a frank giveaway. I knew showing interest quickly was a mistake, but it was hard not to want more.

I signed, *What advice was that?*

She smiled wider as she leaned away from me, back in her seat next to her son. *I shall let him tell you.*

The Conceiver spoke only of pleasantries for the remainder of our trip, the few moments she did speak, as I escorted the carriage and its passengers safely to the Sanctuary at last.

Aching for my own release from this mission.

CHAPTER 13

WILSIRA DID NOT TRY FOR ANY LAST-MOMENT BONDING, SECRET-SHARING, OR whatnot. She was finished with the trip, thinking ahead about something. Formal in her thanks to me and to the Sisterhood, she bid me safe passage back to the Prime, her body language quite different in a place where other Priestesses and their informants could see her.

Kerse behaved as well. I could believe he had gotten his fill of me on this trip and, like other Sathoet, had forgotten the distraction and was again wholly devoted to his Mother. His "patterns" were re-anchored, or whatever it was Auslan had been trying to describe.

I could believe it, but was it true? Wouldn't it be much better for me if that was the case? I wouldn't be at the center of a petition to the Valsharess, trying to convince Her to order the execution of the eldest Priestess Son of the second-highest ranking Priestess in the Sanctuary.

Yes, that's getting too far ahead of ourselves.

Except that I couldn't ignore my own instincts, D'Shea's misgivings, and Auslan's inside knowledge with his warning, in addition to every small thing Kerse had done of his own volition, seemingly without his dam's knowledge.

No. The Sathoet was still a Dragon-sized pile of trouble, propped to bring negative attention from the Priesthood down on me as Wilsira claimed Shyntre had drawn from the Sisterhood.

And I thanked neither her nor my wandering thoughts for the comparison.

My mind kept running this circle but felt numbed as I made my way back to the Sisterhood's Cloister on foot. The lizard mount wasn't from our stables and walking was how I'd first arrived ten cycles ago.

I tripped over a jutting stone, ungracefully but effectively catching myself from a hard nose-plant on bare rock. A moment later, I realized I had no memory of walking the last quarter-mark or so. I'd been drifting.

Drider shit ... Watch it. You'll be putting your hand blindly on a pincerworm next.

The numbness which fast crept in was from my lack of true Reverie for all that time. One very long rest period, cradled by a warm, demon-bred Elf, and several, tiny naps either sitting or standing up. That was it.

Would D'Shea demand full reports first, or might I eat and rest first? Would I ask for that delay or just get it over with?

When I had at last reached one of the hidden entrances, I went beneath a rocky ledge to deal with the ward. I didn't get it on my first try.

Come on ...

Ward suspended, I opened the door when someone grabbed my shoulder. I blurted a startled cry, throwing myself backward and drawing a dagger.

"Sirana!" Gaelan scowled at me. "Don't you threaten me."

Oh, Braqth fuck me sideways ...

"Gaelan," I gasped, swallowing my heart back in its rightful place. I sheathed my dagger. "Sorry. You surprised me. What would you expect?"

Muddled though my thoughts were, it occurred to me to wonder how she had known to expect me. She must have read it on my face. Taking my arm, she began leading me down the curves and ramps of our Cloister's hallways.

"D'Shea's not here yet but soon," she said. "We're going to her quarters. Be quiet."

Acquiescing, I followed and soon found myself shoved into D'Shea's quarters. For the first time, it was in her absence. Gaelan had been able to get in.

The thought barely completed itself before I noticed Reishel was here, too, sitting on the edge of an empty tub. My body jumped again as she stood up and smiled at us.

Had something changed in my absence?

"Strip down slowly," said the Dark Elf older than Gaelan and me, the Red Sister lowest in rank but for Jael. "And hand me each piece as you take it off."

Even noting the long, clean workbench prepared for this, I quirked one eyebrow and did not move. Gaelan folded her arms.

"Everything on you is evidence, Sirana," she said. "We've been instructed to have you prepared and your possessions laid out before Elder D'Shea gets here."

"Oh, you are?" I asked skeptically.

Gaelan nodded once, studying me with a frown, while Reishel maintained her encouraging smile. They'd known I was returning in plenty of time, then.

Someone had been watching the roads. Or spying somehow.

"Say nothing," Reishel said. "Remove everything you have on you. One bit at a time."

I muttered a curse under my breath and started removing my gear, handing pieces to each of them to inspect as I did so. Neither were talkative during the process, and I was to save my words for my Elder. Gaelan blinked when I handed her Shyntre's bloodstone from one of my pouches.

Later, when I removed my shirt, Reishel's mouth opened a little when she saw Shyntre's pendant around my neck and between naked breasts. "What … where did you get that?"

I frowned. Hadn't she seen it before in the barracks, one of the times we'd fucked? Granted, I hadn't drawn attention to it, but I hadn't been as careful or desperate to hide it as I'd been with Wilsira.

A bit loath to do so, I removed it and handed it out to her, the final adornment before I was completely nude, as it had been whenever Wilsira ordered me naked and kneeling while Kerse fucked me.

"The wizard from my trials," I said. "He gave it to me."

Gaelan exchanged a look with Reishel, her face screwed up in confusion. "Wait, the one you said you found?

"When? Was he there?"

I smiled, not answering the first question. "He was, yes. Do you know who he really is?"

Both my Sisters wiped all expression from their faces and stopped asking questions about my mission which I knew they shouldn't be without D'Shea here.

Heh.

Gaelan placed the necklace down with my other items and helped unplait my braids so that my hair was smooth and loose down my back. Then she took a deep breath as she picked up a small purple jar from D'Shea's shelves. Unscrewing the lid, she dipped her gloved finger into a glittering powder and touched it to her tongue. After letting it dissolve in her mouth, she put the jar back and looked me over.

I watched her warily until she stepped directly behind me, and I couldn't see her anymore.

"Look straight ahead," she ordered.

I did, Reishel facing me with obvious curiosity.

Cool, dry gloves rested on the back of my neck. They moved lightly over my skin, my back, my shoulders, and arms, tickling until she reached around and touched my breasts. The nipples grew hard at the light touch. She ignored that and continued down my ribs, my stomach, my flanks and hips. She inspected my legs and buttocks and feet, seeming not to see what she touched.

Finally, Gaelan stepped to my side and lifted her hand, nudging her finger inside my mouth.

"Um, *ngh.*"

"Shush."

She pressed her index finger onto my tongue. She chanted a spell a few times, and when she removed her finger, it shimmered briefly in iridescent green. I didn't know what that meant, but she repeated it after moving her hand between my legs, inserting her middle finger familiarly into my hard-used sex. I sucked in my breath, discovering I was still sore, and her finger shone a brighter green when she removed it.

Like the first, the color faded within a few breaths.

"What are you — ?"

As she moved around behind me again, I had a guess.

"Last time, Sirana," she murmured.

Of course.

I arched my back a little and relaxed to make the probing of my netherhole tolerable. All these probes had been dry; she used a different finger each time and hadn't so much as licked them before pressing in. I glimpsed the same emerald color again before it faded, then Gaelan went over to a table to pour water from a pitcher into a washbowl to cleanse her gloves.

Reishel stood watching, tense like she couldn't wait for an answer. "Gaelan?"

"Almost," the mage replied, patting gloves dry enough to take them off and lay them to the side of my equipment. "Don't talk."

Gaelan approached me and took to one knee in front of me, gently placing both naked hands gently over my womb. She closed her eyes and started chanting.

I was sure I wasn't ...

Pretty sure.

I didn't remember a time I'd failed to take prevention.

But then, I don't remember a lot of little moments on this trip.

I waited as tensely as Reishel for Gaelan to finish. Eventually, she stood up and shook her head in the negative, and Reishel relaxed to show visible relief. My cheeks warmed to see it and the easy smile which followed.

It really mattered to her. The Red Sister whom I'd helped my Elder save, the one who had been the first in our history to awaken and recover from that coma, she cared about my fate. My sometimes roommate, my frequent playmate.

I was sure Reishel wanted to kiss me then, or touch me, the way she looked at me. She did neither. I knew why; we were waiting for D'Shea, and we couldn't spoil anything the Elder Sorceress might deduce from my body having returned from Wilsira's service.

It was a longer wait as we remained quiet and thinking our own thoughts.

When the door slid open, Elder D'Shea came through, and we straightened up. She was dressed in her full reds, and her face was set and serious. Nodding first to Gaelan and Reishel, then to me, she removed her cloak to hang it up, tugging off her gloves and undoing her belt to add them to the wall. She continued to undress as she walked past us father back into her room, seeming to want comfort first thing.

"Gaelan, report," she said.

Her subordinate spoke as the Sorceress continued to change. Reishel glanced briefly at me.

"Some bruising healed from the inside," Gaelan began, "some topical healing done on her flank, no major injuries."

Ah, yes. They'd be talking about me like an object to begin; I would speak only afterward. It might've been more irritating except that I'd just spent a journey with all others around me trying to pretend I wasn't there.

"Residual semen is in all three of her orifices, from within the last two cycles. The most recent was in her sex."

Of course. Neat trick.

"However, she's not pregnant."

D'Shea looked at me directly, and I smiled to hear that spoken aloud, then my Elder looked back to Gaelan with wordless expectation.

"She either used or lost all of her issued prevention draughts but possesses the empties of others not issued to her. She carried a bloodstone not previously issued, and a blue pendant around her neck. None of her equipment is missing, only a handful of empty vials."

Because I'd disposed of them after running out of room on my belt.

Gaelan next listed that equipment laid out, piece by piece, and I listened, only to realize that there *was* something missing.

"Hold," D'Shea said to Gaelan, lifting her hand for her silence. She had stared at me the whole time Gaelan was talking. "What is it, Sirana? Speak on this point only."

I swallowed. "I had a cloth, Elder. White, stained with blood."

"Whose blood?"

"Mine. Used to tend the wound on my side. It's not in one of my pouches?"

D'Shea looked at Gaelan, who shook her head. "No. No bloody cloth."

Our Elder grunted in annoyance. "I figure explaining that cloth will require some context?"

"Yes, Elder."

"Which do you think most likely: you may have dropped it, or someone took it?"

I thought about it. I'd taken it from Auslan and put it in my pouch. I'd only pulled it out again to wipe Kerse's fluids off my face before putting it back in the same pouch and lifting the miscarrying Curgia to remove her from that nursery room.

No one had gotten close enough to take it, unless …

Well, there was the one last time Kerse had mounted me at House Itlaun before we left for House Thalluen. I'd been fully naked on my back; Shyntre had watched my gear as before. Wilsira had decided to include herself and straddle my face. I flinched at the memory of how her scars had felt. Worse than my sister ever was.

I wanted to put it out of my mind.

But I'd *checked* my equipment afterward, as always; the cloth had been there then.

"Perhaps I dropped it on the journey back, Elder," I said, my stomach a little cold. "I don't see the opportunity for someone to take it. It would have only been a few marks ago. I had it earlier."

"I'll send a team out to retrace your path," she said. "It's unlikely we'll find it. If it had blood on it, it could have been found quickly by many hungry things, but we will try. Anything else they should know of this item?"

"Mm. Semen stains. I used it later to wipe my face."

D'Shea left that for the report with context as well. She plucked out a basic map from her scrolls, had me show her the path the carriage had taken, and summoned one of the teams with a message pellet to give them their assignment outside her quarters. It was done with high efficiency and the four of us were soon alone again.

"Alright," D'Shea sat down to be comfortable and left the three of us standing. "If you please, Sirana. Start from the beginning."

Easier said …

One of my most difficult and convoluted recitals. If I had thought my hunt to find Jael and the Tragar was bad for sounding in control, this was worse. It started out well enough; I'd taken my Elder's knowledge and advice, and my time meeting the Priestess for the first time at Sanctuary went well enough.

My Elder did not seem surprised when I mentioned Shyntre was made to come with us, nor was she anywhere near as shocked by my description of how I'd found Qivni than I had been at the time. She asked me few questions about them.

Noted.

The Sorceress listened avidly to the details of the journey, of the tortured and poisoned Davrin whose body I'd purified, and of arriving at House D'Verin. She frowned to hear about Wilsira's incense and spells tying up the three of us, and as I continued, I found that I couldn't answer many of my Elder's questions, either because I hadn't been able to trust my senses or because I hadn't witnessed it.

My Elder refrained from reprimanding me on several points where my will had clearly been tested to its limits, but she wasn't thrilled with my performance under pressure.

"You see how dangerous she is now, don't you?" she asked.

I nodded urgently. "Yes, Elder, I do."

"Well done in returning to us with an empty womb," she said, glancing at the other two Sisters present, and I relaxed a little. "Is Kerse the only bua you coupled with? Gaelan's magic says you took semen in your mouth and backside as well."

My face heated up. "The Priestess commanded the wizard to spurt in my mouth a few times, Elder, but he was never allowed in another hole. Other times, it was Kerse, as I did not have time to allow a prevention draught to take effect. It was necessary."

D'Shea nodded. "I believe you. Keep going."

My Elder listened intently to my interactions with Shyntre through the trip, her face not betraying much besides the interest in the intrigue and his baffling motivation to help me. The Sorceress knew I was extremely curious about the Headmaster' son, but I couldn't say that I "knew" he was birthed by someone in the Sisterhood — maybe by her — while Gaelan and Reishel stood there.

Therefore, the one point where I deviated in my report was with Auslan. I'd given so much lurid and intimate detail, admitted to fuzzy memories and repeated humiliations by then, that when I portrayed my report from the Consort as similar to my previous visits aside from asking him for healing — very much downplaying how inquisitive he'd been about me while never mentioning the information we'd traded — D'Shea didn't notice.

I didn't know if this meant D'Shea did not know about Auslan's connection to the wizard, but at the lack of reaction, I also left out the part of them talking alone in the garden. I had seen what the Prime enjoyed doing with buas accused of mating each other instead of females, and I didn't even know if it was true here.

No reason to expose them to the Sisterhood.

I had reached the point in my report where we would leave House Itlaun to head to the next place, and my Elder paused there to call back to an earlier point. It threw me off, as I'd been about to mention my Mother.

"The Consort was able to save Curgia's life," D'Shea said for confirmation.

I blinked. "Yes, Elder."

"Huh." She considered. "That Consort was never reported before as having this ability. Did you witness the process?"

"No, Elder, though Shyntre did. I was summoned by the Priestess and required to leave the room."

"So, it's only what you overheard the Matron telling the Priestess."

"No, Elder, you'll recall I heard Matron Itlaun ask a servant to wake the Consort and bring him to her. He touched her forehead and behaved like he intended to take action, reassuring her and asking her to stay awake. This was whole marks before that conversation."

"Of course. And you never saw the stillborn?"

"No. I did see Matron Itlaun's face when she referred to it. It was not pureblood. You know it wasn't."

"I know. But you didn't *see* it dead."

I breathed out. "No, Elder. Wilsira ordered me to guard her during Reverie, so she could recover from the ritual before she met with the Matron. Kerse enforced it, I never left the room. She didn't want me sneaking out to search for the stillborn or what they did with it."

"Wise of her," D'Shea commented. "Though you should have tried harder."

"I did. She set her trap before I arrived. I could barely stay awake to watch Kerse. He may have mounted me if I passed out. He prevented me from leaving. Twice."

"Hm," was the most D'Shea would grant on that. "And Wilsira did not ask you what might have caused the disruption to that ritual?"

I paused. "No, Elder. She didn't ask me."

"She didn't suspect you?"

"Maybe, maybe not. She didn't know I was there at first, and for all I know, she believed I came into the nursery only after it failed, hearing the screams. I don't know what Kerse might have told her, but he can't have told her the truth."

D'Shea looked wary. "You are sure now. Kerse acts on his own."

"The pendant would be hers now if he obeyed and told her everything," I insisted. "I would be hers. I go so far as to say the Sathoet *and* the wizard each made efforts to keep me out of her claws. They knew her tricks much better than I did."

D'Shea's eyes flicked to Gaelan and Reishel, as if she considered sending my Sisters away for this part. They understood that the pendant was magical, like so many pieces we used, but not why I was the only one who could get any benefit from it. My Elder didn't seem to mind Gaelan and Reishel knowing about Kerse's changing behavior, but Elder Rausery's warning about not letting anyone know how the encounter with Kain had changed me still rang loudly in my head.

Perhaps the warning rang for D'Shea as well, for she opted to skip delving into the details of the ritual entirely. At least, for now.

"So, the Sathoet gouged you in returning the bloodstone, and you went to the Consort for healing. After that, you used the Consort's cloth to wipe Kerse's semen from your face."

"Correct, Elder."

D'Shea said, tapping her fingers on the arm of her chair. "What had you intended to do with it?"

I shrugged slightly. "Throw it away, eventually. Maybe burn it. I didn't want to leave it behind in Itlaunia's garbage."

"Generally a good idea."

"But I forgot about it with where we went next."

"Which was?"

I inhaled and let it out. "House Thalluen. To visit the Matron and her newborn heir."

Gaelan stiffened, and my Elder frowned very deeply. "You visited a fourth House before returning here? You can't have stayed long."

"No. Barely the eve. About three marks."

"And you didn't stay in any guest rooms."

"No, Elder."

"So short." The Sorceress considered. "Wilsira decided to push on and return to the Sanctuary late to release you."

"Yes. And here I am, Elder." I shrugged at the obvious remark. My mind felt misty; I was still drastically short on sleep.

"Tell me what happened at House Thalluen," D'Shea commanded. "As much detail as you recall, no matter how small."

Argh ... Truly?

I didn't even recall most of the early conversation, as it had seemed wandering and pointless. I knew better than to argue and voice this opinion out loud, however.

As I stumbled through this, my exhaustion must have really started to show. Reishel looked concerned and Gaelan had her jaw locked and mouth tight, eyes approaching a distracted glare, like she grew bored and impatient of the details, too.

D'Shea was merciless, however, and the revelation of the deep trader link and bartered scraps of scroll — one of them now in Wilsira's possession and probably why she left my Mother's House so quickly — at least seemed to satisfy her.

I had neared the finish when Gaelan made a noise, like she tried to speak but then something had jabbed her in the back. I paused, looking at her.

"Continue," D'Shea said gruffly, motioning that I ignore distraction. "Kerse did what?"

"Noticed the orphan, Natia, spying on us as we were leaving," I finished.

"And then?"

"Kerse stayed in his place, and she hid when I looked her way."

"Would you say Matron Thalluen is caring well for these new servants that you've noticed?"

I frowned. "The cait looked fine. Fed and properly clothed, with no visible injuries, if that's what you mean. I only had a glimpse, though. She was fast."

D'Shea opted to smile a little at this. "Very good." The Elder looked to the others in the room. "The bloodstone, Gaelan. Bring it to me."

My Sister obeyed stiffly, and we watched as D'Shea turned it over in her hand, studying it, whispering an odd word here and there, the fingernail on her thumb scraping at the specks of my blood that yet remained on it. She did not take her eyes off it even when she spoke on a different topic altogether.

"The last battle against the Ornilleth thralls," she said.

Reishel, Gaelan, and I showed our surprise at the abrupt shift. Our Elder lifted crimson eyes, pinning her gaze on each of us for a few moments before saying, "Each of you experienced something unusual in that event. You must describe it to each other before I may accomplish what I wish to with this bloodstone Sirana so wisely saved for me."

Or there could be nothing on it.

We exchanged looks, my clothed Red Sisters and me, while I tried not to panic. Rausery had *warned* me. Don't tell anyone I was sensitive to psionics, not even Sisters. Would D'Shea override her? Should I resist? I thought the Elders had agreed—

"Reishel, you first."

She'd had it simplest, if probably the harshest. "Well, Elder, for all practical purpose, I died. I was a shell without a mind. But the Sisterhood somehow brought me back, tested me, and kept me." Reishel's ruby eyes landed on me. "Sirana was the first Sister I saw upon waking."

D'Shea nodded that she was satisfied, and Reishel stopped short of mentioning the healing trance I'd shared with her and the Sorceress, with me in the middle. A conduit, she had said.

"Gaelan?" our Elder prompted.

The potion maker wasn't pleased. "I was used by you and Lelinahdara to enhance your collective spell, so the Red Sisters could hear yours and Elder Rausery's orders anywhere in the cavern. It was my first time … and it was invasive."

"I know," D'Shea replied. "Sirana experienced something similar on the Priestess Lelinahdara's altar, and you watched it, Gaelan."

Reishel and Gaelan nodded.

"More interesting is that Sirana was instructed to undergo a test like this again with the Liaison, around the time we recovered Reishel. I alone witnessed it, but that is what I want to discuss here."

I relaxed to know I wouldn't be asked for share my unusual experience in the flayer battle like the other two. "What do you mean, Elder?"

I could have sworn D'Shea was tempted to wink at me as her lips stretched into a smile. "You were stronger the second time. The Priestess *withdrew* her power rather than openly fail in front of me. It was one of the only times I've seen it happen."

We glanced at each other and waited.

"There is a rank for our Liaison in the Sanctuary. It isn't spoken much, though I've always known it, and I understand how to train you now, after watching her with Gaelan and Sirana."

"Train us, Elder?"

"Lelinahdara is a Confessor." D'Shea's eyes studied us. "She is very powerful in a ritual when she learns a secret, something private that explains something about how you are. Something she can exploit to tear down your will's defenses. Do you agree, Gaelan, Sirana?"

I had certainly been left exposed the first time, following submission. Gaelan nodded, and then I did as well.

The Priestess learned something personal about Gaelan ... Something about the dead bua she misses, maybe?

Meanwhile, my elder Sister asked aloud, "You said Sirana resisted the Priestess a second time, Elder?"

"Even better," said our Elder with a humorous smirk. "Sirana uncovered something personal of our Liaison instead, exploiting *that* in return. The Confessor got a taste of her own methods."

Reishel laughed. "Jaunda would be proud."

"Yes, although I do not think it was a conscious choice on our novice's part, but part of her potential to the Sisterhood." My Elder looked at me. "Nonetheless, Sirana, you confirmed for me that Tarra can be far *less* effective when she learns nothing new about her target. This would have always made her motivated to be very nosy, yet also not likely to climb very high in the Priesthood, as her history suggests. She puts up an excellent front, don't you think?"

Reishel nodded. "And a good reason Lelinahdara was selected as a Liaison for the Sisterhood. Discover a soft spot about each of the new Sisters brought in."

"Mm-hm. Exactly, Reishel."

"You're telling us this, Elder," Gaelan said with open skepticism. "The three lowest Sisters, apart from Jael. What are we to do with this knowledge?"

"Use it to learn not to fear her," D'Shea answered calmly. "You have an early start, Gaelan, and Sirana to thank for learning how, should the Prime insist you submit again."

"Why would she, Elder?"

Reishel answered that. "Loyalty test. The Prime threatened me with it."

"Correct," D'Shea said. "One way the Sanctuary creeps their restrictions into the Sisterhood. Lelinahdara learns personal things of the new recruits, and the Conceiver Wilsira plays on our Eldest's old fears and contempt of the younger Sisters."

"But we're only getting younger," I said, "compared to the Prime."

D'Shea nodded, turning the bloodstone over in her hand. "Well put. And the Priesthood still wishes to control us, that we may not investigate independently of their approval. They partly succeeded when we were no longer allowed to place our own children, and this decision was in the hands of the Priestesses. They still try for more."

I bit down on my cheek, hard, rather than bring up Shyntre right then. I still didn't *know* that he was her son. I only had Auslan's claim and my Elder's treatment of Headmaster Phaelous as my "proof." I recalled Wilsira's taunt as the bua returned to the Wizard's Tower as well, but it was all words.

He is more yours than mine.

What had the Priestess meant? My own Sisters had said he was a "Priesthood favorite." The two views of this wizard didn't seem to mesh.

"Now this," the Elder Sorceress lifted the young wizard's bloodstone for us to see. "Shyntre never asked for it back?"

"He said I owe him something."

"Have you paid it?"

"No. We never agreed on anything."

D'Shea smirked. "And you haven't spoken the command word he gave you?"

I shook my head. "No, Elder."

"A conversation between Curgia and Wilsira." My Elder smiled at the stone. "Earlier the same evening that she miscarried her hybrid after Wilsira failed in her ritual. I do commend you for this one, Sirana, even with missed opportunities. Let us hope something useful is on it."

She looked at us. "More than suspicion must be brought to the Valsharess. Proof too weak only tempts retaliation. Saying that Wilsira is up to something is like telling the Valsharess that fire is hot."

Even Gaelan smiled a little at that one.

"If we can prove Kerse is becoming dangerous and willful — thus far he has not shown himself to be the first, but he surely becomes the second — or if we can prove Wilsira is trying for Abyssal power that could threaten the Queen, one of those two things could bring her down."

"Is Elder Rausery aware you are targeting the Conceiver, Elder?" I asked.

"She is." My Elder quirked her eyebrow as if she was insulted. "Wilsira is one of many being watched in the Sanctuary, Sirana, for over four hundred years now. We keep watch always on the powerful and those positioned to become so. Finding the right Red Sister to handle the right situation is what the Sisterhood does, but it takes time."

True, but somehow this still felt very personal to my Elder.

I nodded. "Understood, Elder."

"Only a bit, but it's enough for now." D'Shea gestured to each of us. "Now, I want to test a theory. With you three as conduits, I want more than one of us to listen to this bloodstone."

"Not possible," Gaelan blurted. "Everyone knows the limitations —"

The sharp look from the Sorceress silenced her. I exchanged looks with my Sisters again.

"What would you have us do, Elder?" Reishel asked.

"Much better." D'Shea smiled, standing up out of her chair and motioning me to her bed. "Gaelan, retrieve four pieces of parchment and a stylus for each. I want them ready for afterward. Reishel and Sirana, come here. Everyone strip down, no magic or objects on you."

The other two obeyed, and I waited on the high-propped bed for them to catch up. We weren't to lie down. Reishel joined me while D'Shea signed privately with Gaelan as the young mage stripped down. Then, our Elder shrugged out of her robe as well and directed us so we sat together in a naked chain: back-to-front in between each other's legs, able to grasp the shoulders of the Sister in front of us.

Reishel was at the front, fingers threaded together, with Gaelan behind her, then me. D'Shea was at the back and behind me where none of us could see her without twisting around.

My Elder surprised me when she silently slipped the blue pendant around my neck and passed the bloodstone forward to me. I took the opaque, green-red lump in one hand, covered the sapphire with my other, and tried to turn and make eye contact.

"Face forward, Sirana," D'Shea said brusquely, pushing my jaw away. "You hold and focus on the bloodstone, but do *not* speak the command word, do you understand?"

"Yes, Elder."

"Gaelan, you wait until I've completed my spell. Reishel, meditate on your aura as you've been taught. Sirana, when you feel Gaelan squeeze your right leg for three breaths, listen only to whatever the bloodstone repeats back to you."

"But — ?"

"Focus, Sirana. And listen. Don't miss a word or a sound."

I got comfortable, waiting for the squeeze signal. This took a while as D'Shea altered her breath and chanted. Magic built up in the room. It affected Reishel first as she sat still; her breathing aligned with D'Shea's, and then Gaelan in front of me. It felt different from Wilsira's magic; at least it didn't make me feel sick.

Gaelan deliberately clutched down on my leg, and I counted my breaths.

I heard her say, *"Kannexu."*

The command word.

Without speaking it myself, the bloodstone in my hand activated, becoming warm, and then a charge passed through me. It swept from my arm to my shoulders where D'Shea held me, through her, then back again to me and to my Sisters forward. I heard an echo of magic returning, closing a loop, and the air popped. A hollow space seemed to form near my ear.

A soundless void waiting to be filled.

"Shall we sit, Priestess?"

Curgia sounded as though she had recovered from the scare of a Red Sister ambushing her at her desk. As fabric shifted and two bodies made the sounds of sitting, I heard Kerse's feet before he breathed out, likely crouching low, beside and behind the Priestess.

"How goes your health, my cait? You look a little thin. Have you been eating enough?"

"I've not had much appetite until recently, Priestess. The ... pregnancy has been an unsteady one."

A pause.

"How have your dreams changed?"

"I ... I ..."

"Have they changed?"

"Y-yes, Priestess. How did you know?"

"You carry the blood of the Abyss in your belly. I know, I've been there. My Reverie changed as well." Wilsira shifted but didn't stand up from her chair. *"So tell me, my cait.* **How** *have your dreams changed?"*

This was not the opening of a deal Curgia or I understood very well, if it was a deal at all. I would have been baffled if I didn't know where this would end later the same eve.

"Is ... is it the Abyss, then? That place I dream of."

"Is it? Describe it."

"Cold, black. It is the space in between points of light. All of it is unfathomably far away ..."

"Do you hear anything, or is it empty?"

"Empty, Priestess."

Wilsira breathed in, then out. *"You haven't dreamt of the Abyss directly, child, though you've seen the path that leads there. Is there a high magical strength in your family?"*

"No, Priestess. Only moderate. We are hoping to encourage that strength through the Consort's blood."

Wilsira was very quiet, then she spoke again. *"Why did you not find some way to make your womb bleed itself empty, Curgia? I know you did not want it, but now look at you."*

"I ... *only had one contact I could trust, but she seemed to disappear. Had gone on a trip, she said, and only returned when it would no longer be safe to ... end it."*

If Wilsira hadn't had a hand in that "trip," I'd be very surprised.

"And by then?"

"I had gotten used to hiding it, I suppose."

"And now you don't hide it at all."

Curgia took a couple of careful breaths. *"I started dreaming."*

"Yes? How did that change things?"

"My own magic has gotten stronger. I feel it. Just in the last few spans I've been able to cast ... stronger and more spells than I ever could before."

"Tell me about this."

As Curgia described some of her modest, new abilities, I considered the timing. Soon after the time I found her attempt to kill it, or herself, in the garden. At her lowest point, when she had been given cause to reconsider. By me.

Wilsira sounded triumphant. *"Ah, my dear. You understand."*

"No ... I don't believe so, Priestess, but ... I know what I feel now."

"And your thoughts?"

After a hesitant pause, *"Is it the ... baby giving me this added power?"*

"Certainly. This is fascinating, Curgia," Wilsira said with more excitement than I usually heard from her. *"You are experiencing a lower potency of what a Priestess does carrying her son. It is certainly a male child."*

It seemed Curgia was not sure what to say to that. *"Well ... ah ... You mentioned ... options, Priestess?"*

"Yes. I believe I know the best path for you. You have been touched by our Goddess's power, Curgia. Truly touched. Cutting the life short at this point would harm you, perhaps leave you weaker than you were when you first came to me. You gained power but would lose it and more if that heartbeat were to stop while still connected to you."

Curgia made a fearful sound.

Despite the apparent appeal of having more magical ability within her young lifetime, the Noble was very afraid of the immediate future.

The Priestess had *never* intended to grant the Noble freedom from her pregnancy in exchange for something else, as D'Shea had theorized. The Priestess had been waiting until it was too late to survive the attempt.

"*Priestess ... I don't know how we could take care of it ... him. What if someone saw and killed him? Or took him? How would we control him, or teach him ... I ... there's no support or knowledge of —*"

"*Calm yourself, Curgia, you'll faint if you keep breathing like that.*" Wilsira shifted again in her chair. "*I shall help you. This very eve, I will help you. We only must discover your child's name prior to his birth. If we discover this, then you may keep your new power even if he should die soon after birth.*"

The Noble still sounded quite scared. "*H-how ... what do you mean 'discover' a name? I never thought of a name for —*"

"*I mean its Abyssal name, Curgia. He must have one, or you wouldn't be having these dreams. I know a ritual where we may hear this name, but we need someplace we won't be disturbed as it requires a long trance. Unfathomable distance, as you said, must be travelled.*"

"*I ... I don't —*"

"*Curgia. If you don't let me help you, you won't know this child's name until he can speak, and that would be turns from now, if he lived. He will be lucky to survive his first breath should word get out, and you will suffer with him. You will lose part of your divine magic along with him, at the very least.*"

The Priestess had done an excellent job frightening and trapping the Noble, and I wondered whether Wilsira was so convincing because this was one of her own terrors?

This matched that I'd witnessed later, what Kerse told me. Could it be possible Wilsira was doing exactly as she said? I couldn't believe it easily; she must have another motive, some other benefit that she would get from this. The Valsharess wouldn't allow a Priestess to breed her own demonblood son this way; the Queen couldn't know this was happening.

Could She?

"*Learn the name of your divine unborn, and the separation will be less traumatic,*" the Conceiver said. "*I will help you with a safer birth. Come to me at the Sanctuary when your time is near, and we will take care of it. You can go home and tell your Mother it was stillborn, then you can try again with the Consort.*"

I guarantee you will give birth to a living, full-blood Davrin child by your new Consort before he must leave for another House."

Curgia sniffed. *"Why ... why did you force me to catch this in the first place, if the baby's only going to die ... ?"*

"Don't be a fool, Noble. I just enhanced your magic in a way that is incredibly rare, usually reserved for only an acolyte Priestess! It was important that you experience this prior to catching your real heir by the Consort."

"Why?"

*"Do you not think that your **true** Davrin child won't be more powerful because of what you have gone through on her behalf? It is what you wanted, isn't it? More beautiful and powerful children than either of your sisters, and than any your House has had in the past few generations?"*

The young Davrin was silent; she may have nodded.

"Then Braqth has favored you, child. Well beyond your known desires and comprehension." Clothing rustled as if Wilsira leaned forward. *"But first you must learn his name with me, later this eve. Where would be a good place to meet while the House is in Reverie?"*

There was some quiet before Curgia whispered, *"The nursery."*

"Good. Yes, that makes sense. I — Curgia? Where are you going?"

From the sound of it, Curgia had stood up abruptly from the chair and walked closer to where the bloodstone had been set on her desk. I heard the scrape of paper against stone and then sudden movement, followed by a short scream and a growl.

"Get him away!" the Noble squeaked and stumbled back from the bloodstone. *"I was getting my journal, Priestess! I had written down some of the descriptions in it, I wanted to show you! ... if you ..."*

"Ah. I am sorry, child. My son is protective of me. We did not know what you were doing. Yes, I would like to read those descriptions. Bring it here."

The voices grew louder as if the bloodstone had been brought closer. At this point, Kerse had palmed the bloodstone, and Curgia was now sitting back in her chair with her book in her hand. Exactly as I'd found them when I'd been summoned and opened the door, so I knew this part would end soon.

We heard Curgia's wavering voice reading the abstract descriptions of mystical imagery one did not understand but tried putting into words. Then we heard more encouragement from the Priestess, reconfirmation of the plan, and finally, Wilsira called for me.

I could hear my own voice as I came back in the room. After we'd left, we went on the tour around the estate. Kerse still carried the bloodstone, and so I got to hear and relive that long, boring thing all over again. It faded when the stone ran out of magical flux right before we got to the interesting part.

Where the puglit startled everyone and Kerse pushed me to land atop my Consort.

I GASPED AS THE MAGIC RELEASED ME AT LAST, AS THE HOLLOW POP OF AIR around my head finally filled with normal, living weight. I blinked as if I had been in magical darkness with only my ears working for me for many marks. Slowly did my vision return.

I was aware of D'Shea's hands, now sweaty and hot and atop my bare shoulders. I was chilled, sitting naked between her legs but warmed by Gaelan's naked body in front.

I heard D'Shea laugh softly. "Excellent. Just excellent."

I looked cautiously forward and saw Gaelan and Reishel first. Their half-expressions as they turned their heads toward our Elder's voice were hazy. Strangely, their auras seemed visible to me for a moment, bright and colorful even in the candlelight.

As it had been after the battle with the Ornilleths, Gaelan's eyes were glassy and her breathing deep. She had been used as a conduit again, enhancing the spell, so no wonder I hadn't missed a word of the conversation. But Reishel blinked her eyes clear, and knowledge appeared in her face. Next, I looked back at D'Shea.

Her smile was so wide, she looked so pleased, that I could only think my Elder must have somehow heard it all as well.

"Well done, Sirana. Each of us, take parchment and stylus, write down what you remember. Do not speak or share until we're done."

Gaelan weaved drunkenly and blinked at me, and I croaked a bit as I responded, "Yes, Elder."

D'Shea touched the back of Gaelan's neck possessively as she guided her to sit at her desk and write, her eyes glittering with power and excitement. Reishel and I found our own writing space, seeming steadier.

I knew the Sorceress was aroused as one hand drifted over her own breast, her nipple standing out through her robe. D'Shea threaded her naked fingers into Gaelan's tight bun at the back of her head, gripping and giving it a little jerk that made the younger one moan.

"Write," D'Shea commanded.

We would compare intelligence afterward.

Chapter 14

Elder D'Shea had placed a gag order on us which took little convincing.

"Leave the report to the Prime to me," she said.

Gladly.

I would take the time to catch up on Reverie.

Elder Rausery wasn't going to let that lie, however, as my Sisters and I must. Whatever the Sorceress had conveyed to the Prime of my mission with the Conceiver, her peer had to know how much she was leaving out.

What D'Shea might convey to Rausery afterward, if it was soon enough for her tastes, was left for me to wonder as I took my turn in equipment maintenance and resupply.

The Elder General's response to the Sorceress was to come find me less than two cycles later, with Jael in tow.

"Sirana, with me," Rausery ordered, her voice quiet but strong as marble.

I stared in utter bafflement, and Jael stared back, seeming to know even less about the reason she was here as our Elder led us out of the Cloister and on a good, long run in the Deepearth.

Fucking Abyss ... how long will we be gone?

The Elder took my current measure harshly. While I hadn't been lax in keeping up a Sisterhood-trained body, the recent trip with a Priestess was largely among comforts, standing watch or fucking her son for entertainment. It showed enough to prove Jael was in better shape in this moment, and Rausery could always run circles around the both of us.

Finally, we stopped.

★Catch your breaths, caits,★ the Elder signed as she stepped away, her cloak flowing behind her.

We obeyed, Jael and I, listening to the distant echoes of dripping water and the subtle scuffling and squeaking of smaller creatures. I couldn't hear Rausery's boot steps as she cleared the area, and I was tempted but wary to believe she did this without magical aid.

Very much how she wants it.

Since Jael had been pulled in, given how I first tongued her, I expected our Elder to begin with questions about Wilsira's Sathoet. Or maybe my Dwarf stone pendant, given what she had claimed knowing about it on the Fringe?

We are far out that way already.

Rausery returned to us, satisfied of privacy for the moment. I read her sign.

★What do you know of the Surface, Sirana?★

I gave away my surprise, my face hot in the same instant to know this and to remember that eve Jaunda found me after she had returned from there. The incredible detail my Lead had given me flooded back.

The pale-skinned Elf.

I hadn't thought about the tall blonde cornered underground by my Lead for spans and spans, but the vivid imagining I'd had back then slammed into me now like a fighter's shield. I still didn't know if Jaunda had been instructed to tell a recruit such detail, or if she'd gone against orders somehow.

Jael watched me, her young face screwed up in suspicion and curiosity. I licked my lips, forced my hands to move.

★Not a lot. There's no ceiling. There's more light from a Sun. Blinding, and yet it makes more things grow. Insects, plants, animals. More of everything than down here.★

Rausery smiled a little. ★Can't disagree. Who told you this?★

I trembled a little. ★Jaunda. When she returned last turn.★

The General nodded, and if my Lead was going to be punished for talking, Rausery didn't offer me that tell.

★Anyone else you know has been?★ she asked.

I did, yes. But I was petrified to say.

★Tell me,★ Rausery commanded, staring at me unblinking.

Shyntre talking with Auslan in the garden. The part I had skipped with D'Shea because I didn't want the Prime to discover by accident.

"You trust one," Auslan said.

"Only on the Surface," Shyntre replied.

Again, back to this Goddess-damned wizard!

Another flick of my eyes to Jael. Why was she here? The only link I could see was the Fringe, and her claim about the blue psionic stone on the Tragar weapons.

She was the one who told us it turned blue somehow, and the Headmaster and his son made it so.

I had only one direction I could go, so I might as well go all in.

Slow and deliberate so neither Red Sister would misinterpret my intent, I reached for the black thread to fish the blue pendant out from underneath my armor, letting it rest where Rausery and Jael could see it. The General quirked her eyebrow in question, and I signed my answer to her with as much confidence as I could muster.

★The Headmaster's son, Shyntre. The one who made this and turned it blue somehow. Well, him or his sire.★

Jael's eyes widened and her jaw tightened to prevent dropping open. Rausery looked at me like a Dragon about to pounce. This was true surprise. The Elder knew about the Dwarf stone I'd brought back from my mission to save Jael from the Tragar; Rausery was present to hear Jael's claim about it turning blue on Grey Dwarf weapons in our debriefing.

But I had told Rausery something she hadn't known. I expected D'Shea would be furious with me, but how could they *both* know about my "mind wound," tell me to work with them to keep it secret, and then keep secrets like this pendant from each other?

"Fuck me ..." the Elder whispered with mist-like quiet, turning over her thoughts. She looked at Jael, signed to get her attention. ★I don't need to tell you this is gagged, right?★

★Gagged, Elder,★ Jael confirmed.

I had a "gag" of my own regarding Curgia's miscarriage. Lots of secrets swirling about.

Always have been. You're just noticing them more, Sirana.

★Back up,★ Rausery signed. ★You know Shyntre has been to the Surface.★

★Only that,★ I insisted, ★nothing more, except he admits having respect for exactly *one* Red Sister, because he could 'trust' her on the Surface.★

I didn't dare blink, lest I miss anything in the colorless Radiants which showed me Rausery's expressions in the dark. Her face appeared to soften a little.

★He admitted that to you?★ Rausery signed.

★It's you,★ I jumped on my gut. ★He was talking about *you*, General.★

My Elder shrugged lightly. ★I reckon so. How in the Void did this come up, Sirana? And when?★

★Recently, on my mission with the Conceiver,★ I answered. ★She brought Shyntre along, supposedly because she thought I didn't know who the invisible wizard in my trial was. Or, that's what she said.★

The Elder nodded agreement that it was possible but not necessarily true.

★Either way, we had time to ... talk, now and then★ I continued. ★We sided together against Wilsira and Kerse. Somewhat.★

Rausery grinned to show her teeth like the mental image was very amusing. ★Gotcha.★

★He knows Lead Qivni from before,★ I blurted.

Her teeth vanished as a serious look arose. ★Why do you say?★

★He was already in Wilsira's suites when Qivni arrived to drop me off, but he was hidden,★ I explained. ★The Conceiver offered the Lead a brief fuck with a Consort-in-training before she left, and she accepted.

The two went into a room together, but when I heard something and needed to check on her, I opened the door to that room to find Shyntre there as well.★

Rausery nodded like her Lead had reported this. ★Go on, Sirana. What else did you see?★

I saw myself in Qivni's place, and the abrupt image made me jerk my head. It struck me then that the Consort could have been in Qivni's cunt instead of her ass. He could have spurted there, and Wilsira would have been delighted if our Lead mage caught. I remembered my concern, how she wasn't answering me, how dizzy and confused she seemed.

Yet the Conceiver was furious with Shyntre, and with me, for interrupting.

"What in the Abyss are you doing?!"

*"What she **asked**, Conceiver!"*

Spider shit …

★I … I think Shyntre saved Qivni from Wilsira's tricks, like he would with me, later,★ I signed. ★I saw him with his fingers taking up her slit to the knuckles, the Consort using her netherhole with his prick. The Priestess wasn't pleased with the wizard.★

This also fit the report; Rausery let me see it.

★He did that for you,★ I guessed.

★Don't really know that, novice,★ she answered. ★That wizard isn't big on doing stuff to please females. But he has less reason to hate Qivni than many of us.★

I felt a twinge of jealousy and pushed her. ★But you've taken him to the Surface for some reason. He trusts you to keep him alive up there. He'd follow you again, if you asked it of him.★

★Fair enough. I wouldn't spread that around, if I were you. Some already know, but the Prime doesn't like hearing about the Surface, and you have your enemies who'd be more than happy to make trouble for you.★

The Elder General considered this new knowledge, appraising me once again. Her dark, intelligent eyes landed on Shyntre's pendant again. She looked at Jael in something like a prompt. When the youngest of us didn't quite get it, Rausery signed, ★Tell her what you told me.★

I heard Jael's heart for a few throbs, warmth showing in her throat. She looked at me and exhaled. Raised her hands.

★Traders on the Fringe aren't just other races,★ she said. ★Some are Davrin, barely known by the border patrols and not really acknowledged by the Valsharess. There's … there's been stories since I was a little cait that some of what they bring in comes from the Surface. Books, scrolls, tools, but nothing too exotic it couldn't fit in here.★

I froze at how similar that was to the stories I'd heard between Wilsira and Rohenvi about Low Gate, the other side of the Great Cavern. Except that story nudged at the Black Dragon.

★One reason the Sisterhood goes up now and again, too,★ Rausery signed. ★The Valsharess knows about these Fringe Davrin but listens to me on it. There's no benefit in rounding them up to imprison or cull them yet. Not when we haven't found their Surface contacts.★

I must have looked ridiculous in my hungry curiosity. ★If the Prime doesn't like to hear about the Surface, then are you doing this on the side?★

★Without full resources, yes.★

That would take decades, if not centuries. How long did Humans live, anyway? Most everything around us in the Deepearth seemed to age and die much sooner than us, except possibly the thought-flayers. We could see multiple generations of Pyte and Ketro slaves under the same Matron before she even bore her first heir, and I knew the Tragar always died much sooner from hard labor.

Maybe Rausery hasn't found the contacts because they're dead. She's too late to watch an unbroken trail.

Except having some Davrin to carry the knowledge forward would certainly let a possible trade-way linger as it seemed to be.

And Shyntre and Jaunda had both seen it.

Rausery was smiling at me now. ★I'm glad you and Shyntre have figured out how to talk, Sirana. You two are going to be doing more of that here real soon.★

We are?

★Tell me about this pendant.★

Whoo ... yipe.

★The Dwarf stone seems to counter active or volatile magic in some way.★

★Who says?★

★The Headmaster. But neither he nor Shyntre know the circumstances where I found it, though they want to. D'Shea's order.★

A nod. ★Good. Go on.★

★It's probably related to what the mind mages do, the Tragar and the Ornilleth.★ I motioned toward Jael. ★As she said, they are protective of their bluestone weapons, they won't trade. Maybe they can use them like we use magic items, but we might not get any more benefit than we would a regular axe or blade.★

★Then why are you wearing it?★ Rausery asked, because she had to.

★D'Shea wants me to test it in the field,★ I explained for Jael's benefit and my protection. ★I'm not a mage, so I rely on fewer spells, but it might influence or drain my equipment potency over a period time. She also wants me to see what effect, if any, it has on mages.★

I looked between them, my expression stern. ★No one is to know. I am to observe what happens as I wear it around various Davrin and their magic, that's all.★

Rausery's eyes seemed to glitter for an instant. ★You just spent loads of time around a very powerful Priestess.★

I nodded. ★The stone didn't seem to help much. Her magic was still overwhelming. I ... relied heavily on the mental training instead.★

She seemed to get the hint.

★Though it did lessen the effect of a shock spell Shyntre cast on me,★ I added. ★I should have been paralyzed for a short while. I could still move, but it hurt like fuck then my arm went tingling-numb.★

Rausery's shoulders shook in a silent laugh. She didn't ask about the circumstances where the wizard would try something like that on a Red Sister, but maybe she didn't need to.

★Very interesting. Hold those details for later, Sirana, and we'll do this properly.★

I was more than glad to obey. The more we talked about psionically sensitive objects and races, the more Jael's presence was making me sweat. I tucked Shyntre's pendant out of sight.

We were given a quarter mark to eat, drink, and piss, then it was time for another hard run over rough terrain to make it back to the Great Cavern. Rausery dissuaded a couple of prowlers from stalking us, and Jael and I watched closely how she did it.

When we weren't so deep that we might get lost and came upon a split in the tunnels, Elder Rausery slowed us and turned to my fellow novice. She motioned to the right, from which we'd come.

★Go find Qivni. She'll have your next task for you. Keep all you know sewn to your back.★

★Yes, Elder.★

With a brief nod of farewell to me, Jael took off fearlessly alone, and Rausery led me in the other direction.

★Where are we going, Elder?★ I signed with my arm stretched out as we jogged without urgency.

★No time like now,★ was her reply.

I hadn't really expected more, and Rausery let me come to my own realization.

Ohhh, damn.

Rausery was smirking. ★First Ward in twenty paces, novice. Phaelous likes to eavesdrop.★

So I've heard.

The Headmaster greeted us similarly to how he had greeted me before, actually coming down to the main floor and entrance.

"Greetings and welcome, Elder, Red Sister." He bowed to each of us in turn. "I take it there is no execution order?"

"Not this time, old lizard," Rausery said with more ironic humor than his question carried. "Maybe next time. I'd like your fifth library to use, preferably not wide open to scrying."

The Headmaster smiled. It looked genuine. "Certainly, it will be protected from others, but no part of this Tower is completely warded from my own magic, Elder, you know this."

"But you also know when to point your nose elsewhere, wizard."

The venerable Elf nodded as he acknowledged her. I bet he "knew" nothing of the sort. Could be why he was still alive.

He looked at me, and I pulled out a prevention draught made by D'Shea, showing it to him. He checked it without breaking the seal, Rausery laughed loud enough for it to echo a bit, and Phaelous returned it with a nod and a smile.

I drank the infertility potion with my Elder and the Headmaster watching, my eyes flicking to the former's obvious exemption from this "tower" rule for Red Sisters.

"Come with me, Sisters," Phaelous said pleasantly.

He escorted us to the fifth level, to the smaller, round library lined with scrolls and manuscripts I had been to before. I admired the bright colors and rich nuance of the shelves built into every corner of the walls, the woven carpet on the ground, all under the glow of perpetual, magical light.

Any bit of brush writing was useless in the dark, but magical words intended to be spoken were worse, I'd heard. Such script on a scroll either simply did not show up as Radiants, or they did with special ink but constantly shifted under a mage's gaze. Mages needed light to read any archive or true Elven knowledge, something which set the Davrin apart from all others in the Deepearth.

I traced my leather-bound finger along the ornate edge of a manuscript, missing when Phaelous left without a verbal word. I hadn't been watching their hands.

Rausery stepped deliberately to an area of scrolls and maps, selecting a few to place on one of three tables and the one farthest from the door. Then she selected three fat, bound manuscripts and placed those next to the maps. She did not instruct me to help her, so I stood at attention and watched the room.

Then, we waited.

Elder Rausery did not sit down but she was at ease with the room, much more than D'Shea had been. Ironic, that, given the Sorceress was among her practiced elements. The General knew where to find specific maps and texts, had asked for this location. I tried to speak once, but she gestured for me to be silent. I obeyed.

I had a sure feeling who was about to walk through that door, though.

"Elder General." The young wizard bowed like he was at Court.

"Hai, Shyntre. Took you long enough. Magic sand in your boots?"

I glanced at his sandals then rolled my eyes at myself. No boots. Rausery was in one of her more patient moods, and that teasing had been familiar and personal. The wizard recognized this and smiled.

Just a little.

It took real effort on my part to avoid staring like a dumb Uroan.

"Heard you can still do the right thing under pressure."

Shyntre grimaced. "Far from it, Elder."

"I dunno about that. I got results and two of my Sisters back at the Cloister where they belong. Never asked perfection from anybody, just the guts to keep going."

The bua's mouth tightened under the practical praise fully opposite of D'Shea's exacting remarks that I was used to. He glanced at me like he resented me being there to hear it.

At least I knew we had another thing in common.

Rausery nodded my way, motioning me closer to her. "Need you to train someone for me."

Shyntre couldn't hide his dismay on his face as I walked up. "Elder … Her? We spent more than a span netted together by the Conceiver."

"Holding out in the same frog-hole, yeah, I know."

"This Sister enjoys provoking me too much," he protested. "We won't get anything done. We'll waste time bickering. She'll keep trying to get me naked, and I'll keep trying to avoid punishment for doing something stupid that she deserves. It's a poor use of your time and expectations for both of us, Elder."

I stared in astonishment. Rausery tilted her head back and laughed.

Well. That was refreshingly blunt.

"We'll see," said the Elder General. "I need her trained, Shyntre. You're going to do it. Make it work."

He wanted to growl something at us. He was bursting to.

The bua swallowed it instead. "Yes, Elder."

Rausery nodded over toward the back table. "I've selected the texts to start with. Make sure you stick to them and cover them thoroughly." She then turned to me. "You will report directly back to me in sixteen marks. Twelve of those will be here studying. Four will be in Reverie, so it has a chance to soak in. Phaelous will give you a place to rest and provide food."

The classic dumb Uroan look arose despite my best efforts.

Twelve ... marks? In the same room with him? Alone?!

My Elder smirked, looking directly at my eyes. "We'll see how much you retain the first time, novice. He has a lot to offer. Get comfortable. Take off your boots, at least. You've dirtied the carpet."

My thoughts went to a *very* lewd place, she could see it, and I heard the groan in my own head. "Yes, Elder."

"We'll repeat this as necessary until a certain level of recall is reached, determined by me. Are we clear, Red Sister? Queen's Wizard?"

"Yes, Elder," Shyntre and I said, voices overlapping.

My thoughts in full whirl, I tucked my boots beneath the nearest table. D'Shea wasn't going to like this, and neither would I, I was sure. I'd never spent much time in the library growing up. Being in a small, uncomfortable room with *this* wizard, sitting in a chair for marks on end and—

I glanced at the intimidating pile of fiberstalk parchment.

—studying to retain it? This was not my strength, and to avoid becoming distracted would be a challenge. Rausery knew this, I was sure. The longer it took me to "retain" what I learned, the more time I would sit in this library with Shyntre.

I wasn't sure how to feel about that. No matter how much fun it might be to nudge the wizard's tender spots and learn more of his history, sooner or later I would want to be out. Doing something else.

Which meant, same as him "training" me, I had to make it work. Somehow.

Rausery reached out and took the back of my neck in a firm grip, steering me a few steps away from Shyntre with our cloaked backs to him. Her other hand moved by her chest, blocked from the mage's view:

Don't waste my time, novice. You're smart enough for this, and you'll be a long time paying me back.

I got it. At least part of it. I gestured back, *I will not waste your time, Elder. I will focus.*

With a curt nod, she released me and moved next to Shyntre, except she put her entire arm around his shoulders — a very odd gesture — and pulled him close enough that he could have had his pick of the tools on her belt if he'd dared try. He paid rapt attention to whatever she'd signed out of my view and responded quickly.

What are they saying?

Satisfied, Rausery bid us a productive time and showed herself out. I had to assume Phaelous would meet her, for he did not return.

Once again, Shyntre and I were left alone.

CHAPTER 15

THE FOLLOWING QUIET STARTED HEAVY. SHYNTRE STARED AT ME BEFORE LET-ting out his breath and taking a seat at the far table. He pulled the manuscripts and a few of the scrolls closer to him and scanned them quickly as if to review what it was that he was supposed to teach me. I stepped up to look over his shoulder.

"Sit down, pupil," he grumbled irritably, the command in his voice was unmistakable.

"You're going to enjoy that, aren't you, tutor?" I stayed standing.

"It's true by your Elder's own decree. Now sit."

His tone got to me. I took the seat right next to him, and he scowled, pointing to the other one across from him. "Over there, you know damn well."

"I do not. You were too vague." I peered at the text. "Wouldn't this be easier to read side-by-side?"

"That's not how this works. Now sit across from me, pupil."

"Use that word one more time, and I'll assume it is foreplay, wizard."

He closed the manuscript at which he'd been looking and threaded his fingers together on top of it. He refused to look at me.

"Sirana. Sit over there."

I might not have even then, except for Rausery's warning. I shook the stupid he brought out in me from my head, standing to move to the other side of the table.

Sighing to imagine how the next twelve marks would go, I removed my belt and weapons, placing them on another table entirely, draping my cloak over an empty chair. I removed my bracers, gloves, and the stiff chest piece I was wearing. Last moment, I decided to remove my boot socks.

Get comfortable, she said. I'm going to be here for a while.

The mage arched one white eyebrow, his eyes scanning me head to bare feet, wearing my red undershirt and leather pants, and that was all. I smiled at his expression, wiggling my toes on the plush carpet.

As I finally sat across from him, he carefully unrolled a map and laid it out in front of me. I scanned it but didn't recognize where it was supposed to be or even any of the symbols on it.

Some squiggles for rivers and streams? Notes of rough, stony passage … um, isn't that everywhere?

There were short slashes in groups of three, jagged lines, tiny crosses, and a handful more I didn't know what they were supposed to mean.

"What am I looking at?" I asked, eyes still scanning.

"The Surface, as if you're a bird flying above."

I lifted my head, narrowing my eyes at him. "What?"

Shyntre sighed, turning the map a little more. "Is it the angle of perception or the bird confusing you?"

"The bird," I said.

"Think of a bat at the ceiling of the Great Cavern, then. Same concept."

"Got it. So, what does this symbol mean?"

"It's a forest."

I opened my mouth to ask "what" again but closed it to wait for him to expand.

"Very good, we might get something done," he said a bit snidely and ignored the dirty look I gave him. He leaned forward and traced with his index finger along the parchment. "This symbol indicates a forest. A forest is made up of many interconnected trees and plants."

"Plants?" I tried. "Like fiberstalk and mushroom?"

"Close enough. Except trees can be enormous, some of the largest living things on the Surface."

"Why?"

"Some of them live as long as us. The ancient ones get Dragon-sized."

My mouth sagged a little to imagine.

Shyntre pointed at more symbols spanning most of the map. "This indicates the eternal green forests, and this those trees that drop leaves in turns. On the West is a marsh. You would know it as inundated sediment, although it's not trapped by stone but drains over a vast distance."

I interrupted. "West?"

"Apologies. That's the trade word for which direction the Sun disappears after traveling the sky for a day."

Sun moving across the sky for a day ...

The wizard read my face and anticipated my next question. "East is the word for where the Sun rises again." He smirked a little, pointing at opposite sides of the map. "East and West are on opposing sides of the world. You must turn around full and face the other way to go from Sunset to Sunrise."

"How the fuck does the Sun do that?!"

Shyntre seemed torn between laughing and rubbing his face with a sigh. "You already know the core of our world is a hot center. This is why we even *have* a concept for a floor and a ceiling. You feel the pulling force every time you trip on the rocks, right?"

I nodded slowly, unsure where he was going with this.

"If the world has a center, and it is drawing the elements to it from all sides under equal power and distance ..." He saw my expression. "Alright. Think about it like a mage's light spell, Sirana. What shape would that take, drawing light in around a central magic user?"

I pictured it. "A circle."

"Close. Fill *all* the space, sides, front and back, above and below."

"A sphere. Like a pearl."

"Yes." Shyntre's eyes seemed brighter with his own interest on this topic. "On the Surface, the Sun disappears on one side of the hemisphere, a time called 'night,' and reappears on the other."

I shook my head. "So ... the Sun is circling us?"

"Either that, or the world is circling the Sun. This eternal light is the strongest source of heat and life energy for the Surface. The land is exposed to the Sky and does not have a shield of rock to block it. As a result, the conditions are much more chaotic and very harsh, fluctuating with heat and cold. The day creatures, especially plants, rely on the Sun returning every day to live, while the night creatures have adapted more like the Deepearth, or a mix of both."

Shyntre paused, and I looked up from the map to meet his eyes.

"What this means," he said, "is that we can go up there, and we can adapt and live as night creatures. Survival may not be easy, but it is not poison. Not instant death. We can live up there quite easily, if we wished to."

I didn't even know what to say to that.

"Do you understand the lesson so far, Sirana?"

"Um. Yes."

"Repeat that back to me in your own words, if you will."

I groaned, doing so haltingly and with several corrections; the experience was like sitting with my mage-tutor in the Thalluen nursery.

This was truly basic, I knew, yet I had never thought about this. It captured my imagination even more than Jaunda's descriptions because the wizard was telling me more of how the whole thing was supposed to work, and what it meant for us.

Before this "lesson," for all I'd known, the Surface was a level, Sun-bleached flat of exposed rock that had edges which fell off into the Abyss.

"Where does the Sky go?" I asked. "Why is it wrapped around the world like that?"

"It's an element, too. Air. It's drawn in toward the center like everything else."

"How far does it go up?"

Shyntre pursed his lips. "As far as the Priestesses know, it goes to the Abyss and other places. And it is more accurately described as 'out,' not 'up.' Though you would hear even Surface-dwellers call it up."

"What does the Sky look like if it's just Air?"

"Nothing, unless there's a source of light."

"Well, that's what I meant. When there's Sun?"

He grimaced like I'd asked a difficult question. "Mostly blue."

That fit my dream. "And when there's no Sun?"

Shyntre shrugged. "I read more reports about the night. There are two moons and farther points of light around them — stars — against true blackness. It's a softer light, mostly silver instead of gold. The moons and stars are visible to us only when the Sun is on the other side of the hemisphere."

Something came back to me abruptly from the bloodstone conversation, what Curgia had described to Wilsira. "*Cold, black. It is the space in between points of light. All of it is unfathomably far away … Empty.*"

Wilsira had said Curgia dreamed not of the Abyss itself but the path that led there.

Shyntre tilted his head at me, reading my expression. "*That* makes sense to you?"

I nodded slowly. "There are other worlds?"

The scholar shrugged. "A given, or we wouldn't have half-demons in the Sanctuary boosting our Queen's magic."

True. "Does anyone else have demonbloods?"

"Possible. We don't know if any Surface races do yet." Shyntre leaned forward and tapped the map in front of me pointedly. "Evergreen forest, leafy forest, marsh."

I blinked at the abrupt return to the map. "Got it."

"No, repeat it."

I did. Shyntre was teaching me how to interpret these Surface maps. I had no trouble focusing.

"North, South, East, West. Repeat."

Fascinating. I did.

"Mountains, mountain pass, cave, cliff, hills. Repeat."

I probably sounded more excited that time.

"Farm, village, town, city."

"Farm, village, town, city … What's this?"

"A keep, like the Tragar build but atop a large hill or mountain."

"Out where everyone can see it?"

"Also with a view to see in all directions, farther than you ever see in the Deepearth before hitting a wall." Shyntre smirked. "Many keeps have towers, too, to get even higher. The closer to the Sky one can be, the greater the distance visible, though in less detail and only to a point."

"What point?"

"The curve of the world."

"Oh."

I could hardly imagine, and Shyntre kept talking.

"If you see others coming long before they can get near you, even riding a beast, do you think this would be hard to defend?"

I knew what the answer was supposed to be. I shook my head so that my educated wizard continued.

"The angle of the map is even called a Bird's Eye."

I smiled. "Back to the birds."

His mouth twitched. "Yes. Birds fly somewhat like bats, but bats are gliders floating among the stalactites. Birds have the space to become strong for sustained, distance flight. They have more complex wings, with feathers, perfect for flying high and far. The colors and bodies of birds are innumerable."

Wow.

He pointed at something else. "This is the scale here, you should recognize that, yes?"

I absorbed the distance it implied, and my eyes widened.

"That's a yes," Shyntre said with satisfaction. "This land is more or less above us, and only shows the edges of what the Red Sisters have been able to reach over the last few centuries. There is more, but we don't have the resources or the permission from the Valsharess to go farther."

"Why do we have permission to go even this far?"

"I *do not* know," he said firmly, "I think there is only one or two other Davrin besides Rausery who do."

Shyntre locked eyes with me to make it clear that he was telling the truth and would not discuss it further.

"What's *your* role been, then?" I asked, intensely curious and a little irritated he was so far ahead of me.

Shyntre shrugged again, getting tense. "Studying, archiving, and preserving the reports, mostly."

Fucking lie.

Except he wasn't. I wasn't supposed to have heard what Shyntre said to Auslan. But I had just told Rausery; that was why I was here.

"You *can't* get all this from reading," I said to get us on equal footing there. "Have you been to the Surface? I think you have."

I was relieved and annoyed when he smiled smugly and told me the truth.

"Twice. Escorted by the Sisters."

My eyebrows drew down. "Why?"

That familiar resistance and tension bubbled across his face. "Because Elder Rausery decided I would go, as she's clearly decided you will, too."

I had enough commentary from D'Shea to know that she was not putting a mission to the Surface as a high priority for me. She would rather hold me in to go after the Priestesses and continue spying on them and their Sathoet.

I didn't want to be stuck doing that.

Was D'Shea even aware of where I was or what Rausery had intended to teach me? Would she try to override the Elder General and forbid me from ever seeing for myself what Jaunda and Shyntre had? Rausery could take D'Shea's own fucking *son*, but not me?

"You're not a Red Sister," I snapped, wrestling with the conflicting motives of my Elders, envious that the wizard had been on the Surface *twice* by the time he was ordered to drill my ass. "You're not even a cait! Why would they decide *you* would go?"

Shyntre made real effort to control a glorious flare of temper. "Red Sisters don't have all the skills they need for such a venture! They need mages, too, and Priestesses are forbidden to go, so it's the Tower that's tapped."

I jerked in surprise. "Forbidden? Th-the Valsharess *forbids* the Priesthood something?"

"Surprised me, too," he replied. "And yes. The Queen forbid it ever since one of them disappeared. The Priestess and her Sathoet. Too much sign they were captured, the Red Sisters couldn't track them farther North when the snows came, and we've never seen them again."

Snow? I shook my head not to get distracted. "And it's not talked about *at all* among wizards? I don't buy it."

"It's not often the Red Sisters go," he said tightly, "and those that do know better than to talk."

"But is it only *you* who's 'tapped'? Who else at the Tower has ever gone to the Surface?"

"That's foolish of you to ask!" he barked.

"Is it true you belong to us? To the Sisterhood? We get to use you when we want?"

Shyntre went still, his gaze was piercing. "You're playing with me."

I smiled and shrugged. "Wilsira is one that likes to talk."

"And only the foolish don't question why," he growled. "What did she say?"

"That I should ask you why you didn't take her advice."

His eyes narrowed. "Is that all? The answer is simple. Because it was self-serving advice. All of hers is. You couldn't expect anything more than that from any Priestess with that much power, could you?"

"No, I couldn't. But the result was that the Sisterhood *noticed* you, and from what I've seen, you probably do wish you'd taken her advice now, don't you?"

"No, I don't!" he spat. "If I had, I'd be attending Worship Balls and sacrificial rituals and making beautification potions for Nobles until my fingers bled."

I laughed. "And that's worse than being ridden by Thena and Jaunda? And all the rest of the Feldeus, as far as I know, as if you were a recruit, too?"

A muscle flexed in his jaw.

Leaning forward aggressively, I hissed, "The Sisterhood turned your role as a male Davrin on its head and still left you without *any* power to use it. You've been a cock and a cunt and something else, something only the Red Sisters are in this City, you've been to the Surface and defy the fucking *Conceiver's* wishes, but don't wear the uniform.

"At least the Consorts know how to gain something from their value as a possession, but you reject all of it! The strength of your will and your power is wasted on you, wizard. It should have been given to a cait. I'll bet your Sorceress dam and the Headmaster *both* agree on that!"

His hand moved, and I didn't recognize the words that left his mouth.

A force blast struck so quickly I'd barely half-stood before it hit my chest and sent me and the chair flying backward. I landed hard, by training alone was rolling toward my gear before I'd managed to regain any breath. I aimed low and out of the way of another attack like that. I thought it had cracked a rib.

Instead of casting again, however, Shyntre vaulted over the table, avoiding the parchments, and kept me from reaching my belt or weapons. We collapsed to the floor with him mostly on top. His hands dove under my shirt, planting skin-to-skin on my sides and he gave me another magic shock. My body bucked and my back arched as pain lanced through me.

"Cunt," he hissed, pure acid.

I managed to strike somewhere on his head with my elbow, and I forced first one roll, then another, trying to keep him from another spell until more feeling had come back in my fingers. At least the shock hadn't been paralyzing.

My arms and legs wrapped around him as I sought a good hold, even neither face-to-face nor behind him, as he fought hard not to lose the dominant position. Out of my armor and with him in his robe, I detected his erection quickly and might have laughed at him if I could have managed the breath.

I hooked my arm behind his neck and grabbed his jaw in my free hand, squeezing hard and forcing his face up. Soon, I had him in place, enough to press a bruising kiss on his mouth, sucking and biting his lips as we each struggled to get enough air through our noses.

At first, he tried to pull away but I made sure doing so hurt more than to kiss back. It did not take him long to try turning it around, forcing his tongue into my mouth and reaching to grip my left breast before giving the nipple a brutal twist through my shirt.

He could only have learned to fuck like this in the Sisterhood.

I responded with a delirious, muffled squeal and reached to tear as much of his robe open at the front as possible. It was enough to let me grasp his scrotum in my fist; I was sporting enough to give him a warning squeeze, and he stopped the abuse of my nipple.

His cock remained firm and hot against my wrist and inner thigh, and when he released my breast, he massaged it a bit as if to encourage the blood to flow back in — which it did in abundance, firm and full against his palm. I let go of his testicles in return, giving up the advantage because I didn't want it to be over so soon.

Breaking the kiss, I brought my hand up to strike him across the face.

"Oh, fuck you!" he growled hoarsely, recovering quickly as he tore at the leather ties of my right hip. He meant to strip my leathers down and expose me.

He really meant it.

I laughed and growled back at him with lust, biting his neck and plucking the ties at my left hip to make it easier for him. I helped him shove my leathers down my thighs, and I could feel the cool air hit the moisture on my netherlips.

Groaning, I stripped his robe down his shoulders, trapping his arms and holding him there until he roared in frustration and twisted to free one arm from its sleeve entirely. I let him shed the rest of the robe to toss to the side.

Shyntre wedged his knees between mine, forcing my legs apart and my leathers further down to my shins, trapping my ankles. His hips were between my thighs; he was in position. The only thing that slowed him down was his trying to grab my wrists, to control my hands as we struggled.

His hips and mine were guiding any possible penetration.

I writhed to pull up my red shirt, so our bellies touched, so my breasts pressed against him before he squeezed both my wrists in a grip so tight his hands were trembling. I did not struggle as hard as I could have against his pinning my arms near my head.

The next moment the alignment was right, and he penetrated me in one thrust.

I cursed lewdly, reacted with such force I struck the back of my head against the floor — I was glad for the carpet then. Shyntre put his weight on his hands, on my wrists, and fucked me so hard I'd probably have bruises on my inner thighs from his hip bones.

"Ah, Goddess, yes!" I cried.

"Crazy slit!" he growled, pounding my sex with his cock.

I encouraged him, planted my feet to lift my hips a bit and spread my legs wider as he wallowed in me. We lost control so completely, I shrieked with joy in that quiet room. All that stress from the trip with the Conceiver burst its dam, and I grunted and growled with him, matching the pace thrust for thrust until I hit my peak.

He felt when I climaxed around him, my sex fluttering and squeezing along his raging member.

"Still cumming from force, novice?" he gasped, the derision and venom palpable.

I shook beneath the impacts, grinning. "The Sisters taught you well, bua."

He barely paused before thrusting in hard again. He was trying to make it hurt; I was too high on a massive release to care.

My eyes rolled upward, and I groaned. "Ah! Again! Ah, ah! D-Don't pull out!"

Shyntre stopped abruptly, pressing his erection all the way in but holding still, panting. I sensed the shift; he had begun to think again.

Tightening my legs in desperation, I prevented him from withdrawing, from throwing himself back from me in disgust or fear.

"No, not yet!" I panted.

He only fought harder. He was slipping out.

"I took a potion! It's safe! Finish! Cream me!"

"Let me go!" he roared next to my ear.

Oww!

The wizard escaped my thighs, his cock withdrawing from my soaking hole as he released my wrists, beyond reason or will to take a risk for release.

I felt instant regret as Shyntre rolled and pulled himself back on his elbows, his white pubic thatch matted down with dampness, cock glistening as it softened. Considering the scare he'd had, I thought his deflation was not as quick as it would have been if he hadn't been so close to the edge.

"Stupid Sister!" he sneered, his hand lightly stroking himself. "You know what happens to you if you catch from a bua!"

"I told you, I took a vial!" I retorted. "You think Phaelous would let me in here without it? His rule!"

"Yes, well, it won't last much longer, will it?"

"Long enough to get you naked and in my twat. As I promised I would."

"That's what you thought was important?" He rolled his eyes. "You are *insane*, Sirana."

"I'm glad *you* have the baseline to be able to tell."

Smirking, my gaze landed on his cock, and the corners of my mouth fell. I thought his motions had been thoughtless to maintain his rod, but then I realized he was serious. He stroked harder, masturbating openly, meaning to steal his own moment of release.

To spite me.

I couldn't stand the challenge.

I rolled to my knees quickly. My long-sleeved shirt fell back down to cover me to the waist, and I tugged up my leathers to sit haphazardly on my hips. Then I crawled toward him.

He left off stroking and scrambled backward beneath the table. "Get the fuck … away from me!"

"No."

"ARGH!"

He yelled and groaned at once as I darted forward and grabbed his hips, dragging him toward me. Then I seized his wrists as he'd done me but quickly pinned them near his waist instead. My elbows kept his legs open enough that I could settle my head down and nuzzle at the stiff, fragrant cock.

"Can't help it, can you?" I teased, licking him, tasting both my sex and his. "You get off on fighting as much as I do."

He tried to break my hold, tried to kick me, but mostly I enjoyed the struggle until he tired himself out further.

"Come, you must be aching by now," I murmured, closing my lips around the head in a sucking kiss. "Let me —"

The coaxing didn't help; I received an awkward but effective knee to my sore rib, which sent my head bumping into the table. Time also pressed on me for how long this could last, and I knew we had more studying to do, or Rausery would have both our hides.

"Stop fighting me, Shyntre, we have to study! Think of it as my gratitude for helping me against Wilsira, if that helps."

"Let go of my wrists and I will!" he said, his body quivering.

Close enough.

I did this only after I had dragged him into the middle beneath the table, where there wasn't anything for him within arm's reach, not even a chair leg. Once he was in position on his back, I released his wrists, took his hips in my hands and his cock in my mouth, the first time he wasn't standing or kneeling above me.

With relish, I tasted my cunt on him again; he was leaking his own juice from the tip, and my tongue darted out, curling around the ridge to make him squirm.

Mmmm …

Shyntre's freed hands went to the back of my head the next instant; for a while we were fighting to control the pace and the depth of the act. I allowed several deep thrusts that blocked my air because they excited me but, after I'd had enough, peeled his hands from my ears and used faster, shorter strokes to bring him over.

The wizard was holding himself back; he had been for a while, but eventually the bua's breathing changed. He sucked in a single draw of air before falling utterly silent like before when we entertained Wilsira.

In the next instant, several pulses of semen squirted into my mouth, and at last the damned wizard was coasting down from his peak.

Unlike before, however, the near-constant tension in his body finally drained out. His hands were resting on his torso as he caught his breath.

I slurped his offering carefully as I lifted my mouth up, shifting further over him and smiling down. He caught my deviant expression and immediately rolled away, knocking my arm to the side.

"Fucking not!" he declared and skittered naked out to grab his robe.

I bumped my head again, trying to keep my balance. Underneath tables wasn't the most comfortable place to mate.

"Mmph!" Nearly choked, I swallowed to finish laughing. "Oh my fucking … ! Your face! Hahaha!"

"Shut the Void up."

I made a rude gesture. "An impossible curse."

"Bah!"

My wizard used the excuse of retrieving food and drink from the kitchens to collect his head again. It wasn't a bad idea; even I knew things had gotten out of hand, and after the sex, now I was quite hungry.

By the time he returned, I was willing to eat and focus again on the next map, which showed three interesting landmarks and something else of which I'd never heard.

"Ley Lines?" I asked, scanning the vague, imprecise outlines that looked like impossibly giant rivers meandering over the Surface.

"These 'interesting' landmarks aren't there by chance," Shyntre said testily, as if I had openly doubted him — which I hadn't. "Those magically sensitive can feel them. They exist in the Deepearth, too, but the pulse of the core can obscure it for most of us. On the Surface, the Ley Lines have been known to move, so sometimes a landmark falls into ruin when the magic isn't as strong anymore. It's always the same, remember: follow the Ley Lines and you'll find the powerful magic users on the Surface."

I nodded.

Later, Phaelous dropped by the library, heralded by a polite knock. The Headmaster saw the disheveled state of my braids and my relaxed state of dress first, though I had at least straightened my clothing to be presentable. Shyntre had cleaned himself up completely before returning with our meal, and looked his normal, sullen self.

"How goes it, children?" he asked, a very slight smile on his lips.

"It goes well, Headmaster," Shyntre answered respectfully enough, but he wasn't overjoyed to have his sire checking in on him.

"And you, young Sister?" he turned those gold-flecked eyes on me.

I smiled warmly. "Revealing. If this is just a fraction of your archives, I cannot imagine what else is here."

Phaelous chuckled low. "This small library is the only one with these particular details, young Sister. Only three sons of the Tower have been allowed to study here, Shyntre one of them. You have a gifted instructor, young Sister."

"I am aware, Headmaster." I glanced cheekily at the wizard, and he focused very hard on his text.

"I believe you have nine marks yet to go, and I will come get you for your Reverie."

"My thanks, Headmaster."

Shyntre had been introducing many foreign words to me as we discussed the Surface, I asked questions while he referenced his material. He was the faster reader and only made me read wholes pages myself if there was a cluster of interrelated subjects that were too difficult to speak of individually.

Otherwise he was a very good lecturer and held my attention — complete with backhanded compliments and subtle, snide remarks, which sometimes distracted us and sometimes sharpened my interest in the subject matter.

By the time he began practicing the most common "trade" Surface language with me, my head had begun to hurt from the overload of information. I offered a suggestion for a break, and he thought I was teasing. Again.

"I'm serious, Shyntre I need a break."

He shook his head. "Sirana, we're running out of time, we're not going to reach the goal Elder Rausery set."

"You're not going to be rid of me in one session, you know," I countered. "You think I'm going to retain it all the first time? We can go over it and more the next time."

His face lifted, and his expression had my crotch burning.

I grinned. "Come on, Shyntre. You want to practice tongues, practice on me for a while and then we can have something to eat and resume. The study that's left will be better spent."

He shook his head, even as he seemed to agree. "I can't believe your appetite."

"Appetites. Plural." I showed him my focus, my desire wholly on him. It wouldn't budge.

Shyntre breathed out in frustration. I readied another argument or two, anticipating his next protest, when my wizard surprised me. He slammed his manuscript closed and threw up his hands. Standing up, he came around to my side of the table, looking down at me.

"Well? Take down your pants and sit on the table, unless you've changed your mind."

Holy fuck.

I most certainly hadn't. I stood up, moved my chair to the side, and turned to rest my bottom on the sturdy table, tugging on my leather's ties again. I smiled like a fool as he helped me get the red leather down around my knees for the second time.

I enjoyed the impatient way he pushed my thighs apart and started stubbornly licking me; it was pure amusement at first, but then I was made to remember that he didn't have to be seduced, or even *like* the cait very much, and still display breath-stopping talent with that mouth and tongue.

He and I had this in common, although I would admit from experience that liking the cait one was sucking was more fun.

"Oh … ." I breathed out, threading my hands behind his head but unlike him refrained from mashing his face into my snatch.

I massaged his scalp through his short hair instead, closing my eyes, neither fighting the rise nor trying to draw it out. He had a good point about running out of time, but one more climax should also give me a third or fourth wind that I needed for this much studying.

My wizard chose a good time to use his fingers, and I shifted to open my legs wider for him without hesitation.

Good bua, oh, good …

My legs started to tremble as that coil tightened up inside me, waiting for release. I mewled softly, crying out in delight when a small spark went off inside me where his fingers caressed.

"Oh, Braqth!" I blurted. "Do that again, whatever it was!"

I white-knuckled the edge of the table when he did; another pop came from his fingers as he kept sucking on my slit. My ass slipped from the table as I bucked.

Oh, yes!

His fingers popped twice more in quick succession, tiny shocks not nearly what he'd dealt out earlier in our fight, yet they practically shoved me over the proverbial edge now. I screamed, quivering, and squirted all over his face. He jolted in muffled surprise.

At first, I thought that I pissed on him, but the fluid was clear and did not smell like waste, nor did the wizard seem as baffled as I was. He wasn't disgusted, either, just needed to cough some of the fluid out of his windpipe when we'd finished.

Gasping and trembling, I showed him some gratitude by shuffling over to retrieve a cloth from my belt. He accepted and wiped his face and throat thoroughly, getting to his feet. He slipped the cloth in a pocket on his robe, in case we needed it later.

"I didn't know you could do that," he commented.

"Neither did I." My smile felt languid and lop-sided.

Shyntre gave me a look but did not pursue that subject. I was too drained to care.

When Phaelous returned for the final time to take me to a very small, secure room with a cot where I could rest, I was well on my way to commanding the basics of a new language. I said as much, feeling excited with all I'd learned.

"My compliments on the progress, Sirana," Phaelous said with a wrinkled smile. "I will return after your Reverie and release you to report to your Elder."

I wouldn't see Shyntre again, then. And I hadn't even *thought* about

Callitro and the golden ring on this visit. *Oops. Embarrassing.*

I spoke on impulse before the elder wizard opened the door.

"Headmaster?"

"Yes, young Sister?"

I swallowed. "Shyntre's Mother."

Phaelous's golden brows lifted a little, and he folded his hands together in front of him. He waited patiently but volunteered nothing.

Intangibles and doubt made me waver, but I pushed it out anyway. Might as well know if I was wrong.

"Is she Varessa D'Shea?"

The old male watched me without expression as silence filled the tiny room. It seemed like he waited longer to answer than it really was.

He nodded once. "She is, young Sister."

One breath. Then two.

"Does he know?"

"He does. Now rest well in Reverie, Sirana. I shall return."

Chapter 16

Elder D'Shea contemplated the bloodstone ritual for spans. Possibly doing her own research, for certain making her own plans. Wilsira was quiet as well, perhaps occupied with whatever lead my Mother had given her at our visit.

In that time, Elder Rausery slipped me into the Wizard's Tower to sit with Shyntre as my teacher of what we knew about the Surface. He and I were better behaved in these latter lessons, having gotten something primal out of our systems. My new awareness of D'Shea's son had altered how I viewed him.

So damned intelligent. Powerfully willed and educated.

And so fucking trapped.

No wonder the young wizard was so angry and defiant, even when it brought him more punishment. Especially that they refused to kill him for it. I saw more likeness between Shyntre and D'Shea than not, especially to imagine a Davrin like my Elder Sorceress imprisoned against her will for two turns in the Sanctuary, held underneath the Priesthood's thumb as she grew a baby for them.

At the end of it, when she was at her weakest, they stole him fresh from her womb.

That broke the unspoken rules of the Nobles in so many ways, like what my sister Kaltra had done to warrant me coming to kill her. Among the Nobility, even Matrons could be put in the dungeon for this, but the Priestesses got away with it. More than once. My Elder was the last one to be imprisoned for pregnancy, and both D'Shea and Rausery had ways to enforce prevention within the Sisterhood.

And they are both worried about Wilsira and her son's interest in me.

So was I.

I didn't know exactly where Phaelous fit into all this beyond, some-how, helping my Elder to catch in the first place. But I moderated my mouth and allowed Shyntre to teach. I sucked in all the knowledge the wizards of the Tower could give me of what lay beyond our bor-ders. I didn't want to live out my life as a Red Sister warring with the manipulative cunts and their Sathoet in the Sanctuary.

I wanted to see the Surface, but I worried that I wouldn't get the choice.

Rausery and D'Shea have different goals for me.

Shyntre could tell.

Even not speaking any of this aloud, I wagered the sapphire pendant he'd made for me — for I had confirmed this from his own grudging mouth — that he knew I wanted a choice but knew I didn't really have one. He understood the conflict in a way I would never have thought a bua could before I met him.

Elder Rausery tested my retention as she said she would, and she seemed pleased. I learned a lot and we continued my every spare moment. I never reached that level she had mentioned, where she determined I was done.

At one of those lessons, I could visit Callitro as well, claiming at last the gold ring Phaelous said was finished and fully tested to the Headmas-ter's satisfaction.

"This is imbued with one recurring spell," the young battlemage explained, waiting as I removed my red glove before slipping it onto the finger he'd fitted the ring for quad-spans ago. "Use the command word, and it will enhance your senses such that whatever you aim at, you will hit it. The spell will last only a few moments and you will not get a second try the same cycle if it dissipates, so always take your strike."

I nodded, studying the plain band closely, trying to sense if it felt different from regular jewelry. "Ranged attack only? Arrows, throwing daggers?"

"More, Red Sister. Any strike. A stabbing blade. A web pellet which absolutely *must* ensnare your prey. Your fist, if necessary."

A huge smile spread across my face to think of such a useful tool. Callitro grinned back.

"Can I use it in here?" His smile dissipated like the spell, and I laughed. "No, no, you aren't the target, Callitro. I want to try it the first time while you're here. Then we can fuck."

The grin returned, ear-to-cute-pointed-ear, and I jumped him, pushing the battlemage onto his back in his bed. He melted when I claimed his mouth, thrust my tongue inside, and he instantly tented his robes. The younger wizard was not even close to the work it took to get Shyntre deep into my holes, but I wasn't complaining. I still remembered my aimless conquests at Court.

A contrast in available buas is always nice.

A third bua provided a starker contrast still, starting with the irksome point that he *wasn't* available, and yet I kept coming back. He was the eldest of those males who kept my interest most as a Red Sister.

Auslan stood somewhere in between Shyntre and Callitro. Yielding and submissive to a cait's desires, and yet able to convince me to reconsider my own temptations, holding fast to a boundary best for both of us. Proven observant and intelligent, even educated in his way, yet he wore the mask of a pretty, vapid breeding toy to perfection when needed for his own survival.

So few females know who he is. Not even Wilsira.

Following my glut of lessons about the Surface, knowing Shyntre had said to *this* Consort that he'd been there, knowing that both had likely been talking about *me* in the garden … I had to go back before D'Shea lost interest in the merchant Nobles. The Sorceress had the answers she wanted from Curgia and House Itlaun. She might stop sending me here. Or worse, forbid it.

I must go back.

My Elder wasn't the least interested in my attempts to bring up the subject.

"How goes your practice and knowledge of wards, Sirana?"

"Very well, Elder."

I glanced at Reishel beside me, who was smiling with pride and she spoke up, "She progresses well beyond where I was in her place."

D'Shea nodded, checked a few things on her desk, set them aside for later. She stood to collect objects from a few of her locked chests and boxes, donned her belt and cloak, and motioned to the door.

"Let's run an exercise."

Quietly, we left the Cloister and our sparsely populated area of the Great Cavern, and my mouth twisted to think how similar this was to Elder Rausery calling me out with Jael.

But for a very different purpose, no doubt.

Elder D'Shea also didn't run us ragged first; her demands on us were our stealth skills, and we did not hurry. To return even more memories, I recognized the path.

Gaelan led me this way to meet D'Shea. My first debriefing after I'd executed Kaltra.

Eventually, we reached that same area outside the sentry point on the edge of the wilderness, where darkness was complete, each cave a bubble of silence but for the throb of the world's heart. For a moment, it seemed louder than the bustle of Sivaraus.

We kept going until we found that source of running water, which at least provided sound and a way to muffle voices and steps. My eyes were fully adjusted to the ever-present Radiants without color, though I could barely make out D'Shea's form separate from the water-carved stone around us because she kept moving. Her energy at the middle of her chest was brighter, as if she was tense; mine was likely the same to her eyes.

★The last time you stood here,★ she began, ★you described one sister's death. We are here again so you may describe the death of the other at last.★

I could not hide my dislike of her demand. Her intense eyes tried to pierce me as they stared back.

I will know what happened, Sirana.

You were there! I tossed at her. *You arrived to investigate when my Mother called! *You* deemed it an accident.*

There are many 'accidents,' Sirana.

Tell me about my Grand Matron, Elder.

A muscle flexed in the Sorceress's jaw. *What?*

Lead Jaunda knew her, I said. *The Matron made an impression on her. I know you've been watching my House for generations. Three, at least.*

D'Shea recovered and now smiled calmly at me. *It is not your place to demand your answers before I get mine, Red Sister. This is your only warning.*

I quivered with that old, habitual sense of threat, of secrecy, when I could not speak of what Jilrina was doing if I tried. It was ridiculous to think I could squeeze information or distract my Elder from this, yet I was tempted.

I glanced at Reishel, though I didn't know why or what I sought.

You're my Sister, she signed in reassurance. *Our Elder has been watching my family, too. She has good reason to choose and protect us. Tell her. Tell us. Speaking it will lift some weight, helping us all succeed.*

If by succeeding, she meant surviving.

Nothing which has defined your life began with you, Sirana, D'Shea signed. *Too many Nobles choose to think so, and that is why they are so easy to control. I *must* know the real reason Jilrina died. You are capable of speaking it now, and you *will.**

I had so many questions of my own yet could not bank on any trade. Knowing this stuck in my throat; it was just as well that my hands would do the speaking.

We were quarrelling again, Jilrina and I, I signed. *This was frequent. Often, she would force her demands on me during or soon after a quarrel — whether that demand was to submit to a beating, my 'participation' in another false ritual, or … other humiliations.★

D'Shea nodded; Reishel kept still to read my gestures.

★During the cycle she died, I had escaped her room — something I always tried but did not always succeed — and she pursued me. There were no servants in the barn when I entered, there were no witnesses, it was her and me.★

I paused as I brought the memory forward in my mind; it had been a long time since I had reveled in it.

★In the past, I had climbed up a ladder to the loft, and she had trapped me there, releasing frustrations on me instead of dragging me away to her 'altar.' I had fled there twice more with the same result.★

My Elder's gaze sharpened, her eyes seeming to glint in the darkness as she lifted her hands. ★You do not strike me as a youth who would make the same mistake three times, Sirana.★

I bared my teeth in a smile. ★The second and third times were not mistakes, Elder. My sister was a creature of habit, and the third time I only did not have the distance I needed before she caught up.★

★What do you mean?★

★There would be a fourth time. I had enough distance to start climbing and make the noise and to jump off and roll behind a large crock. Jilrina assumed I had made it to the top and had hidden up there, like the three times before. She climbed up, and as she taunted and searched for me in the loft, I knocked over the ladder. She cursed at me, and I left her in the barn and returned to the manor.★

The Sorceress tilted her head a little. ★Yes, I saw the fallen ladder. The drop was not far enough to kill for certain but could certainly injure limbs. You gambled on her jumping and somehow landing on her neck?★

I shook my head. ★I imagine Jilrina may have discovered a pincerworm when she lifted the coil of rope that we stored in the loft. In case the ladder fell.★

Goddess help me, I enjoyed the look on her face.

★Pincerworm. I performed the inspection. There were no insect bites on the First Daughter's body.★

★Then she was lucky,★ I replied. ★Not so lucky in how she landed on the barn floor when the creature startled her. As I've always said, I did not touch her.★

My Elder narrowed her eyes at me. ★How long was the pincer-worm?★

★Tiny when I collected it. By the time she died?★ I demonstrated by showing her the space between my index fingers, about the length of my hand from heel to fingertip.

D'Shea measured with her eyes. ★Large enough for its venom to be lethal. Did you know that?★

★No, but I hoped so, Elder.★

★You let Braqth's Hand take it from there?★

I shrugged indifferently to that. ★I had decided I could work with what circumstance gave me, even if it was just a large scare. Braqth proved more generous than that. If I ever prayed, it was always for Jilrina's death, Elder.★

D'Shea went still after that. Perhaps she was reflecting, as I had, that even if there had been pincer marks visible — for those worms were known to attack repeatedly when subjected to loud noise — it could still have been a simple case of stupidity: Jilrina stumbling onto a sensitive, poisonous creature and screaming, startling it. It still would have been an unfortunate accident for the First Daughter.

The little box where I had kept and fed the worm wasn't an obvious place for a "pet" but, regardless, it had disappeared before Kaltra had cornered me about Jilrina being missing. The simplicity of my plan had never been fully tested because the worm hadn't managed one strike. Jilrina had simply broken her neck, and it had crawled off to freedom.

I had always maintained that I did not kill my eldest sister, but now D'Shea knew, as most had probably suspected, that was only a technicality.

The proud and satisfied smile that appeared on my Elder's face told me I still had a place in Sivaraus despite that. Or because of it.

★Very good,★ the Sorceress signed, satisfied at last. ★Did you know that her death would release the compulsion she set on you?"

★Yes, Elder.★

How did you know?

I paused. I tried to think. *When?*

Compulsion spells that strong are not sold in any merchant shop, Sirana, D'Shea explained. *The Sisterhood finds and destroys such contraband, executes those who make or distribute it. They are uncommon, rarely spoken of, and many do not know what it takes to free themselves.*

I stared at her. My hands hesitated, choosing words. *I just knew.*

Since when?

Since she stabbed me in the shed. I remembered that much. *I woke up in my bed after passing out from bleeding. I … knew she had to die. Or I'd never be released.*

D'Shea smiled wryly. *Had we known, Sirana, the Sisterhood would back the Matron Thalluen on this, but the Priesthood wouldn't.*

I shrugged. *Consort-bred Daughters seem stupider to me, so that makes sense.*

D'Shea chuckled in silence, and Reishel showed her teeth. Then, my Elder signed, *I want to go back to the ward you found in your game with Jaunda. Its discovery was what got you sent to Wilsira in the first place.*

It seemed our Sorceress had had her fill of probing my childhood while I still knew nothing about why she watched us. But at least that explained why Reishel was here, too. I had never understood why Jael was present with Elder Rausery when they came to get me to poke me about the Surface.

I nodded. *You want to refine the report, Elder?*

The Sorceress shook her head. *No. I want to go there. Lead me where you found it.*

My mouth opened in mute surprise.

Reishel signed, *But the Drider, Elder.*

And Wilsira will know, again, I added.

So little faith in your Elder, novice? D'Shea smirked. *This is an order as well. We return. Show me the way.*

This is Abyssal smoke. Jaunda could have led D'Shea back much easier, any time she wished. The Lead knew those tunnels in which she'd been hunting us much better than either Reishel or me. *Jaunda knew them well enough to save my naked ass in time.*

But I understood D'Shea enough to know that wasn't the point. The "easy" way was rarely the Sorceress's way. An insistent trait inherited by her wizard son.

I took point at a sustainable pace, Reishel behind me and D'Shea covering the rear. I basically remembered how to get there, but Reishel tapped my shoulder once when we would have gone down the wrong tunnel.

A few times the area squeezed down tight and vertical to reach through to the next network of caverns, and we had to crawl single file. I witnessed D'Shea competent as any of us in feats of strength and stealth in the wilderness, despite my first introduction being her sitting in a spider silk robe with a glass of wine.

We stopped when a shudder raced up my spine, and I spotted the mouth of the tunnel which led to the Drider's den. While I had not sensed the danger the first time this far out, it had changed quite a bit in the quad-spans since I'd last stumbled here.

Whispers, distant and intimate, folded around me. Warning and welcoming me in unintelligible gossip. Pain and delirium I hadn't recognized before now wept in its clarity. I took a step backward, and my Elder gripped my shoulder in her hand, holding me in place. My heartbeat grew audible in the darkness, subtle tremors in my body passing through to her. Tensely, Reishel looked around as if she felt eyes upon us.

D'Shea signed over my shoulder. ★What do you sense?★

★Don't know!★ I signed, my emphasis crossing over into angry fear. ★Voices?★

★Thoughts? Like the Tragar?★

★No. Worse. The Drider, for certain.★ I hesitated. ★Madness ... fermenting.★

Her hand over my shoulder stilled. The Sorceress once trapped pregnant in the Sanctuary signed approval. ★Good description.★

Then she turned me around, put my back to the danger, and I panicked.

~No! It's coming!~

She took my jaw in her hand. *Look at me, Sirana! At my eyes.*

I looked.

Found a quiet place within them. A place she had jealously protected for centuries.

I fled there.

We connected.

D'Shea gasped at how deep the link went; she nearly pushed me out, wanting to throw me off her before I violated her again. With reluctance and effort, she yielded her will, the mindlink holding strong. A strange, wordless understanding slowly mixing between us, like silt meeting water, to create a temporary moment of free-floating thought and suspension.

Good. Come with me.

D'Shea reached out for Reishel's hand without breaking eye contact with me. Though it was out of my periphery, I knew when it happened, when our recovered Sister clasped the Sorceress's hand and, somehow, Reishel entered in that suspension.

Away from the den, D'Shea thought, and we both understood. *It has done what I wanted for you.*

D'Shea led us somewhere specific, and I did not need to wonder where. I knew. She must have scouted this area while I had been gone with Wilsira. She found a small place three Davrin could hide; she had cleared it first and set a ward and illusion on its entrance to keep it unoccupied. Far enough away from the tunnel which led to the Drider den that the whispers faded and the quiet thrum of the Deepearth returned.

The Sorceress suspended her own spells, we entered, and once inside, we would likely remain undisturbed.

Hold Reishel, my Elder instructed, *as we did before with the bloodstone. Same position.*

Reishel and I obeyed; I sat facing our Elder with my back to the rock wall, and my Sister got down between my open legs, sitting and leaning against me while I put my arms around her. As D'Shea watched us, nodding approval, I noted how carefully the Sorceress tread, how rigid was her discipline against allowing her mind to wander.

We remained in a mindlink, wide awake and unaltered by any magic or substance — a first-time accomplishment — yet I remained in that "quiet place" from which her inner voice arose. I could not search beyond it. I neither witnessed nor eavesdropped on any memories of her own.

I looked at Reishel. My Sisters had been used many times as conduits and shields, and this was no different. I could sense both the vulnerability and determination in D'Shea, recognized it in my own story, in the confession of the lengths I'd gone to be freed of Jilrina's control. My Elder recognized that we were the same in this.

Someone controlled a secret deep within my Elder, a compulsion like mine, and she sought to break those chains, too. I *knew* this, but I had to wait for her thoughts to come to me in that quiet place. I was not allowed to dive in and look for myself.

D'Shea smirked as if she knew. She sat down next to us on a boulder, facing us. *Swim that deep without illumination or experience, Sirana, and you may become lost in a life much longer and stranger than yours.*

I did not doubt her.

We hovered in that suspension. Holding that precarious balance through will alone. We were not merged into one mind, yet a path remained open, a channel of experience without voice, flowing both ways through the recovered Red Sister between us.

Reishel squeezed my hands in hers as she watched our Elder as if in a dream. She was the focal point between two more powerful wills; she became the quivering conduit for the Sorceress, and the anchor for me, whatever I was. She may comprehend what passed through her, but she was more likely to relive it only in Reverie.

~I am listening, Elder. What do you ache to speak aloud but cannot?~

D'Shea did not have to ask me if Kain was there; she looked at my eyes and knew it was me. As Lana had said, the shard of him within me was almost absorbed into non-existence.

Almost.

Shyntre is my son, and Phaelous is his sire, she began. *I know you uncovered this. I know Phaelous would answer truthfully if you asked, which you did. He informed me.* ⋆

She paused, sensing my concern, and she shook her head once. ⋆*I was not impregnated against my will, Sirana. For a time, I visited the Headmaster often in his Tower. I **was** tricked, however, and Phaelous quickly learned which weaknesses to exploit. My own arrogance had me believe the desire to conceive by him was my own but, as you may expect, the Priestesses were behind it. Phaelous acted against me on their demands, and he will always obey to protect the buas in his care. He is easily coerced into betrayal for the sake of the young wizards.* ⋆

I nodded. ~*You said you were the last Red Sister to be held in the Sanctuary until giving birth, Elder, so it had happened before. How did you not see the consequence of coupling with him?*~

⋆*The Prime calls this stupidity, and perhaps she is correct. Phaelous's mage aura was attractive to me in a way I find difficult to describe. Nothing to do with his appearance or his age. Rarely, a Davrin feels the incredible urge to breed with a specific male, and I felt this with him. Once discovered, manipulation of this truth came from all sides. Both the Prime and Wilsira Tachnathon suggested I would be allowed to place the child myself. I did not believe them, but then the Valsharess Herself told me the same. As the last of my House, She offered me proof of that truth! Goddess help me, I believed that I could place my Daughter, and I embraced Phaelous and the urge then.* ⋆

The last of her House. So she did remember where she came from.

I tilted my head. ~*You could place ... a Daughter? Was that taken away because he was a Son?*~

A wrinkle appeared on her forehead. ⋆*No. I carried a First Daughter, Sirana. I tested with a spell. I **know** I did. I do not know how it happened that I gave birth to a son in the Sanctuary. I dream ... that while I was held there, heavy enough to feel the kicking, that there was a ritual ... somewhere ... It hurt. ... they did something to my unborn.* ⋆

D'Shea's focus wavered, those careful mental shields cracking, a shape like a door opening, enough for a sound to come through.

Chanting. Endless echoes.

And screaming. *Hers.*

The Sorceress's eyes and jaw hardened. The iron door slammed shut. Silence.

D'Shea swallowed. Breathed. *I have been unable to speak anything of this for the whole of Shyntre's life. I cannot speak directly to him, either, nor be in the same room with him, because the Conceiver still lives and thus, so does the compulsion.*

~You confess it now. You can speak.~

*Yes. This linking of minds ... passes through that magic. You **know** in your mind without true voice. Without words. As I've prayed to find before I died. This is not a counter spell. I have tried, and they have all failed. This is true psionics, what you've done with me. More than once.*

My back broke out in waves of bumps. My own report from what I witnessed with Curgia and Wilsira flowed back and forth between us. ~You understand better than any what that bloodstone told us.~

D'Shea smiled a little. *Fascinating how each report after was different, based on your experience at the time. There is no absolute view, even with psionics, but I suspected as much.*

I considered. ~Do you really believe they changed your Daughter to a Son?~

I don't know. I cannot get near Shyntre even to know his aura. Somehow, the Priestesses have always assured only Sathoet Sons are born of ritual. Once Wilsira gained her title as Conceiver, the Sanctuary also revealed the pure-blood Consorts would be only buas. This was shortly after Shyntre's birth, so I worry that I was part of whatever Wilsira discovered. If she can select the sex of any Davrin child, or force its change after conception, as it appears that she can, then Wilsira grows too powerful. We now know she breeds Kerse intentionally and seeks Abyssal names from his offspring. And we know that Kerse becomes willful. All signs that the Conceiver will soon threaten the Queen's Order.

~But I could not gain proof to convince the Valsharess, Elder.~

We will keep trying. We grow short on time to convince the Valsharess before Wilsira creates another deflection. You will not learn anything new from studying with my son, Sirana, so these sessions with which Rausery has kept you occupied must stop.

She knew I was displeased without having to think it. Her mouth tightened.

*You cannot go to the Surface any time soon. There is no benefit, only risk. Jaunda earned her trip, but you have not. The time is now that you will help me *bring down Wilsira. You have a bond with Kerse, you can use him as no one else can. You have this gift, this way to communicate in secret which the Priestesses do not have. I **need** you if I am ever to free myself. I know you understand.* ★

My eyes were wet, I realized. I did not remember them becoming so, but yes, I did understand. I would be sent to the Sanctuary again very soon. Damn them all to the Abyss.

~*If I may not visit the wizards for now,*~ I thought, ~*let me visit the Consort Auslan before I go on another Sanctuary mission.*~

D'Shea arched a brow. ★*A well-timed pounce. You are still dangerously fascinated with him, as I was with Phaelous. Your auras merged with each other when you attacked him, and they will never forget. I've seen it since you found him. You should not be around him. The temptation could get the best of you, as it did me.* ★

I shook my head, knowing she was right.

~*Auslan spoke with his Mother about things he shouldn't know, and she was a Priestess destroyed by Wilsira. He is not loyal to the Conceiver, and he has seen things inside the Sanctuary. He will speak to me. Let me question him, now knowing what you've told me.*~

My Elder scowled, displeased with me, but my logic and strategy were unbreakable despite my desire, and we knew it. She also knew I wouldn't betray her. I was in as much danger from the Conceiver as she had once been. Wilsira's death meant D'Shea's freedom from her compulsion, and my avoiding the same pit. Again.

But Kerse was changing, and my Elder was right.

Time grew short.

★LET HER REVERIE WITH YOU,★ THE SORCERESS INSTRUCTED ME AS SHE AND I finally reached our Cloister with Reishel. ★*She will feel better soon, but don't let anyone see her until she is coherent. Then, talk to her.*★

D'Shea was back to hand-signing. The mindlink which had allowed me to know the truth of her mood, which granted her the ability to "speak" despite the magical gag was now broken between us, and I felt very odd.

Cold and drifting. Alone.

Part of me wanted to reform it somehow, wanted to maintain it indefinitely as reassurance that we were allies who could not betray the other, yet neither of us would survive the Davrin ways if I clung to her like that.

My Elder would kill me herself if I tried.

Reishel was worse off for having been the bridge between us, her own will suppressed as she sat in a trance within my arms. She may have been aware of all or part of the conversation, but I wouldn't know until we talked.

I had guided the silent flayer survivor through the tunnels, who was willing if withdrawn. D'Shea had signed that, between the four versions of the bloodstone report, Reishel's was the least detailed, though not inaccurate. Simpler, observant, with fewer conclusions drawn for having less experience with magic overall.

Gaelan's was only as strong as her magical extrapolations, though she had less working knowledge of the Priestesses having been a common merchant before the Sisterhood recruited her.

★You,★ she'd continued, ★having been there and being what you are, where you grew up in Court, were second only after me.★

A short while ago, that would have sounded arrogant.

No longer because, in this, I didn't want to be first.

D'SHEA AIDED ME IN GETTING REISHEL INSIDE MY ROOM UNSEEN, AND THEN she disappeared. I quickly retrieved some fresh water from our well and returned to her, securing the door to the tiny barracks room. I looked down at my resting Sister with a sense of having been here before.

Gaelan. She blamed Lelinahdara's 'invasive' use of her aura, but either D'Shea is just as harsh, or …

Or, it was me. I wish I knew what I was doing. If Kerse was changing, so was I, and either of us being found out by the wrong power too soon only meant death and torture for us and our current "Matron" figure.

Then I grimaced, annoyed with myself for the comparison. *Argh! Don't think like that!*

It was either D'Shea and me, or Wilsira and Kerse. Sisterhood or Sanctuary. As it had been for centuries. I was a tiny, new piece on the game board.

I'll not lie down on the altar and give up. I never have, even suffering upon it.

Reishel was responsive enough to help me undress her, and I soon followed her into the nude, bathing myself with a cloth, and then her. She smiled a little while I ran the cool dampness without hurry over her entire body. Her eyes were open. She looked in my direction but still appeared the same kind of distracted, unfocused conduit that Gaelan had been.

What did she say … ? She 'relived' parts of her life in Reverie.

A vivid memory for the mage. Gaelan had tried to call out someone's name, I was sure. Yet she hadn't; something held her back. If Reishel experienced similar now, her dreams seemed fuzzy and peaceful rather than clear and loud; there was nothing to make her thrash or cry out. My eyes landed between her legs, slightly open. Impulse suggested I settle there and pleasure her.

It might help wake her up.

Yet, neither Gaelan nor D'Shea had been approving when the potion-maker had been woken up like that. My motives had been selfish, looking for entertainment, and a vulnerable Sister was undeserving of the treatment. I had promised I'd never do it again.

Yet in watching Reishel now, I wanted to touch her.

I wanted to make her feel good. Help bring her back.

What is it with you and pawing sleeping Sisters, Sirana?

Maybe because that was when Davrin seemed most real. Beautiful and honest. Their guard was down, their face relaxed. It wasn't just Sisters, I realized. I had admired and kissed Shyntre under those circumstances. He had also been furious with me for forcing him with his guard down.

And it had been funny.

Reishel wasn't asleep, though; she just wasn't alert.

I reached out and placed my palm on her thigh, rubbed gently. "Reishel?"

"Hmm?"

"I want to suck you till you cum."

That took a moment, and then, she chuckled softly. Her legs opened a little more. She hummed like she sat at a table of delicious food. Willing.

Or, close enough.

I settled down on my belly between her smooth thighs and enjoyed tracing her folds with my fingers for a bit, priming and prepping her with alternating, teasing licks.

She moaned; her legs stayed open, a quiver passing through when my mouth finally attached. Her hand reached to touch my head, my hair. She neither pulled nor grasped, and her hips thrust up only a tiny bit, still languid.

"*Ah*," she exhaled, her sex becoming swollen and hot beneath my tongue as I nuzzled and mouthed and sucked her. I didn't care how long it took her to peak; given enough time, she'd have a finger in her netherhole when she did.

Before that could happen, Gaelan caught us in the act. She had suspended the ward and entered alone, startling me. She swiftly closed the door and warded it, standing still, watching. After a few surging heartbeats, I refocused to make Reishel moan and shiver.

Our ranking Sister became aroused, I thought, for she soon stripped down as well. She removed her Feldeu from her gear and stepped around behind me to caress my buttocks.

"On your knees?" she whispered the question.

No reason not to.

I brought my ass up, my knees comfortably apart. With my tongue, I stroked Reishel's nub harder and faster.

"Oh, Goddess," she moaned while Gaelan squeezed my haunches, lightly touched my slippery netherlips with her other hand and chuckled.

Then my elder Sister leaned down and tasted my asshole, swirling around as it clutched and squeezed her tongue in response. My own tongue went deep into Reishel's slit, a rumbling groan my tight throat.

Then my mage Sister stopped. Straightened up.

I heard her say, "Ra'velishta."

There was a subtle magical pop in the room following the command word for Gaelan's Feldeu. She touched my buttocks again, the blunt head of a prick sliding along my sex, nudging for the breeding hole.

Oh, fuck …

Gaelan hadn't serviced me with the magic phallus since she insisted that I start doing her instead.

Are you sure? I wanted to ask. *You want to?*

But I kept my mouth attached to Reishel, who was close, and instead waited for the answer. A few moments later, Gaelan filled me deep; my back arched, hips tilted to receive her.

Nnnnngh! Yes!

"Sirana … !" Reishel gasped, grinding her mound against me the same moment Gaelan started pounding my back end.

Oh fuck! Yeah, harder!

Reishel and I teetered on the edge; one of us struck our climax and set off the other. I'd be hard pressed to say which one. It didn't matter.

My eyes mostly closed, my body quaking under sensations and thrusts, my Sister's juices oozed into my mouth and smeared across my cheeks as her thighs squeezed down, trapping my head. Gaelan's finger penetrated my pucker midway through my high, and I jerked as my pleasure spiked again; Reishel squealed simultaneously.

Then we came down, Reishel and I, and Gaelan withdrew from my cunt without getting off. I gasped for breath, turning to look back at her while resting my head against Reishel's sweating thigh.

"Thank you," I said.

Gaelan smirked, lightly stroking a glistening, black Feldeu jutting up from between her folds. "You needed it."

"Wanna trade?" I offered.

She considered then shook her head. "No, I'm too close. Would you ride me? We've never done that."

I smiled, quite relaxed but willing to muster the effort. "Sure."

Reishel was alert enough to shift and make space for Gaelan on the pallet, resting on her side so that the other lay on her back. I straddled the mage, took her life-like, magic pole in my grip, heard her gasp, and guided it into me as I slowly sat down on her. Her hands rested on my thighs, caressing my hips as my body gripped and squeezed her.

My thoughts drifted unbidden to Auslan.

He's been beneath me like this. Gaelan was the one to stop me.

With a shake of my head, I reached for her tits. Mauled them, squeezing the nipples.

"Ohhh, yeah," she encouraged, settling in for a good ride as I moved in earnest, my mouth tight in concentration. I watched her eyes roll up, felt fingers press deep into my leg muscle, listened to her breath become erratic. She turned her head to the side, eyes closed as she, perhaps, imagined something else.

Someone else.

She wouldn't be the only one.

Her dark, maroon eyes opened when she was about to cum; we locked eyes by accident.

Locked and linked, as I had with D'Shea.

I saw Gaelan riding a bua, just like this, in a storage shed somewhere. There was another bua behind her, spreading and penetrating her ass. They doubled up on her and fucked with an enthusiasm she welcomed, unmarked by threat of any kind. Even with this other male present, however, it was the Davrin beneath her who held most of her attention.

And much of her genuine affection.

The sire of her only Daughter.

Conceived—

Now. Let it be now! Yes!

"*Oh my Goddess!*" Gaelan cried, her back bowing, her grip on my hips like metal as she came.

"Oh, fuck!" I barked, swept along with her as the threads of her memories entangled me. I had never climaxed that hard with her, nor her with me. I shook at the end of it.

She kissed me in exhausted gratitude, soon to fall into a nap, and Reishel helped me get off her and roll to the side to cuddle. Gaelan didn't seem to know what I'd seen, and I said nothing to break that rare moment of peace as she slipped fast into Reverie.

I stayed awake long enough to be sure I wasn't still bonded with her, with either one of them. Just to be sure. I would sleep on my own in good time, with one thought lingering in the dim Cloister.

Gaelan's a Mother.

Her Daughter was still alive.

CHAPTER 17

I GAINED BOTH OPPORTUNITY AND MY ELDER'S PERMISSION TO RETURN TO House Itlaun at last when news came that Curgia had caught — which was less impressive as the realization that it must have been very soon after her tragic miscarriage.

The Court was buzzing about the "divine magic" of their new Consort, though only briefly. Curgia's sister, Tulia, was about ready to burst, but this middle sister was early, still, and she made sure all who would listen knew exactly how far along she was in carrying this new unborn she desired so very much.

"Interesting," my Elder pondered. "Close enough to have happened the same eve you were there."

I grimaced at that mental image, and D'Shea smirked. She wasn't entirely serious.

"Go find out what you can from Auslan about what happened, what he witnessed. See if he knows what happened to the stillborn."

"Yes, Elder."

The Sorceress read the willingness in my face and frowned. "Be careful how you ask for the rest. Discover what you can, but don't force him or reveal our hand. We can try again, based on how he responds to you this first time."

"Yes, Elder."

I returned to House Itlaun with surety in my step, not having to sneak out here unbidden. I entered the privacy of the Consort's warded room when most of the House Nobles were in Reverie. The beautiful Davrin greeted me and we exchanged a pleasantry, but he seemed troubled by something before I'd arrived, the expression lingering after I had secured the room.

"Are you well, Auslan?" I asked, mostly to keep him talking.

"Yes, Sister. I have only not been sleeping well."

"Oh? Why is that?"

He shook his head. "It happens sometimes. The dreams of Reverie are too real to allow deep rest."

"What kind of dreams?" I shouldn't be interested, but I was.

Auslan watched me in silence for a few pulses, unblinking. "A ... walking trance. It keeps the pathway open."

Pathway? What pathway?

"A healer's trance," he clarified, looking at my face. "When I put my hands on someone in pain ... the pain tends to return in Reverie for a while."

I frowned, sniffing a partial lie. *Walking trance, huh?* "Mm-hm. And when these dreams seem 'too real'?"

"It feels as if Braqth herself punishes me, and the sheets usually need washing when I awaken."

I glanced over at his rumpled bed. There weren't any dark stains. "It doesn't look too bad."

Softly, he huffed, looking at his vanity. "Try dreaming my dreams sometime, Sister, and tell me you feel otherwise."

On the outside, I grinned. Inside, I was shocked. He almost sounded like Shyntre right there, with that bold defensiveness. It was cute.

Damnit, so tempting ...

"I'd love to," I teased back, "but seeing as that's impossible, I'll have to stick with my own dreams and leave you to yours."

He didn't respond, and in the following lull, I could have sworn I heard someone laugh. Probably me. I knew I was lying; I dared not imagine what it would be like to dream with him.

We'd have to be resting naked in the same bed.

Auslan looked back from the vanity to see me staring at him. He read my expression well because it was the one with which he was most familiar. "You still desire me."

I shrugged, ignoring a pinch of unease at the back of my mind. "Why wouldn't I?"

"I have not seen you since the eve Curgia miscarried."

"You could have seen me off the next cycle as we left."

"I was ... resting."

"The healing took much out of you. I want to hear more about that eve, Auslan. And, tell me when Curgia conceived. My Elder wants to know."

Auslan looked wary, started to shake his head. I took a step forward, closing in on his space. He backed up.

"Fertility magic like yours can heal, too," I said, stepping again. "And you *said* it can take fertility away as well."

"No, I said it can have that side effect on a healthy womb," he corrected, sudden panic on his face as he moved to keep two lounging chairs between us. "*If* both the mage and ritual is powerful enough. It is not a direct occurrence, nor something that happens in the weaker spells. But you had been barren. Now, you are not. I know a powerful Priestess healed you."

"Very good," I said, starting to circle around. "So you claim to be as powerful as a Priestess to understand this? Did you perform a similar ritual to get the stillborn out and save Curgia from bleeding to death?"

The Consort glanced away as if making sure he didn't stub his toe on a fiberstalk leg. "I have no idea if it was like what you experienced, Red Sister. I cannot claim to be as powerful as a Priestess. That is blasphemy."

"So exact in your wording, Auslan."

"I must be in my role, Sister."

"Curgia caught by you immediately, didn't she? You must have been powerful, or she was constantly grateful in your bed."

We still moved around Auslan's room during this back-and-forth.

We each wanted to maintain the same distance from each other, but we disagreed on what that distance should be. Perhaps Auslan thought I was stalking him, and he merely responded like prey.

He could be right.

"I fail to see how that is relevant to this report, Sister," he said.

"Don't hide behind your mask now, Consort. Your act doesn't fool me, it never has. You *are* powerful, I *felt* it. And you're smarter than they know."

We drew near the bed, but Auslan realized it and took several steps sharply in the other direction.

"You agreed to leave me be," he gasped.

I could hear his heart.

"You got too curious about me last time," I replied. "Tell me, have you told Wilsira what you know of me in the wilderness?"

"No!" he replied, shocked. "I have said what will happen to me if she discovers I was 'poached' by you while under House D'Verin."

"You couldn't give it to her without implicating yourself?"

"She would ask how I could *possibly* know. I do not think she would believe you simply loosened your tongue around me on her visit for no reason. Not when she wasn't even aware that you and I knew each other before you fell upon me in the garden."

I flushed in that memory. *Oh, yeah …* He'd smelled good.

"At best," he continued, "she would assume you had taken me *during* her visit and engaged in pillow talk, and the consequences for me would have been the same. I will say nothing of you to her. I gain nothing. I lose everything."

His voice had risen in frustration, and my blood rushed to hear it. Auslan chose to keep this room secure and did not open his hallway doors to escape into public. He passed them.

"Then why ask me what you did in the first place?" I pressed. "You seemed desperate to know something about me. About what the Sisterhood was doing with our wombs. You mentioned Shyntre being 'the last.'"

Auslan's face tightened. He was being backed into a corner in more ways than one, and he knew it.

"You said you would not lie by omission," I added, breathing faster. "This is your last chance to uphold our agreement, so I may do the same."

He showed me on that pretty face his honest opinion, who *really* was straining the agreement, but I still hadn't touched him. Yet. He was trying to think of something evasive; I could tell.

"Does your probing my past have anything to do with Wilsira?" I asked directly. "Anything to do with Shyntre?"

Because it was what I *really* wanted to know.

The Consort blinked, swallowed with little moisture in his mouth. "Yes. But … never on the Conceiver's behalf. Never, Sister. She killed my first Priestess. I loathe her."

I nodded; I could believe that. "Then whose behalf?"

He was quivering with fear. "My own."

Lying.

I only had to tell him I'd seen him and the wizard in the garden.

Instead, I asked, "To what purpose?"

"To discover the Conceiver's true reach," he said. "To avoid stepping into her trap. To avoid *dying*. I grow older, Red Sister. Consorts never live long before we are discarded. I am not ready to die."

Harsh. But also truth. For the first time, I imagined living on without him. If it was a trickle of fear now, I wondered what void he would leave if it became to be. I paused, both in my conversation and my step, listening to the quiet of the room. My Consort ceased roaming as well.

"What if you discovered something that compromised the Conceiver?" I asked, creeping closer to that line D'Shea had told me not to cross. "Or might threaten her power? What would you do with it?"

His eyes slid evasively to one side, and I stepped forward, clapped in front of his face, startling him. "Look at me. Answer."

He shook his head, watching my face carefully. I imagined he could read me quite well by now. Instead, he asked, "What would *you* do with it?"

I smiled a little and took the risk. "I'd bring her down before she comes after me again."

Auslan blinked slowly, his expression carefully controlled. He did not try for either defense of her actions or shock at the thought of mine. He had said he loathed her, that was enough.

"What happens to *you* when she falls?" I asked.

I caught his attention with my wording. *When.* He understood what I was saying for certain now, and his next answer mattered quite a bit.

"It would depend on *how* she falls, Sister," he answered, "but, as you have said before, I am not made of crystal. Let her face her fate, and I will accept what comes for me."

I narrowed my eyes slightly and smirked. "Not so afraid as to try to prevent it? Keep things the same as they are now, Consort?"

"No, Sister."

"Why not? Does it have anything to do with the wizard you were talking to when last I was here?"

I managed to shock him very much, that was clear, but I had to commend his short recovery time. "No, it is still for my first Priestess. Shyntre knew her, too."

"Huh." I couldn't quite swallow that because of what he asked next.

"Who knows about the garden, other than you?"

That was a deft riposte, I realized.

If I admitted to Auslan that no one knew but me, I'd be telling him I withheld that information from my Elders. If I told him otherwise, I could scare him enough that our conversation would be over. I'd impulsively dropped a figurative flare at his feet, but he'd deflected the burst back at me like a mirror, blinding me as well, and I wasn't ready with a reply. It would lead us into another deal, another secret held only between him and me.

Damn. Need to stop trying for honest responses out of Consorts!

"If I said that no one did, would it save your life?" I said in mild threat.

He watched me. "You did not report that part of your journey to your Elders."

"Not yet," I corrected.

He smiled a little. "It has been half a turn, Red Sister. They will want to know why."

"I did not have enough information yet."

"You wanted to learn more ahead of them," he interpreted.

If his tiny smile got any wider, I'd probably slap him.

"Do you know who Shyntre's Mother is?" I retorted.

"How can I not, when the Sanctuary is one large hive of gossip? The children conceived outside of it are talked about the most, especially with outsider Matas of high-status being kept there until they bear."

"Such a clever description without giving me a name."

"I am not in the habit of calling Red Sisters by their names," he said with a smile that made me flush. "But as you wish. Your Elder Sorceress D'Shea is his Mother."

Fuck!

"Then the Sisterhood knows that you know him," I said.

"They do. I do not believe they care."

Meaning I could have told D'Shea about Shyntre and Auslan talking in the garden, and it would not have threatened them. I only hadn't understood the connection well enough at the time. Now I would have difficulty explaining why I left it out, if D'Shea ever knew I did, and Auslan had gleaned far more about my situation than I had of his.

Damn him. He's good at this.

"Perhaps none care," I grumbled, "except for me."

"Why?" he asked. "Because of the Conceiver?"

"No, because you were giving him advice on how to deal with me," I said, deciding to show my irritation. "He is *my* prey, you meddler!"

I was not in complete control of the conversation here, but neither would I allow Auslan to be. Better that we *both* reveal more than we intended.

He looked confused. "Your ... prey?"

"You knew that. I heard you. You told him I'd lose interest the sooner he submitted, but I was enjoying the game." I smirked. "It doesn't matter now, though, he was anything *but* submissive when I finally got him, so he ignored *your* advice."

Auslan watched intently. "Shyntre has been of ... lasting interest to you?"

"Jealous?" I teased, mostly to block him.

He shook his head, showing me an odd smile. "*That* is the least useful of emotions to a Consort, Sister."

"How pleasant for you that you may pick and choose your most *useful* emotions," I commented snidely.

Auslan laughed. The first one from him I'd ever heard. It was music on my ears, but I had to shake it off.

He fucking laughed at me!

"Shyntre," I barked. "How well do you know him? How often do you see him?"

I waited expectantly and did not open my mouth again until he answered the question. No more distracting myself or making it so easy for him to do it.

Auslan watched me carefully, his eyes now bright as his mind. "You never told me what he is to you."

"Why would that matter?"

"You are asking me the same thing."

"So he means something to you."

"Implying he does to you, as well. If you saw us in the garden, you could not come to that conclusion yourself?"

"I'd say you were allies, at least."

"We are brothers, young Sister."

I blinked. It was as surprising for him to admit as it was for me to hear.

"It could not be by blood?"

"No. But we were raised together, we have a bond." My Consort shrugged. "The Consorts are encouraged to listen and watch the Nobles but not to interact much beyond mating signals and seduction. Nor are we encouraged to think too much. Or to read. Even though I was older than him by half a century, the son of your Elder Sorceress possessed thoughts which were challenging. And in time, I awoke to see how mine were ... not."

I smirked. "And you have a latent competitive streak to catch up?"

251

He smiled at me. "Not really. But having him around made my existence more interesting and worthwhile. This indirectly made me one of the more useful Consorts when I worked my mind on occasion. But as I said, I do not believe either the Elders or my Priestess care much about our past association."

"Or present?" I asked again. "How often do you see him?"

"Very rarely, these times." He gave it some thought for context. "Once per Worship Ball, in the cycles preparing for it. If he isn't being kept elsewhere. It was a true and wondrous surprise when both you and he arrived together at the House I serve now."

"Both?"

"Yes."

He smiled again, eyes alive and so lovely.

Stop that.

Mentally, I knew I *must* step back, although this Consort was truly someone from whom I could learn about Court and the Sanctuary, as I could learn from Shyntre about the Surface. If I might be stuck on missions at Court or poking into Priestess and Sathoet business in the near future, Auslan's observations and memory upended my dim view by strengthening the torch.

I slowly let out a breath, moving closer without threatening his space, matching gazes with him for several moments and not looking away. I enunciated my words, "I am searching for anything to bring about Wilsira's decline sooner rather than later. Will you offer me anything?"

Auslan was quiet for a few moments as he considered, and he smiled a bit.

Then he reached out and touched my face.

The warm, soft palm cupping my jaw and smooth fingers sliding behind my ear felt far more intense than it should. I sucked in my breath, frozen for an endless instant. Like Shyntre's fingers sending a magical charge through my sex while he serviced me, Auslan so gently and chastely touching my skin shocked me. In the most pleasant of ways.

Why?

My gut told me he was doing *something*; his eyes were slightly unfocused as if his mind was elsewhere. I found the will to knock his arm to the side and step back, glaring, hating how my breath shook.

Goddess, I wanted him!

"What was that?"

He blinked and focused on me. His throat flashed as he swallowed. "I'm sorry, Sister, I wanted to .... thank you, if the Sisterhood is targeting Wilsira now."

"I should treasure a touch from you that much, hm?" I said irritably. "You cunt tease. Don't do that again unless you're prepared to *show* your thanks much more than that."

I saw clear regret. "My humblest apologies. I'd forgotten to ask ... Um. What of Kerse's interest in you? Has that changed?"

I shrugged impatiently. *Fine, let's change direction.*

If it was a change in direction.

"I don't know. I haven't seen him since I left him and the Conceiver at the Sanctuary."

Auslan nodded. "I will wager that if it has not, then I cannot give you a better key than that which you have, Sister. Though, it can as easily kill you."

Or worse, his expression seemed to add.

"Tell me something I don't know, Auslan," I said.

And I meant it. I stared expectantly. He frowned slightly.

"Tell me something new," I repeated. "Surprise me. Or I'll surprise you."

"What I see in your eyes is hardly a surprise, Red Sister."

"Try me. I'll remind you that you touched me first. I should get a return touch."

He finally looked wary. "That is not a good idea."

"Then *surprise* me."

His lovely mouth was open, trying to decide what to say, when the ward on the door sounded. We both jumped.

"Enoquis?" I heard Curgia's voice. "Are you awake?"

Fuck! I scowled at the door — *Enoquis? Really? Surely they can do better than that!* — but Auslan grabbed my shoulder and signed quickly in front of my eyes, his expression intense:

★She can break the ward if she wants. She has sometimes come in while I sleep.★

Braqth damn her.

★Answer her,★ I signed grudgingly.

Or she would wonder why he didn't when she realized he was not asleep.

"No, Mistress, I am awake. Allow me a moment, please."

I darted for the dark corner where I entered and exited by way of his laundry shaft. A false panel above my head would lead me to the roof of the manor, on the back side above the garden. The magically curved design of stone and fired clay afforded blind spots even to one standing in the garden.

I couldn't escape yet; the panel would make too much noise to move right now. Instead, I pulled myself atop his wardrobe right next to the laundry shaft. Its flattop frame was solid stone, decorated high with ornate whorls of fruit and fertility signs, with sliding, fiberstalk doors with a polished, mirrored surface. I lay upon my belly. With my cloak and hood covering and dampening my body, I was invisible to the casual observer.

Auslan quickly lit two real candles with a spark rod which, given their placement, further helped to mask me by casting longer shadows above the wardrobe and obscuring life heat and Radiants from sensitive eyes with their bright, burning light. I approved.

Curgia was allowed in and immediately wrapped her arms around his shoulders to kiss him. I was still but heard that internal groan. If Auslan didn't persuade her to leave quickly, I could be in for a long and frustrating spy session.

"You are up late," she commented.

"I was awakened," he admitted, which surprised me because that was exactly what happened.

"Dreams again?" she asked. "Poor beauty."

She stroked his arms and looked at his silken, white robe that he'd used to cover himself when I'd arrived. Otherwise he slept nude — which had been pleasant to discover. She was wearing a robe, too — a rich blue — and her baby bump was barely there.

"I am having unsettling dreams as well," the Noble Daughter said, still holding his arms. "Do as you have done and make me forget them for an eve?"

"Are the techniques I taught you not working, Mistress?" he asked, his voice soft although his body language wasn't melting into her.

"I've told you, use my name when we are alone, Enoquis. And I have tried but still dream of that terrible place before you saved me from it. I feel so weak still, body and magic …"

I heard the unbecoming whine in her voice, and it occurred to me that she could be playing the weakness part but still made note. The Noble's hands slid up to Auslan's collar bones and her dark fingers slid beneath his white robe as she parted it to expose more of his chest.

"Mistress. Curgia. Would you like me to instruct you how —"

"No! I want you to do what you did once to save my life. Do it again."

His face tensed. "I cannot, Curgia, I've said before … that's the divine influence, I cannot use it at will. Braqth saw fit to have it happen."

She kissed the skin of his chest, inhaled his scent, and moaned softly in taking his wrists and placing his hands on her swelling belly. Auslan's face was expressionless, and he took little initiative, but he kept his hands where she had placed them and let her continue to taste his skin as she licked his dark purple nipples.

I was envious, crouching lower on the wardrobe and scowling.

"This baby is yours. Conceived that eve I nearly died, I'm sure of it. We are truly blessed, Enoquis."

"You are blessed, Curgia, your House is," he said quietly. "I have many offspring and know none of them. They are the Goddess's gifts to you, to the Mothers who bear them, not to me. I am just the spark. You must wean yourself from me because I won't be here much longer."

The Noble looked up angrily then, and the Consort took his hands from her middle. After a moment, she reached to tug loose the knot at his waist.

"Curgia, this will not help!" he said, some alarm in his voice as she stripped him of his robe and pushed him toward his bed. "The more often you visit, the worse it will be."

"Be silent. We have time yet, I'm not going to waste it!"

I wished I could have left then; I didn't like entertaining thoughts of violence against a pregnant Davrin regardless, but neither would my action hold up under scrutiny later.

I heard Auslan and believed him. Curgia was making a mistake in becoming overly attached to the sire of her child, particularly *this* one. But again, some of my best lapses in judgment had been under some impairing influence, when I should have known better. Other times, it was my right as a Noble, as it was Curgia's whether I liked it or not.

I looked around for something, anything, to distract the pregnant cait, to stop what was happening below me, but anything I could have done would be at the expense of revealing myself or harming her. She still owed me a favor; perhaps I could insist that she never entered his room again? Except I could not enforce that and, as I watched, realized this was unusual for one I'd been watching for a long time.

I didn't recognize her.

Auslan had been slow in becoming erect despite her frantic fondling and sucking, so the Noble had stripped herself, showing her belly proudly, and straddled him on the bed. She ground herself on him as she reached to wrap both hands around his neck.

I knew about playing with air deprivation during sex, and generally it *did* help a bua increase his stiffness, but there was too much desperation in her body language, too much aggression for it to be play. Her self-control was not there, it was violent. It was as if she thought if he would not give her what she needed, then she would wring it from him instead.

I tensed while my eyes locked on the coupling pair as I read my Consort's signs of distress. She wouldn't kill him, would she?

Show yourself. Stop her. Do it!

Deal with the consequences later.

I tensed to leap out, but then Auslan did something to save himself, though I was not completely sure what.

His hands left trying to loosen his Mistress's hold around his throat and went to her belly first, stroking her like one might brush a Uroan's coat to make it shine, and she cooed. Then one graceful hand slipped beneath the bulge to her hidden mound, the other to her pregnancy-tender breast, stroking that as she grimaced and groaned.

He alternated, going next from her snatch to stroking her side, her waist and back, the other her buttocks and thighs. He couldn't speak and was wheezing, but the touches were bizarre, deliberate and complex enough, repeated in the same order starting with the belly again, very much like a spider weaving an invisible web.

The actions themselves seemed like the cause when Curgia calmed down, riding him less frantically.

The warm spot at my chest distracted me. My sapphire glowed again beneath my armor, like when I'd been wrestling with Shyntre. I smothered that light promptly but was fascinated to watch Auslan finally loosen Curgia's hands without my interference.

She kept rocking for her own pleasure, and he took one deep breath, and another, and the stone beneath my shirt went cool and dark once again.

As far as I could tell, Auslan didn't climax although Curgia did sooner than I expected. She was disoriented and lax after she coasted down, rolling off to the side and promptly falling asleep.

His sex remained turgid as he escaped the bed and quickly lifted his robe, carrying it with him over to the vanity. He looked at himself in the mirror, at the darkening marks around his neck, then he selected a bottle from which to take a healthy sip.

The Consort donned his robe and sat down abruptly with his eyes downcast, adjusting to hide the softening erection. He didn't look at the mirror again though he would have seen me climbing down from the wardrobe if he had.

"She will not wake for the rest of the rest cycle," he murmured. "You may leave safely, Red Sister."

Near the bed I leaned over, looking at Curgia's face and her form in repose, my fingers dipped into my sleep powder I could blow over her face if her eyes fluttered. She was down for the time, motionless and deep in Reverie. I removed my fingers and cinched my pouch again, dusting off my gloves.

"How often does this happen?" I asked, trying to control that concerning anger in my chest.

Auslan shrugged, his hands resting still in his lap. "Every few cycles, when she dreams of the Abyssal ritual the Priestess put her through yet manages to tear her out of Reverie. She is convinced sex with me helps her sleep peacefully. I cannot convince her otherwise, so at least I know a sleep spell that works on her."

I quirked my brow and stepped toward him. His gaze lifted to the mirror and watched me warily, though I stopped while a few steps from him. I noticed the finger-shaped bruises on his neck were already fading.

"You know about the Conceiver's ritual, too?"

Auslan nodded, his neck a bit stiff. "I knew from the beginning that you had not caused the miscarriage as Wilsira claimed. I did not find that kind of damage when I examined her. I have, however, heard Curgia talking in her sleep. She had experienced something like a Priestess does when dreaming of the Abyss, seeing it, hearing it, one might as well be there, but she does not know how to tolerate it. Wilsira has … condemned her to a particularly cruel fate."

"And she looks to you as her healer and comfort," I commented.

"You wanted me to surprise you, Red Sister," the Consort said, turning around slowly in his seat to look directly at me. I saw a side of him that I hadn't seen before; an anger like cold iron, different from Shyntre's white hot flashes of temper.

It was the first time I was wary of him, even a little.

"Would it surprise you to know that something like this," he indicated the sleeping Mother-to-be, "is what could have happened to you had I not fought you? I could have made you addicted to me, as she is. You were vulnerable, thanks to whatever the Priestess had done to you. I could have not only given you my seed as you demanded but made you *long* for me far into your pregnancy. To a point you may forget who you had been."

Okay, yes, he had done it. He surprised me.

I shivered at what would have been a very effective punishment for my actions against him. "Did you see the stillborn? I must ask."

"I *held* it, Sister," he replied frankly. "And yes. She must have been Kerse's seed. A female."

Again, the bloodstone conversation came back. "Wilsira told Curgia it must be male, to feel the added power to her magic as she did."

The Consort shook his head. "Female. I saw it."

Shit.

"What happened to the — ? Uh, her?"

Auslan squeezed his eyes shut, disliking the memory behind his eyelids. "Shyntre offered to burn the body for the Matron. She accepted and wanted both of us as witness to convince the Priestess when she emerged from her chambers."

"And you omit nothing?" I asked. "You delivered the stillborn, you confirmed the demon's seed, and you watched Shyntre burn it alongside the Matron?"

"Yes, Red Sister. That is what happened."

"How did you heal Curgia?"

"A ... form of the ritual 'Braqth's Threshold,' " he murmured. "Only the 'dagger' wasn't metal. I made her fertile again after the Abyssal birth would have scarred her. Yes, she did conceive that same eve." He glanced with something approaching self-loathing at the bed. "But look at her now."

I held very still; my mind blanked of all following questions. I only had a thought.

*He **is** as powerful as a Priestess. Whether they made him to be or not.*

Yet he had no other place to go. He said he was only trying not to die as he grew older, with younger Consorts offered every Worship Ball to replace him. Surely there was some other role where we could use such buas? Except the Nobles were as likely to tear him apart fighting over him, like the healer-youth abducted last turn.

At my silence, the Consort said, "I am trying to bring Curgia back to something of what she was before Wilsira damaged her, but I'm not sure it is possible. You may have limited time to continue using me, Sister, and if you plan to target the Conceiver soon, then may our Goddess favor you in that fight. I do not know if this will benefit me or not, but it may not matter. I will tell you some things anyway."

I perked up and kept my mouth shut.

"Beware of any incense she lights, or any thought that doesn't seem your own in her presence. Also do not accept any token or article of clothing from her if you can help it. Her strength has been in mind bending but she needs some fluid from her target first, each time, as her element is in water. Kerse amplifies the effects when he's near, which he so often is."

Most of this I had experienced, but there was a level of unease in my middle when I thought again about that cloth I had lost, which had had both my blood and Kerse's semen on it. The search team had never found it, and even knowing it was a long shot, my Elder hadn't been happy about it.

"I see. Anything else?"

"There's a dungeon in the Sanctuary."

"Yes, I am aware."

"There is something else beneath it."

Silent, I tilted my head.

He said, "Do not go there, or let anyone take or lead you there."

I stared at him. "You're stoking my curiosity and expect me to ignore it? You won't say what's there?"

His fine, scarlet eyes looked around the room, back at the bed where Curgia hadn't moved a sliver, then back at me. "What is there is … where I was made. Only grown females and infants see it, and any female there who is not also a Priestess does not leave it again."

A swarm of creeps swept down my back. "A sub-room where you were … 'made'?"

He smiled, but it wasn't one of his beautiful smiles. It had the same slant tinged with bitterness as my wizard. "Consorts are not accidents of birth, Sister. I thought you knew that."

"Well, specialized breeding, yes," I replied.

"How the Priesthood and the Valsharess want all to see it. But have you wondered how Priestesses have additional sons *after* their Sathoet is born, after seeing the Conceiver's scars for yourself?"

I thought about the mad commoner in the city, the one ranting about a stolen Daughter fed to the Abyss, whom Wilsira ordered me to kill. *Daleina.*

"They're stealing commoners to ... bear for them?"

His mouth quirked upward but was too tired to make it. "Indeed. I am impressed, Red Sister."

"But how is that possible? Are Consorts commoners' sons, not Priestesses?"

He shook his head. "This, I genuinely don't know. But the truth is the Consorts like us are a new introduction to the Sanctuary's ceremonies. Three centuries, perhaps?"

Then my sisters, Jilrina and Kaltra, were among the first born as a result.

Rotten as they come.

I narrowed my eyes slightly as something odd struck me. "How are you able to talk about this? Did they not use a compulsion or a forgetting spell? I know how those work."

"Magic wears differently on us all over time, Red Sister," he said, sounding much older than two hundred and fifty. "There is always change, even with a Queen that aims for stagnation in the center of a maelstrom." He smiled again, and this one was more suited to his face. "I enjoy a waking dream where it may be one as young as you to bring a deep earthquake to Sivaraus. It needs it so. Although, we should never presume to do it alone."

Before I could truly absorb that, he said, "That is all I have to say, Red Sister. If you would, please bid me good eve? I am very tired."

Only when he said that did I realize that I was well past my check-in time for D'Shea. Yes, I needed to leave.

"Very well. Get some rest." I smirked. "Enoquis."

The Consort snorted, reaching for what I assumed was a bottle of wine set by the leg of his vanity. "Please, do not call me that. Of the last five names the Nobles have given me, I dislike this one most."

"What is your real name, then?"

"What is yours, Red Sister?" he returned smoothly with a wry smirk.

I considered a few things then. I would be going to the Sanctuary sooner rather than later, for certain before I went to the Surface. I had no idea if I would return from either place or, if I did, whether this particular Consort would even still be alive.

And if we succeed ... When we succeed, and Wilsira is brought down, this Consort's life will be one of many to change as a result.

And if I failed, I would have either much more or absolutely nothing to worry about, no matter how I answered this question right now.

"My name is Sirana, my Consort."

I grinned at his expression. I had surprised him. His eyes swept over my face and hair and figure, as if he was trying to decide if he could match a name with my appearance.

Finally he nodded. "A true pleasure, Sirana."

"And yours?"

He hadn't opened the wine bottle yet; he set it back down and shook his head gently. "Forgive me, I cannot tell you. It has power over me a bit like a Sathoet's name, though not as binding. But honestly, Sirana? I do treasure 'Auslan.' I consider it my own 'free' name, because neither the Priestesses nor the Nobles gave it to me. If I should never see you again, I can still take that with me. And I'm grateful."

I struggled to respond. He liked the name I'd chosen for him best. That did much to stroke my ego, and I smiled. It took a moment to recall I was late.

"Um ... I should go."

He nodded. "Of course."

"Care to give me a kiss for that Goddess's favor you mentioned earlier?" I teased, expecting yet another polite decline; I'd even lifted my boot to step backward to my exit.

Then he stood out of his chair.

I froze, the instant pulse of desire in my chest. I was sure he would have seen it light up if the room had been darker. Auslan leaned in to offer me his mouth — relaxed, soft, and slightly open — and I could not turn down the invitation.

He kept his hands out and open, and I cradled his face with my own gloved ones, tasting him deeply. It felt the same as when he had responded to me before, pressed trembling against the wardrobe yet somehow with an even greater intensity for *not* being trapped now.

It took all my willpower and some of his to step apart and keep it from going farther.

My Consort said, "May the Woven Webs trip up your rival, but Goddess grant that they glide harmless beneath your feet."

Although I did not tend to use them much myself, I smiled at the formal blessing.

I could leave now knowing that, of all the times he may or may not have been acting, that first kiss and this last one had been genuine.

Chapter 18

After sharing a secret with her compulsion still unbroken, D'Shea proved remarkably patient as we waited for Wilsira to ask for me. My Elder and I prepared together, planning and practicing, but she also had to focus on the other plans and plots spread out before her. There were too many from which to choose.

Elder Rausery stepped in more than once to nudge me about my Tower lessons as well, often speaking in that "Surface Common" language to see how well I understood her. One time, D'Shea was close enough to overhear and confront us.

"You'll not be sending her out, Rausery," my Elder growled. "I need her here."

The General smirked. "Always training, D'Shea, like you are. Red Sisters are never finished. She's more than suitable for the job."

"Stop poaching my novice. You're not going to find that missing Priestess after all this time. She must be dead."

"I wager you know as much about that as I know what you are next planning at Court."

"The Surface is not important enough to be draining our best resources on simple fascination."

"Something you and the Prime agree on. Amazing." The General grinned at D'Shea's expression, adding, "You know we wouldn't go at all without the Valsharess's approval. There's something there She wants."

"Oh? Has She asked for some Pale Elves to be brought back?"

"No, She hasn't."

Rausery offered nothing more, and D'Shea's mouth tightened. I stood there, looking at the ground, trying not to squirm. I *wanted* Rausery's mission, but I *knew* what no one else could about D'Shea's own struggles and chains. I knew our Elder had to be freed from the Priesthood, and Wilsira had to be stopped.

Maybe then, I could go to the Surface. I would keep practicing. Keep training.

Red Sisters are never finished.

"Whatever you're planning next, D'Shea, indulge me with a lesson per span for Sirana at the Tower," Rausery said. "You pick the time. Just keep her going back to Shyntre, he has his instructions. I'm not about to spring another Surface mission on you in the next turn, Sorceress, I can say that much, but this is as important. She needs broader training than whatever you're cooking."

D'Shea glanced at me, and my eyebrows lifted with obvious interest. I held my breath.

"Very well," she agreed, probably to avoid talking more about her "cooking." She gestured to me to come with her. "If you will excuse us, General."

Rausery shrugged like she didn't care one way or another, watching us leave with a lingering smirk on her face.

Wilsira Tachnathon waited for over half a turn before we heard from her through the Prime. In that time, Jael had earned her red uniform, we managed not to lose any Red Sisters to casualties, and in addition to my language lessons with the wizard, I made ever-increasing attempts to break wards without the help of my bracers.

I was motivated for both, learning to accept my fast-changing mind and the indescribable stress of the strongest wards Gaelan and D'Shea could set to test me. My performance was decent when nude but stronger wearing the blue pendant, where I suffered less aftereffects. In time, my

Elder saw me break one of Priestess-strength naked from will and mental training alone. She displayed a rare delight in my success, despite me collapsing and passing out afterward.

The Sorceress also instructed Lead Jaunda to make time to train me as a team with Gaelan, Reishel, and Jael as well. A welcome contrast, all physical, where I didn't have to think so much. I also thought D'Shea might be getting back at Rausery, snatching Jael away from her tasks as many times as I was sent back to the Tower.

It seemed like they were born to work together, one's expertise shoring up the other in a view which gathered the most factors of Davrin living I could think of, but I hadn't been a Red Sister long enough to tell if they disagreed on focus and tactics frequently with new, promising Sisters, or if it was just me and my fucked head.

★So, have you been sent to the Fringe?★ I asked my youngest Sister curiously during a brief rest.

I refrained from asking about the Dwarf stone or Tragar weapons with Gaelan and Reishel nearby, but Jael nodded and probably made the connection.

★Yeah, I'm more familiar than most. The Prime likes the reporting, too. I think she's planning to cull the Davrin laying low among them, but Rausery's keeping her from acting too fast.★

Jaunda glanced our way; she knew, but Jael had gotten the other two caught up quickly. Gaelan and Reishel paid attention.

★You don't wear your uniform, do you?★ the latter asked.

Jael signed a negative.

★And you aren't recognized as Aurenthin snatched by the Sisterhood?★ Gaelan added. ★I'd think you'd be known as a plant.★

Jael's mouth twisted a little, lifted a hand to reply, then Jaunda's heavy boots made noise in their approach. The Lead flicked Gaelan's and my ears in quick succession.

★Enough of that,★ she signed, throwing shut that trap door. ★If you're rested enough to gossip, you're ready to race to the next cavern and fight over who gets the water first.★

I'd long noticed Red Sisters had perfected the art of voiceless groaning, thanks to Jaunda.

Much of the cycle had passed, filled with endurance tests and drills, before we could rest again. My entire body ached, I'd passed by simple hunger marks ago, and my mouth wouldn't stay moist enough to tongue a clit without sticking. My three Sisters were in the same condition, and Jaunda smiled at us.

What the matter, caits? she signed. *Too many foot massages growing up?*

Jael snorted audibly, and the rest of us made a face. Even the pampered luxury I might have claimed was paid for in unwanted attention by vicious females.

Where'd you come from, Lead? I signed back, panting. *Did D'Shea carve you from sheer rock or something?*

Maybe. She winked. *I know I'm fucking hard for your ass right now, novice.*

Uh-oh. Pucker up, then?

The appearance of her normal, booming laughter performed in silence made me smile, and my other three Sisters relaxed into the banter. It was a good sign of a team; I knew it in my gut. We didn't have someone here who would stab us in the back to get ahead. I couldn't think of anywhere else in Sivaraus where I might find that.

Our Lead was serious about getting off before we headed back, however, and she clearly had a preference as she took my arm.

Keep watch, you three, Jaunda ordered the others as she pulled me away.

Before a cluster of heartbeats passed, I stood gripping the nearest rock wall with my belt off and leathers down, cloak swept to one side as Jaunda spread my cheeks and soon had her Feldeu seated full length in my ass. Given how thirsty I was, I was grateful she carried a vial of slippery oil and decided to use it this time.

Jaunda reached around and took hold of my sex with her full gloved grip, nuzzling my ear as she panted and fucked me. Quick and hard, with minimal noise.

My blood roared in my ears; my lips pursed tight as she nipped my nape and sucked in my scent through her nose. I suppressed my moans by necessity, not desire, as my body loosened up and opened to her, as my netherlips plumped up in her hand and grew damp with each jolt.

I had a moment to reflect how well she'd trained me to enjoy this from her. But only from her.

Because she had never really hurt me doing it.

"Aw, yeah ..."

I heard her barest whisper, and it made me sweat. A tremor passed through her as she got close. It wouldn't take long. It couldn't.

~*Yes ... my Lead. Fuck me ... !*~ I begged in my head.

She responded like she heard me, biting where my neck met my shoulder to stay silent as she managed five more hard thrusts before holding her oily Feldeu still, deep in my asshole as she shuddered. I felt pleasure like a warm bath wash all along my back, rising to the back of my head, despite not peaking myself, and I shivered against her as well.

I had the sense that several minds were focused on us. A couple not my Sisters.

Cheering Jaunda on. They recognize her.

I sucked in air, eyes coming open as I looked around the dark, quiet cavern at what little I could see. There was nothing yet, and I waited until the Feldeu was out to quickly right my uniform and arm myself, trying to find that spot again where I thought I'd sensed the others.

Jaunda tilted her head, still catching her breath with soiled cock poking out. ★What's down?★

I hesitated as I glanced at the other three standing watch. Nothing held their attention. Should I say someone might have been watching us fuck? Suggest we spread out to search? How would I have been the one to notice when the other three didn't have someone breathing in her ear as her netherhole got reamed?

Don't tell anyone. Not even a Sister.

★Nothing,★ I signed. ★Thought I heard something, but it's gone now.★

It was true enough. Maybe I'd imagined it in my heated state. Or sensed her own fuck-dream instead. I couldn't be sure.

Jaunda glanced at our temporary bodyguards, saw Jael and Reishel shrug, and smirked, working to wipe herself down and putting her cock away in her pants without detaching it. It poked up through the band in this state.

Time's done, she announced. *Back to the Cloister.*

She made us run halfway, but it was too far to reach the end before collapse if we didn't stop. I enjoyed the more leisurely walk as we reentered familiar territory. Never an excuse for a Red Sister to let her guard down completely, but we fast approached methods for summoning backup if we needed it. My confidence rose again, and I chose to nudge my Lead again, just to see what happened.

If we've had enough of the Fringe, I signed where all my Sisters could read, *what about Low Gate?*

Jaunda shrugged. *What about it?*

I learned House Thalluen has deep trader links there, too, I signed, *which the Conceiver is interested in somehow. They somehow produce scraps of scrolls with the mages' language on them which don't come from the Palace. Story seems to go back a while, to the time of the current Matron's Mother, perhaps.*

My Lead cuffed me at the back of my head. Rightly so.

Coy ass, she somehow growled with her hand, glaring at me.

I smiled. *Look who's signing, Lead.*

The glare turned into that familiar smirk, and she glanced at the others who had their eyes glued to the conversation. She mouthed, "Fuck you," as she considered what to say. She didn't have to say anything.

I know that way leads to the Black Dragon's territory, she signed. *I've seen the drakes hopping around when something weird is happening to the pulse of the Deepearth. It doesn't surprise me if 'scraps' are showing up in trade to tempt and fuck with the mages here. Especially greedy Priestesses. Even the Valsharess.*

She smirked, continuing, *Serves them right thinking they got that under control. None of us were born the last time he was awake, but I heard stories growing up. Everyone else in Sivaraus seems to have forgotten about him. The stories went away.*

My eagerness showed.

★You are from Low Gate?★ I guessed. ★Or near it?★

Jaunda nodded. ★How I made connection with the late Matron Thalluen, by odd luck. It was the start of getting me out of the slum, though the Prime and Rausery had to be pointed that way first, how I understood it.★

★Pointed that way? By whom?★

My Lead waggled her eyebrows. ★Who do you think, novice?★

★D'Shea found you in Low Gate?★

★Because of your Grand Matron, yeah. I know you figured out she has a link with your family, though we're not talking about that.★

I exchanged looks with Gaelan and the others, although her expression was the one most intense. She looked like she wanted to say something but didn't. Then Jaunda's hand struck out, her palm slapping my ass hard and making me jump. We all cringed at the noise in the quiet dark, and our Lead laughed.

Aloud.

"Hope it was worth it, caits," she said. "This time, you won't stop until you're all in the sluicers lined up naked, legs wide, and bending over for inspection. Now *move!*"

We moved.

THE PRIME HAD ACCEPTED THE SUMMONS FROM THE SANCTUARY ON MY BEHALF.

"Seems you're gaining a rep as a Sathoet Soother, Sirana," the eldest Sister chortled in the briefing. "Unlike the little Aurenthin scrapper who hates their guts."

She reached down and rubbed herself through her leathers, either not noticing or not caring that we saw it, the Elders and me.

"What would you have me do, Prime?"

"Let the Conceiver figure out the best place for you. The Sisters don't get an inside look at their little breeding hive unless it's been to squeeze one out herself."

The Prime glanced at D'Shea. It was so brief I nearly missed it. I would remember how her eyes had narrowed in contemptible enjoyment of the remark. Even if D'Shea had wanted to say something, she couldn't. She maintained her poise instead. Not even she knew if the Prime understood why she didn't.

The Prime finished quickly. "I could use an updated map of who sleeps where. Priestesses and a headcount of the youths they've got now. Consorts, if you can find them but they're low priority."

"Yes, Prime."

Just a map and a headcount?

She has no idea.

Later, D'Shea had given me a different set of objectives. She couldn't manage it without Reishel, though, and me wearing her Feldeu, buried in my Sister's slit. It was the only way to quickly "spin up" our auras and let them merge again.

So I could hear her thoughts again.

Focus on Kerse but watch for any opportunity. Try to find proof I can use. Don't get trapped. If you find nothing this time, we can try again. Just come back.

~Yes, Elder.~

I triple-checked my equipment and went over again what details D'Shea was able in words or signs after the link broke. More than I had known before, enough to satisfy the Prime if I had no time to make that map or take that headcount.

Lelinahdara met me at the Sanctuary's back entrance when I arrived, same as before. She wore her purple robes and her silver jewelry on her hands and around her neck, her ears pierced with the usual studs and delicate chains and dangles, but she was not wearing her headpiece or her ceremonial dagger. She looked relaxed and casual, though the green of her eyes glinted with sharp cunning as she resealed the door behind me.

"Welcome once again, young Sister," she said with a smile.

"Priestess." I bowed.

"Wilsira is unavailable at this very moment, but she will be pleased to meet you on the fourth floor."

The fourth had been of several floors that we'd skipped the last time I was here, my having been guided into a subtle jump circle that went from the blue Third Floor to the Sathoet chamber on the Twelfth.

More recently, Qivni had taken me from Third to Sixth, where Wilsira's bedchambers were. Perhaps the Conceiver also having space right above the children's floor made an amount of sense.

"As you wish it, Priestess."

We passed the main purple floor, then the gold one, and my ears automatically strained for sounds of children with the third blue floor. I did not hesitate as before.

The Fourth floor was red. Not the blood-red of the Sisters, but a lighter, more playful red, as if blood had been mixed with a little white and the barest touch of blue, lightened to a delicate yet excited color.

The expected tapestries and decorations were all erotic, pieces of art that celebrated and glorified the swollen belly and the act which led to it. I inhaled at the scents, then did so again more deeply than I should.

Shit. Careful.

The perfume of the place could have one's head spinning in a few ticks. Some of it was manufactured — whether by magic or mundane skill — but another layer of it reminded me strongly of Auslan's scent near his neck. It was sweet and made my mouth water.

"Why have me wait for the Conceiver on the Consorts' floor, Leli-nahdara?" I asked without much amusement.

Tarra smiled at me. "A gift. You are not one to spurn divine gifts, are you, Sirana?"

I hesitated to reply. My spine itched, and I thought about Qivni's "gift," and Shyntre being there to make sure her cunt was properly blocked while the Consort-in-training took her ass. My aggravating, educated wizard wasn't here now.

I wished he was.

"Whom should I thank?" I asked. "You or the Conceiver?"

"That is best revealed after I see your response."

I squinted at her, trying to read a face as evasively beautiful as D'Shea's could be. Especially when it was clear in those emerald eyes that she plotted something fierce.

Like everyone in this 'hive.'

"Wait here while I inform Wilsira," Tarra said, straightening her back, lifting her breasts. "Look around at the art, if you like, but, oh … you know the Consorts are off limits, correct?"

I stared at her, trying to see the jest. Or did she know?

"Yes, Priestess. I know."

Her smile turned a little sour. "And you did not bring a Feldeu, I trust?"

"No, Priestess. Not part of my issued equipment."

"Show me."

I opened my cloak and held it out of the way so she could see my belt from all angles, and she nodded.

"Excellent. Then you are as safe as they are."

My cloak dropped back into place. *Drider fucking shit.*

"I shall only be a moment, Red Sister."

"Thank you, Priestess. I shall wait."

I turned away as she left in a swish of silk, my eyes drifting to a small portrait of a young bua with piercing gold eyes. Moving closer I studied it, wondering if this was a "real-to-life" Consort or a painter's imagination.

The only Davrin I had ever seen with eyes close to this color was the Queen Herself, but as a translucent yellow and orange, like a tawny copper but without the metallic sheen. The Davrin in the portrait had eyes like the true metal mined from the rock.

Strange.

I drifted farther down the warm colors of the hallway, finding it easy to admire the masculine beauty and posing, as well as the images of rutting. Many images of pregnant females as well, worshipped and pampered for the blessed weight in their womb.

After my trip with Wilsira and Kerse, after learning of D'Shea's confession and being able to imagine what had probably happened to Daleina's abducted Daughter from Auslan's own mouth, the swollen bellies did not look glorious to me.

They looked …

Damned.

Soft music and a quiet drone of voices arose the longer I studied the art. It was coming from a larger room at the end, before the hall bent to the right. There were four other closed doors, but this one was open, and candlelight spilled out into the hall. The first order I followed by indulging my curiosity, ironically, was the Prime's.

The young male Davrin did not hear me or realize I was there as I sneaked up and peeked around the frame. The sight was as beautiful, as one might expect. Four nubile bodies dressed to appeal to the feminine eye, so much clean skin and well-groomed, pure white hair.

But also very odd.

They were languishing, idle, and entertained easily with mirrors. Their eyes were vacant. Docile. Most Davrin around this age would be searching for something to do, perhaps pacing if kept in a room for a long time. They should be eyeing each other to gauge the entertainment value of any sort of reaction. They were not.

The contrast to Auslan was strong; his matured experience and his interactions with the outside world appeared in his stance, his every move, expression, and change that showed in those eyes. Did all Consorts grow into what Auslan had become with time? Not for certain, perhaps. What was it he'd said about Shyntre?

We are not encouraged to think too much. Or to read. Even though I was older than him by half a century, the son of your Elder Sorceress possessed thoughts which were challenging. And in time, I awoke to see how mine were … not.

These new, young adults before me had the spirit of domestic livestock, so it was not hard to believe my Consort about Shyntre, who must have appeared a firebrand by comparison. But would the wizard's anger and resistance to obeying have so affected one Consort but not all of them? It implied something unusual about Auslan as well, even if I didn't know how he tasted.

"Who is there?"

After my lingering so long, one of the Consorts had sensed my presence. I did not retreat but stepped out boldly where they could see me, and the reaction made me want to laugh aloud. Their shocked gasps collided with each other and, to a one, the buas looked so prettily frightened.

Only one of them looked at another door at the back of the room. I could have stopped him, but I let him escape through the door and to whatever safety he could find.

Of the remaining three lovelies, two were frozen to their couch and the last was nervous but fascinated. He placed his hands on either side of him, his body language open and non-threatening as I'd seen in Auslan, posing, with no attempt to cover the erection beneath his wrap.

"What are you?" he asked.

I recognized his voice; he had been the one to call me out. It was smooth and tender; I could bet he might also sing to arrest an audience at the altar. He had perfect hair and skin, his eyes closely resembling the main body of a candle flame in color.

"A guardian. What are you?"

The young bua blinked. "A Consort?"

He had mimicked my own answer, wanted my approval. I nodded, and he relaxed.

"Do you have a name, Consort?"

His mouth opened to answer, then his throat constricted. His face showed a sharp discomfort that surprised and frightened him, and he gasped for air when his throat opened again. Memories of that same pain and sickness, that forced silence, rushed back and I ground my teeth.

"N- ... no, no, guardian," he gasped, slowly recovering. "I have no name but what you give me."

Auslan could have told me his name. He chose not to.

A youth who had been frozen on the couch suddenly thawed and gave a muffled cry, hissing at his nest brother. "Stop talking to her. She's not a Priestess!"

"She was sent here." The bolder one glanced at him then back at me. "*Were* you sent to us, guardian?"

I smiled a bit. "Yes. Lelinahdara let me in."

The other two buas relaxed a bit more, and the bolder Consort looked their way, biting his lip and lifting fine, elegant eyebrows in question. I wondered what had passed between them when the bolder one stood up and approached me on bare, sensitive feet. He stopped a few paces away and smoothly removed his wrap, letting it drop to the floor.

I was struck both by the sudden nudity and his overall form displaying every sign of health and desirable beauty if a cait sought a suitable sire. His scent seemed to grow stronger, and I drank it in, wanting one more sniff.

His motions showed nothing but grace and sensuality, his sex blatantly ready. He caressed his pole in that gentle way which could not be mistaken. He offered it to me, asking without words that I decide when to claim it.

For Braqth's sake, I did not know what to do.

Off limits.

"Are you here for a child?" he asked.

No. Absolutely not.

"Possibly," I murmured. "Have you fulfilled such requests before?"

The Consort nodded. "Though none have looked as you do, guardian, or come in alone."

"Here?"

"Well —"

His brothers hissed behind him.

"Stop talking!"

"They can hear you!"

The nude Consort turned his head slightly and nodded then as he finally agreed. In place of answering questions, he moved closer and reached for me. I blocked his fine hands from reaching anything near my belt, pushing them to the side without taking hold of him.

"What are you doing?" My voice was thick.

"I will help you undress," the Consort said patiently. "Though you may have to instruct me. I have never seen this clothing before. The others were undressed already."

"Were they?" I said hoarsely.

He nodded, blinked those wide eyes. "Will you kiss me, guardian? I miss that part when they are sleeping."

The Consort moved this time to touch my face, and I wanted to let him. If he smelled this good, how would he taste? Of course I would kiss him when I had him underneath—

His touch set every nerve I had on fire; there was a flash inside my head. It was like a ward, warning me not to move yet welcoming me home. I had only to give in, to let myself fall.

Let him touch me. Let all of them touch me, if they wish. Kneel ... and open up. Honor Braqth with your willing wombs, Daughters.

In my memory, I kneeled once again upon the floor of the Sanctuary, in the center of that ritual orgy. Complete loss of control. Broken order. Then so much like now, except for one more thing.

Unlike the Noble buas who'd been dragged in that swarm with me, I could feel the thoughts of this one. The Consort genuinely, and innocently, believed that I would never leave. That I belonged here.\

And that I would soon be carrying a baby.

His touch felt like Darkness.

Hastily, I formed a shield inside my head and hurled my body backward out into the hall, bumping into the tapestry on the far wall. The Consort was startled as well and skittered farther into his room, staring at me wide-eyed through the open doorway.

"Mother? What have I done?"

I couldn't answer. Trembling. *No words for this.*

I shook my head and stalked down the blushing hallway toward the main foyer, my breath unsteady, my brain buzzing. I was sure he had meant "Mother" as an honorary title, but it sounded so strange. I wasn't his Mistress or a Priestess. Did he see me as someone his Priestesses had only one purpose for?

A Davrin cait to be made into a Mata, an expectant Mother.

The adult females never leave.

Auslan was telling the truth. May I hop by my big toe upon the head of a needle if he wasn't. But this wasn't the sub-room beneath the dungeon he described. It didn't happen here.

The healer feels nothing like this one. What is wrong with them?

I reached the end of the hall, able to breathe a bit easier. I carried yet more knowledge which wasn't proof for my Elder. Where could I find *proof?*

The Liaison stepped out of a dark shadow and made me jump. I hissed a curse that edged toward blasphemous then added, "Forgiveness, Priestess."

Tarra was smiling; she enjoyed seeing me shaken. "You didn't taste him, did you?"

"Fuck, no!"

"Very good, Sirana."

"Have *you*, Priestess? Is he yours?"

Her mouth twitched; her green eyes sharp. "Why would you ask that?"

"Or does the Conceiver own *all* Consorts?" I continued, deflecting that. "I watched her give them all away at the Worship Ball."

The Liaison's gaze narrowed a little. "Hm. I am genuinely impressed you broke the Consort's touch so readily. How did you do it?"

"And if I hadn't been able?" I asked instead, incensed.

"I would have commanded him to step away. I was watching. How is it you resisted him?" She winked. "Does the Tragar not like him?"

Now *my* eyes narrowed. "Nice try, Liaison. I know my Elder updated you. That part is faded away, along with your ritual."

"Yet I overheard the Conceiver herself say how resistant you are to will-bending. You've offered her a challenge she hasn't seen in a few hundred years. Otherwise you'd not be here."

"My request to train, Priestess," I said. "My focus. After being on your altar, I'm motivated to learn how to resist all of that."

Never mind that not even Qivni or D'Shea could resist forever once wrapped inside a Priestess's web.

Tarra's face changed; it was sympathetic. "After what your sister did to you, this only makes sense. Need I remind you again I am not your enemy?"

"You tried to tempt me just now, Priestess."

The Liaison nodded. "Before Wilsira does. Which she will. Giving you a warning would have spoiled the knowledge you gained. The real response. Was that bua not strange to you?"

We studied each other warily, and I said nothing.

I had a very good idea what had happened to Qivni at a wave of Wilsira's hand.

Was this "Confessor" trying the same thing on me? Not to make me catch but to learn a new vulnerability before Wilsira found me?

Probably. But she might also be offering an aim toward proof. I asked no more questions, however, because the answers would only be self-serving. Shyntre was right about that.

"I'll see the Conceiver now, Lelinahdara," I said.

Her mouth ticked up with grace. "Very well. Follow me."

CHAPTER 19

THE CONCEIVER HADN'T BEEN ON THE FOURTH FLOOR; THAT HAD BEEN A LIE. Tarra led me to the Sixth floor without commenting on this, and neither did I.

Unlike the first time I had caught the Conceiver busily packing her trunks to leave, Wilsira lounged in her spacious quarters, enjoying them to their fullest. A selection of fine finger foods lay on a tray awaiting her attention, her large bed was still rumpled, the silken sheets unmade, and incense had been lit.

I'd swallowed the first dose of a concoction D'Shea had given me to slow any sedative effects, now that she knew a bit more how the airborne drug affected me. I'd taken this, and a prevention draught. Just in case.

From the level of humidity in the air and other things, Wilsira had recently taken a long, hot bath. Her gold-streaked hair was loose and hung down to her waist, still damp but brushed straight. She wore a comfortable lounge robe and matching slippers — purple threaded with gold and silver, of course — and wore none of her jewelry. She sat at her vanity with her back blatantly to me, though she could see me in her mirror.

I might also guess that Kerse had bathed as well, given the way his mane was spiking in clumps as if it, too, were very damp. The mental image made me smile; had they both been primping for their new arrival? Not likely. Tarra probably knew they were busy and took me on that side-tour to fill the time.

Better than my walking in on them in the bath together.

"Ah, here she is," Kerse's Mother said, standing up and turning to face me. The cleavage of her full, dark breasts within her robe was on blatant display as she took a deep breath of the scented air, maroon eyes glimmering in the candlelight. "Thank you, Tarra. You are dismissed."

Not even an announcement this time. The Liaison bowed, a little stiff, and glanced at me as if trying to tell the future. Tarra didn't seem to have any greater idea than I did when she left.

Wilsira glided by me on bare, silent feet, hips swaying as she checked the door. Kerse crouched still as a statue and paid me no attention, looking elsewhere amid the many pretty things. The Priestess came up behind me; my boots upon the plush carpet didn't move but I turned my ear toward her, seeing her from the corner of my eye.

She adjusted one breast, lifting its weight briefly in her left palm. "How have these past quad-spans been for you, young Sister?"

"Challenging, Conceiver, thank you."

"I've heard you have been taking lessons at the Tower," she said.

I waited, letting the silence stretch.

"Are Rausery and Varessa fighting again?"

I unstuck my mouth. "I don't understand, Conceiver."

How had she heard? Had she cornered Shyntre and forced the wizard to talk?

"It's rare that the Elders want the same novice for wildly different tasks so soon," she said, moving up and around me like a prowler, so we could meet eyes. I watched her mouth instead. "But then, there is something unusual about you. I'm glad the ancient Order of the Sisterhood hasn't grown so dull at *all* ranks as to fail to see it."

Heh.

"I may have to toss my case before the Valsharess as well. I do not want to see you trudge up top so soon. Sivaraus still needs you."

My tiny smile vanished. Not what I wanted to hear upon first stepping in this room, but what had I expected? No protest I considered would have an effect, and no clever retort came to mind. I stayed silent, and perhaps it surprised and annoyed her a little after chattering pleasantries so long with my Mother.

"What were you told was the purpose of this summons?" she asked.

"That you wanted me to work with the Sathoet somehow, Conceiver."

"Indeed. That is exactly so."

Wilsira's son finally moved out of the corner of my eye. It took every drop of willpower to stay focused on his Mother. She watched me without blinking.

"You remember the first three in the chamber, I presume," she said with a little smirk.

The three surrounding me. Hissing, yellow eyes glowing. One with his tongue darting between my open legs as soon as my pants came down, each jerking his rod until they spewed all over me.

"Yes, Priestess, I remember."

Wilsira had not expected it to happen that way, that I held my defense yet allowed them to play — not unlike her own Kerse during my trials. The Conceiver hadn't been sure she could control the entire host of them if the Sathoet went any farther with me. I'd seen fear on her face and had wagered even then that she had never indulged with any other except her son.

That was why she had commanded them to stop, and why we left so quickly. So she could return to him.

I didn't like the smile on her face.

"The Prime and I agree," said the Conceiver, "that another Red Sister with a skill like Qivni's to manipulate the demonbloods, but as a non-mage, would be in order."

Why in the Deepearth would you want that?

"A balance in power beneath the Valsharess to manage the city," she continued, perhaps reading my face. "That is the long-standing agreement between the Sisterhood and the Sanctuary."

"How long?" I asked.

Her brow quirked. "Far longer than my life, little Sister, and I am seven times your senior. How much farther back would it matter?"

Well. Surely even the Valsharess had a Mother at some point.

I felt warmth between my breasts then. I kept my mouth closed and nodded. "And you want to train me with the Sathoet?"

"Yes. Sirana. I am ready to teach you."

Trying to snatch some demons' sons from your sisters?

She didn't react. I was relieved.

I asked aloud, "Do the other Priestesses agree?"

Wilsira chuckled, a pure indulgent sound. "Why would we? We didn't agree that Qivni learn, but she paid the cost for her Prime. As shall you. It is always an even trade with your Eldest."

"Will I know the cost in advance?"

Besides my ass?

The corners of her mouth tilted up and her eyes glinted like a stalking spider about to jump. "No one does, Red Sister. Not even the Divine Daughters of Braqth. This is for the Valsharess. Serving Her is why we exist."

When convenient and adds more power.

"Yes, Priestess."

Wilsira looked away, considering her next step. She couldn't hear any of my thoughts. I tried not to smile.

"Give me a moment to dress. Keep my son company, won't you?"

"Is he coming with us to the Sathoet chamber?"

Wilsira tilted back her back and laughed, her sensual backside outlined by her thin robe. "He certainly isn't! He tends to start fights with his brothers if any get too close to me. He shall stay here, won't you, my bua?"

"Yess, Motherrr," Kerse rumbled.

Finally, I had the excuse to look at him as the Conceiver walked away.

He watched me, yellow eyes glowing subtly. I believed he would start a fight in the Sathoet chamber above us; he was ready for one.

His white mane had dried more and was starting to rise along his spine as it did when he felt threatened. His lip was curled back on one side. I detected more heat coming off him, could smell his musk even from where I stood. His long arms reached out, and clawed fingers lightly touched the ornate carpet; he crept forward, toward me.

Uh-oh.

When I stepped back, Kerse paused, lifting one gnarled finger to the front of his mouth. He didn't move his lips to shush — perhaps because he couldn't — but I recognized the child's sign for quiet. We didn't blink, and he crept forward again. The sapphire pendant burned at my skin, and I didn't know why.

~*What do you want?*~

*Can helllp ... *

~*Help how? With what?*~

Getting hurrrt by goets.

~*Goets?*~

*Brrotherrs ... *

Kerse had closed the distance as I stood there, my limbs frozen. He stood up straight in front of me — *so tall!* — no longer crouching or crawling. His erection was plain and large through his green groin wrap.

I looked up at his face, into his eyes again, and saw his mental image of me bent over while he humped between my ass cheeks, until he sprayed his seed and scent all over my dark buttocks and swollen crotch.

Afterward, he would rub it in with his palm until it was tacky, mostly dry.

I would stink to all the others in that chamber. I wouldn't be pressed to the floor and gang-fucked, as the Conceiver had expected to happen the first time. As she wanted to *watch*. She expected failure, and there was an infirmary one floor down, on the Fifth, if I needed tending afterward.

~*No ... Not here. Not first thing.*~

To be so vulnerable to multiple Priestesses after taking multiple Sath-oet? At least Jael had been dragged back to the Cloister by the Elders to recover!

Bennnd overrr.

Elders help me, I removed my belt and kept it close to my chest as I bent over the nearest table. Kerse wasted not a moment; he stood behind me, pushed my cloak to one side, and tugged my pants loose as he had several times before. He pushed them down swiftly.

His cock was long and scalding hot between my bare buttocks, sliding along my netherlips. I gasped at how good it felt, and he reached to cover my mouth with his palm, long fingers extended across my cheek and sharp points resting along the edge of my left jaw.

*Quiet … *

~Oh, Goddess — ~

Biting back his growls, his phallus caressed my swelling slit lengthwise first, his tip pointed at the floor, an intense texture along the ridge of his glans grazing my nub in brief shocks.

~Argh! Tease!~

Then he reversed direction and teased my netherhole from his tip to his base, his dribbling cock now pointed above my lower back as he fucked between my ass cheeks, exactly as he'd imagined himself doing.

He humped me quickly, anxious to get off, enveloping me in his scent and eager lust. Given the proximity, I waited eagerly for him to slip into a hole to speed things up; I vaguely wondered which he'd choose.

He never dipped so much as a finger-width inside.

*Rrrr, yesss! … *

I lost his body heat, felt my own sweat start to chill along with my frustration as he leaned back to aim his cock. He painted my buttocks with his cum, sure to get both sides and my crotch. Then he rubbed it into my skin, into my pubic fur where he gave it a little tug.

I hadn't climaxed at all.

~Fuck! Don't stop — ~

Dress. Motherrr.

Yes, damn it all. She was coming.

Kerse wrapped up his quivering erection, and I pulled up my leathers, secured them and my belt as he kept watch. I wiped the scowl from my face as soon as Wilsira stepped out of her bedroom door. I petted the crouching Sathoet's mane as he whined his usual greeting to her.

"My pretty bua," she said with affection, glancing with arched brow at my hand in the coarse white hair. "I shall be back soon."

That first time I went to the Sathoet chamber with Wilsira, leaving her son behind. I mostly thought about finishing what we started. I didn't want the other Sathoet in front of me. Those all around me. And they knew it.

It was clear to me they were young and didn't know how to use their dicks.

I wanted *him* to do it.

"YOU MUST FOCUS IF WE ARE TO TRY AGAIN NEXT EVE," THE CONCEIVER scolded me. "This is dangerous."

I nodded. "I'm not afraid, Priestess."

"Indeed, you aren't." Her eyes narrowed. "A foolish trait in most."

I shrugged. "I don't think it went poorly."

"You didn't succeed in controlling a single one."

"Yes, but I'm also still clothed."

Wilsira almost smiled, covering it with a roll of her eyes. "A great deal of touch and go. You confirmed for me that you see each magical son as a type of 'ward,' for lack of better imagery, and you press your will on him as such. But you can only focus on one at a time and another can easily distract you."

Closer to the truth than Lelinahdara had gotten so far.

"Well, I also haven't yet learned to take on multiple wards at once, Priestess."

Could any Red Sisters even do that?

"That is why I am here." Now, Wilsira grinned. "I *know* it's possible with the right aptitude. And you have it. You *must* be taught."

"Thank you, Priestess."

How long would I be trapped here this time? How long would I go without Reverie? Would I get a moment alone to discover anything to help D'Shea?

The answer to the last was, "No."

With the Conceiver and her son present, I witnessed more strange sights and interactions that cycle; I met more Priestesses than ever I would care to. Wilsira would subtly question them about the last time they had used their Sathoet's magic and allowed me to listen to their answers, but I disliked that three of those Priestesses remarked both on my unusual blue eyes and how I looked like Matron Thalluen.

Why do you remember my Mother? Why does it matter?

I was claustrophobic in the Sanctuary, even more than when I'd been sharing the guest rooms at the Noble Houses with this same Priestess. Nothing surpassed that very first unsettling interaction with the youngest Consort, but I could not stop imagining being forced to stay here for two solid turns to carry and birth a child.

I was right in thinking that it would be among my worse fates, whether it proved temporary or not.

The Sanctuary was behind closed doors, shut tight, and felt like it was some place outside the Deepearth. Sounds and smells that I couldn't always identify seemed to occur randomly, coming from nowhere, and the energy was unpredictable, always humming and surrounding the rooms and hall and bodies.

I could get lost here, like I could in the spy ways without regular practice.

There was also the unusual quiet; a shushed, depressive feeling that sapped my spirit and dissuaded me from maintaining my reflexes. It did not seem to affect everyone equally, but it was noticeable to me.

If D'Shea had been here before, I could see even her strong will being at the Priestess's mercy. It would have slowly worn her down, as it would me. Eventually.

I can't stay.

Kerse had given me a few signals that he wanted to couple if we could get alone again and, Web wrap me, *that* was the familiar dose of excitement I wanted to wake me up.

I had felt his aura before but had only come to learn what this meant after D'Shea had tutored me more about it and the aftermath of that ritual that had nearly killed Curgia. When the Conceiver tried a few times to push at my mental defenses outside the demonblood chamber, her own Sathoet's magic seemed … suppressed.

He was not helping her. Whatever the Sathoet wanted, he did not want me by *any* means, mentally incapacitated or otherwise drugged.

I tried to follow Auslan's advice, refusing offers of tokens or clothing and being careful about personal liquids around the Priestess. The third cycle without sleep saw me no closer to grabbing any evidence I could use, but I did finally have an opportunity to slip into a small storeroom to be alone.

I hoped the quiet would soothe my pounding head.

It didn't last long.

Without the door opening and letting in any torchlight from the hallway, Kerse was there, and he put his arms around me, scenting and licking my clean skin as we stood. I had finally taken a bath, cleansing off the stale semen, but hadn't taken a preventative.

Shit.

"Goet chammberr again," he whispered. *"Thiss eve."*

Drider shit.

This would be the third time.

Turning around to face the wall, I removed my belt while the Sathoet pulled down my leathers, greatly familiarity by now. Braced on my elbows, I rested my fevered forehead against the cool stone, and Kerse knelt behind me, parting my buttocks. He began lapping from clit to pucker. I relaxed into it as much as I could.

"You going to leave me wanting again?" I murmured.

I hadn't found time to get off, despite everything. I'd never been so aching.

He slobbered on his own palm and wetted his cock nicely as he stood up. He leaned close to my ear. *"Wannnt me?"*

I shifted my feet wider, presented my ass in answer. He squeezed a buttock with his dry hand, spread it, and I felt the tip nudge around my netherhole.

I smirked. "Not going to try to breed me?"

"No viall, yesss?"

He pushed. The tip burrowed in, stretching me.

~*Ungh! Goddess, yes!*~

He popped back out.

~*Fffff — argh!*~

Pushing again, his thumb kept me open to watch it sinking in. He didn't even threaten to put it in my vulnerable cunt.

"We don't have much time," I whispered.

He responded to that, sliding a bumpy, non-Davrin cock deep into my body, reaching around to hold my mound while he plundered me. He was very wide, and rough toward the base. We didn't have time for the bulge to be worked in.

He came in my ass, squirting a full load that would leak out as I faced his "brothers" soon after. His spunk would help keep them wrinkling their muzzles; they would back off whenever they got anywhere near my crotch.

Wilsira called him then, and Kerse had pulled out and vanished.

Leaving me empty without peaking again.

Chapter 20

"You're doing well with the Sathoet, Red Sister. The Prime will be pleased with your progress when I tell her."

"Thank you, Priestess."

"But you do need to rest. And your uniform is becoming ripe. It must be washed."

"Th' cantrips aren't enough?"

Her nose wrinkled. "They can only go so far, Red Sister."

I'd been here before.

Wilsira smiled. "Why don't you use my bath and rest on my bed while we have your uniform tended?"

I shook my head. "No, Conceiver, that's ... disrespectful."

"Far more disrespectful to refuse."

Her voice was chilly.

"Not allowed," I mumbled. "Must tend my equipment, Priestess."

Not that I couldn't do without the extra weight and count. None of the stimulants worked as well as they had.

"Just this once, Sirana. Just this once. I won't tell the Prime."

How long had I been here? I should have left before now. I should have seen what was happening and simply escaped the Sanctuary while I had the strength. Fuck the Prime, D'Shea and Rausery knew what went on here, they would have helped me …

Wilsira's hand covered my glove. Her voice was soothing. "Come, little cait. I am astonished you're even still conscious."

She leaned over, took my arm, tried to pull me up. I resisted getting out of my chair. Only a slight delay.

With a chuffing noise, she motioned to Kerse, who came up behind me and slipped his large hands underneath my pits. He lifted me out of my chair with little effort, putting me on my feet and pushing gently against my back.

"Sleeeep," he murmured.

Same trap. Very simple. Very patient and spider-like. Her only mistake last time had been bringing Shyntre with us. Otherwise, it would have worked.

~Help me. Help me!~

When we stepped into the Conceiver's opulent suite, the same Consort once offered to Qivni was now lying upon the well-made luxury bed. He was nude and achingly beautiful. As soon as he rolled over and saw us, his red eyes landing on me, his prick thickened.

He caressed himself to make it swell faster.

"Mother?" he asked.

~No!~

I jerked free of Kerse and ran. He caught me, tackled me before I could reach the hall door. He started dragging me back.

"N-no!" I cried out hoarsely. I rolled and thrashed with an uncooperative body, managed to make eye contact with the demonblood. ~H-help me, Kerse! Don't let her!~

Wilsira sighed dramatically in the door frame, watching as her powerful son wrangled me under control on the carpet.

"I'd hoped one of Rohenvi's Consort-bred Daughters would have come to me as an acolyte," she said, "but that is not to be. Instead, I shall gladly accept a new baby from the Sisterhood through the Matron's plain Noble."

She strutted forward, pulling out of her pouch a familiar cloth, smeared with dried blood and dotted with semen. As she held it up, her satisfied smile spread out to its widest yet. "Especially a child from out between the thighs of Varessa's current favorite. I have waited long enough since the last one, and what a disappointment he turned out to be."

Kerse had me pinned, though I thrashed my head and screamed, snapping my teeth at her when she reached for my jaw. She jerked her fingers back, assured they were still whole, and glared.

"My son?" she asked.

The Sathoet reached and clutched my jaw in one hand, squeezing hard enough to force it open. I moaned as she stuffed the cloth in my mouth, tucking it mostly underneath my tongue. It tasted bitter and burned a little as she whispered a command.

"*Uthrenchi'k raushulvess*," she hissed.

Abruptly, I lost any ability to move, or fight back.

But I was awake, and I could still feel.

I tried to move. To scream.

"Consort!" Wilsira called. "Come here! Now!"

I heard his soft, naked steps.

"You will make this one a Mother."

~NO!~

"Yes, Conceiver."

"Kerse, move back a little. Let us strip her."

Sharp, white teeth bared above me. The dark demonblood swatted away her fingers questing at my belt. I bet Wilsira had never looked so shocked in her life.

"How dare you, you deformed brute!" she exclaimed, and I cringed inside.

Kerse snarled, "*Me!* Not him!"

"Absolutely not! No child of yours has *ever* lived!"

Kerse charged off me, aiming for the Consort, and Wilsira shot to her feet in a whirl of silk.

"*Stop!*"

I couldn't turn my neck to see as they stumbled beyond my periphery, but there was an exchange of magic. I didn't know what the intent was, or whose, but felt the pulses of energy and a slight vibration in the room as I was blinded by a flash of light. A physical struggle before Wilsira howled in pain.

Then she screamed in rage.

"*Kerser'yn'czael!*" she bellowed.

Her son shrieked in response as if she'd flayed his back with a spiked lash.

"Pick her up!" she demanded. "On the circle! Now!"

Kerse resisted her command for a few moments, growling and whining at once, but ultimately obeyed. He arrived to gather me up in his arms.

"N-no —" I moaned around the cloth in my mouth, my useless body leaving the floor.

Wilsira paused and stared wide-eyed. "You spoke … Impossible." She eyed her son suspiciously. "What have you done?"

The Sathoet growled deeply, his chest vibrating against me. I stared, afraid to blink as yellow eyes burned in clear hatred. For the first time, his Mother could see it.

Oh, Goddess …

Although my flesh was dead weight, my mind was on fire. I could sense the depth of her shock, her pain and confusion, and her fear. It washed over me one after another like a filthy stream filling up a dry canal. She stood there for a time, trembling.

Then the Priestess snapped her fingers, summoning the silent, beautiful Consort, who came with a bow but hid behind her. She spoke with the deepest cold to her demon's son.

"Bring her, Kerser'yn'czael."

He flinched. Briefly, her eyes glowed a dark red.

"Stand on the circle. You'll *watch* as this bua *I've* chosen fills her womb, and your blue-eyed slit is *never* climbing out of the Forming Pit again."

Unlike the rest of the well-lit and decorated Sanctuary, the "Forming Pit" was all bare stone and iron.

A dungeon beneath the existing one, with walls roughly hewn. Spots of condensation, evidence of chains and other restraints, a cabinet containing who knew what.

The rock was covered in runes showing both as Radiants and by luminescence. The atmosphere was oppressive; one could choke on the fetid magic which collected here like water in a sinkhole. Off to the side was a hallway where I could hear bare movement and a single moan. Someone living was back there.

What chilled me most was the altar in the center.

"Place her there," Wilsira demanded. "Chain her wrists, then strip her legs bare."

Manic protests remained inside my head. Breathing harder around the fabric, I couldn't protest again. Even a pathetic whimper had taken monumental will, and my strength was waning. I was even more helpless than I'd been with my sister.

Kerse obeyed to the letter, his lip twitching in resentment as his Mother coaxed and caressed the younger bua, preparing him to impregnate me. The demonblood was still intimidating enough that the Consort needed the help, and Wilsira flaunted her lavish attention.

"That's it, beauty. Does that feel good? We'll make you ready, then I want you to climb between her thighs and do what our Goddess made you to do."

"Y-Yes, Mother."

Kerse had removed my belt, my boots, and my leather bottoms, snarling under his breath. He avoided eye contact with me, though I pushed thoughts toward him to help me, to free me. I knew he heard me.

~You are proof she's lost control,~ I said, flailing. ~The Sisterhood can stop her. Bear witness for us, perhaps my Elder can save you — "

Kerse had been ignoring me, but at this point he smiled. I peed what little was left in my bladder. He was holding two pellets he had taken from my belt; he let me see them along with his glowing, yellow eyes.

We have a betterrr plan, Sirranna.

He pitched them to the side, and I heard the pellets plop onto the ground.

Both the Priestess and Consort were instantly covered in a mass of sticky webs.

"Argh! Kerse — !"

He darted out of my sight, his mane spiking straight out. He snarled, and I recognized the sound of a fist striking flesh. Wilsira shrieked, and he hit her again. Again. She went quiet. Didn't speak his name. There was a little blood on the half-Elf's knuckles when he returned to me, climbing onto the altar between my lax and open thighs.

~Ker — ~

Sstop!

He mounted me urgently, pushed his hard, knobby cock into my cunt more like he had a task to complete than because he was overtaken by lust. His dark pole felt different again, like it was changing shape with each passing cycle.

The blood of the Abyss is not stable.

Small, hard bumps on his staff scraped the engorged walls of my birth canal. After cycles of him teasing me, of my never climaxing, the intense pleasure of these first thrusts shocked me. My eyes rolled back, and I drooled as my head flopped to the side. Something strange and invisible plucked at my skin, made it prickle. Hyper-aware. I could feel *everything* … !

He took my jaw and turned my eyes back to him. *Miiine, Sirranna.*

He fucked me, his drool splattering on my belly as two smaller arms broke free of their camouflage on his torso to grip my thighs. Terror churned lust, and within moments of this surreal sight, I climaxed. I went blind as my head went off like a light burst, and his aura …

Not just his cock but his very *magic*—

My eyes widened. Entered me. *Invaded* me!

~Goddess, augh, stop! Get out!~

He ignored me, rutting, roaring as he spurted deep inside. Grunting and wallowing, without any barrier whatsoever. We blended together.

Fucking Braqth, that shouldn't feel so *good!*

I should have been shaking after an orgasm like that, yet I still couldn't move when he pulled out. Somehow, I was even weaker, exhausted, as the strain of a cacophonic song pulsed in my ears. I could hear his thoughts drifting as the pendant warmed beneath my armor. It seemed like there were two of him, debating with each other.

Herre?

~No, not here.~

Sstrong gateway herre.

~You must free us, or you will not survive that gateway. We need her as you do. Bring her to us.~

Kerse rumbled, shook his mane, then turned away from me, spoke aloud to someone I couldn't see. "Witness?"

"Y-yes, Divine Son," the Consort whispered. He was curled small and bound on the floor. He sounded terrified.

"Tell herr. She will hurrt even morre. Very sssoon."

" … Yes, Kerse. I will."

The Sathoet quickly gathered everything which was mine, put it back in place on my body, and unchained me. I whimpered aloud again.

~Please, Ker — ~

Three hands and arms were ready to catch me as the fourth drew me off the stone platform.

"Resst," he murmured. "Quiet."

I felt his command deeply. I couldn't fight it.

I relaxed and was quiet. I concentrated on drawing one breath after another as he lifted me into his arms and carried me out of the Forming Pit.

KERSE KNEW HOW TO USE THE JUMP CIRCLE TO RETURN TO HIS MOTHER'S ROOM. From there, he used it to get us out of the Sanctuary.

I could smell that we had somehow skipped most of Sivaraus; he now carried me through the outskirts and rural areas. I was still paralyzed but not numb, aware of his body heat and his scent, the expansion of his chest as he hurried us out of the Great Cavern.

~Where are we going?~

Wait.

I had to obey him, and I had no choice but to wait. I had to wait for something to change without fighting. Without screaming. No one I wanted to hear me could, anyway. The fact that there were others I wished I could call only made it hurt worse than when it had been just me and Jilrina.

The demon son didn't worry much about being seen. Not only was the population sparse enough, the view from any distance fuzzy and unreliable, but he also bent any natural light around us, cloaking us and confusing his movement whenever he might be visible.

He knew where we were headed as we made the trek farther out into the wilderness.

The climbing became awkward as the passageways grew smaller and twisted about; at one point, Kerse had to throw me over his shoulder so that he could use both primary hands to pass us over and down boulders, slides, and into tunnels, with his smaller hands clutching tightly to my waist.

I could only stare down at the ground passing beneath us and work harder at breathing as blood pooled in my head.

Finally, the Sathoet laid me down in what seemed a random place in a random tunnel, until I detected a faint, lingering scent of alchemist's fire. Scorch marks on some of the stones as well.

We were near the Drider's lair. Even worse, Kerse went to the spot where I had taken D'Shea's confession with Reishel, as if he'd long known it was there. He shifted a small stone to the side and reached in to pull out another Davrin.

She followed the Sathoet to me in a sleepwalk.

~Oh, Goddess, no. Reishel! Reishel, can you hear me?!~

Pushed to her knees, she stared and didn't look at me. She possessed the wilderness equipment I hadn't been allowed to take into the Sanctuary, and Kerse removed one of her long daggers from her belt.

~No.~

Kerse kneeled by my side, his right, smaller hand stroking my ear once in a bizarre show of gentleness as my heart slammed against my ribs, waiting for him to use it on me. He looked away from me to my Sister.

"Prrotect herrr," he rumbled, and Reishel nodded.

Then he left my field of vision. Went farther down the tunnel. I couldn't gain Reishel's attention even then; I could only listen, straining to know what was happening. I needn't have bothered.

The noise erupted in rage and combat. It was pure agony not being able to cover my ears against the dual shrieks of two Abyssal creatures, yet Reishel didn't flinch, either. Short and fierce, the Sathoet won. The skittering sound of the disfigured Davrin stopped; she collapsed with a thump, bubbling gases escaping from a warped, diseased body.

The tunnel was blessedly quiet but for the pounding of my heart.

Would the Drider Keeper have felt the demise of one of her children? Would she tell the Valsharess? Would the Queen send the Red Sisters to investigate, and would they make it in time for me and Reishel?

When he returned to pick me up again, Kerse was splattered in spider guts. They smeared my cloak and my uniform, the foul stuff entering my nostrils. I lost sight of Reishel as we entered the cavern but heard her boot steps follow.

As I feared, the Sathoet walked toward the large, quartz-shot stone set with a very powerful ward. I protested with shrill desperation inside my head, but I could not prevent his setting me down and — after some rough handling to hold me vertical — placing my hands on the quartz stone.

Unimaginable pain shot through me and the demonblood. He pulled us back, catching his breath. About to try again.

~No! Don't make me touch it!~

Finally, he acknowledged he could hear me. "Nneed touch to brreakk it."

~I can't!~

"Nnot trrue."

~*It is true! I can't do it! You'll kill me!*~

He growled in frustration, hesitating enough to imply he didn't want to do that. At least, not yet, which was no comfort. I was struck by how very close the *other* mind was.

It had kept very quiet until now.

~*Patience, Sathoet. She will give us the solution.*~

Kerse gave a mental nod, and they both waited. I did not like it and wasn't sure what they expected to happen. I had been practicing for over a turn, and I had broken one as powerful as this — D'Shea's last challenge where I passed out — but I couldn't even try in my condition.

~*Why?*~

I had my bracers on, which helped; they were the only reason I was still conscious after a shock that bad. But I possessed no way to prepare my body, no control over managing its stress. It wasn't a matter of wearing the tools and putting my hands on it, as Kerse had thought. I had to have control over my body to break this ward.

~*Unfortunate,*~ the presence commented. ~*Sathoet, you must free her. It is not by her will alone that this is done. She must have connection to her body.*~

I was in between Kerse and the warded stone, constantly battered by its crashing spell song as Kerse considered and discarded a few thoughts. After a few moments, he spoke aloud.

"Mmove. You cannot harrm mme."

Only when I caught my own balance before losing it again, falling onto the floor, did I realize it had been a magical command. That simple, I had my body back. Though heavy, sluggish, and weak, I could move my own limbs again.

Goddess, it *hurt!*

My joints and my back. The Dwarf stone at my neck burning at my chest. My gut and my cunt felt raw and unsettled, cramping like they contained lumps of fire-heated pebbles.

I lifted and turned my head to at my captor. "Ker —"

"Do nnot sspeakk," he added.

I lost the ability to form words with my mouth, although I could still vocalize.

"You cannot thinnk mmy true nname."

That worked.

My vision blurred for a moment, and I blinked, moisture escaping to land on my cheeks. I feared enough under a spell this strong that I could ignore shame for the tears. I had enough will and mental resistance to frustrate the Conceiver, a Priestess of Braqth, and keep my privacy. Kerse demonstrated that it was not enough here. *Not enough*.

~*What are you?*~

"Nnot Elff anymorre," he answered, curling his bestial muzzle, his pride and hatred palatable. "Brreak thiss ward, Sirranna. *Obey*."

I had to.

The planning to break this prison had begun turns ago.

Even the eldest Sathoet in the Sanctuary should not have been able to focus on a goal this complex for that long. This could only happen if he had help, and I was about to meet it.

I would be releasing another prisoner: the mind which the Priestesses had locked up and set a mindless Drider as guard.

I knew this as I focused on a task at which I had so recently become skilled. Such a fortunate bonus for them.

Kerse did not touch me as I worked. Reishel did not speak or move to save us; she may as well have been dead. It took a long time; it was complicated and strong, and I was still trying to resist, to stop myself from accomplishing this.

I listened to the song and knew that it was not old; the ward had only been set in the past few spans. How could that be? I had first found it on my Hunt with Jaunda a whole turn ago, and it had been set sometime before that.

The one possibility was that this prison had regular visitors who removed the ward only to reweave it again before leaving.

~*Very good, thrall. Now obey your new master and remove it for us.*~

Kerse repeated this command, and soon after, no longer able to delay, to stand the stress or resist, I found the combination of runes that I needed. Mentally, I tapped them in order, felt the magic swell and become unstable. My nose started to bleed; the ward was failing. My gut ached and twisted strangely.

~*Arrrgh, noooo — !*~

I blurted a scream at the implosion of magic; it sucked out most of my failing strength, at last collapsing and dissipating, and the thick vein of quartz lit up in ragged magical light like a wound. Kerse caught me as I went limp, my imprisoned body trembling as I tried to stay awake. Wetness gushed once in the crotch of my pants. I pretended I had pissed myself.

~*Move the stone, demon,*~ said the prisoner.

I imagined this desperate creature scratching at the boulder on the other side, so close now to freedom. The Sathoet lay me down and turned, using raw strength to lift and roll the glowing boulder to the side.

By the smell, there was no doubt this had been a small and torturous prison for a long while, half-turns if not full. The frail, bony body inside was able to unfold itself completely for the first time since the ward had been replaced. Putrid slime coated the rocks inside the hole, and while an attempt to dig out had been made, that effort had been abandoned some time ago.

I stared at what crawled out, and Kerse returned to pull me back and make room.

The limbs were long and incredibly thin, sinewy muscle barely seeming to hold the skeleton together; the soiled flesh was ashen grey or perhaps an impure purple. With only four fingers and needle-like claws probably not used for hunting, the hands and arms were as skinny as the rest of it.

Those trembling limbs grabbed and scraped at the stone, pulled a spasming, wasted body out and into the cavern. I saw the bald, oblong skull and the wide-set, milky eyes, the sensory frills, and tentacles formed around what should have been the lower jaw and mouth.

I had seen this creature only one time before.

An Ornilleth. *A thought-flayer.*

Only three of them had commanded an entire army of thralls. We had killed them from afar without touching their bodies, and they had *still* taken down three of the Red Sisters.

Including Reishel.

The flayer's body was near death, and so close it could reach out and touch me.

An even more powerful psion than Kain had hoped to be.

CHAPTER 21

I EMITTED ONE SHRIEK AND NEARLY SCRAMBLED AWAY, SWEPT INTO ACTION BY the intensity of my fear. The sudden movement surprised Kerse but he was quick to grab my upper arms in his larger set of hands, hauling me closer to him and farther from the emerging mindbender.

It paused long enough for me to wonder why hadn't it shredded both our consciousnesses the moment the boulder was lifted.

Then I noticed the collar around its neck. A polished mixture of stone and metal which I didn't recognize, loaded with runes and formed from two halves with a hinge. No latch or lock to be seen on the other side; it was magically welded on.

For the briefest moment, our eyes met.

~*So hungry.*~

The Ornilleth wanted to crack my skull open with the beak hidden within those fleshy tendrils; it wanted to consume what it found. It let me see it.

Frantically, I shook my head and fumbled back onto my rear end and partially into Kerse's lap. I lashed out with a clumsy kick, though I missed because Kerse jerked me hard before he growled loudly. With a word, he took away my ability to act. Although I went slack, my eyes were still wide open.

"Mine!" the Sathoet barked at it. "Killl yyou firrst!"

The Ornilleth blinked its empty eyes, looking to the demonblood. Naked, abraded, covered in pressure sores, it waved its emaciated hand dismissively.

~We recall our deal, demon. Pardon our severe hunger. We shall take these, instead.~

The flayer reached out slowly with trembling hand, and the half-blood held me while watching its every move. The bony fingers went to my belt and removed my healing draughts; it had known right where they were. I sensed its amusement, and amazement, as it observed me.

~She is locked awake. A thrall fully aware. Unlike the other.~

It quaffed the slow healing potion, dribbling the bottle messily beneath its facial tendrils and between the sharp points of its beak, and I heard a mental sigh. It was a test with uncertainty how it would work on a non-Davrin body but felt some improvement soon enough.

It intended to keep the second in reserve, and glanced at Reishel.

White, pupil-less eyes focused on Kerse as it rose painfully to its knees. *~We do not have much time. Our deal: if you will remove the collar, we shall remove your 'mother's' last block on your true power. After that, let us leave with the new thrall, and you may keep your chosen female. Do as you must. Attack us instead, and we do not have to touch your mate to kill her. Betray us and, with our last Thought, we will replace **all** the chains from which you have been freed in your recent revolutions.~*

"Agrreed," Kerse said with a determined glare. "No attack. Both ffree."

~Then do it.~

The Sathoet set me onto my back upon the stones where I couldn't see Reishel at all. One large hand pressed firmly to my chest, and he commanded me not to rise. I groaned in wordless protest, staring up at the ceiling, barely able to see the two creatures standing. I was wide-eyed, hating every moment of this helplessness. This *compulsion*.

Once again, a prisoner inside my own body. Inside my head.

~Ahhh,~ the Ornilleth sighed, coming closer, looking down at me. If it had a gender, I couldn't tell. I didn't know how thought-flayers

made more of themselves. I could have sworn it smiled somehow.

~*You know this suffering, Davrin. We comprehend it well on account of your 'Priestesses.' We have studied you, as you studied us. Davrin thrive on destruction and singularity, and your Abyssal hybrids even more.*

~*When the inevitable catalyst brings change quickly to realign our Great Work, we see it coalescing before us while you are blind. We know the cause and destiny as one, far out from your will but not from ours. Your minds are far too splintered to ever guide it. That is why we are here.*~

~*Wh-what are you saying?*~

Kerse distracted the Ornilleth from answering by reaching to touch the collar; the flayer held still and allowed it. The half-breed's magic rise around us, my breath shallow and quick.

Energy whirled around us as the Sathoet chanted something in a low bass. Tension rose steadily and more strain entered Kerse's voice, which had taken on that impossibly deep undertone, an echo coming from a chasm ...

As I'd heard at House Itlaun from Wilsira's own lips.

Something snapped. The tall, gaunt creature flinched then stilled again. The next moment, Kerse removed the collar.

Fuck. Fuck ... fuck ...

I never stopped trying to lift my head or my arm, to touch something, anything on my belt. I remained as I'd been at the time the Ornilleth was truly free.

~*Our gratitude, demon.*~

"Repay mme."

The Ornilleth reached up with two hooked fingers, lightly touching the Sathoet's temple. Kerse's yellow eyes stared for a few moments, then he grimaced and roared. His smaller, secondary arms struck out at air, barely missing the thought-flayer.

And I watched the Sathoet's form begin to shift.

The muscles on his back shifted and bulged, and something sharp broke through the skin at his shoulder blades — a talon, I thought — and it continued to grow as he screeched in pain. The demonblood shuddered and shook, twin malformations jutting straight out of his back. They rose to a height above his head; they were wet, ribbons of fresh life-light shining in the dark.

My stomach clutched and heaved with cold. I trembled as I felt part of that transformation through the link we shared; the flesh tearing and reforming, bones bending, his pain and the surges of power. The link seemed to be strengthening, tightening between us.

It was true; Kerse became less like Wilsira and more like his sire, whatever that had been. His exaltation in knowing this, to feel it happening at last, stopped my breath.

These newest limbs unfolded and stretched out with webbed skin stretched between long, thin bones and multiple joints. They were huge, meant for gliding through vast space.

Wings meant to fly.

But he would never fly far on wings down here. Not in these cramped spaces.

He must leave. Find another place.

*Yesss ... *

It was over. Kerse trembled from the abrupt shift; he huffed heavily but managed a scowl and a nod to the Ornilleth.

"Lleavve."

~*Were we stronger, we would stay and observe.*~

The Ornilleth motioned to Reishel, and she came forward to crouch before it, facing away to show her back. The flayer removed a pouch from her belt, handed it to Kerse, and then climbed onto her, its muscles stringy, every boney edge showing.

~*Stop!*~ I cried. ~*No, don't take her!*~

Reishel stood up with the prisoner balanced on her back, holding its legs. Her familiar face was vacant, but her gaze pointed briefly in my direction.

~*Reishel, listen to me! Whatever it is holding you, **fight it!***~

She blinked and stumbled, nearly dropping her passenger. The Ornilleth hissed, wrapping tentacles around her neck to regain control. Its enormous, empty eyes looked directly at me.

~*Enough.*~

A thin, desperate bond snapped like a single spider thread.

No ...

~*We must get far from here,*~ it said to Kerse.

"Then go."

The prisoner vanished from my sight, and I listened to heavy boots as my Sister carried her added weight away.

The larger consequences of that prisoner escaping didn't even cross my mind when Kerse removed my belt and remaining weapons, tossing them to the side. Then he methodically removed my bracers, my boots, and my armor.

"N-n — !" I stuttered when he loosened the thongs at my hips and soon tugged my pants over the swell of my hips and down my thighs. I chomped at the damned cloth in my mouth, felt the relatively cool air of the cavern on my sex, and my skin knew every measure of bare exposure as Kerse peeled my pants off my legs.

Slowly, deliberately, he raised my arms above my head for me and lifted my shirt next. While the shirt briefly covered my face and my eyes, Kerse's tongue flicked one of my nipples. It responded, tightening into a hard nub.

~*Stop!*~

I wanted to show him my teeth, to stare defiantly at his eyes when he removed the shirt, but even that freedom had been taken from me. My face felt passive and expressionless.

He loomed over me, more than ever before; those massive, dark wings cast a shadow even in darkness. He took everything from me. He unplaited all the smaller braids in my hair, leaving it loose, and he slipped Callitro's ring from my finger. Shyntre's blue pendant had caught his attention as the very last thing, and he held it curiously for a few moments, rubbing his thumb across it as if to polish it.

Smiling a little, he left it around my neck.

"Forr noww," he said ominously.

All my clothing and other possessions he placed far from me, at a far side of the cavern, and I lay helpless and nude on the hard, stone floor. For the next while, Kerse created his own magical circle using chalk, salt, and other things handed to him from Reishel's belt. I lay where he had placed me, several long paces away from the open prison hole.

~*Ker* — *Ker* — !~

As he'd commanded, I couldn't think the entire name. I kept thinking anyway, since he couldn't stop that completely; I was locked awake.

~*Please talk to me! What are you doing?*~

A slight pause, and he murmured under his breath as he drew a circle large enough to circumscribe both of us. I tried to cajole him, coax him, even tried opening a bargain, but as soon as I saw that expression on his face — like the bitter resentment he'd given Wilsira — I stopped. I swallowed as I stared at the ceiling. A little bit at a time, I was able to shift my eyes around more easily, and I could follow his progress.

~*Are you going to kill me?*~

Stupid question.

He watched me a moment, and answered, "Killl meanns eatt. No. Ssacrifficce."

I would have preferred being eaten.

~*No. Please, don't, not like that.*~

He continued his circle.

~*Wouldn't your Mother be the greater sacrifice? We could go back to that room where she's bound.*~

Pathetic and desperate. I knew he could never go back to Sivaraus.

He paused again then continued both drawing his symbols and sprinkling his salt. "She ssufferrs more thiss way. Sseverr Motherr's bond forreverr. Nneed yyou, Ssirranna."

My death would literally come between Mother and son? Assuming he wasn't straight-up Abyssal insane, which was still a possibility. Not that it mattered; knowing which wouldn't change his actions. No amount of begging would save me, so what now? How had this happened?

Kerse was so much less like the simple-minded half-breed I'd first met in the candle chamber and again at the Worship Ball. His maturity reflected his true age as if he were fully Davrin. I shuddered to acknowledge a half-blood older than Jaunda, who was now fully aware of this fact.

~*You said you weren't Elf anymore, but you are.*~

"Abysss." He hissed it as a warning. "Five *centuries,* Ssiranna ... Now, the chainss break. I crosss overr."

If he opened a gate here, he'd be able to use those wings on the other side. Only an Ornilleth could have held this motive, this steady course, the entire time. They had met sometime between my trials and the thrall battle where Reishel was struck down and later awoke.

I had never been given a reason by my Elders why the thrall army had attacked, nothing beyond wanting more slaves and resources. Yet, they hadn't attacked an area easily looted; we'd been both on the outskirts and the wrong side to gain much.

The army they'd brought with them was a shock force, I'd always thought, intended more for swift penetration and retreat, as if they had come for something small and specific.

Like a missing mind of their conclave.

How had the Priestesses come upon that creature? When had they sealed it up like that?

Kerse finished with his circle while I fretted, and he wasted no more time to begin his ritual. He parted my legs and kneeled between them again, hunched over and chanting while I lay damnably still for him. He caressed my bare skin, my hips and belly up to my breasts, over my throat and added a stroke across my cheek.

Making eye contact.

"Ssirranna Thhallennssarrecci," he whispered my name in that Abyssal voice.

I shuddered involuntarily.

He did something to me. To us.

I could feel both his slower breath and my panic at the same time. I was frightened mindless, as I had been during Braqth's Threshold, as I had often been under Jilrina. I could feel the build of energy, the dark, slow rise. I heard the droning hum of low voices and whispers that seemed far away and shrouded in black.

Kerse may have been making all these sounds, or perhaps he was only one of many to join them; I couldn't tell. My vision swam but I tried to focus on the Sathoet and what he was doing as arousal and anticipation grew stronger.

That must be his. I only became aware of it. Felt it.

When sufficient magic coursed through the runes and within the circle around us, Kerse rose up on his knees, one smaller hand holding an erection. He proudly showed me why he wasn't an Elf anymore.

His genitals had changed as much as his back had by sprouting wings. He was erect, and the bulge at the base was still there, but now the pointed tip had two collapsible spikes protruding, one on each side that seemed able to stand up at will. The shaft itself possessed bony bumps I'd felt recently, but more than a few had risen to sharp points in these last few marks. It appeared like claws growing through. The knot at the base now possessed three fine rows of small barbs.

If this was what all Priestesses had meant about a demonic coupling being "scarring," then I did not see how they even survived it.

Though, perhaps this *did* explain why they were all insane.

Warped out of their fucking minds.

Tears fell out of my eyes and trailed into my ears, though like everything else, I could do nothing about it.

~*Ker — Please, no … ~*

He opened his yellow eyes and looked at me as he leaned forward and lined himself up with my sex. I whined; I could feel it, feel everything, and I couldn't fight or run away!

Ssorry, he thought, and pushed half of his reformed weapon inside me.

I cried out only once at first, the soiled rag in my mouth flopping out halfway, sticking against my sweaty cheek. I realized then I felt his pleasure mixed perfectly with my pain, and the other way around. Like me and Kain.

Kerse would suffer everything alongside me. He wasn't afraid. He was willing.

Ssacrifice. The price musst be paid to my ssires.

He would pay the price. Wilsira's mature son admired me; he would rather I live and be his companion for much longer than this.

But he wanted his freedom too much to stop now.

I lost any self-control, started screaming long before we got to the barbs at the base. He allowed this and did not silence me this time.

Perhaps I screamed for the both of us.

THE DARK SILHOUETTE WARMED HER BARE FEET IN RED SAND. HER DRESS WAS white, a stark contrast to the bare, dark skin of her elegant arms and shoulders and throat. The cloth fluttered in the dry breeze.

Stepping to her left, she turned to look back at a narrow fissure of orange stone, as if the underground had cracked open beneath the Sun's Gaze only to be scorched bright, to all the colors of fire.

No longer hidden in the dark, now open, and alight with heat and flame.

The wind whipped up and spilled down from deep within the fissure, hurling into her like a battering ram, scouring her skin as she lost her balance with her feet buried in the deep sand.

She peered at the dreamer with a sense of wonder and dread. Her eyes almost golden.

Her lips moved without sound.

Do we try again, sacred treasure? You don't have much time. If it is to be, you must save her from the Abyss.

So that she may return and save you in kind.

I HAD THOUGHT, IN MY DELIRIOUS STATE, THAT WHEN HE WITHDREW, WHEN the pain spiked viciously and pleasure fell abruptly, that the gate to the Void must have been opened.

I thought he didn't need my body anymore; he was finished, and somehow my mind had survived like the imprisoned Ornilleth.

If only for the short time that it would take to bleed out.

I heard a high, loud scream of hot anger. Too high to be him.

It sounded familiar.

"Get away from her!!"

"Jael! Damn you, stop!"

"Brilliant tactics."

"Shut up and shield her, mage!"

"Yes, Lead."

It couldn't be.

A trick.

The calls of the Abyss. Demons could be very good mimicking those voices that one knew best.

Cared about most.

Don't ...

Afraid to see, I had to know.

My lids were so heavy to lift, but I managed to make out Kerse crouching over me. He was splattered with blood from the waist down, and the white stripe of his mane stood up as he roared in answer. A magical blast from his fist, blinding me and leaving the cavern quaking with echoes.

"Jael ... you up?"

"Yeah. What the fuck are those?"

"They're wings, you fool! Gaelan, break the circle!"

"Lead?"

"Do what he says!"

They were closer.

Real boots on stone.

There *were* intruders.

I pushed the last of the soiled cloth from my mouth with my tongue. Within a breath, a small bolt from a crossbow pistol struck the edge of Kerse's circle near my head.

The attached pellet burst.

I turned a stiff neck to see a thick, viscous fluid filled with fine particulates spread rapidly over the runes, chasing them as if they were fuel catching fire, strong enough to dissolve the salt.

Aching pain flowed across my chest as the magic began to collapse.

Loss. Isolation. Failure.

The anger and encroaching despair swarmed me through our fading bond, sapping away any elation or hope.

Yet I, Sirana, might have a chance to live.

The Sathoet howled and stood over me, grinding out something I didn't understand. A blast struck from his hand, and I heard more familiar curses.

"Keep those shields up, wizard! Gaelan, Jael, flank him and try not to get hit in the teeth. Force him away from her."

That wasn't happening at first; Kerse wouldn't give ground. Jael engaged so closely that she was within my view, and they nearly stomped on me. With even more fury than I'd heard about in her Sathoet trial, my youngest Sister attacked, pushing the offensive hard. Her sword ripped through one of his newborn wings.

I threw back my head and screamed at the same time he did.

Then someone hit the half-breed with their own concussive blast, finally forcing some distance between his body and mine as my Lead caught up to the novice. The space didn't help my mind; I felt every strike that Jaunda and Jael landed as they flanked him, and I could do nothing but moan in agony with my head pounding a double beat.

I had begun to wonder why I hadn't bled to death.

But now I knew.

He was still alive.

"Where is it?!" Shyntre demanded, kneeling next to me and fumbling with one of his gems. "Sirana, where is it?"

My mouth was open, but no words would come out. My vision faded fast; although I blinked, I couldn't see any Radiants, couldn't make out the wizard's face. My ears remained sensitive despite my rapid weakening. I flicked my eyes to the side of my head where I'd spit out the cloth.

Shyntre snatched it up wet with fresh blood.

"Jaunda, a talisman links them!" he yelled. "You kill him, she dies with him! I heal her, and he heals, too!"

"What?!" Jael cried.

"Fucking lovely!" my Lead growled. "Stop the fucking bleeding, then find a way to break that spell!"

The wizard pressed something very small into my palm, closing my fist around it, though I could barely feel anything else that wasn't happening to Kerse by this point. A hint of warmth seeped into my body, settling deep enough in my ruined core to know this was somehow separate from the Sathoet.

The sensation of my life draining away first slowed then ceased, and my vision began to return at a cave slug's pace. No stronger and still unable to move, I could at least breathe without agony.

"Sirana!" The mage shook my shoulder, as if that would help. "Can you hear me?"

My eyes shifted toward him. I could see life sign within his face but not his expression.

"Good. Good. Just hold on. Don't give up."

He worked on the talisman kneeling next to me, but I couldn't see what he was doing. Kerse knew, however. He spoke another blast spell to get the Red Sisters off him so that he could turn and charge Shyntre straight on.

"Mage, look out!" Jaunda bellowed.

The wizard jerked his head up and his eyes widened. Strong fingers flicked two precise gestures, and the quick evocation saved his life when Kerse collided with a magical shield.

"You can't fucking have her!" my wizard growled.

Shyntre remained on his knees and low to the ground, giving no sign that he meant to retreat. He maintained beside me with that legendary stubbornness and concentration.

The Sathoet tried to force his way through, hurling blasts at the magical shield, covering himself in sparks which burned our skin. I watched Shyntre force him back by expanding the perimeter of protection a little at a time. Talons on demonic feet scraped against the stone as Kerse tried to push back.

Finally, trapped by Shyntre's spell and with Red Sisters at his back, Kerse had to sprint off to the side again and loose another attack. His next blast was for the wizard but aimed too high. He was trying not to hit me, too. This gave my three Sisters the chance to close with him again.

I moaned a loud protest when they hurt him again. When they hurt me.

"Gaelan, I need a conduit!" the wizard yelled, setting the talisman on my chest.

Jaunda ordered, "Go! We got this!"

Gaelan broke away from the fight and soon fell to her knees in front of Shyntre, who reached above me and grabbed her face in both bloody hands, the only place he could make skin contact. She gasped audibly as the wizard aggressively funneled the power needed from them both.

"Pick up the cloth," he commanded.

She did.

"Spit on it, it needs some of your saliva."

Hers?

"N-n-!"

Desperate to speak, I still couldn't. My head pounded, and pain shot through as if my skull had split open when I finally found the way.

~No, you damned wizard! Don't pass it off onto her!~

Shyntre and Gaelan jerked their gazes to me. The shock of my voice in their heads was real.

The wizard glanced at the blue stone glowing around my neck, but the horror of my condition and the waning time overrode any hesitation. I watched Gaelan ignore my warning and spit on the cloth, knowing full-well the risk she posed to herself. I understood enough what they were doing because of D'Shea's stern leadership.

Shyntre's power and ability might push the bond between me and Kerse hard enough to break it. As with his Mother before, Gaelan braced to absorb the inevitable backlash, so the primary mage could maintain his concentration.

If he failed, Gaelan could get tangled up in it with me.

~Don't. No! Wait!~

Shyntre shook his head — his only answer — and cast his spell, chanting with hands still planted on my Sister's face. The phantom hooks inside my head and chest appeared from an invisible vapor; the intangible threads Wilsira and Kerse had placed on my will and body lit up like a glittering maze of barbed chains.

The wizard was none too gentle as he hurried to disentangle the hooks and free me from each one.

Kerse cried out in denial of the fraying connection.

Ssirranna, hhellp uss!

I obeyed, holding tightly to our connection, fighting Shyntre's goal.

Keep him close, don't let go —

"Ffuck, Sirana, don't help him!" the wizard growled hoarsely, trembling from unseen effort. "Let go!"

Jael jabbed a knife into my side, and I screamed.

As did Gaelan.

~No.~

Gaelan's desperate plea sounded as she joined with my bleeding mind. *Sirana, it's not you! Let him go! Look at me, Sister!*

With supreme effort, I did.

Remember me! I've helped you before you knew me, and I'll do it again. I'm so sorry for what I did! Let me take the brunt for you this time.

I saw a face in her mind: *Jilrina.*

Gaelan was … *there?*

The last time I bled out like this.

In the shed on House Thalluen lands.

~How … ?~

Live, and I will tell you somehow! I swear!

I concentrated on Gaelan's pain-streaked face to keep myself from slipping, from losing a mindlink which scorched me like I held my hand over a candle. I resisted giving strength to the half-breed, wanting nothing more than to release that deadly bond and all its centuries of poison. Like pushing two massive boulders apart, my two sources of agony became separate.

For the moment. I shook with the strain.

~I c–can't hold it — ~

Shyntre seized his chance, increasing the magical pressure sevenfold in one vicious push. The ritual bond snapped.

Kerse's shriek reverberated in the cavern as Gaelan shrieked, absorbing the burst of magic in my stead, saving me *and* Kerse the added pain.

My Sister slumped to one side, Shyntre lunging to soften her fall. I moved my hand toward her, clumsy and uncoordinated.

~*Gaelan! Gaelan!*~

I tapped her thigh, trying to get her attention as Shyntre straightened back up.

~*Are you caught? Answer me!*~

She trembled, pushed herself up, smirking at my pitiful attempt at a smack. She lifted her hand which had held the talisman; its destruction had burned off her red glove to the wrist. Ash fell silently from her palm, and her skin was blistered.

She smiled anyway. "Sirana. You're moving …"

"K-kill him," I croaked weakly. My throat was raw from screaming but preferable to the sharp pain stabbing into my skull like a Tragar's hammer and chisel. "Kill, p-please. He w-won't go back …"

Shyntre yelled out to Jaunda. "She's free!"

"About damned time! Gaelan, on me!"

The ragged mage answered the summons. I was concerned as she stumbled to her feet.

"R-range only!" I stuttered after her. I didn't know if she heard me.

Shyntre kneeled in between me and the fight, which dragged on far too long for it to be a good thing. Shadows darted along the wall as Kerse tried to fly, and the wizard split his focus between shielding us and aiding my Sisters. He let some spells be destroyed only to raise another shield in their place.

The wizard seemed to be looking for an opening.

"D-don't you sh-shoot," I said.

He didn't look at me. "If they're going to lose, I will. Kerse will kill us next."

I licked dry, cracked lips. "*Kerser'yn'czael* … "

My heart stuttered, and I winced even to whisper that name, and Shyntre glanced down before quickly looking back.

"What?"

"He's more demon th-than Elf now ..."

Shyntre huffed on a smirk. "Yes, the four arms and wings are big hints, Sirana."

"U-use his name."

His body stilled, the sarcasm fading from his face and tone. "I can't use Abyssal magic, Sirana. It's useless to me."

Damn it all. I hurt everywhere; my head and below my waist was the worst. I couldn't even roll over.

Four arms and wings.

That reminded me.

"Is he h-holding ... a c-collar?"

"A collar?" Shyntre tried to see but shook his head. "I don't know. Where would it have come from?"

"F-Flayer ... prisoner. Kerse removed it. Freed them both."

"What?!" My wizard was aghast. "They kept an Ornilleth hostage? How could they be so *stupid?!"*

Leave it to him to blurt out the most obvious, least useful thing. I wanted to roll my eyes but couldn't waste the energy.

"WIZARD! SHIELDS!" Jaunda roared.

Shyntre got back on his role. "You can't die, Sirana. You hear me?"

"Th-thank you, wizard, will d-do. J-just for you."

He almost smiled. "Stay alive. Stay awake. My Mother can use this to bring down Wilsira."

Maybe. Not the sort of proof I had been hoping to find when I first stepped in the Sanctuary.

I understood his demands, however. I was not actively bleeding, he had stopped that with a gem, but my body was far from healthy. I couldn't last in this state indefinitely; sooner or later my internal organs would fail from the bruising and tissue destroyed which remained unhealed.

"H-hope they hurry, w-wizard."

At that, Shyntre fumbled in a pouch with one hand. He set one gem between us without looking away from my Sisters. "Can't hold the shields and use one of these at the same time, but maybe you can help me.

Take it. Just hold it. I'll watch for an opening to speak the command."

Weak, numbed fingers scraped for the gem. I found it, couldn't quite clutch it. Cool and hard in my palm; it wasn't active yet. I waited. My mind drifted.

Why had I thought of that collar?

It was something ...

Something had gone through Kerse's mind before Shyntre broke our bond.

Something about being able to choose his time.

His choice when to die.

As it had never been before living with his powerful Mother.

I gasped. "He's d-drawing them in! He c-can take us with him!"

Shyntre didn't look at me. "How?"

"M-magic c-collar!"

The mage's attention was still on the fight, which was now edging toward us. He gasped, too. "I see it!"

Kerser'yn'czael came into my straining view. He was severely injured as the Red Sisters did not hold back once he and I were separated. The Sathoet knew it was only a matter of time now. He snarled, lifted the collar in both primary hands.

"Jaunda!" Shyntre shouted. *"Fall back!"*

The demonblood used his strength, physical and magical, to snap the collar into two pieces and release the binding magic uncontrolled.

A retributive strike.

Shyntre threw his body over mine as the shock wave deafened us. The explosion shook the cavern.

Then the rocks began to fall.

Chapter 22

I was aware but couldn't remember why I had not been before. I wasn't sure if I could speak. Or what I would say if I could.

The room was dark and quiet except for soft shifting over a smooth surface.

Soft.

Everything was ... soft.

The bed. The blanket. The pillow.

Gentle lips.

A light touch. *So light.*

It hurts ...

Suddenly, everything hurt intensely. Someone was touching me.

"N-nooo," I moaned, failing even to lift an arm to push the hand away. "No m-more."

"Shhh, you are safe."

His voice.

"If it hurts, it is healing at last. This is good."

Through gritted teeth I choked out, "*L-liar ...*"

This searing, screaming agony inside couldn't possibly be *good!*

A chuckle, and even that was soft. "Rest, beloved. No need to fight now. I will help you, and I am not the only one."

He spoke the truth. Somehow, I knew.

I stopped resisting and slipped back into Reverie.

Trusting him that I'd awaken again.

THE NEXT TIME MY THOUGHTS AROSE TO FORM SOME COHERENCE AND CON-nection to my body, it wasn't the pain of it, but aching fire.

Want. Want!

I wasn't alone in this. I heard his answer. *Yes.*

A familiar hum wrapped me like a blanket; it was a beautiful song. My skin was flushed, hot, sweating. Someone was with me, holding me close. Mouth tracing my throat, my jaw, kissing my lips but letting me breathe in between them. Without demand. Arms embracing me without wariness, open and vulnerable, in no hurry to pull away.

~Oh, Goddess, more!!~

My arms slipped around, clutched at his back, and I dug in my fingers so he couldn't get away. Pulling him flush against me, I rolled onto my back so that he lay atop of me. My legs opened, wrapped around him, my ankles hooked near his knees. His hard prick dragged along my thigh and pressed to the cleft; the desperate sound which escaped him when he did was delicious. I licked salt from his cheek.

He was as exhausted as I was, needing comfort. Sensation before thought.

Trembling, we shared what little strength was left. We reaffirmed life. We were *alive.*

~Yes! Now!~

His prick pushed inside me with a grunt, he held my hips to the mattress with his weight. My legs clasped to him as he moved inside me, testing at first, then gradually thrusting harder.

He kissed me again, gasped for breath, both of us moaning, trying to be quiet. I licked at his mouth and gathered him closer for a deeper kiss, his long hair spreading across my hands. I moved my hips against him, undulating. Matching the rhythm and the rolling pleasure of the song. I could not think past how perfect the pattern was.

I'd never cum so hard as when he gasped a passionate cry and spurted inside me.

"Yes!" he whispered.

I growled, equally breathless. "M-more! Give me more!"

~*Ta'suil!*~

He heard me. He was willing.

He would do anything to please me.

His cock didn't soften; he was still hard. I rolled us again to be on top. He let slip an adorable sound as I straddled him, grabbing his wrists, and pinning them by his head. He arched his back. Encouraging.

He didn't fight me at all this time.

"Goddess, yes, beloved!"

~*Ta'suil … *~

HOW HEAVY THE REAL WORLD SEEMED WHEN MAGIC INEVITABLY DRAINED BACK into its pool, withdrawing behind whatever veil always hid it away.

I opened my eyes to a low-burning candle, long shadows waving at me from the walls. I was warm and comfortable, and lay on my side in a Noble bed with a fine, soft blanket keeping the draft off me. The absence of pain struck me at about the same time as the heat source behind me, which cradled me from neck to thigh. A lax arm rested on the curve of my waist.

A vague memory of being held like this by something else spurred my heart into double time; for a moment, I felt sick. I breathed deep and slow, trying to still my quivering stomach.

Eventually I could lift myself to a sitting position. The Davrin behind me did not awaken, even being so jostled; he rolled onto his back more by accident, his beautiful face relaxed and eyes closed.

Where … ?

I looked down at both hands, at my torso, folding back the blanket from my legs, letting it sink in that I seemed whole. No injuries; nothing was broken or missing.

I had been given a cursory cleaning, I thought, quick because of the odd smear or two of dried blood that colored my hair and was underneath my fingernails and toenails. A small amount of red also dotted and streaked the fine, white sheets, although my bedmate seemed much better scrubbed.

I touched my belly and my thighs and touched between them gingerly, anticipating pain. I felt none.

I am whole. Healed.

My sex was puffy and very wet, but the stain on my fingers was not blood. As I lifted them in front of my eyes, the subtle glow implied a mix of living Radiants and …

Magic.

I had not simply woken up from an intensely erotic dream. I had coupled with someone. I glanced behind me.

With the pure Davrin bua in this bed? Not a half-blood …

Even so, why did I have this dead-certain feeling that this was a *bad* thing?

Finally I stared at my bedmate.

He was beautiful but looked haggard even in sleep, as if he'd been under a lot of stress. He may have been about three centuries old, still in his prime, and yet something about him seemed older. Perhaps because he had a solid gold streak in his hair, running back from his right temple. Gold did not begin to appear in our pure white hair until our fifth or sixth century.

As far as I'd seen, it didn't tend to arrive in singular, broad stripes like that.

I know you, do I not?

I looked around the dimly lit room. How did I get here? I had been injured for sure. That story was there before my eyes, on the bloodied sheets and my body, but I had been healed. I was warm and strong and very glad to be alive.

But I couldn't remember my name, or that of my companion. I was safe for the moment but how long could I rest here? I didn't know if anyone was looking for me, whether they had ill intentions or not. I had no knowledge of events to help me prepare to meet them.

Maybe I should leave. Just go. Figure things out later.

I slipped out of the bed. It felt strange putting weight on my feet, as if it had been a sensation to which I was unaccustomed. However, my body worked, and I moved as quietly as possible, searching for my clothing. It had to be here somewhere.

Nowhere on the floor or chairs.

I moved toward the wardrobe, intending to look inside but pausing in front of the mirror. I looked how I thought I should look, even knowing the blue eyes were odd. Nowhere near the color of my bed companion's eyes.

Scarlet red.

I shook that flash of memory away and looked inside the wardrobe, frustrated to see only male clothing.

Not my room. Where am I?

I was fine with the idea of sneaking out naked if necessary, but the lack of knowledge was a disadvantage to me greater than no supplies, no tools, no weapons or armor, and not knowing how far I had to go.

I blinked. *Weapons? Armor?*

I was a fighter, then. So where was my stuff?

My beautiful bedmate drew in a deeper breath suddenly, and his legs shifted beneath the blanket as he rolled over, his hand questing where I had been. His reach came up empty, and his eyes fluttered open. As he sat up, I was struck how his face changed from peaceful to wary.

"Sirana?"

I blinked. *My name.*

Yes, this sound was right.

"Where am I? Who are you?"

Instant understanding in those eyes. He kept his voice patient and calm. "You are in my room, inside a Noble's House. You call me 'Auslan.'"

My heart began pounding harder. This was bad.

"What happened?"

He swallowed, and my eyes were drawn to the marks of passion on his throat, as if someone had been biting or sucking on his skin. That someone had probably been me.

"Your Sisters brought you here. You needed healing, and they knew that I could heal you. I think one still waits atop the roof."

Where I stood now began to make sense, it felt right, but my stomach felt so tight. I still didn't remember how I'd become so injured as to be dragged to one of those rare, hands-on healers.

"Where are my clothes?" I asked.

"You had none when you arrived."

I clenched my jaw. "And what injuries did I have that needed healing?"

Auslan's perfect brows drew down, and he shook his head. "That is not important now."

My voice raised in anxiety. "Yes, it is. It might tell me what happened."

The healer clearly had reservations about telling me, but I repeated it as a brusque command and did not relent.

"Tell me how I looked when I arrived!"

Ultimately, Auslan answered my question as a matter of fact.

"You had bruising and scrapes on your arms and legs, but that was the least of it. You had been ... assaulted with a phallic torture device. Internal injuries. You were near death from loss of blood. No sign of restraints used, no marks on your wrists or ankles and no defensive wounds on your hands or arms. Nothing under your fingernails except your own blood."

My body trembled, growing worse as my eyes widened as far as they could, as if my vision was large enough to see it all at once. Everything came back to me in a rush: Wilsira losing control of her son, the Ornilleth breaking free, Kerse sprouting wings.

And me ... unable to fight him.

The ritual, and the rescue.

Shyntre covering me, protecting me from the explosion.

I knew that at least one of my Sisters was gone. Worse than dead.

My head swam and my knees buckled. I collapsed onto the floor with a mourning cry that I didn't recognize in my ears.

Auslan surged out of the bed and kneeled next to me, gathering my uncooperative weight with a grunt, and wrapping his arms around me. He held me tight as he could, and I was still shaking too hard to push him away; my hair fell into my face as I tried to use him as a still point for my spinning head.

He waited for what seemed a long time before the shakes lessened even a little. "Your Elder knows about the Sathoet, Sirana," he whispered. "You do not have much time, and I am sorry for that. I did all I could."

Yes, he had.

Amid painful memories and flashes of red and black, there were the white of his wrap and his sheets, and the golden light of the candle. That odd streak in his hair.

Auslan had never had gold in his hair before.

"What did you do?" I asked breathlessly, my forehead resting on his shoulder, my hot breath bouncing back at me from the skin of his chest.

My Consort was silent for too long.

In that time, I finally noticed the odd, enhanced warmth deeper down. Low in my belly. It felt tight, magical ... alive. As if someone had placed a fire-warmed bloodstone in place of my womb. It was an utter opposite feeling to Jilrina and Kerse wounding me. It was like Tarra's magic, the fertility rituals, except ...

I wasn't desperate to breed like before.

I lifted my head to glare at Auslan; he looked wary again but didn't draw away.

"Tell me you didn't use that 'version' of Braqth's Threshold that saved Curgia."

He swallowed. "That is ... all I could do. You would have died, Sirana."

A cold, dull horror formed in my chest to counterbalance the new heat in my abdomen. My voice shook. "Y-you couldn't have used your healing potions? I know you have them!"

"I tried that first, Sirana, I promise you." His voice strained, trying not to panic like I was. "You were tainted by the Abyss. The potions did not work. You were dying, and the Spider Queen was ready for you."

"I don't believe you!" I spat, pushing him away, collapsing heavily onto my arms without the support. The fear, the flashes of cold and heat that spread through me now stole any strength I'd regained.

"The taint was the same as when Curgia miscarried, only stronger," he said. "You had to be purged, and there was no time. I had the power to do it."

"Should've just let me die!" I cried. "You've killed me anyway! Kerse is dead and Wilsira may still live, and I w-will go to the Sanctuary to bear *your* seed there before they execute me anyway!"

He did not reply. He knew this, as others did. I wanted to strike him, to take all my anger and fear out on him, to force from him something as raw as I was right then. I did not want to have to look at that too-beautiful mask always hiding what he really was!

I didn't hit him, however, because I looked slightly beyond my own misery to other possibilities and a few reasons why he was holding his tongue.

I asked, "Did *she* instruct you to do this?"

"No!" he answered immediately and without looking away. He didn't blink. "Wilsira did not. I told you the truth. Your Sisters brought you to me. There was no time to take you anywhere else."

Sisters. Jaunda, Gaelan, Jael ... Which of them still live?

I squinted at him. "Have you decided your fate, then? You are ready to die?"

His eyes lowered, drifted along the floor before lifting back up. "I decided nothing. My fate is not my own. You know that."

It was my turn to be silent.

Then, "Is there *any* possibility I didn't catch?"

Auslan hesitated but shook his head and didn't lie to me. "I ... know when I have healed a broken womb. I know when I have fulfilled my purpose. What I was created for."

I huffed an ironic laugh. From scarred to fertile to scarred and back again.

Braqth fucking damn it, make up your fucking mind!

Jaunda slipped into the room through the laundry chute then. I spotted her over Auslan's shoulder and jolted. He whipped his head around behind him and gasped.

My Lead was in uniform. Her face and stance both looked hale and healthy, but a large portion of her reds and equipment were badly damaged by scorch marks and soot streaks as well as rips, breaks, and tears.

She didn't have her original cloak; she wore a discreet grey one that had not been put through a grinder. She may have stolen it. Her hair had always been cut short, but now it was barely a layer of fuzz covering her skull, growing in from full-bald. She had no burn marks that I could see now, easily the results of our most powerful healing potions.

My Lead pulled out a small black bag and a ball gag, stepping closer as she murmured, "You going to cooperate, pretty bua?"

Auslan shrank away. "W-what?"

"Wait — !" I said.

Jaunda kneeled and firmly pushed the hard, black ball between his teeth and secured it behind his head; he made only one small sound of protest. Then she snapped the black bag over his head and cinched it shut, using it as a hold to push him belly down onto the ground. He didn't struggle as she tied his wrists together behind his back. She also took the time to stuff all his hair up inside the black bag so it wouldn't show.

"Got you some dark clothes and cloak," she told me brusquely. "They're tucked in the false panel in the chute. Get dressed now."

Shaken, I obeyed her order, unable to think past the moment. Jaunda saw fit to put a distinctly non-Consort wrap around Auslan's waist before hauling him up and pushing him toward the chute. He had been amazingly quiet; perhaps he was simply that scared.

"What are you doing, Lead?" I asked after slipping on the plain shirt and pants, stuffing my feet into the plain boots before donning the cloak.

"Simple. He knows you're pregnant, so he's not talking to anyone any time soon. Gives our Elder more options before the shit hits the ceiling."

My mouth gaped. Auslan shuddered but did not protest.

"Keep him upright and still," she said, setting him to stand next to me.

I watched as she first removed the soiled sheets from his bed, balled them up, and remade it with fresh ones. She searched the room quickly after that, picking out several empty healing bottles from the waste bin and adding them to a larger, generic sack she had taken from somewhere.

Next, she added several of the relatively plainer clothing from his wardrobe. She found all his unused vials as well, healing and prevention and possibly others, seated neatly in two padded boxes. She took the entire thing.

There would be enough missing from the room to imply that the Consort may have left on his own. A runaway. Although I had not heard of one successfully escaping before, that didn't mean none had ever made the attempt.

The Sisterhood is stealing one of the Sanctuary's Consorts.

I couldn't believe it, yet I was glad that Auslan was going with us. I didn't have to leave him here. D'Shea would say it was smart not to leave loose ends anyway.

I just wished I knew if she intended to kill him herself.

Jaunda found a bloodstone in the vanity, eyeballed it, and stalked over to us. She set the bag down with minimal noise and then her hand darted out beneath Auslan's wrap to seize him by the testicles. He hadn't been expecting it and jumped, hunched over, and made a plaintive sound through the gag.

A strong need to protect him coursed through me. I quivered with the high effort that it took to resist throwing a punch at my Lead. Jaunda narrowed her eyes as she noted it.

Her mouth near Auslan's ear, she spoke low and strong. "I've got a bloodstone here from your chest of niceties. Yes or no, can this be used to track you?"

He deliberately shook his head in the negative, his balls still clutched in her fist although she didn't seem to be squeezing hard. Yet.

"This bloodstone does *not* track you," she tested again.

He nodded the affirmative.

"Is it dangerous in any way?"

He shook his head. *No.*

"Mind if I take it?" Auslan hesitated but shook his head, and Jaunda smirked. "Good. Does anything track your whereabouts?"

He nodded. *Yes.*

"Is it something that can be removed?"

He hesitated, then nodded.

"By me?"

Negative.

"By a mage?"

Affirmative.

"Got it."

She let go of his scrotum, added the bloodstone to the bag, and looked at me. "Use the hood, cover your face," she ordered, doing the same. "Let's go."

CHAPTER 23

To discreetly lower a bound and blind Auslan plus the sheets down from the roof was a challenge, even when he knew better than to struggle lest he be dropped. Jaunda and I had to work together, a slow task to purloin the Grandson of Braqth from the Itlaun estate. He was tense but cooperative.

Eventually we reached the two lizards waiting far out from the manor. Gaelan was there waiting for us, and something ached behind my eyes to recognize her, to see her well. She smiled but said nothing, only stuffed the dirty sheets into her saddle bags and signed that I should mount up behind her.

Auslan went with Jaunda. She placed on his belly over the saddle in front of her, and I couldn't help but think how I'd once been carried exactly so by Gaelan. I sat upright, holding her waist instead.

With his whole head covered and the basic, servant-grade wrap he was wearing, he wouldn't look like anyone of importance from a distance. Neither would we.

As we got moving, Jaunda used one of her message pellets. I didn't know what message she sent, but I could guess it had been to our Elder even if I knew not what she would say. Or had said.

Jaunda had been waiting for a while from what I understood, stealing clothing and hiding out — she could have been updating D'Shea as well. It would have been hard to justify not doing so.

We were not headed directly for our Cloister, the Tower, or the Court, but took the long road out, figuratively speaking. Jaunda guided us through field and rock, using what dips and crevasses were available to help camouflage us.

We had covered a lot of ground before I finally thought it safe enough to extend my arm forward and sign to Gaelan.

Jael?

Alive, she gestured shortly. *Sent ahead.*

I hesitated. Then, *The wizard?*

Sent him, too.

Alive?

Of course. She turned her head and smirked a little as the path widened and the lizards didn't have to go single file. *His shield is the only reason you aren't paste.*

I phrased my next question. *Why was it necessary to bring me to House Itlaun?*

Jaunda saw that and expelled a breath, motioning Gaelan to be still. She was brusque as always in answering. *After that blast, there was nothing to spare for you. Everyone used everything on them to save their own life first, even the wizard.*

I nodded, felt no surprise or disappointment. I was glad. *Who suggested it?*

Her mouth curled into a sneer. *Shyntre. Made his case, like he did to search for you in the first place.*

He ... what?

He knew you were in trouble. Where to look. She shrugged. *Claimed it was counter-magic, he knew Wilsira was after you. And he was right. Gaelan vouched for the wizard's next claim about the Consort being a healer. I didn't have any better ideas. You didn't have the time.*

I trembled on the inside. I was pregnant because of that idea. *Do you think Shyntre knew what would happen?*

*If he did, I'm going to toss his robed ass out of the top floor of the

Tower,★ she signed. ★But he mentioned the spare potions first, that this bua had a lot of them. And I heard this pretty one say he tried those first. The only reason he's not dead yet.★

I fell still, trying to regain my discipline and focus in front of Jaunda, regardless of how weak and shaken I was on the inside.

I had noticed how easily Auslan distracted me whenever he moved his head or shifted and breathed so that I could hear him. Maybe I would end up "addicted" to his aura, as he'd threatened, as D'Shea had warned me. Maybe I would have a fate like Curgia's.

How had Shyntre known where to find Kerse and me? How had they made it there in time?

★Wait,★ I signed. ★Lead?★

Jaunda cocked a brow, expectant.

★D'Shea didn't send you?★

Jaunda shook her head. ★Bad timing. Gone somewhere. Rausery, too. Shyntre came to the Cloister.★

★He can do that?★

★Sure. Been before. He knows his netherhole is fucked if he does uninvited.★ Jaunda shrugged, and Gaelan picked it up.

★He found me and Jael first. We got Jaunda, because Reishel was missing, too. We were looking for her.★

Jaunda saw my expression better than Gaelan, even in the dark. ★You know what happened?★

Gaelan tensed when my one arm tightened around her. I was glad I didn't have to speak around the lump in my throat. ★Taken by the Ornilleth. When it escaped. Forced her to carry it on her back.★

"*Fuuuuck,*" Jaunda hissed aloud.

★Prime isn't going to let that go,★ Gaelan signed, every motion lined with tension. ★When she finds out — ★

★Let D'Shea worry about that first,★ Jaunda cut her off.

We fell still after that, lost in our own thoughts as we kept on the move. Eventually we sensed that someone approached.

Jaunda muttered, "At last."

Elder D'Shea met us within the circle of a rock outcropping, far afield but not quite to the sentry border. Her face was set and determined; she neither spoke nor signed as she slid off her mount and went directly to pull the Consort off Jaunda's lizard.

Auslan made a muffled sound of fear as Jaunda helped lower him to the ground. I clutched at my Sister, giving away my reaction, and worked to slow my breathing when my heart rate picked up dramatically. As Jaunda dismounted, so did we, and Gaelan was clearly concerned.

★Watch her,★ D'Shea signed to Jaunda, throwing a look in my direction.

My face burned with heat, but I resolved to stand still. Knowing why D'Shea had given her Lead that order didn't change the outcome.

D'Shea lifted the hood off Auslan, his chin and much of his face wet from his own saliva as the ball effectively prevented him from swallowing. My distress spiked as she gathered up his hair and gave it a twist at the nape of his neck. She withdrew an obsidian dagger and cut off his hair in two quick slices. The fearful surprise and shock caused my chest to hurt in terror for him.

I clenched my fists, stood stiff and tense.

No, not like Curgia … Not another forced bond like Kerse. I hate this …

My Elder next grabbed what was left of his hair and used it to force him down and chest-first against one of the boulders, so he knelt with his wrists tied behind his back. He struggled a little but D'Shea didn't dawdle as she spoke a few quiet, magical words and dug the point of her dagger into his back, to the left of his spine between his shoulder blades.

Auslan's body jerked as she broke skin and blood welled up. He made sound even around the gag.

"No — !"

Jaunda seized me by the back of my neck and dragged me to her, covering my mouth with one ragged, gloved hand to keep me quiet.

D'Shea chose to ignore my insubordination as she focused on her slow, agonizing cut until it was about a hand's length long and vertical down the Consort's back. He was bleeding and quivering from the pain but did not try to jerk away from her again. He stayed still and suffered, biting down, his body breaking out into a sweat.

Soon, the tip of the dagger began to glow a pale purple inside his flesh, and the Elder Sorceress slowly withdrew her weapon as if coaxing the glow to follow it.

Held tightly by my Lead, my eyes wide, I saw this was exactly what happened. The magic was visible, even to me, and seemed to stretch out in a thread like so much syrup, connecting the obsidian dagger to the open wound, and eventually the blade absorbed all that glow.

Auslan went slack as the pain seemed to stop then, leaving only the normal, oozing knife wound.

I watched my Elder burn the Consort's length of hair, letting the small, smelly flame lick the blade of her dagger as well, and then smother and scatter the ashes with her boot. Auslan had settled onto his hip and leaned against the rock, breathing hard through his nose, looking drained.

Jaunda still held me though I had stopped fighting her by the time D'Shea sheathed her dagger.

Release her, she signed, and her Lead obeyed.

Both my Sisters watching me for sudden moves toward the Sorceress as I caught my feet, tremors passing through me from the aborted surge of violence. I met her eyes, and it was clear my Elder was not happy with what she saw. However, she saved it for later.

At a sign, Jaunda replaced the hood to cover Auslan's face after he'd regained some breath, and D'Shea stood between me and the bleeding Consort.

She signed to us, *They can't track him now. Back to the Cloister. We don't have much time, and I still need to understand what in the Abyss happened.*

I winced inside.

The Abyss *was* what happened.

D'SHEA TOOK OVER GUARDING THE CONSORT HERSELF AND SENT JAUNDA AHEAD to make sure we could get him into the Cloister without witnesses.

★The fewer Sisters who know he is here, the better,★ she signed.

Auslan's blood would have eventually dripped onto the ground or leave smeared arches from his bare feet. Only by these facts did D'Shea see fit to wipe the Consort's wound with a mild topical healer while we were out in the field. He was quite surprised to discover that the healing process *hurt* with a less refined potion and left a raw scab rather than new skin.

My Elder kept most of her attention on me during that event, and the part of me that wasn't demanding I protest that unnecessary pain was instead weighing the benefit of remaining stoic versus simply showing my Elder how I was being affected.

D'Shea may systematically increase the strain on Auslan to get me to react, to find exactly where the breaking point was. She could also simply punish us both as she saw fit whether I showed it or not, and my reactions would be the gauge for what hurt us most.

It was hard enough to think straight. Every step, I was too aware of an unnervingly warm womb and caught myself wondering if it was cait or bua. At a stalemate, I clung without words to Gaelan on her lizard.

Quickly, we made it to the Cloister, Gaelan and I dismounting when D'Shea did. She dragged our bagged bua roughly off the beast, catching him when he would have stumbled.

★Take the lizards to the stable,★ she signed curtly to Gaelan when my Lead reappeared to guide us through one of the less used entrances. ★Then find Jael. And Rausery, if you can.★

★Yes, Elder.★

D'Shea, Jaunda, and I moved with the Consort into one of the small interrogation rooms. Inside was a simple chair for one Davrin to sit down; the rest had to stand or sit on the rough stone ground or be chained to the wall.

A Sister could sprint across the room in three or four long strides; the ceiling was high enough to hang a chain or bar from the large iron hooks anchored above our heads to stretch the average Davrin to their tiptoes.

The Sorceress set what had to be a powerful privacy spell, given how long it took her to complete it. She turned around, small beads of sweat on her forehead as she watched us all with a flinty gaze.

"I don't know why the Prime's not breathing down my neck, or why we haven't been summoned to the Palace yet but let us get through this at least once. Sirana, what happened at the Sanctuary before Jaunda found you and Kerse in the Drider's cave?"

I was concerned that I couldn't remember at first. "How many cycles was I gone?"

D'Shea frowned. "A full span. I asked for updates but was being put off if the Prime didn't say she wanted you back for something specific. What happened?"

I shook my head. "Wilsira forgot all restraints and subtlety. She wanted me pregnant to get back at you, and … something about my Mother and sister."

My Elder's eyes narrowed. "Continue."

"Shyntre was there to help me against her before; he wasn't now. She kept me isolated. I only met other Priestesses or faced the Sathoet in their chamber. Kerse helped me with the other Sathoet."

"How?"

"He didn't want them touching me, and they didn't like the scent of his seed on my skin."

"He didn't try to breed you?"

"No. He was waiting for his Mother to make her move. She kept me awake too long without Reverie and had made a … a talisman to sap my willpower. The cloth that we couldn't find."

D'Shea's gaze pierced Jaunda, who shrugged. The Sorceress growled, "Continue."

I nodded. "Eventually the pendant didn't help anymore. When I couldn't resist her further, she had a Consort in the suites ready to obey her."

My Elder stared as if to bore holes through me. "And then?"

I swallowed. "Kerse rebelled, intimidated the Consort. Wilsira used his true name against him, forced him to heel, and took us both to … the …"

"Yes?"

I glanced at Auslan. "The Forming Pit. The room where Wilsira makes the Consorts somehow. There was someone down there besides us."

My Consort shifted uncomfortably, as I would expect him to, but it was D'Shea's expression that took me by surprise.

It was as naked as I've ever seen her.

"You've seen it," she murmured, careful with her tone around the others, but I still heard the unspoken: *You've seen it, too.*

My Elder had been in that place before? When? It must have been while she carried Shyntre, but why? The sire was Phaelous, not a Consort.

"What happened?" she demanded, jolting me out of my thoughts.

I felt dizzy to recall. "Kerse used my web pellets to trap his Mother and the Consort. He … beat her unconscious."

"Impossible."

I chuffed, tears touching me eyes. "You dare say that, even now?"

With a stiff nod, she acquiesced. "Very well. Kerse abducted you. He escaped Sivaraus with you."

"He wanted to open a gate to the Abyss," I said. "He wanted to do it in the Forming Pit, said it was a powerful place. There were runes everywhere."

"Why didn't he?"

"He needed to free his full demonic magic, first. The Priestesses place mental blocks on them."

D'Shea nodded confirmation.

"He needed me to free the Ornilleth, so it could free Kerse from his stunted magic." I swallowed. "And that's exactly what happened, Elder. I *had* to obey. I couldn't stop them; they used both Abyssal magic and psionics! A-and the flayer somehow called Reishel back, too! She waited for Kerse and me in a daze, I couldn't reach her, the mind control was too strong. The creature *took* her. Rode away on her like a Uroan!"

I shook, and my eyes blurred. D'Shea watched me steadily, and Jaunda flexed her fist, listening with a deep frown.

"Then Kerse began his ritual to escape the Deepearth," my Elder said.

So weak, I was ready to sink down on the floor but resisted the heavy pull. "And your son knew, somehow. Shyntre left the Tower and came here, probably to find you, but he found Jaunda, Jael and Gaelan. They saved me. They kept a gate to the Abyss from being opened by a Sathoet." I hesitated. "No matter what happens next, that has to count in the Sisterhood's favor with the Valshoress?"

"Perhaps, but never assume that means it counts in any single Sister's favor." My Elder paced, ending up on Auslan's side of the room with her boots very close to his head. She looked down at him. "And you, Consort, were somehow able to heal such damage on her."

She nudged him with her boot, and he shook his head with a muffled moan. Before Jaunda or I could offer to do so, D'Shea kneeled to tug the hood off his head once again, his shorn hair falling into his face. She also removed the soggy gag, uncaring of how stiff his jaw must be.

He moaned and grimaced as he gingerly closed his mouth, licking his lips and swallowing repeatedly. He stayed mute.

"Look at me, Consort."

Auslan obeyed. His fear was evident, but he made eye contact.

"What do we call you?"

He hesitated. "Whatever you wish, Elder Sister."

D'Shea smirked. "I understand one of us prefers 'Auslan.' Do you like it?"

"If it pleases you, Elder."

"You're avoiding my questions, Consort."

"That is not my intention, Elder."

"Of course not. You're one of the 'yes-whores' when you're scared, aren't you? You have no thoughts of your own?"

He was caught on how to answer — to agree or show her otherwise — and he glanced at me. That was the first time D'Shea struck him, kicking him in the ribs with her boot. I jumped and lifted my fists, but Jaunda grasped my right shoulder hard in her hand.

"Don't," my Lead said shortly.

Of course, she was right.

"An interesting side-effect of your healing, don't you think, Consort?" D'Shea asked, her anger evident. "Have you ruined one of my Red Sisters in more ways than one?"

Auslan gasped against the pain in his ribs, his hands still bound behind his back, and eventually lifted his chin again to look at her. "Elder Sister?"

"Have you caused her to conceive?" she asked, slowly, so he would understand. "Is my novice pregnant?"

"Y-yes, Elder Sister," he answered.

"For certain?"

He trembled in dread and still answered the truth. "Yes, Elder."

"I see."

Another strike; a kick square in the gut. He curled up and couldn't breathe.

"You fucking whore."

She landed a glancing hit on his head next, snapping his neck back and he groaned. She'd ripped a gash by his temple, and I could see red stain his hair.

"Elder, stop!" I growled hoarsely, leaning against Jaunda's tightening grasp.

"Quiet, Sirana!"

"No, Elder!"

She whirled on me. "He planned this for that cunt Priestess!"

"No, he didn't! I thought of that, but I *know* he didn't. He has only *obeyed* the Red Sisters since I found him. Every time, to the word!" We stared unblinking. "You said we don't have much time before the Valsharess could summon us. Will you spend it beating a helpless bua who hates that same Priestess?"

D'Shea laughed. "This one? Hate a Priestess?"

"T-truth, Elder," he whispered. "I confessed this to Sirana. Anything I know of her is yours."

She glared at him, and I rushed my next pitch.

"Wilsira may still be in a mass of tangled webs, or she may be freeing herself this moment to get out of the Forming Pit."

D'Shea reacted to my mention of that place beneath the dungeon.

I glimpsed the haunted look on her face, but it was banished a moment later.

"She was probably down there still when she *felt* her son die," I said, willing to feel that satisfaction. "Killed by the Sisterhood. Very fitting, I think."

The Elder kept her face impassive and shook her head. "You are trying to distract me."

"Well, I am slow to see how beating him helps your immediate concerns, Elder, but even if you have a reason, there is more to consider."

"Oh?" she challenged, lowering her chin, her gaze sharp.

"Yes, Elder. When Kerse and I were bonded through the talisman, Shyntre and Gaelan couldn't break it without my cooperation. I was *willing*, then." My voice became aggressive. "I'm *not* willing to endure more pain on account of your frustration. Tormenting Auslan only hurts me! Provided we finish off Wilsira, as we *should* be planning, there will be time yet to find the best way to deal with this. Meanwhile, let him be!"

My breath was ragged. I stood trembling at my conviction to own such a weakness, disbelieving I'd taken such a tone with her. Jaunda was dead silent behind me, not interfering beyond keeping me from engaging D'Shea in a fistfight.

The Sorceress tilted her head and approached me instead, leaving Auslan where he was. Her crimson eyes glowed with anger and suspicion as she gazed at me.

"I hear you, Sirana. However, know this: I have no use for a Red Sister who is overly protective of *any* Davrin. If we win this conflict and are somehow neither locked up by the Valsharess nor run through by the Prime, and your behavior around him does not change? He dies, or you do." She paused significantly. "*After* you give the Priestesses your child."

I couldn't speak for the white-hot burn that spilled into my chest. I stood shaking with anger, nodded with extreme effort and silently thanked Jaunda for never letting go, for holding me back.

There must be another way.

Someone chose that moment to push the ward on the door.

CHAPTER 24

D'SHEA MIGHT'VE HEARD SOMETHING MORE SPECIFIC THAN MY GENERAL SENSE that someone was determined to enter. She moved to the door and, after putting her hand on it a few moments, allowed it to slide open.

Rausery strode in, convincing in her confidence. The taller Elder held Jael by her neck and Gaelan by the arm, hauling them through before D'Shea closed the door behind them again. My Sisters were not fighting the tight grasp, though they knew it was not the most dignified way to enter, dragged in like naughty children.

Jael wasn't wearing her reds; she had been redressed in her earlier blacks — probably from extensive damage to her actual uniform as she had been closer to Kerse when the collar broke. Gaelan's reds looked like Jaunda's: as if a thousand creepers had been chewing on them.

"Ohhh, this is going to be fun, D'Shea," Rausery said with unmistakable glee in her voice and on that grinning face. "I can't wait to hear how you're going to handle this one."

"Hmph," the Sorceress scoffed.

The General's eyes swept the rest of us. Rausery tilted her head at my completely missing uniform and substitute drab clothing, along with how plainly roughed up Jaunda was.

"Looks like you two fared even worse than these two."

Elder Rausery noticed the Consort last. He lay very still, bound on the floor, and she blinked at him, frowned a bit, letting go of Jael and Gaelan so they could stand at attention. She folded her arms in reprimand to her peer.

"Since when have we started stealing the Priestesses' sluts, D'Shea?"

The Sorceress presented a solid image for her peer, a contrast to the frustrated Elder lashing out on a helpless male whom I'd seen moments before. She kept her chin high, her face placid, and her stance the one of elegant poise I remembered upon first seeing her.

"Since one learned far more than he should have."

"About what?"

"Have you really no idea?"

Rausery shrugged. "He healed a Red Sister, right? Might have seen the injuries. Big deal. They'll just track him."

D'Shea shook her head once. "I've taken care of that."

"Oh, have you?"

"I know how they do it. And I can undo it."

Rausery tilted her head. "So now he's untraceable? D'Shea, they're *still* going to be looking at you."

"You are going to help me dissuade them. He's not going anywhere else for now, and there is more to be concerned about than one aging breeder."

"Yeah?" Rausery grinned like she knew but glanced down at her feet. "You gonna tell with or without him lying there on the floor?"

"With."

Though, with that, I watched as my Elder crouched by his still-bleeding head and pushed something squishy into each of his ears before gagging and bagging him again. The Sorceress stood up. "There. Now."

"Yeah?"

"Wilsira must have our focus." D'Shea smiled back with a mean tilt. "Other bonds tend to break in quick succession when a Priestess loses her Sathoet."

"So, it's true, then. Jael tells that we're in deep dung because she helped kill a Sathoet without the Queen's writ to do so."

"If there had been time to inform the Valsharess, She would have granted the writ. Kerse had grown into a powerful threat, and Wilsira has been hiding that fact from us all. Now, an Ornilleth has escaped because of *her* demonblood. We'll have her pinned. The Conceiver's fall has begun."

"You'd better hope so," Rausery commented wryly. "And yeah, Shyntre mentioned the flayer escaping. That's right up there with killing the half-breed without an order if we take the fall instead. I've sent a tracking team out, but let's figure out how we're going to hold up against that one first."

"Auranka's Drider was killed by the Sathoet, and the Priestess's ward was broken. Where is our failing? The Red Sisters arrived to prevent Kerse from completing his plan *long* before Auranka responded at all. You've beaten the Sanctuary to a first response tracking the prisoner as well."

"Pardon me if I'm wrong, Sorceress, but aren't the Priestesses' wards tailored *against* those of demonic blood to prevent exactly outcomes like these? So who broke it? Not Kerse." Rausery's deep red eyes slid to me. "And where is Reishel?"

Cold illness then seemed to drift about the room, on Gaelan's face first, then Jaunda, with Jael coming to a slower conclusion. If anywhere, *this* was where we would lose the Prime and the Valsharess in favoring our case against the Priesthood.

D'Shea didn't have an immediate reply. Auslan lay utterly silent and still, curled up and presumably hearing nothing the Red Sisters said.

Rausery exhaled. "Look. I can't watch your backs in the shit-landing if you don't tell everything. What the fuck happened?"

Jaunda was no longer holding me back. She had taken her hand away a while ago, but I wished it was still there.

"I was forced to break the ward for him, Elder," I said. "And Reishel was forced to carry the Ornilleth away into the deep. Sh-she's gone with it."

"Tell me how both those things happened."

Rausery did not blink in her demand. She had heard some version of this prior to now; she wasn't shocked, but she was disturbed.

I swallowed. "Kerse usurped control of a talisman Wilsira made to overpower me. She ... she wanted me pregnant and under her control. The flayer exploited that, told Kerse what to do, helped him rebel, and it must have ... I don't know. *Done* something to Reishel. Planted an earlier suggestion?"

Rausery nodded; I watched her humor drain away. "When did it have the opportunity?"

I looked at D'Shea, and her mouth tightened. She still couldn't speak what she had confessed to me.

"Training out that way," she admitted. "Myself with Sirana and Reishel."

Rausery scowled. "You *knew* about the Priesthood's prisoner, D'Shea."

"Sirana stumbled on it as well. Little point in ignoring it when she sensed it with the wizard's pendant but couldn't speak to it because it wore the collar."

The General jerked her head, rejecting that. "Don't buy it. For this to happen, it stopped working at some point, like the Prime said it would."

D'Shea sneered. "She doesn't know magic."

"And *we* don't know psionics. We haven't had enough time." Rausery's jaw ticked. "*How* did it get Reishel, of all Sisters, and not Sirana?"

"Reishel was sensitive as a conduit for Sirana, the same way Gaelan is for me," D'Shea said. "A suggestive mind amplifying her reach. I confirmed it, I had plans."

Rausery grimaced. "Which got fucked fast as liquid shit. One thing in our favor is the Prime was against holding that prisoner from the start. She's proven right, and she'll like that, but it was two low-ranking Sisters and a negligent Elder that allowed it to happen. Now a conclave of flayers will have deep knowledge of parts of Sivaraus."

"Then the Prime can be glad it was a low-born who was taken," D'Shea retorted, "and *I* can ask if it learned far more from Wilsira herself. Kerse was changing regardless, and the Conceiver hid her son's instability, becoming too distracted by her status to keep a proper eye on the changes in that prison. The responsibility was hers; the failing is hers."

"Better hope we can convince the Prime of that, you and me."

D'Shea glanced at us, then back to her peer. "Let us speak in private."

Rausery nodded but jerked her chin toward Auslan. "If we're holding on to this one for the time being, stash him. Unless you think he knows something the Prime ought to?"

An immediate shake of the head. "No, let her not see him. He'll go to solitary. If we have time before going to the Palace, I'll question him further."

D'Shea began a gesture to Jaunda.

"We need the Lead in on this, too," Rausery interjected. "It's a simple task. Let the other three move him. They should stay low until we have a plan."

A stubborn line entered my Elder's back; grudgingly, she looked at me. The General still hadn't revealed how much she might know about why Auslan was here. It depended on what Rausery had learned from Shyntre, and D'Shea was about to find out.

"Gaelan," the Sorceress ordered, gesturing to her.

Jael and I looked at each other awkwardly as Gaelan stepped forward to lift Auslan from the ground and D'Shea removed the black bag to retrieve her ear plugs from the Consort. She removed the gag as well, handing it and the bag to Jaunda.

Auslan looked dizzy, and I hurried forward to take his other arm. The scent of him and my two closest Sisters mixing in proximity was cruel. I swallowed as saliva quickly formed in my mouth; even in *these* circumstances, it felt good to touch his skin. He even relaxed a little himself, an unconscious smile touching his lips.

And D'Shea noticed.

Damn it.

The ward on the door was impressive. D'Shea didn't realize that Shyntre had been waiting outside until she'd stepped out into the hall. I recognized the hard strike of a decades-long compulsion overtaking body and mind. She was about to vomit, though I could only tell because I knew what to look for.

The wizard had looked at Rausery first, meaning to say something, but jerked in surprise to see Auslan and the patch of blood staining his hair and face. Anger boiled up, and Shyntre completely missed his birth Mother's moment of weakness before she, too, threw up an angry wall in her defense.

"Rausery!" she barked. "Get him out of here!"

"Enough of this, D'Shea, I want him in the meeting. He can explain the most to the Leads — "

"So he'll do so after I'm done," she snarled. "Send him elsewhere. Now. He's not a Red Sister, we're not changing that rule. What if the Prime walks in?"

Rausery acquiesced in the face of the fire, but she was displeased. At the same time, the Sorceress refused to acknowledge her son directly, wouldn't even look at him. I knew why she couldn't, what she was feeling, but I could also see how that fact got to the bua who'd been teaching me about the Surface. I saw the last few centuries in that moment.

No wonder Shyntre held something like trust for Rausery. The sour wizard could manage a smile for the General but only anger for any other Red Sister.

And now Auslan was in the mix.

"What have you done, Elder?" Shyntre asked the General. "Why is this Consort here?"

Rausery's mouth quirked at his tone while me and my Sisters' mouths gaped. She missed the way D'Shea touched her hand to the wall to keep herself upright.

"Not my doing, bua. Ask the Sorceress."

Shyntre did. He flagged a hand in my direction but was focused on D'Shea. "He brought your favorite novice back from certain Abyssal death, Elder, and this is how you repay him? By abducting him and beating him? Why didn't you leave him where he was?"

D'Shea didn't look at him, her jaw like stone. "Rausery, we don't have time for this."

Her voice sounded cold, though I knew that was a cover-up. Her body and mind were in violent upheaval; I could never hide it as well as she did now.

Rausery would let this go on, I could tell, thinking it the time to force a confrontation longtime brewing. With me pregnant, Wilsira gathering what strength she had left, and the Prime breathing down our necks, it really, *really* wasn't.

But I couldn't tell the General that.

I caught Jael's eye, pushed Auslan into her, so she and Gaelan held on to him. I reached to grab Shyntre, who resisted but he lost his feet with the force of my pull.

"Let me go!"

"No. You're coming with us." I looked at his Mother. "I'll stay with him, Elder. You and Elder Rausery get to it. We're running out of time."

"Do that, Sirana," D'Shea said before Rausery could belay my direction.

The Elders glared at each other, and we left them and Jaunda behind. I encouraged and sometimes pushed the two buas down the dark hall. Shyntre stopped resisting before too long; perhaps he recognized the opportunity to see Auslan wasn't further abused by Red Sisters.

A large storage area lay beneath our main barracks. Most of it was for equipment and supplies, but one hallway shot straight out away from everything else. Halfway down, a small, warded stone door would slide to one side with the right command; Gaelan knew it, as did I, and Jael picked it up right then.

This doorway led down some shallow steps to a dead-end path with a few cells on either side, only five in all. Vertical iron bars stretched from floor to ceiling to form the separation between captive and captor for each cell. A guard could see every corner of the confinement room; there was no place for a prisoner to hide from view.

"Welcome to solitary," Gaelan said.

"Been here, thank you," Shyntre muttered.

Jael blinked at him. "When?"

"Not your privilege to know, recruit," he said snidely.

I caught her wrist when she would have punched him. "Complicated, Jael, don't make it worse."

Gaelan snorted with ironic laughter. Jael quirked an eyebrow.

"Queen's pet cock, indeed," the youngest bit out.

I heard Shyntre's teeth grind, but at least my Sister lowered her fist, and it wasn't a feint.

The Red Sisters could not rely on servants. We did everything ourselves, even the basic cleaning, and it made us very selective in whether we took on a prisoner of our own over simply sending the doomed prisoner to the Palace or Sanctuary dungeons. Those dungeons had more bodies and servants to assist with running the place, including skilled torturers and mongrels scrubbing filth off the walls.

If someone was kept here, there had to be a good reason.

Each cell contained a small cot as well as a small stone basin for washing or drinking. The basin filled itself by way of a trickle of fresh water from our main source in the main level and was designed to stop automatically when it had reached a certain level rather than overflow, pure construction over magic to make this happen.

In addition, there was a second basin intended to collect and flush down all waste. The only thing that lacked any means of regular maintenance was food. Someone must be assigned feeding duties, or a prisoner could be forgotten and left to go hungry.

I had heard that a Red Sister could be thrown into solitary confinement for whatever reason the Prime chose that span, although I knew of another small clutch of rooms outside of the barracks, designed for harsher punishment and interrogation that led to death eventually.

I was too new to know how often the Prime chose to use that over this place. The First Sister may not have much respect for young caits in general, but she barely noticed buas at all.

Hopefully she doesn't find the Consort interesting enough to mess with.

Auslan would be the only captive for the moment and was lucky we were putting him down here. From the look on Shyntre's face, he was aware of this and relieved on his "brother's" behalf.

"Release his hands before you lock him in there," the wizard said to me as Gaelan opened the iron door.

I had withdrawn a blade already to slice the tight straps. One cut and Auslan's hands were free before Jael pushed him harder than necessary through the door. Gaelan closed it behind him to secure it.

"And whose tongue-pet are *you* to be telling us what to do?" Jael snarled at the wizard.

"He points out the obvious, Jael, pay him no mind," I said, as my Consort returned to the iron bars, stiffly massaging feeling back into his arms.

He looked as saddened as I'd ever seen him, and I swallowed the impulse to open the door again. How was he doing this? Was this how all Consorts survived, making females feel so protective over their comfort?

"Sounds like he didn't get enough slaps in the jaw growing up," Jael said to Shyntre, facing him. "Doesn't know when to shut his mouth."

"If this one had kept his mouth shut," Gaelan interjected, "Sirana would be dead now."

I could feel Shyntre vibrating behind me, and I waited a little longer to see his response. To my surprise, the mage let Jael's remark go. There had to be a strong motivation for that.

I turned my head to look; Shyntre was already watching at me.

"May I get something to keep the Consort warm, Red Sister? There is moisture down here, and he's wearing very little."

Good point.

"No need, wizard."

I removed my own borrowed, grey cloak that Jaunda had snatched from somewhere and passed it through the bars. Auslan accepted the offering, bowing his head slightly to me, and wrapped himself in it. It covered all of him but his feet. I was sorry for that, but at least Shyntre relaxed a little. He tried for more.

"May I retrieve something to clean his cuts and get him some food, Red Sister? I can do so through the bars."

"Didn't realize this was an infirmary and an inn," Jael grumbled. "Shall I get the wine and blooms as well?"

"At ease, Jael," I said softly, feeling conflicted and tired. "Guard him while I escort the mage to get some basic supplies. We won't be long."

Gaelan nodded to me — I knew she'd keep Jael in line — and Shyntre held no hesitation in following me back upstairs.

What happened? Why is he here? the wizard signed the moment we were alone. *You're alive. You look hale. It worked.*

Oh, yes, it did.

My gut heated up again at the memory of Auslan crying out as he climaxed inside me. As I'd begged him to. My stomach trembled, and I grew nauseated when I thought next of the seed planted.

And how the Prime and every Priestess in the Sanctuary would react to that news.

My Lead decided he knew too much and my Elder agreed, I signed. *D'Shea doesn't want anyone to interrogate him.*

Except her, he added harshly. *Why beat him? He did nothing wrong, he only did as he was told!*

I shook my head and kept silent.

Why did she cut his hair?

So he couldn't be tracked. She cut into his back with an obsidian blade at the same time, burned hair and blood in a spell.

His face told me that D'Shea had done something that made sense to another mage. *Did you try to help him?*

I convinced her to stop hitting him, I replied. *I'm not a high-ranking Sister, Shyntre, you know that.*

She still favors you.

I still can't tell her what to do. She's not pleased with me.

Again, why?! You're alive!

And because of me, an Ornilleth has escaped, and a Sathoet is dead. Many well above my Elder won't be pleased with either of us.

We had reached a storeroom, and it contained what we needed: a kit with plain, clean cloths and a mild solution for cleaning wounds, and rations which lasted a long time on the shelf. The wizard collected the cleaning supplies, and I picked up a few bags of the food. Three would last six cycles if it was rationed well, maybe longer for a non-fighter like Auslan.

I understand he was a playmate of yours growing up?

The wizard frowned at me. *How would you know?*

*He confessed. I saw you talking in the garden at Itlaun. You are certainly concerned for his wellbeing.★

★I dislike watching the Red Sisters abuse those weaker than them,★ he replied with teeth bared. ★He's *valuable* if you put your minds past his looks.★

I smiled wryly. ★I'm listening, mage.★

★Nothing you haven't thought of. He knows Wilsira, knows a great deal of the Sanctuary, the Sathoet, and much else about the Noble Houses where he's stayed. If you keep him here past a cycle, I can't see you giving him back any time soon. It's better he is healthy and cooperative, isn't it?★

I nodded slowly. ★What do you suggest about his dreams? I understand they drain on him when he heals.★

Even though it had been my intent to put him off his guard, I was surprised to see Shyntre's face flush with heat as much as it did. He added a few more cloths to his kit before he signed to me. ★His dreams are part of his healing magic. Just keep him able to bathe himself and stay clean. That's all.★

Odd request.

★And if a few Red Sisters wanted to take advantage of his being here?★

That visibly upset him; Shyntre had trouble controlling his breathing, and I saw his pulse in his throat. ★They shouldn't risk it. He's one of the most fertile Consorts the Sanctuary has.★

Yes, I know.

★He's helped quicken twenty-two living offspring.★

Twenty-three.

I signed, ★We have prevention.★

★And he has divine magic that mends torn wombs!★ the wizard retorted. ★Draughts can fail with him. Make sure your Sisters know that, and don't whine to me when one of them must go to the Sanctuary to squeeze out a babe!★

I suppressed my own reaction to that and shrugged. ★There's more than one way to fuck, Shyntre. You know that.★

A muscle ticked in his jaw. ★It's not necessary. He doesn't have to go through what I did, there would be no reason to test him like that.★

★You won't have the decision any more than I will,★ I said.

Shyntre watched me with narrowed eyes. ★Meaning you wouldn't enjoy seeing him tortured?★

I shook my head, and he believed me. I'd earned a decent opening for where I had been aiming. ★It's clear he means more to you than a long-past nest sibling, though. Why?★

Shyntre tried to brush that off. ★He was one of the least vapid Consorts I knew, but he's more fragile than I am. I don't want your kind breaking him just because you can. It's not as it should be.★

My eyes narrowed. ★As it should be? That's an odd concept, Shyntre, and that's never persuaded anyone in Sivaraus.★

★Would you help me protect him? He saved you.★

★By using a few healing potions,★ I lied, testing him, my eyes never leaving his face. ★I can't promise, Shyntre. I don't know what the Elders plan even now.★

He plunged ahead. ★Then help me find out and make sure he doesn't die.★

You really don't know what it took to heal me.

★I'll give you whatever you want in exchange,★ the wizard continued. ★Anything.★

★Anything?★ I signed, unable to prevent the suggestive smirk.

He wasn't surprised at all, but he answered. ★Yes. Anything.★

Argh. I did *not* need that temptation. No matter the justification, I'd be more a failure as a Red Sister than I was.

I sighed, trying to withdraw. Evade. ★We have a lot going on right now.★

My wizard wouldn't accept that. ★You're smart, Sirana. You can even be subtle, sometimes. You can help me, help him, as I helped you against the Conceiver.★

★I *will* help, Shyntre, but know I might be dead or gone before you can react again.★

He blinked. His mouth opened but no sound came out.

★Jaunda told me you came to the Cloister to persuade her,★ I signed intensely. ★She told me you *knew* I was in trouble, and which direction to go. How? *How* did you know?★

He licked his lips. Slowly, he raised his hands. He was thinking too much. ★I made something. The first time you left the Tower, when you drenched my face. The cloth you gave me to wipe down. Like the talisman I found.★

My mouth fell open. The Vast Web as my witness, I would *never* leave another cum-soaked cloth behind again!

★Is it so easy?!★ I snapped.

I flat out did not want to believe him. It was terrifying.

★It's *not* easy, no,★ he replied. ★But I knew Wilsira wanted you. I knew your aura well enough to try a counter-spell. To prepare.★

★If you knew I was in trouble,★ I challenged, ★why didn't the Sisterhood come to the Sanctuary first? That's where it got bad!★

★Too many wards and strong mages crammed in one fortress!★ he snapped back. ★Something 'bad' is always happening there. It's a miasma no wizard or sorceress can cut through! I knew when someone *removed* you from the Sanctuary, and I know the Conceiver's methods. Anticipation out of an educated guess.★

Sounded reasonable. Well-planned and enough to convince Jaunda, lucky me. I knew it was enough for Rausery. This was the story he'd be telling the Valsharess, too.

So why didn't I believe him?

★You'll protect him while you can,★ Shyntre repeated.

I nodded, hating myself for this hook of weakness, but I didn't know what was going to happen next anyway.

The wizard was satisfied. ★Thank you. You're one of the few Sisters with any brains. Even some effort on your part is worth full effort in others.★

My brows rose at what was the most generous thing he'd *ever* said about me, but the mage picked up his supplies and opened the door. Motioning with his chin for me to go first, we left to return to solitary.

Auslan sat on the stone ground wrapped in his gifted cloak when we returned, leaning against the bars, as Gaelan and Jael stood guard above him. The Consort looked tired and resigned, patient as he waited for what would become of him.

"What took so long?" Jael asked me as Shyntre knelt to hand a cloth through the bars.

"We couldn't find the finishing powder," I remarked, half-smiling.

"*Pfft!*"

I watched Auslan accept the clean rag and stand up to wet it in the basin. He began wiping the blood off his face, tenderly dabbing at the gash under his hair while I pushed three bags of rations through the bars, their drawstrings cut and removed. Just in case.

Jael scowled at me but glanced at the Consort again before looking back. "Why does he have that gold streak?"

I shrugged even though I had a good guess, but I could see Shyntre wanted to know as well.

"I have said, young Sister," Auslan murmured, avoiding eye contact with anyone as he rinsed his cloth and wiped more of the dried salvia from his throat after getting the blood. "It required a great deal of magic to heal your fallen Sister. I believe it aged me in a short time."

Jael blinked in surprise, and I was guessing there was more information there than she'd gotten before now. Also a curiosity that she wanted to ask me first thing when I returned. Was that Auslan's doing, his encouragement? I thought it likely. The beautiful bua was nimble in conversation.

Returning to the iron bars, Auslan added with a small bow to Jael, "The potions did not work against the Sathoet's taint. I had to use a healing trance."

That answer wasn't meant for Jael or Gaelan. Shyntre was the one who stiffened, looking like he'd been slapped. The wizard looked at me then grabbed the second, less soiled cloth from Auslan through the bars, took his chin, and began wiping the dirt off more brusquely, holding the Consort's eyes up where they could meet. There was some communication there. I couldn't be sure what beyond my certainty that Shyntre now knew what D'Shea wanted no one else to learn about my present state.

"Hmph," Jael said. "Well, glad to hear the Priestesses aren't breeding for gold hair. It's not flattering on you."

The Consort chuckled while Shyntre was probably biting the inside of his cheek to keep from saying anything. I smiled at my younger companion, testing her mood toward me, and she smiled back. It was nice to see.

"Thank you for watching him," I said to both my Sisters. "He did save my life."

Gaelan nodded, a touch of concern on her face, but Jael only shrugged.

"As mages like him are supposed to," she said. "Glad he didn't fail you. I'd have had to get in line to hurt him."

She said this so blithely casual, it was almost funny to me. Shyntre didn't take it well after the first jibe about the Consort's hair.

"Too bad he can't purge the Sathoet out of you," the mage muttered.

I couldn't stop her fist this time; Jael nailed him right in the jaw. Gaelan and I quickly got them separated. The brewer hooked her arms beneath the wizard's, and I caught Jael in a headlock.

"Stop!" I said. "This won't help anything!"

"I. Hate. *Sathoet!*" my younger Sister seethed, trying to get free of my hold.

"Calm down!"

"This sour 'shroom says *anything* like that again, I'll gut him! I hate seeing half-bloods fucking, Sirana, but especially *you* when you can't fight back!" Her voice was shaking, her breath powerful bursts. "I don't have to justify shit. That fucker shouldn't even *be* here!"

"I'll wager I've been inside the Cloister more spans than you, cait," he sniped.

Gaelan had the good sense to drag the wizard back a few more steps but not force him to silence by covering his mouth.

Jael raged back. "Yeah, as some spoiled whelp! Who the fuck are you to get so many passes by Priestesses *and* Sisters? What I've heard, the skin on your back should be a solid layer of scars by now!"

"What makes you think it isn't?!" he snarled.

"Enough!" I barked, scrambling to calm them down. "I'm alive because of *all* of you. I know it, I won't forget! I don't know what's going to happen next, but I'm glad you came to get me! Red Sisters don't leave each other to die."

They both went blessedly quiet. But then Gaelan murmured, "What about Reishel?"

My eyes teared up. "If Rausery's team can't catch up to the flayer ... I don't know."

Auslan observed us in silence from behind the bars; he wasn't taking sides. He watched Jael and me with that same, strange sadness as he did Shyntre.

"Gaelan, Sirana, Jael," Qivni spoke from atop the stairs, and I released my headlock as Gaelan let go of the wizard. "Our Elders need you now."

My stomach tightened. Already? That wasn't nearly enough time to plan.

"Bring the wizard," she added before going quiet.

Neither Shyntre nor I wanted to leave Auslan down here alone, I knew, but we had no choice. It helped that the Consort nodded to us in agreement.

"Go. I shall wait here. As long as you need me to wait."

"As if you can do anything else," Jael muttered grouchily, turning toward the stairs and rubbing her neck.

I motioned Gaelan to follow her, moving to take Shyntre's arm, volunteering to be the one to lead him. He didn't protest. Shrugging, my Sister headed toward the stairs. After she was out of sight, I released his arm.

Catch up, I signed. *Don't push it.*

I turned my back and walked slowly without looking behind, staying out of sight of the top stair until I heard the wizard's steps behind me. He didn't risk more trouble by dawdling; Shyntre stepped in front and cooperatively left solitary confinement ahead of me.\

He'd had a few moments with Auslan without any eyes on him, to use as he saw fit. I hoped he used them well.

We exited and secured the basement then trooped as a group to where the Elders were in debriefing with the glowering Prime. Rausery smirked at us as we entered, her back straight and her uniform glorious as ever. D'Shea stood with grace, arms folded, and stepped casually away from both Prime and General as Shyntre entered, letting her peer do the talking.

"The summons from the Queen has come. We're going to the Palace to answer the Conceiver's accusations. Everyone, play your role, and we might live to see the next cycle."

The Prime narrowed her eyes at me. I wondered how much of that last statement was Rausery's bluff.

CHAPTER 25

NEITHER D'SHEA NOR RAUSERY COULD HAVE HAD ENOUGH TIME TO TALK OR plan, to gather evidence before the Prime came charging back from the Palace. We stood here now because the Valsharess and the Conceiver wouldn't wait. Political blood was drawn, flowing, and ready to gush. It brought out an intensity in the Prime I had never seen before.

I'd been foolish to think I'd seen all her worst moods.

"Sisters ranks Lead and down, strip," the Eldest, near-blonde Sister ordered, darting a sharp look at the only male with us. "Not you, worm."

Shyntre bowed and stepped to the side closer to Rausery and away from D'Shea, eyes on the stone. He was silent and still; I wagered he knew he was the lucky one.

Jaunda, Gaelan, Jael, all shed their damaged equipment and uniforms. I stood out from them, wearing simple, stolen clothing, not even a cloak after giving it to Auslan.

I was finished first, and the Prime focused on me, eyes scouring my nudity. I waited for her to comment on the lack of scars between my thighs, but her gaze kept going as Jael, Gaelan, and Jaunda showed their magic-healed bodies as well.

Despite myself, I imagined some baby-positive glow to match the heat in my gut. I was never more thankful the Prime wasn't a mage.

Was it possible she hadn't yet been debriefed on exactly *how* Kerse had intended to sacrifice me? Or if she had, perhaps she hadn't heard at what point in the ritual the Red Sisters interfered.

"One Sister missing," stated our Eldest. Her harsh, creased eyes shifted to Elder Rausery. "Where's Qivni?"

"She and her team were tracking that missing Sister," the General answered.

"Were? Update?"

"I called 'em back," Rausery said soberly. "They went any deeper, we could lose the whole team."

"So our greatest enemy now has one of us." The Prime looked at D'Shea with clear blame. "A slit we should've killed along with the other two."

"I fully backed the goal of the Elder Sorceress, Prime," Rausery reminded her. "D'Shea and Reishel passed your standards. How could we know?"

"Because they're fuckin' *flayers!*" The Prime slammed her fist on the table, making us jump. Her shoulders and chest expanded with the rising aggression."Never again! Any Red Sister is compromised by an Ornilleth, Elders, you cut their throats yourself out there in the dark. No second chances. Got me?"

"Yes, Prime."

They both answered, though D'Shea was quieter. The Prime looked at the Sorceress, resting her weight on her fists.

"This includes the one standing in this room. The one who let the fucking thing out."

My entire body spread with cold; for a moment, I felt nothing. Hollow and sick. Shyntre's eyes widened, Gaelan gritted her teeth, and Jael shook her head without thinking. Fortunately the Prime wasn't looking at them, as the Sorceress held her attention.

My Elder straightened up and elegantly turned to face her superior, folding her hands in front of her. "Will you use the same argument for the Conceiver? For Kerse to have been so compromised, to be instructed as he was to abduct Sirana, Wilsira had to have gotten close to that prison with her son. More than once."

"My only concern is the Sisterhood, D'Shea."

"Whose purpose for existence is to protect the Queen. Will you allow a Priestess compromised by an Elder Mind to stay so close to Her?"

"I'll do what the Valsharess commands. Wouldn't be the first time the Priestesses lunge for a new pecking order as they eat one of their own. I don't carry two turds for them, but no matter what goes down there, my say of the rank and file of the Sisterhood is final. Sirana will bear her witness to the Queen. Then, after she is released, you will execute her, D'Shea. And I will watch."

No.

The Sorceress offered no expression to this. The Prime grinned a challenge at her.

"Well?"

"Understood, Prime," D'Shea replied without emotion.

The only twitch of hope that kept me from panicking or passing out was a subtle wink Rausery threw at the wizard when he looked to her. Whatever went through his mind, he was the only one of us to bow his head and close his eyes for a heartbeat.

When he looked up again, he he'd found more strength from somewhere. I still felt like I was going to puke.

Don't give up.

THE PRIME MADE CERTAIN NEITHER ELDER HAD A CHANCE TO TALK WITH ME alone before we left for the Palace, which wasn't immediately. We still waited on Qivni, and all four Red Sisters involved in the Sathoet's death needed to be redressed and outfitted properly to stand before the Queen. Jael and I wore the black recruits' uniforms again, and Gaelan and Jaunda wore familiar-looking "borrowed" reds. We were given useable belts, some tools and weapons at least for show.

A signal came at the door, and Qivni's team returned at last to provide more information and help refine the details of our testimony.

"Did you find Reishel, Lead?" Rausery asked directly.

"No, Elder," she said. "But we did find a group of five slain peches, throats cut, and craniums cracked open. Circular bruises on the skin, brain gone."

"Quite a feast."

"Our Sister helped it eat. We could have tracked them farther but —"

Rausery shook her head. "No, you made the right call. Not enough defense if the Ornilleth revitalized itself."

The Prime grunted, unimpressed. "So it got away."

My superior's boiling eyes landed on me. In case I thought the confirmation that Reishel was taken to a fate I knew nothing about wasn't bad enough, regret and grief clawed at my heart while terror and denial struggled in turn to change it to stone. I could barely think, but I listened. And watched.

Rausery asked, "Anything else of note?"

Qivni nodded at her support, three of whom stepped forward and each poured the contents of their black sacks across the table. I recognized my equipment and warmth overran my face.

Indeed, not yet bad enough.

I'd been helpless to stop Kerse from removing every item and placing it far from me; there had been no struggle. Having it spread before me in its sorry state only enhanced the shame in front of the Sisterhood. If I hadn't been sentenced to death after the Queen's Hearing, I was stuck how I would climb any rank in the next five hundred years after this.

Qivni spoke. "Suna and Koreth stayed to search the rubble before any of the Priestess servants could arrive. The rest of us tracked Reishel and the Ornilleth. They found these buried all in one spot, and a lot of bloody rocks on the other side of the cavern. It looked to Koreth like a protective circle or shield had kept the blood from being scorched. That's why the color was still there."

Rausery glanced at Shyntre, who nodded to confirm, and that apparently was all that the Elder needed, but D'Shea wanted more.

"Did you recover a white wipe cloth stained with old blood?" the Sorceress said to the two Sisters, her voice tight.

"Um. No, Elder."

"It disintegrated after the will-bending spell was broken," Shyntre interjected.

D'Shea stiffened, didn't turn to him, but managed a nod. I saw the frustration and regret having lost that evidence. She and the General could have heard that before now except neither Shyntre nor Gaelan were part of the talks. With a soft sigh, Rausery rooted through the badly damaged pile as if to see what was left. Watching her, suddenly, I had something to know.

"Did your team find a blue pendant or a gold ring, Elder?"

My gaze was drawn to an overly clueless expression on Suna's face. Qivni noticed it as well. She bared her teeth and slapped her subordinate upside the head.

"I said no skimming, Suna!"

"I didn't realize it was part of her tack, Lead!"

Thena's sycophant Sister fumbled to take off her left glove and remove Callitro's ring from her finger, swiftly dropping it into Qivni's waiting palm.

"Spider dung, Suna," Rausery snorted, gesturing for Qivni to return my ring to me before the Prime could voice an opinion.

I gratefully accepted and tugged off a glove to slip it on my own finger.

"Wait, what's that do?" the Prime growled, a bit slow to catch up to the General.

"Sensory enhancer," Rausery said with a casual shrug.

"Hmph."

I stood at attention, stiff as a pillar, and gave away nothing.

Sensory enhancer ... Maybe that *would* have been more useful in the Sanctuary, given I had not been able to use Callitro's ring even once in this last fight. More than that, though, the General gave it back and had lied to the Prime. D'Shea, Shyntre, and I knew it.

Suna had no reaction, however, so I had to assume she hadn't figured out its purpose when she palmed it.

The Prime said, "What about the other? She asked for a blue pendant?"

Rausery frowned in an excellent display of bafflement. She looked at Qivni, who looked at her subordinates. They all shook their heads.

"We didn't find one, Lead," Koreth answered.

I grew dizzy trying to recall where I'd last seen it. It had been the only thing I was wearing when Kerse mounted me that final time. He had left it around my neck, as he had confirmed its properties linked our minds, bound our sensations together. I had been wearing it still when Shyntre knelt beside me, when he shielded me from the Sathoet's attacks. It was there when he had thrown himself down to cover me.

Unhurriedly, I let my eyes drift toward the wizard. He was waiting for that; he reached up and scratched a spot on his chest, letting me see the lump beneath his robe.

Son of a Dwarf ...

At least I knew where it was.

Although, on second thought, I wasn't sure if I ever wanted to wear it again.

THE VALSHARESS TOOK HER AUDIENCE IN A STRANGE CHAMBER FAR FROM THE main doings of the Palace. Small compared to the one in which I'd once stood, listening to the plans for the Worship Ball, the first time I had seen the fine lines of Her ancient face and glimpsed those strange, tawny eyes.

This room would contain far fewer Davrin, standing room only.

The Prime and Elders, the Leads and only those three younger Red Sisters who had witnessed Kerse's death were there along with Shyntre. I had gathered from gestures that we stood on the very top floor of the Palace after using a transport circle in the basement. We were above even the Sathoet floor of the Sanctuary in elevation.

The chamber itself was opulent and showed no stone. There was a comfortable violet and gold throne set upon a staging area to one side of the room, the decorations both sensual and threatening in their curves of breast and claw. The throne was empty.

Royal purple drapery framed complex tapestries, many themed in some fashion after the Spider Queen alongside those which either reminded me of erotic and violent images I'd seen on the Sathoet floor. In addition, some were simply beautiful, like the innocent, sensual buas, on the floor of the Consorts.

The images on the ceiling were distracting.

Blue sky and red waves? The curve of the world?

A horizon, perhaps, such as Shyntre had described to me in the library at the Wizard's Tower. Or like that dream I had which woke Qivni.

I frowned, reminding myself it could also be abstract art. Me seeing what I wanted in it, still wishing for escape from execution at my own Elder's hand after this audience. Was there anything my Elders could do, or was the Prime's say, indeed, final?

Our scrubbed and polished boots sank into a thickly woven rug made of interlinking webs in purple, gold, red, and blue shades. Four yellow candles, so thick that I wouldn't have been able to wrap both hands around them, sat in their golden stanchions at equal distances around the perimeter of the circular room.

The firelight was real. I could smell it smoking a little now and then, but the light was not overwhelming; instead, it enriched the colors to an astonishing degree. These candles might last for cycles without burning down and out.

The Red Sisters weren't alone for long. On the opposite side of where we had arrived, there was another small jump circle, though I only became aware of it when I heard the suck of air and hum of magic.

Three Priestesses arrived: Wilsira, Lelinahdara, and the current eldest, Roshen Byu'Felathon, the "High" Priestess to whom I'd been introduced recently and under Wilsira's influence. Roshen was nominally above Wilsira because she was First House instead of Second and a little older. She got into the luxury position first and worked only to secure it.

D'Shea once remarked that Roshen didn't do much with it.

Kerse's Mother made certain she kept her feet then looked for me, eschewing any pretense of why she was here.

The hatred in her eyes burned brighter than the candles, but she looked much older and weaker. Her hair was all blonde, with loose skin around her jaw and neck and arms as if it had lost significant elasticity in a short time. Her hands seemed bonier as well, showing a vein or two, her knuckles were larger knobs unable to wear her rings.

Wilsira at only seven hundred now had actual wrinkles like Phaelous and the Valsharess.

We stared at each other for several heavy moments, Wilsira and me. She had been ready to chain me in that sub-room with my belly forcibly stuffed. She would have left me down there to give birth and, according to her and the peasant she had once ordered me to kill, I would never have left again.

I couldn't know yet if I would end up back under her thumb again if anyone discovered my condition during this audience, but I smiled at her to acknowledge how much she had suffered when Kerse died.

Fuck you for dragging me down, too, just when I found a purpose in this fucking city.

We heard a subtle shift of stone and a surge of magic, then the Drider Keeper herself stepped out from behind a tapestry in the form of a loose-haired, Davrin cait. Every younger Red Sister tensed.

The Braqth-touched Elf smiled playfully at us, her eyes like hard rubies. She had fangs, and there were very dark purple spots around her Davrin eyes, mimicking the multiple sets of a spider's eyes.

She wore a simple, purple robe-gown like a Priestess except that it was sleeveless to show her arms, shoulders, and part of her ribs. She was far more muscular than any Priestess, with thick, black hairs growing out of her forearms and elbows. Her full white hair fell down her back with no decoration whatsoever. She wore no jewelry, looking better placed in the wilderness, not the Palace.

This was the first time I had ever seen Auranka, though I'd always known of her existence. I caught more than one Davrin in the room suppressing a shudder. Auranka tittered with pleasure. She drew back the tapestry and spoke.

"Your Valsharresss."

We bowed as the Queen entered wearing the elegant, venerable body wrap of gold and purple which She'd worn the last time.

Her crown was still interwoven into Her solid blonde hair, diamonds and amethysts and rubies glittering in candlelight. Matching necklace, rings, and a bracelet around Her left wrist completed the ensemble, and this time She wore a ceremonial dagger at Her waist.

Our Queen remained standing, facing us in silence.

The Priestesses shifted, clearly wishing to be asked to speak, to begin spinning the threads of their story. The Prime looked annoyed to be standing here, Rausery waited patiently, and D'Shea was in no hurry to speak as she considered her proximity both to her tormentor and her son.

The Valsharess did not seem to note any specific female from amongst Her more powerful officers of Sivaraus. Her encompassing gaze moved once across the room and readily stopped on the one bua among us, standing at the very back.

"Fadele," the Queen said.

I had no idea who was being addressed.

"Prime, my Queen," the Eldest Sister corrected.

The Valsharess smiled without humor. "Fadele. Retrieve Our elder Son. Bring him to Us."

I witnessed the strangest thing. Centuries peeling back in an instant, a hint of a younger Queen and even younger Red Sister Prime facing off. It vanished as soon as Rausery stepped out of the way to make room for her superior as "Fadele" spun around and stalked to the back of the line to snatch Shyntre roughly by his neck.

"Move, worm," she growled, dragging him past me.

The Prime shoved him so hard that the wizard stumbled onto his knees with a hoarse cry, landing short of the Queen's gown. Shyntre righted himself quickly but took the lowest kneeling bow he could, curling up in a ball, interlocking his fingers on the back of his head.

"Majesty," he whispered.

He did not even attempt to look up, shuddering when the Valsharess leaned down to caress his hair, plucking it as if She noticed how short it was. Far too short to thread into a proper grip.

I stared, a shiver running up my spine as I witnessed *terror* in my fiery mage. It seemed unreal.

I had seen him bow low to Wilsira, obeying her commands, but I thought each time that Shyntre was less afraid of the Conceiver than reluctant to endure her whimsical punishments for nothing. I also didn't believe he was truly afraid of any of the Red Sisters; we held even fewer unknowns for him than a Priestess would.

This is true fear. The Queen has given attention to him before.

I looked at D'Shea as if she could tell me anything. The Elder Sorceress wasn't looking at him; she held her gaze fixed on Wilsira, who still glowered at me. The curving room was a veritable vortex of trouble with no clear way out.

The Valsharess leaned down, using Her bare hands to peel Shyntre's fingers apart so She could raise him up and cradle his face in Her palms.

"Eyes, Son. Look at Us."

The wizard resisted but it was very brief. Soon he craned his neck to peer up at Her tawny gaze. He flinched, gasping before a crash of tension ripped through him; it looked like someone unseen was pressing forge-glowing metal to his back.

"N-no," he groaned.

Auranka stepped closer, peering curiously at him like he might be food.

"Shhh," the Valsharess murmured. "Confess, child. You are Our untainted witness."

"M-Ma —" he stuttered, clutching at the heavily decorated hands. "Majesty! Goddess! *Aaa!"*

Shyntre howled, jolted once more, and went slack. The Valsharess allowed him to drop to the plush, carpeted floor, unconscious.

Each of us stared at Her and the young mage; not even Wilsira could think of what to say as our Queen stood in contemplation, a frown growing gradually upon Her face. I had the feeling that She wasn't interested in a preliminary briefing of what happened.

She already had it.

"You lost control of your son, Wilsira," the Valsharess said, sounding troubled. "Your Sathoet broke his blood bond with you. How is this possible?"

"Ruthless and irresponsible tampering from the Sisterhood!" the aged Priestess answered, flinging her fingers to point at D'Shea and me as the words spilled to fill the thick air of the chamber. "They've been experimenting with a new will-bending magic from a forbidden source! The result was *this!*"

The Queen tilted Her crowned head in mild curiosity while Auranka still watched Shyntre, subtly licking her lips. I worked to focus on what accusation was being laid at our feet.

"The Elder Sorceress found an adept, Sirana of House Thalluen, and recruited her. D'Shea chose to practice this unknown on *my* son, starting at *that* cait's trials. The Elder Sorceress caused a willful vulnerability, an unknown to me when I visited the prisoner in the Drider cave.

"This ... this foolishness *lost* Sivaraus both our eldest Sathoet and allowed a dangerous leak back to an Elder Mind. Such a great mistake cannot be let go with mere punishment or imprisonment. I urge you, my Queen, sacrifice the last of her fouled House to Braqth, once and for all! Give her to Auranka!"

The Valsharess glanced down at Shyntre's body, as if noting that expunging the "last" of D'Shea's House included him. She did not appear convinced and looked at my Elder. "Have you a response, Varessa?"

D'Shea couldn't speak. Not what she *really* wanted to say. I could see it on her face. I knew how ill she felt as well; how it was building without relief, yet she tried to hide the tremors. The Prime made a scoffing noise. D'Shea forced her throat to clear; her voice had to be strong.

"This goes back farther, Valsharess," the Sorceress said, lowering a scroll case from her shoulder. "Wilsira Tachnathon has knowingly and successfully bred her Sathoet at least once, and she did *not* purge the unborn before it had an Abyssal name. This, she tried to wrest from the young Mother by trickery and intimidation before the Noble could learn it herself."

"Lies," Wilsira hissed. "How dare you?"

D'Shea ignored her and lifted the case. "Sister Sirana captured the conversation by bloodstone, and I heard it. I have it transcribed here."

Roshen the High Priestess sneered, her back straight. "I'm sure it's a lovely poem, Elder."

The Sorceress ignored her. "If this breeding and bonding has happened more than once, then Wilsira forced Kerse's maturity on her own, and his demon sire's blood frayed the bond, made him unpredictable and willful, until it broke. The Sisterhood is meant to execute these Priestess Sons *before* this happens."

"Always with permission from your Valsharess," interjected Roshen, the High Priestess, with clear disapproval.

"Yes, Your Highness. By the time Sirana confirmed it, Wilsira forced her into the Forming Pit, intending to silence her and cover up the changes in her son."

"My Queen," said Roshen, "they spin fanciful tapestries."

The Valsharess lifted one hand to the High Priestess. The room fell quiet, and D'Shea waited for the signal to continue. She received it a moment later.

"There, Kerse made his move," the Sorceress said. "He rebelled, overtook his Mother's spell on Sirana, wrapped the Conceiver alive in a mass of webs. He abducted one of our Red Sisters to later force her to free the Ornilleth before attempting to sacrifice her to open a gateway to the Elsewhere.

"We did not have time to seek your permission, Valsharess. For the sake of our *entire* city, we acted without regret to prevent a demonblood from summoning the Abyss outside of the Sanctuary, in service to himself, not to Braqth and You."

D'Shea bowed her head. "The Sisterhood will accept the Queen's Judgment, as we always have, but beg you hear the entirety of our case first. The Conceiver has broken your Law for simple lust for power, and she is a threat to You."

"The Sisterhood exposed their weakest members to psionic vulnerability as well, Your Majesty," Wilsira countered. Roshen beside her looked truly surprised. "They failed to deal with them effectively. Sirana was attacked by a Tragar during her trials, and D'Shea covered that up for her own foolish greed to control what we know cannot be controlled!"

It took everything for me to stay still, but my eyes flicked to the Liaison. Lelinahdara kept her eyes on the Queen, lifting her chin in agreement as Roshen scowled at them both.

Fuck.

"Red Sister Reishel," Wilsira rushed forward, "the one being ridden by the escaped Ornilleth, whom the Sisters *failed* to recover, was one of those struck down in the last attempt the Elder Mind made to recover its creature! Both these Sisters should not have been allowed to live. The Prime went against her own judgment because of this manipulative Sorceress challenging the Sanctuary.

"*That* is why the Ornilleth escaped, Your Highness! *That* is why my Son rebelled against me, and why he is dead!"

Admitting now that the Prime hadn't known about the Tragar attack while D'Shea had would be even worse; our Eldest scowled but said nothing.

Now I knew why I hadn't welcomed a Priestess inside the Cloister. *Goddess, we're in trouble.*

Wilsira shook badly despite her air of certain victory, gasping for breath as wetness leaked from her eyes. Her determination was set deep in every new line on her face.

"I was *testing* the new Red Sister Sirana for you, my Queen, to discover what the Sisterhood was hiding, even as they plotted against me. This cait is strange, resistant to *all* my suggestion spells, as none this age should be! When I knew her limits at last, and the Confessor shared that she had the shadow of a Grey Dwarf inside her mind, yes! I put this threat in the Forming Pit where she would harm no one ever again.

"But it was too late for my Son, Highness, he changed too quickly. I demand the execution of both Elder D'Shea and Red Sister Sirana for this atrocity against our divine Davrin magic!"

The Prime nodded, clearly in agreement with the Conceiver. She opened and closed her fists several times, a tic in her jaw relaying her fury.

Rausery motioned for permission to speak and was granted it by the Valsharess. She began simply. Her calm voice somehow neutralized the violence threatening to spill.

"Lead Jaunda witnessed the Second Daughter of Itlaun conceive by Wilsira's Sathoet only a few cycles before the last Worship Ball, Your Highness. This was done in the Conceiver's presence, at her command. A bribe to grant the cait's House a Consort."

The Queen's ancient eyes glanced at Jaunda, who bowed her head and voiced respectful confirmation. A nod. "Go on, Elder."

Rausery bowed as well. "Shyntre witnessed the miscarriage of that child, Kerse's offspring. It was more than a turn later; she was over halfway. Sirana had been sent by Elder D'Shea to find out why. She has a transcript of a bloodstone confession from the Conceiver's own mouth."

"Yes, General," the Queen acknowledged. "We saw this in Our Son's memories."

"Thank you, Your Highness. No amount of web-spinning now explains the Conceiver's motive except either the spread of Sathoet-blooded mages, which Your Highness has forbidden, or gathering more demonic names outside the Sanctuary's rituals to increase her power, an action which is troubling for the one who claims the credit for the arrival of our Consorts. This investigation has nothing to do with any novice Red Sister or our perceived failings training them."

Wilsira snarled, "And an Elder Mind understanding the inner work-ings of Sivaraus isn't troubling as well, General?"

Rausery smiled, turned, and bowed to the Conceiver. "I'd remind my peers that *any* Davrin or half-Davrin can be used by an Ornilleth, and we've fought both them and the Tragar before *without* culling our Sisters simply for doing their duty to engage them. That's a slippery path to begin walking.

"The Prime herself has fought flayers and Dwarves in the past to keep us all safe. By these cries now, the entire Sisterhood should be executed for doing as we've been trained to do by the Prime for the last fifteen hundred years. I dare say it's an easy cry for a Priestess who never risks contact with the Fringe at all, yet the Sisterhood remains loyal to Your

Highness and the Throne even now.

"No matter what happens, the Red Sister won't stand helpless against the flayers, regardless of the fallout from Kerse's rebellion. The Sathoet knew *exactly* how to hurt his Mother, and the rest of us, the most. So be it. We can only prepare for what comes now."

The Elder General was the portrait of reason, dispersing the hot air of accusation and pushing us forward out of the haze. Even the Prime smirked in satisfaction, her back straightening with pride at Rausery's speech, as if she *hadn't* ordered the exact same sentence in the Cloister with the same justification as Wilsira.

As if 'Fadele' didn't order D'Shea to slit my throat after this audience.

The Valsharess still listened. "What would you say of the Conceiver's statement, of your recruit suffering multiple shadows in her mind?"

The way She said that caused groups of bumps to arise on my back.

Rausery nodded, ignoring the look from the Priestess. "Perhaps the Conceiver *was* testing our novice of unusual talent, finding the limits at the same time D'Shea was increasing her skills in ward-breaking and resistance to will-bending. Clearly, Kerse saw it and took advantage.

"I would state that it could be expected, Your Highness. Sirana came to us as a child survivor of a contraband compulsion which lasted for decades. Her older sister, who placed it upon her, was intended to become an acolyte of the Sanctuary before her accident. Our new Red Sister has prior experience with will-bending and resisting those methods with Sanctuary origins. That was the main reason we recruited her."

Wilsira scoffed, glancing at Tarra, whose mouth twisted a bit. Roshen looked left out.

"But the Sathoet had been bred with a Noble and had encountered the flayer well before Sirana's special training began, Your Majesty. Let's not conflate the two. Kerse was a different matter which escalated quickly and pulled in those most vulnerable.

"Why *wouldn't* the Sathoet and the Ornilleth choose two competent Sisters to help break them out? Wilsira gave the Sathoet ample opportunity to discover Sirana's limits for himself, and he would have learned all those skills he used against us from her. The Ornilleth simply gave him the will to use them independently of her."

"Not true!" the Priestess barked, her face twisting in denial. "It was D'Shea's pettiness and greed, distracting my son with her new pet slit!"

Elder Rausery paused and looked at her in surprise. "I'd like to remind the Conceiver that underestimating an Abyssal Son's determination to slip his bonds has ended up here before. It's in the blood, a constant test of worthiness from the Spider Queen herself, and the only risk I see demanded of the Daughters of Braqth in exchange for their power. Blaming the rupture of this one bond on a cait barely a century old and a Sorceress doing her due diligence, as per her rank, is blind hubris."

"You —"

"A good reminder, General," our ancient Queen interjected. "You've stated your case."

Rausery bowed her head one last time, and the room fell into silence. Our ruler further contemplated this without interruption for some time, the High Priestess motioning more than once for the Conceiver to hold her tongue and wait. The Queen's gaze drifted down to the wizard who'd fainted at Her feet, then up, studying me.

"Red Sister Sirana."

A staggering rush like liquid fire flooded out from my chest as I crushed the impulse to run. As if I could flee out of this room. I didn't know what to do or say, so I took to a knee.

"Y-Your Highness?"

"Come forward, Sister. Bring your Elder's scroll case."

I rose again, accepted the strap as D'Shea handed it to me, and took four silent steps on the springy mat beneath me. I kneeled to the left of Shyntre's still body and presented it to Her, wishing he would wake up and convince me he was alright.

What has She done to him?

"We have seen you before," the Queen muttered absently, accepting the case. "Blue eyes. Yes."

My stomach clenched in response; I kept my head bowed. She removed four fiberstalk parchments, which I presumed to be the four versions of the bloodstone conversation that my Elder and I had shared with

Gaelan and Reishel. The Queen read through each of them, seemingly in their entirety, giving away nothing in Her body language or expression.

"Hm."

The Valsharess rolled them up again and slid them back in their tube, closing it and handing it to Auranka, who slung it across her torso like a satchel. The Queen spoke to me.

"Have you any tangible proof against the Conceiver, Red Sister?"

My heart pounded in my ears. I hadn't had the time in the Sanctuary, my focus had been destroyed as thoroughly as that damned cloth. The Conceiver and her son ganging up on me without Shyntre there had been so much worse; I barely remembered anything but the lust and fear.

If only the stubborn wizard had been there again.

A moth's wing seemed to brush my head. It didn't hurt. *Why do you wish this, child?*

He protected Qivni from catching. I know he did. He knows those Priestess sons aren't right …

Are not right? In what way?

A lurid memory returned without my conscious thought.

The young Consort offered to my Lead; his plunging deep into her netherhole, holding flush against her bottom. After the spurting was done, he maintained a tired balance long after any bua would have withdrawn. The Conceiver had hustled us out of the room, and I heard again Qivni protesting behind a closed door, pleading with him, squealing in pain:

"*Get it … out. Just … p-pull it — … aaa!*"

Wilsira had laughed dismissively, claiming the Lead was out of practice, but I *knew* why it might hurt so much to pull out.

I'd had one of those cocks lodged in my ass a few cycles later.

Did you, child?

Yes.

The time alone in bed with Wilsira's son arose as vividly as when I'd discovered Qivni bent over the bed. Every sensation returned, the pleasure, the scent. The Sathoet's new, smaller hands touched me again, and his bulge stretched my asshole wider than it had ever been.

We became locked together, and had we tried to disconnect right after he'd climaxed, I would have been squealing like Qivni.

A massive shadow seemed to pull back as the candlelight flickered around me. I heard a soft gasp.

Kerse had changed shape since my trials, Your Highness, I thought, trying to explain. *He showed me as he set the foundation for the binding spell which would force me to release the Ornilleth. I didn't know. I was too focused on Wilsira trying to fill my womb and trap me away from the Sisterhood.*

Our Queen loomed over me. The ethereal flutter now applied galvanized pressure.

⋆Speak what you've not told your Elders. What Wilsira has not yet heard. We would hear them spoken aloud.⋆

Yes, my Queen.

I licked my lips. "There was a Consort with us when Kerse rebelled, Valsharess. Chosen by the Conceiver to stuff me in the Forming Pit. Kerse bound him up with his Mother but left him alive."

"Strange," the Valsharess acknowledged. "Was he rushed?"

"No, Your Majesty. He had the time to complete the binding upon the a-altar. I heard the Sathoet say to this Consort that he was to bear witness when the Conceiver awakened. That she would suffer very much, very soon."

"He did not!" Wilsira denied.

"Silence!"

The Valsharess' voice landed upon us like a collapsing tunnel. After the dust settled, another mental push.

⋆Speak your accusation, Red Sister. Let it begin.⋆

"They were brothers," I said. "The Sathoet and the Consort, both Wilsira's sons, and much closer in form than it appears at first. Centuries apart but maturing at the same time. I … don't know how or why."

The Valsharess lifted her tawny eyes away from me at last, addressing Wilsira before the Priestess had time to react. "We shall meet this Consort of whom she speaks, Conceiver. Summon him."

"My Queen, should we allow serving buas in on our private affairs?"

"Do you defy Our command, Conceiver?"

"No, your Grace, I —"

"I know where this Consort is, Your Majesty," the Liaison spoke up then. "I will retrieve him for you."

The look on the Conceiver's face could have dissolved stone.

And there it is.

The backstab we all expected in battle, sooner or later. It seemed we could never be sure who would break rank first.

But here, in this room, I wasn't surprised.

CHAPTER 26

We waited in simmering tension.

I had been instructed to stand again with my Elders, and I made eye contact with D'Shea and Rausery, saw their curiosity and minor annoyance that I hadn't mentioned this Consort sooner. There hadn't been time, nor had I been sure of what I'd seen until now.

The next Davrin to enter the Queen's chamber wasn't Lelinahdara returning with Wilsira's pet, however. It was the Headmaster, whom no one had been expecting except, it seemed, the Valsharess. He went directly to Shyntre.

At last, my wizard stirred with the proximity of his sire. Shyntre's gold-flecked eyes opened with the light touch to his forehead; he stared at those strange red waves on the ceiling, looking lost. Phaelous reached for his son's hand, pulling him up and urging him to stand without a word spoken. Shyntre got to his feet yet still didn't appear to know where he was.

"Return him to the Tower, Headmaster," ordered the Valsharess, and the subtle lines of terror returned to Shyntre's face. "Keep this *bua* safe from *all* females. Make certain he does not leave your care. We shall summon him again when We are ready."

"Yes, my Queen."

The Headmaster didn't look at D'Shea, nor did she look at him, as the two males made their way to the jump circle. They disappeared a moment later, leaving only the Priestesses and Red Sisters in the audience chamber, and the Elder Sorceress took a deeper breath. Something inside her uncoiled. I sensed her mentally preparing for what happened next.

The Liaison finally returned, and more than one of us inhaled deeply as the new fragrance spilled in from the magic circle. Tarra escorted a mostly naked Consort wearing only a pale blue loincloth.

This was the same bua I'd seen twice in Wilsira's suites, now possessing fresh burn marks around his wrists and ankles. He was beautiful and graceful as before but wary and in pain. He did not make a peep, standing cooperative and obedient.

The Valsharess motioned them forward, every Red Sister watching the Conceiver in case she panicked. The Conceiver lifted her chin against us. She spoke.

"My greatest achievement, my Queen," she said. "A new path for the Davrin people, if You but wish it."

The Valsharess took a step down from Her platform, studying the young male. She seemed to be looking at something beyond his face.

"Sirana is correct, he *is* my son, born and matured well after I was told I would have no more. Indeed, Kerse's brother, but only through me, Your Majesty. This one has a *Davrin* sire, and I can prove it if your Grace but gives me the opportunity."

"You still possess the scars," our Queen stated without looking at her. Without asking proof.

"Yes, Your Highness. Another Mata incubated and bore him on my behalf." Wilsira licked her lips, holding her hands in respectful supplication. "The next step, when I could be certain of success and make this joyous announcement to You, was when this one healed my scars.

"After the Consorts, I meant to create healer buas to return our fertility. A gift from Braqth for all my sisters who resent and ignore their firstborn sons in the Twelfth-Floor chamber. We would cease having to farm our closest servants from the Sisterhood. The Red Sisters could *return* to placing their own Daughters and sons."

The Conceiver managed to get a reaction from everyone in that room, though it wasn't uniform.

Dread stole through Jael, Gaelan, and me first, and I heard a soft curse from Jaunda as she exchanged a glance with Qivni. The Prime snorted and shook her head, indifferent to the news, but I glimpsed both doubt and reluctant interest on both D'Shea's and Rausery's faces — for a moment — before anger at some memory wiped it out.

A real smile came to the High Priestess's face; she nodded with regal pride. Tarra, in contrast, struggled to hold her confidence at the front of the room, holding the silent bua by his arm but now uncertain if she'd made an advancing choice.

Behind the Queen, the Drider Keeper chuckled, standing as a guard with no skin in the game, her bare, spider-haired arms crossed in ease.

We each awaited the Queen's response. Her faraway look pierced Wilsira's new son even as I dared imagine Her thoughts drifted.

"The perfect son," She murmured.

The remark sounded absent to me, rhetorical, not spoken of the bua before Her. I could not grasp the length of memory She must have, nor could I imagine the convoluted way that She might find attraction in this claim, yet Wilsira jumped upon it as tangible barter.

"Forgive me being discreet," she said. "I did not wish to raise hopes too soon. W-without the jealous distraction of my Sathoet, I can continue this work, Your Highness."

"With half your power gone in a suicidal blast, Priestess?" D'Shea said, cutting to the quick.

Rage arose on Wilsira's face, now beyond control already made brittle. The Sorceress smirked defiantly in the face of it. Any sense of those "raised hopes" fizzled.

"Lead Qivni," the Valsharess said, watching the Consort. "Come forward. Confessor, remove his loincloth."

Our Lead wasn't eager for this, although Elder Rausery's light touch at her back helped cover any impulse to keep her distance from the pretty little bua who had drilled her on her knees in the Conceiver's suites. Qivni passed me, moving forward with her back straight. Then she bowed.

The Valsharess peered at her for a few instants. "Yes. We remember you, too."

"Valsharess," the Lead mage murmured.

By now, Tarra had stripped the Consort. He looked only bewildered, not aware enough of the situation to be afraid but glancing at Wilsira for direction. She offered him none; I caught a tremor pass through her. She was thinking too hard. Or not enough.

With the lack of directive even being surrounded by ranking females, the Consort looked at Qivni, the one closest and one he knew. He smiled, turning slightly toward her, where I could see his genitals clearly. He began to lengthen, to stiffen being near her again. His prick looked normal to me; there wasn't a bulge like Kerse's demonic change. He was as perfect as any desirable Davrin.

I swallowed the rising nerves trying to seize my throat.

"Touch him, Lead," the Queen commanded, gesturing to that responsive pole.

Qivni's face tightened to be on such display before both superiors and subordinates, but she obeyed the Queen, stepping closer to wrap a gloved hand around his cock. He stepped closer, eager for it, his eyes soft with suggestion. His mouth opened to a seductive and submissive invitation for a kiss.

I was mesmerized when he moaned as Qivni stroked him harder. Pulled him closer. Her lips hovered above his, hesitant and quivering, when the Consort stood up on his toes, stretching his chin and neck to take the initiative and close the distance.

They kissed, and Qivni was caught. We could all see our Sister's behavior under the Consort's influence, but the mages saw something much, much more which pulled striking reactions from D'Shea, Gaelan, Tarra and the High Priestess—

And the Valsharess.

Those tawny, translucent eyes were wide open with a very present horror.

Qivni moaned in despair, trying to pull away as I had on the Fourth floor when I had wandered into a collective bedroom of young buas. She was reaching for her belt, fumbling to remove it with one hand while the other still held a turgid erection.

He grunted a protest, pressing in to kiss the Red Sister again and again as if he would consume her very breath.

Power swelled to fill the room, hot and scorching to our heightened senses. An ancient Davrin stepped off her stage, drawing Her ceremonial dagger. The Valsharess clutched the bua's neck and delivered a magical shock which threw Qivni back and away with a cry. The Queen squeezed, cutting off his breath and the blood flow to his head, and he gripped at Her bejeweled hand.

Now there was a bulge swelling at the base of his cock.

Unthinking, Wilsira protested. "No — !"

The Valsharess plunged the dagger in, straight up and behind the breeder's sternum, piercing the heart with precision in one stroke. His lithe body jerked; She twisted her wrist, and it jerked again.

Dropped to the carpet. Dead.

The Queen's eyes blazed as they swept over us. Although She paused briefly on the Conceiver, Her focus turned on Auranka, gripping Her bloody blade.

The Drider Keeper was smiling, showing fangs as her shoulders shook in silent laughter. "Your Command, my Queen?"

"Hold the thought, Dread Mistress."

Tarra skittered backward out of the way as the Valsharess stalked forward. The Priestess Roshen reacted the same way, backing away like a scavenger giving ground to an approaching predator over a wounded animal.

In my periphery, Jaunda darted forward to grab Qivni by her shoulders and get her to her feet. By the time Wilsira was backed against a tapestry on the wall, whimpering with her Queen's hand around her throat, Qivni was back within our wary circle as we waited on a blade's edge for the next action.

Hold, D'Shea signed so all Red Sisters could see, her eyes fixed intensely on the Conceiver and Valsharess.

I doubted any one of us would have chosen to do anything else.

"How long?" the Valsharess demanded, interrogating the Priestess directly.

"I-I don't ... ?"

"WHEN?!"

Wilsira shrieked as arcs of violet lightning, tinged with bloody red, pierced her, and her body withered more before our eyes.

"Th-The last Red — *argh* — !"

The Valsharess quivered in rage. "Varessa D'Shea?"

"And Ja'Prohn, Your Grace! No pairing had been more potent in centuries. We are *losing* mage strength in the newly born! It was necessary! It worked, you've seen it! You approved!"

"The youngest Consorts are all affected, my Queen," Lelinahdara put in.

I bet it took all she had to sound so bold; I still wasn't sure if she'd been heard.

"Fadele," the Valsharess said without looking away from the Conceiver.

The Prime was wide awake now. I'd never seen this smile on her face before. It was gleeful. "Yes, my Queen?"

"We shall need you. Soon."

"Always, Majesty."

Auranka hissed upon the stage, purring in contentment, her eyes glittering in hunger. "Give her to usss, my Queen. We will make thisss one suffer for a very ... *long* ... time. She shall not die."

"Yes. That is best. A warning to all in the Sanctuary who would flaunt the Queen's Law."

Our Valsharess did not use the dagger again but stepped back to pull Wilsira with Her, throwing the crippled Priestess to one side. Wilsira landed in the open area between our ruler and her Drider enforcer. With a delighted, squealing exhale, Auranka sauntered forward, the black hairs on her arms rising.

"No, no, not this!" Wilsira scrambled away, but anyone could see it was only a delay.

D'Shea shook her head in denial. She tried but couldn't speak. She looked at me, crimson eyes pleading for connection. My head hurt just glimpsing that deep; it pounded in silent protest as I merely *thought* to bridge the gap between us. With the unbearable tension rising, with Wilsira wailing out loud, I wasn't sure I could, but I had to try.

We are her — !

I barely heard her.

*--she is **my** only way out!*

I understood. *No demons but us.*

I guffawed once at the spectacle of Auranka stalking a doomed Priestess around the stage; I belted it loud enough to gain their attention. Wilsira twisted abruptly to look at me. The old terror met my aching eyes for an instant. I pushed as hard for her to hear me now as Shyntre must have pushed to set me free.

~Kerser'yn'czael chose **me**, you wrinkled son-abuser. You weren't **enough** for his sire's altar a second time!~

Whatever fear held Wilsira to the floor now shattered; I staggered under such vile loathing. New strength filled the withered body, and the Conceiver howled as her red eyes became liquid rage.

She charged me, and I braced to block her from reaching my Elder. We collided, and I kicked her gut as something small and tickling streaked up the back of my head, rushing cross the tips of my ears.

Suddenly, Wilsira's outstretched arms scratching at me were the bridge for three black spiders. They reached her neck and face.

And bit her.

With a scream of shock, the Priestess staggered and fell away from me onto her back. The venom acted quickly, seizures taking her body. The wrinkled skin of her jaw, neck, and chest swelled as her throat closed; she could no longer breathe.

Auranka took one quick step forward, her weird eyes wide as she watched the Priestess suffocate.

When Wilsira went still, succumbing to the poison, Auranka looked at me and D'Shea with a curious expression. The Drider Keeper had stopped smiling for once. Slowly, she stepped back to her original waiting spot as if knowing she was no longer needed.

The next moment, D'Shea collapsed to her knees, shuddering and coughing before vomiting up something black and thick onto the lush padding beneath her.

"What the fuck, Varessa?" the Prime snarled, but the Valsharess raised Her hand to silence her.

"We see it, Red Sister Prime. Wait. An old spell is being undone."

The formal use of her title calmed the First Sister. Although her vicious scowl remained, the Prime stood at attention with fists tight as she waited on her ruler.

I was still on my feet but trembled to watch my Elder be released at last. I'd been there. I knew what it was like.

The Elder Sorceress heaved one more time, spat another clog out, took her first breath as if drawing air down to her toes, then pushed herself up enough to take to one knee. She weaved a little side-to-side. "Valsharess ... my ... apology. I'd prepared."

The Queen stepped closer, around the Consort's body, still holding the blade that killed him. "Show Us, Varessa."

D'Shea nodded, and I heard an odd sound in my ear, something like a chime without a source of crystal or metal. The three spiders which had executed Wilsira rushed back to me, climbing my legs. I opened my hands without thinking, letting them rest there. I generally didn't enjoy holding spiders, but these were alright.

Wait.

What the fuck just happened?

The Valsharess displayed a minute smile. "We have not seen guardians so capably formed in a very long time. The Headmaster?"

"Me and my own study, Your Majesty," D'Shea said with firm pride, calling the spiders to her next. I let them go.

The Queen nodded once, watching as they were tucked back in their pouch. "And your Confession held back by force, Elder?"

"I regret to say it is too late now, Your Highness. The Conceiver used me while I was pregnant with my s-son to remake that Forming Pit first approved by You. I do not know how long I was there rebuilding parts of it, but I know she made a deal with the Abyss to garner more magic among the Consorts in exchange for stripping some protective runes.

"She couldn't do it alone, she needed me. The corruption would spread faster, I *knew* it would … But I couldn't *speak* it. I couldn't remember in full. Until now."

The Prime snarled something about weakness, skeptically glancing at the foul stains on the carpet. They were starting to smell like the infection it was.

"Your son's birth is the still point," the Valsharess said, nodding, and She turned away to join Auranka, standing before Her throne to face us all. She settled on Lelinahdara. "Confessor, guide the Red Sisters to the Fourth Level of the Sanctuary. We shall meet you there."

"Valsharess," Roshen cried. "Our sons —"

The Queen silenced her with a threatening gesture, calling a ball of purple light to Her palm, not yet releasing it. "Return to your quarters, High Priestess. Await Our Word."

Never in my young life had I imagined *any* Priestess could look so helpless.

TARRA'S FACE WAS SET IN STONE AS SHE STEPPED OUT OF THE JUMP CIRCLE AND led us through the second hallway to the left. The Prime stayed at her shoulder, chuckling now and then. With the rest of us at her back, we watched our superior reach up to twice brush her heavy palm on the back of the Confessor's neck. She stiffened both times.

"Stop," she said.

"What's the matter," the Eldest Sister snickered. "That ragged cunt only getting tapped by the satin bows on this floor, Priestess? Don't know what real fuck is, do ya?"

If Tarra hadn't enjoyed me wearing a Feldeu the last time, she shuddered in disgust just glancing at the Prime. Fadele seemed to enjoy the look too much; her lip curled back like a predator.

We marched past the various erotic images, past the portrait of the bua with metallic gold eyes and arrived to find the Queen in the first room, standing contemplatively over four buas who were kneeling on the floor, hiding their eyes.

Without looking around, She said, "Fadele?"

The Prime grinned this time. As Tarra shuffled backward to get out of our way, the First Red Sister displayed an eager lean forward in her shoulders, a lowering of her gaze as if acquiring a new target. It was also a bow of respect. And loyalty.

"Yes, my Valsharess."

"Cull these buas before they enter our bloodline. Make it quick."

"Sisters," the Prime said, her voice roughening with bloodlust, drawing a blade to raise it above the four males in front of her. "Spread out. Clear the floor. Bring the bodies all back here when you're done."

I saw the look on Gaelan's and Jael's faces as we backed up out of the Prime's sight. Qivni turn away quickly, lowering her head and stalking off down the hall by herself, drawing a weapon as well. Her hand shook. Rausery looked after her then focused on D'Shea and Jaunda, who nodded their support, though without the glee of the Prime slaying the buas in the next room.

"Damage control," Rausery said, making eye contact with each of us, making sure we understood. She signed, *The faster, the better. You don't want the Prime to catch up and do it for you.*

Yes, Elder, we signed as one.

CHAPTER 27

THE FOURTH LEVEL OF THE SANCTUARY SMELLED THICKLY OF BLOOD AND FEAR. It was choking, and I had vomited in the waste room, sure one of the Elders saw me. She said nothing. The Prime kicked some bodies after we dragged them all to her and seemed satisfied. Or, satiated. The Valsharess somehow seemed relaxed.

"Confessor."

"My Queen?" A slight tremor in her voice.

"Convene with the Prime and Ourselves. We shall retrieve the genealogy records from the last two hundred-fifty years. We shall look at them carefully." Her gaze drifted our way. "Elders?"

Rausery and D'Shea bowed. "Valsharess."

"Prepare the Sisterhood for a purge. Speak to no one, wait for the report. Be ready."

"Yes, Your Majesty."

We left, and I guessed that the servants and acolytes of the Priesthood would be the ones left to clean up after us, rather than the Priestesses themselves.

Later, when the Prime had returned from her conference with the Queen and Lelinahdara, she carried her list of targets and the official Queen's Writ. Her Elders General and Sorceress were prepared to act, and all thirty-six of us were present and equipped.

Internal bickering was forgotten as we waited to be released into Sivaraus. The Prime did not give the order for D'Shea to slit my throat when she saw me. None of my superiors mentioned it. When D'Shea and Rausery picked their own targets first and the Sorceress claimed House Itlaun, I did not react.

Neither did Rausery.

The Red Sisters next moved in a long chain through the spyways from the Cloister to an elevated courtyard of the Palace I'd never seen before. There, amid decorative spider webs, mushroom rings, pools and stone, we were met by the Valsharess.

She authorized the Sisterhood to use a powerful tool to accomplish our mission as quickly as possible. I didn't know if we always had this access or if it had just been created for this threat. I knew Jael had an opinion on the matter, given the intensity of her frown as she listened.

"Six teams jump to Twelve Houses," our Queen announced. "This circle will take you inside each manor. Seize all Consorts and offspring of Consorts, bring them here alive and whole if they cooperate, dead if they do not. The Matas you shall bring alive, they and their unborn unharmed, or face punishment of sacrifice."

The Prime looked *so* eager. She bowed. "Of course, Your Majesty."

We had a mage with each team who could use the circle, plus five more Red Sisters who would make the arrests. In most cases, that meant only one or two targets per Sister, so a high chance of success. We were prepared to take any female servants who might have dallied with the Consort behind the Matron's back as well, though those would be rare.

Equipped with rope, manacles, gags and bags, knock-out powder, and intoxicating darts, we were ready to jump.

"Team One. Get on the mark."

We hit hard and fast, taking them by surprise before gossip could spread.

I WAS GONE AND BACK WITH JAUNDA'S TEAM, HAULING THE UNCONSCIOUS weight of a Noble child of a scant thirty years, chilled by our astounding success. I could not help but hear the rise and fall of wailing in the courtyard.

Elder D'Shea was back from her first jump. She held an infant in her arms and a naked, male body with a scorched face lay at her feet. Curgia, with her second swollen belly, was shrieking in horror, her arms gripped by Kiren and Lawret.

"Enoquis! Enoquis, my sire!"

"Sloppy, D'Shea," the Prime remarked, although for once she wasn't displeased with my Elder, who'd shrugged.

"He ran," she said shortly. "We found him high in a nearby cave. He wouldn't come out, so we burned him out."

The Prime tapped the toe of her boot to the body, grunting. She nodded. "Prepare your next run."

The Palace Guards took the prisoners, leading them down below into the dungeons to secure them. I passed my prisoner over to them and returned to Jaunda's side, my heart slamming against my chest. She slammed her palm into my back for good measure.

"Focus on the next target, novice," she murmured.

"Yes, Lead."

I did my damnedest. Shut out the wailing. Strangle those emotions in me struggling to escape their bindings. I couldn't panic or stumble like Curgia. There was no choice.

The Red Sisters would collect every Davrin sired by a Consort, and every female presently pregnant by one.

Except me.

THE SISTERHOOD'S PART IN THE PURGE WAS FINISHED FOR NOW, THOUGH WE could be called again at any time to help control pockets of unrest in the city.

After we'd regained the Cloister, the Sorceress wouldn't let me out of her sight. We had shed filthy boots, armor, and clothing on her clean floor.

Now, we sat in her bath together, sharing the heated water.

The images in my mind played through over and over, not just the mass arrests but what came next in the Sanctuary. I'd watched and I'd prevented anyone from leaving, as directed. What else could I have done and still be alive?

"You need the pendant back," said Elder D'Shea.

"Huh?" I blinked out of my stupor. "What did you say, Elder?"

"Sirana," she sighed, though with less frustration than usual when repeating herself.

Her arms dripped water as she braced her elbows on the side to sit up straight, rolling the water around us. I glimpsed the unhealed scar beneath her breast. She leaned toward me, silently commanding that I look her in the eyes.

"The Valsharess has dealt with the Priesthood over the Conceiver's treachery."

Oh yes, She did. By the Ice Pit, She did.

I shivered. Stayed silent.

"Listen, Sirana. She has *not* yet dealt with the Sisterhood over the escape of the Ornilleth. Rausery was right, that was a different matter. She eschewed its focus at the time, but it shall return."

D'Shea licked her lips, betraying nerves. She spoke with care.

"I need you to go to the Wizard's Tower and get your pendant back from Shyntre. While you are there, talk to Headmaster Phaelous. Tell him where you found the Dwarf stone on the Fringe, and what Jael has said about it, but not what happened to you. Ask him if he's discovered anything else."

"Why don't you go, Elder?" I asked. "You can speak to Shyntre, now."

There was a flash of fear in her eyes. She blinked and shook her head calmly. "It is not a good time for that. I should not draw unnecessary attention their way."

I didn't reply.

"In any case, the more you stay out of the Prime's sight right now, the better. She is enamored with her present tasks, but she'll remember you soon enough."

I shook my head, stamping down that sense of misery and impending loss of what I'd found here. It was as Rausery warned me, if anyone found out about the Tragar. D'Shea should never have told Lelinahdara. She told Wilsira!

"What am I going to do, Elder?" I murmured in despair. "How can I continue *anywhere*, much less as a Red Sister?"

Her mage's fingers lightly tread the surface of our bath. Her expression tightened, looked determined. "The babe will give us more time. The Prime cannot command me to kill you while you're pregnant. You saw the care the Valsharess took with the Mata prisoners."

My eyes teared up against my wishes, a hard lump in my throat as I looked to the side. That wouldn't help. She didn't know. And reminding me of the Valsharess again didn't convince me.

I whispered, "Their unborn are tainted. All the sires are *dead*. Th-the Queen gathered them all in that giant ritual chamber. Released the Sathoet upon them."

Oh, Goddess. The begging.

The claws and teeth.

D'Shea's reply was stern. "Our Queen did it to remind the Priestesses of their place and not to defy Her Law. Every Priestess there had a firstborn Son. *Any* Priestess who claimed a second bua in a Consort just watched her firstborn destroy him. The Sathoet are rejuvenated, validated."

"So what?!" I barked, prompted to hear again those sounds, those yowls of glee as the Sathoet ruined that soft flesh, tearing it ragged.

D'Shea's mouth tightened; she did not blink. "The Priestesses will no longer have the Consorts to focus their efforts upon. Like us, they may not build families or count their bloodlines. It returns them all to their original oath to serve Sivaraus and the Valsharess first. The sacrifice of their future children is the price for their power, as our heritage and old family bonds are the price for ours.

"This is *good* for the Sisterhood. We are still Her Enforcers, and the Purge returns the balance of past centuries to the city. This means there is hope for your child being placed with another family by *you*. We may be able to change the way it's been before you are forced to make a choice."

My voice was tight. "What choice? How do I even stay in the Sisterhood? Who would take a twice-damned infant, by a tainted Consort and out of a flayer-thrall Mata? Especially if it's a bua. He would be thrice damned!"

D'Shea didn't answer at first, tapping her fingers at the edge of the tub before standing up, rivulets of water streaming down her skin. She motioned for me to get out as well, grabbing two towels and handing me one. With mindless motion, I dried off.

"Your Mother would," she said quietly. "Without hesitation."

I ground my teeth and made a face. D'Shea arched a brow.

"If not her, then perhaps Matron Aurenthin."

"Jael's Mother?" I squinted. "Why?"

"She has so little, she needs all who will live in the lowest House to help run it. Everyone works, and even servants receive a share comparable to the Noble children. It is not as filthy and disease-ridden as the other Houses tell each other, just rustic."

"I *do* know that, Elder."

"But you haven't watched long enough," she said. "They are the only House without mages to contribute to the Priesthood or the Tower. Your child will likely become one, because of the sire. No matter male or female, a mage would be *very* valuable to the Matron."

Give a mageless House an infant who may become one …

Why did that feel like yet another plan of my Elder to disrupt things? There was much she wasn't saying — starting why Matron Aurenthin had no mages. It was either this or my own Mother should take her grandchild, according to her.

Jaunda mentioning my Grand Matron, D'Shea always showing up … what was the link with my Mother?

I didn't want to think about it now, and my Elder wasn't likely to answer. Those things were either a long time ago or still a long time ahead, if it even happened. Something else was more pressing in my mind.

"Why is Auslan still alive down below, Elder?" I asked without straying too far off topic. "Why aren't you as concerned as our Queen what he's quickened in my belly?"

"I was held in that Pit carrying my own son, Sirana," she said, donning her favorite robe. "I know where the Conceiver's taint started, and it was not with him. The Prime was overzealous in her recommendations, wanting to execute all the Consorts 'to be safe.' The Valsharess agreed because She could regain control over the Priestesses and the Nobles all at once. But I saw those records."

She paused to cast a cleaning spell on our equipment. I waited for her to continue.

"At the Purge, there were three living Consorts who would have been 'clean' births from the ritual the Conceiver developed, that the Valsharess approved. One of them is Auslan. He's now the last one. There's *nothing* wrong with your baby, Sirana. She will be pure Davrin."

"The Prime won't let the sire live once she knows he's down there! You lied to her, told her you'd burned him. You showed her a body."

"Because she *forgets* in chaos. As does the Queen when there are greater concerns. Both live in relative dormancy and rely on *us* to run the city cycle-to-cycle!" My Elder's eyes blazed. "Rausery and I need more time to find places for both of you, Sirana. I do not intend to reveal that lie, but if it comes to it, 'Fadele' will be *required* to let him live, as she must you, and she shall hear it from the Queen. I will see to it."

"How can you be sure?"

"This bua is a healer of rare magical strength not seen in centuries. Even had he not somehow saved you, I would never recommend we destroy him. I also wager my most precious scrolls that *all* his Noble children will pass the purity tests in the dungeons and be returned to their Matrons. I have a plan for granting Auslan life and a new role, we only need a little more time to set things in place."

I swallowed, drying my hair to distract myself from the swelling bubble of hope in my chest. "Why would you do that, Elder?"

She frowned. "I am still uncertain how his death might harm you and your baby, given Curgia crumbled to merely *think* that he was dead. And I am also aware …"

She paused. I watched her blink.

"Aware of what, Elder?"

D'Shea crossed her arms. "My son knows this Consort from his childhood trapped in the Sanctuary. I saw the look Shyntre gave at me in the hall when he saw the Consort bleeding. If I am to ever know my bua at all, after Wilsira *stole* him from me, after two centuries of his very presence making me ill through no fault of his, I shall not begin this task by letting the Prime gut this healer. Not when I have clear paths to prevent it."

No doubt it helped that the First Sister and the Sorceress resented everything about each other, and D'Shea wouldn't give up having things her way. Still, I calmed down and, as I began to dress, reflected how my Elder proved why she *was* an Elder.

She keeps thinking, keeps planning no matter what chaos erupts around her.

"Go to the Tower, Sirana," D'Shea ordered. "Retrieve your pendant and anything else you can learn before the Sisterhood stands before the Valsharess again for the loss of Reishel to an Elder Mind."

Solemnly, I nodded and obeyed.

CHAPTER 28

I ARRIVED CARRYING DOUBTS. MANY SMALL ONES, BUT TWO WERE LARGE AND full in my mind.

I handed D'Shea's fertility suppression vial to Phaelous, and he tested it as before, handing it back with a nod of approval. He waited for me to drink it, calm and tired eyes resting upon me. He saw my hesitation, my eyes flicking away on one of those huge doubts. His gaze drifted down to my middle and back up.

He said, "Perhaps we will skip it this once, young Sister."

You're bluffing.

My mouth opened but the denial wouldn't come out.

He offered a tiny smile. "Do not be afraid. Come."

The voice was coaxing, neither aggressive nor conniving. For the moment, unthreatening. I had to shake off the comfort, though, knowing more than ever the danger of those males who appeared harmless. At least Shyntre made it clear when he wanted to fight.

I followed the ancient wizard to the jump circle, went up a few levels without him asking which one. We were at the familiar library in a brief time, presumably with some privacy.

"Did you come to visit Callitro?" he asked.

It had been a long time since I'd had any time for the battlemage. I rubbed the gold ring he had created for me through my glove but shook my head. "Shyntre."

Phaelous displayed mild humor. "The Queen has commanded that he be kept safe from all females."

I shrugged. "He's safe from me."

The old mage chuckled. "He may disagree. But I could be persuaded you would not harm him in a way unacceptable to Her Majesty."

My eyes narrowed. "The Queen owns him. Not the Priestesses, not the Sisters. Why? Because She owns you? And my Elder could not place him herself?"

The ancient wizard bowed his blond head to me. "That is as best one could explain it, Red Sister. Why are you here to see him?"

"Well. How much do you know already, Headmaster?"

Old eyes glinted as they drifted across the script-laden shelves. "We don't ask ourselves this enough, do we?"

I made a face. "That doesn't help, Headmaster."

"True. You could be more specific."

"Fine. What do you know about the Queen's actions of late? When you arrived to take Shyntre back to the Tower. How much do you know of why we were there?"

He considered. "Has your Elder acknowledged her son to you?"

"You must know Wilsira is dead."

"Is that a yes, Sirana?"

I exhaled. "Yes, Phaelous. My Elder can. And she did."

"Good. Thank you." Another bow. "Again, why are you here?"

"Shyntre saved me. He led my Sisters to where I was and shielded me with his magic when I was too injured to move. I need to talk to him." I squinted at his modest expression. "Did you help him?"

Phaelous's mouth quirked. "I removed a few obstacles which would have slowed him, perhaps. I neither direct nor hobble the self-driven or his potential. That is the responsibility of his Mothers and his Queen."

I made a face at that. A mate like this would drive most Matrons I knew mad; a wonder the Queen hadn't gotten tired of him. "Hm. Then may I meet him alone, Headmaster?"

"Persuade me."

That came out so differently from this ancient teacher than it did from so many caits, or even Shyntre himself. Spoken neither in defiance nor challenge, but an offer. I took a breath to give it a try.

"Do you still have the second Dwarf stone? Have you looked at it since Shyntre gave me that pendant?"

"Yes, young Sister. What of it?"

"I found it beyond the Fringe after a battle with Tragar to recover a recruit. We know it's why the Grey Dwarves sometimes come so close to our borders. They mine for it, determined to find new sources, and some Sisters have seen this same stone inlaid in a few of their weapons, but not many. The theory is only those Dwarves born psionic like the Ornilleth would gain any benefit from it."

The Headmaster made no effort to hide his interest. Perhaps he had known some of it or perhaps he hadn't, but it didn't matter. He received the context surrounding it that he had asked for at the beginning. The gold in his eyes seemed brighter in the candlelight.

"How did you find it, Red Sister?"

"I didn't, I discovered the Tragar who did. Watched him dig it out. After a skirmish where we won, I brought some back for my Elder in case it proved useful somehow."

"It responds strangely to Davrin auras," Phaelous said, "unlike any precious stone I've worked with. I'm not certain how useful it is."

Except to you. I feared to read that on his face; he didn't speak it. If he thought it, I didn't hear.

Instead he asked, "And we have never seen the thought-flayers themselves use this stone in some way?"

"I don't know, Headmaster," I said. "That's a good question."

He contemplated as the old wizard did, nodded to himself, and motioned to me.

"I will show you to Shyntre's room. We may speak later."

Good enough for me.

Where Shyntre bedded down in the Wizard's Tower was a place I'd never been. When we got there, however, I was unsurprised to see its layout was the same as any other bua wizard's dormitory in this place.

The young mage was summoned and opened his door in the same way as Callitro. The crackling wariness could have ignited the air with a spark.

"Headmaster," he protested.

"Let her in, bua," Phaelous said.

It was the first time I heard something like a command brooking no argument out of him. I blinked in surprise but readily stepped forward when Shyntre moved out of the way. I glimpsed a brief bow from Phaelous before he turned to go, and Shyntre closed the door, locking and warding it.

The room smelled like my wizard had neither left it nor bathed since the Queen commanded Phaelous to bring him back here. His short, white hair had random spikes from restless Reverie, and I spotted hints of dark bruises beneath his eyes.

He asked curtly, "What do you want?"

"What did She do to you?" I asked in return.

"We're not going there."

His eyes drifted down to my middle, and he remembered. His fingers hovered on a hand sign.

"Yes, I am," I answered. "Still."

He glared at me, but instead of annoyance or impatience, there was only fear.

"He's alive," I said, guessing what he wanted to know. "Still in the Cloister. My Elder means to keep him so. She told me she'd protect him."

"*You lie!*" he burst out, his hands flaring orange. "Don't you dare tell me that!"

I was taken aback.

"I know what happened! The whole fucking Tower is waiting for the next husk to drop! All the Consorts are dead, and you and your fucking Sisters rounded them all up! Them and all the children they quickened! Did you think some of those Consort sons weren't here?! Phaelous had to let the Prime inside and do *nothing* while she dragged the youngest of us to the dungeon!"

Fuck. I hadn't heard this, and I'd been in too many places, bearing witness to and participating in other horrors, to see this coming.

My breath shook. I could only say it again.

"Auslan's alive. Elder D'Shea is keeping him hidden from the Prime. She and Rausery are planning something. I don't know what."

Shyntre shook his head, refusing to believe it. He spun away, turned his back to me and stalked to pour a drink of something which had probably been hot some marks ago.

"Is that what you're calling him?" he said without looking around. "He's had a score of names; this is another."

"Do you know his real one?" I challenged.

"Fuck you."

"Fitting. Almost as cute, I guess."

Shyntre snorted a scoff, slurped whatever was in that cup as if it would fortify him, set it down. He said nothing; his back muscles were probably a network of knots.

"No one denies he's a hands-on healer, and a strong one," I said. "There's as strong an edict against torturing and killing one of them as there is doing the same to a pregnant Mother."

"So what?" he growled, turning around. "Edict or not, it happens anyway, and what's *always* worse is getting the Valsharess involved! Your Elder will hand him over for whatever price she wants."

"She doesn't want to lose me to the Sanctuary," I said. "She wants to change it before that happens. She won't 'hand him over' an instant before it's necessary to keep him and me alive. She *told* me this."

He sneered, "And you believe her."

"What else can I do? Tell the Prime myself that I'm pregnant and the sire is a Consort which my Elder lied about executing during the Purge? That he's really alive and well underneath the Cloister in solitary?"

Shyntre watched me for a moment, reluctant surprise creeping visible. "What?"

"D'Shea lied to the Prime for him," I repeated. "She brought back a body, face unrecognizable, and claimed it was the Consort from House

Itlaun, the one she was sent to retrieve. The Prime doesn't know the difference. Even if she sees Auslan later in another setting, she wouldn't recognize him."

Shyntre looked ill. "The Valsharess will *know* he's a Consort reported dead. How will your Elder explain *that* when cornered?"

"I don't know. She didn't tell me that. She needs more time."

His jaw tightened, some of the gold in his eyes glinted. "Then why are you here?"

Not for the reason I want to be.

I stared at him, surprised by my impulse to step closer. I stayed where I was. "Do you still have my pendant?"

Shyntre looked at a shelf to his right. "Yes. You want it back?"

"Yes, but may I ask why you took it?"

"Simple. I couldn't risk it interfering with healing potions or spells." *Or rituals.*

"I've observed," he continued, "it enhances your will but at the expense of magical potency." Shyntre glanced at me and shrugged. "The Headmaster and I wonder why it works on you versus any other Davrin, but we haven't had time or cooperation to experiment."

And neither he nor Phaelous had been conscious and present when Wilsira made her accusation. Tarra knew, too; that was how the Conceiver found out about the "Dwarf shadow" in the first place.

So, what was the point of *not* telling Phaelous and Shyntre when the Liaison and the Queen had already heard it? Was this habitual distrust on the side of my Elder, or more about their being male than because it made any sense?

Between the Priestesses and the wizards, I knew which had *aided* me over trying to own me.

"I was ..." I stopped.

Suddenly afraid.

Don't tell.

Shyntre lifted his eyes. Listening.

I breathed in. *Out.*

"I was wounded by a psionic Tragar," I confessed. "Our minds were linked when I killed him. Ever since then, my ... will has been acting a little like ... some of our spells. But I'm not a mage."

My wizard said nothing for quite some time, turning that over in his intelligent mind. He seemed troubled and illuminated at once.

"I see," he murmured. "Yes, that could explain what I saw."

"I was awake when the Ornilleth climbed out of its hole," I said, needing to tell someone. "Aware but I couldn't move my own body. The flayer commented on this, I heard its thoughts. I should have been like Reishel ... a puppet. Sleepwalking."

"And you were wearing the pendant," he said. Some dark thought crossed his face. "You were conscious the whole time? For Kerse's ritual, before we found you?"

I flinched to think it. "Worse. I was conscious, and we were mind-linked."

Shyntre looked down, rubbed his face hard. Grimacing and muttering curses. "I'm ... sorry. Again. You should know I'm not ... angry at you. You're young. You didn't do any of this. And I sure as bane have never seen another Red Sister survive anything like it."

He looked up, eyebrow arched like his Mother. "That, *and* who stands here listening to me gripe without slapping me around."

I managed to smile at that. "I'm only here thanks to you and your brother."

"What?" The wizard's eyes widened in alarm. "He's not my brother, we share no blood."

I shrugged. "It's what he called you. I have sisters who share no blood. We aren't allowed our blood family, and maybe we don't want it anyway. It makes sense."

Shyntre was silent, caught between thoughts and not sure which one to take. It was one of the only times he looked vulnerable. Open to being nudged, for once.

Persuade me.

I knew where I wanted to nudge him.

I took those final strides to close the distance, slowly pushing him back against his bookshelf, rattling a stone or two that sat among the scrolls. My lips came to his, and I kissed him with a genuine eagerness as his familiar scent dominated my senses for a few wonderful moments.

He tasted good, and I wanted to keep going.

Shyntre resisted with only a portion of his usual stubbornness. I moved from his mouth along his jaw to his ear, nibbling on it, using my tongue to explore its sensitive edge while holding him tightly in place. His erection grew firm between our bellies, and he let slip a clear noise of reluctant desire.

I froze mid-breath, not wishing to miss such an arousing sound: that of a supremely willful bua losing the battle with himself at last.

Admitting to himself a pure need, answering mine.

Oh, Goddess, why couldn't you have moaned like that before now?

"You w-want me?" I whispered near his ear. "Please, say it."

"Y-Yes … I want you."

I locked my knees to stay upright and braced myself against the case, grabbing his ass with my other hand. We kissed again. If my eyes were open, I couldn't see a damned thing but felt and smelled and tasted *everything*. Pulling at the neckline of his robe to expose his smooth shoulder, I tasted his skin, my lips leading from there up to his neck.

Shyntre reached for something on my belt. Without thought, I gripped and turned his hand, firmly trapping it behind his back. His own belt was gone, part of his chest was exposed as well as most of an arm.

I paused to soak in the sight. He was gorgeous.

"Not teasing me, are you, wizard?" I asked, really hoping he hadn't just lied to me.

"Your belt has to come off to shuck your leathers, Sister," he growled in challenge, the gold flecks in his eyes see molten.

"Fine. Don't take anything."

"Don't need to. I can make better, anyway."

Granting him a chuckle, I released his hand and stroked his cock through the robes, cupping his balls, squeezing and exploring as he over-concentrated on removing my belt.

Once he got this, I tossed both it and my gloves onto his desk; my cloak followed them. He reached for buckles on my bracers and straps on my armor as I slid my bare hand down his stomach and beneath the thick cloth, through the tuft of white hair before grasping his iron-hard sex.

He growled and leaned to bite my neck, his hand snapping onto my buttock.

Oh, Goddess!

I pulled away as if annoyed by the bite — I wasn't, but it gave me space to claim his mouth with even more lust. We kissed, and I sucked with my lips down from his throat to shoulder to chest, at last to lash my tongue in circles around his nipple, moving to shove the rest of his robe down off his waist to pool onto the floor.

"Fucking sexy," I panted.

"Now, you," he rasped.

We got my bracers and chest piece off. I stood in my shirt, leather pants, and boots when I wrapped my arms around his waist and lifted him, naked but for his sandals, to throw him onto his bed. Shyntre bounced and tried to sit up, but I was right there, pushing him back down to cover him, where he would feel my clothing along his skin from neck to thigh.

He couldn't easily forget how naked he was.

His response was to wrap an arm around my neck and force my mouth onto his. Determined fingers jerked at the leather ties at my hips, but I thought we should tackle my shirt first. We wrestled over this choice for a good long time, slapping away each other's grip, huffing, grinding our crotches together.

Eventually, I coaxed him to help me shed my shirt and free my breasts, and I was glad I did. He stoked the fire higher. My eyes rolled at the tingling sensation of what he did next to my nipples. I was surprised they didn't start leaking some pleasure fluid right then!

"Aauugh …" I groaned, his buzzing fingers squeezing my turgid buds again. "Where d-did you learn that, and w-why don't you share?"

"Because Red Sisters are too busy stinking up their fingers first chance they get to learn."

I laughed, he rolled my twin nubs gently, and I almost came in my pants.

We struggled with those leathers next, grunting, eventually working them down. I leaned in, mostly on top of him with my pants barely beneath my ass cheeks now, and Shyntre's hand darted in between us, gripping my mound, pushing two fingers into me. I groaned. My sex was sopping.

I arched my back, parted my knees as wide as they could go.

Then the wizard started thinking again.

"Why name him?" he asked.

"Huh?"

"Auslan."

Oh. Now you ask?

He persuaded me to answer when those fingers began to move. *Just right.*

"*Mmm.* My wilderness trial," I panted. "After killing the Tragar." I paused to swivel my hips, hearing myself squish. "I caught him alone. We fucked. Think he ... healed me ..."

A quiver passed through the wizard, and I looked down to see he stared up at me in shock. His fingers twitched and stroked harder.

"Ohh, yes," I hissed.

He worked me with a practiced hand, as he had Qivni. I floated so nicely in the rhythm that I absently released Shyntre's other wrist, my grip growing slack. He freed it to tug my pants down farther, over my thighs and down to my knees.

He raised up to kiss me again, biting my earlobe, and bumps spread from my neck across my shoulders. "The Priestesses never knew?"

"No, they didn't."

His lips touched my throat. "And he's known you this whole time. Before you found me at the Tower, or when we first met with the Conceiver."

"Yes!"

"That fucking trophy. He never said a thing."

Shyntre regained a second wind and lifted both hands; he gifted me a marvelous wave of controlled, crackling mage-fire along my breasts and arms and ribs — far from my womb or my cunt. I shivered, arching my back on all fours upon his bed.

He kept me in distraction long enough that I barely noticed he had slid out from beneath me until he kneeled on my pants, now bunched between my knees. His weight nailed my legs to the mattress, now in perfect position to penetrate either of my holes.

Once he gripped my torso, pressing his chest to my back and his erection into the crack of my ass, I realized I had a preference.

"Wait!" I gasped.

"What?"

"Want you in my cunt," I said clearly. "I can't catch again, so don't pull out."

Shyntre paused, working for every breath; he said nothing as his mage's hands trailed over my skin.

I clung to his blanket like it was the side of a cliff. With effort, I remained on my elbows with my ass presented to him, like the first time we met in the candle chamber.

Please, don't refuse —

The head of his cock fit between my netherlips, and he pushed, filling me. I sucked in a breath and moaned with indulgent relief as he lunged as deep as he could. He shuddered in pleasure, playing with my breasts.

"Oh, yeah!" I cried. "Right there!"

"You've caught," he breathed, as if reminding himself.

He drew back, lunged in.

"Yes!" I agreed, relaxing into it instead of tensing up. "Caught by your brother ..."

Responding intensely to that, the wizard drove into my sex as it clutched wetly around him, and he didn't stop.

We were too excited to talk more but made an inexorable amount of noise regardless. I reached the point of no return and climaxed before the mage, pulling him over the edge right after me.

He growled and released his seed inside me without hesitation, holding on, pressing in as deep as he could reach. I imagined his offering splashing and coating my insides.

I believed I could feel its scalding heat.

Oh, Goddess!

Like the early times at Court, I lost those next moments to mindless ecstasy. The anxiety with which I'd only recently become familiar was gone now, because …

Well, it had already happened.

Oh … oh …

Shyntre trembled as he peeled away, rolling and landing beside me, trying to catch his breath. I settled belly-down beside him, mopping my forehead on his pillow.

Hot in here.

"Do you know his name?" I whispered.

The wizard shook his head. "No."

"Lying."

"So certain?"

"Yes. Because you *knew* he had a true name."

"You're reaching. I grew up around them."

"I know you when you're insulting, wizard. Auslan has said your thoughts were 'challenging' even as a child."

Shyntre tensed. "Sirana … No."

"Why not?"

He initiated something like afterward cuddling, pulling me close, but he was tense. Maybe he wanted to make sure his sire couldn't read his lips if he was peeping in on us.

"Because I sometimes wished I'd never tricked him into telling me," he whispered. "He didn't know better. You're linked now in a different way, and I can't know either of you will survive this. Don't make it harder than it is."

Either of us?

Was he so certain that *he* would survive, then? Interesting if he did.

"Very well," I said.

Shyntre lifted his head and stared into my eyes for a moment, waiting, and when I said no more, he let it go. He offered, "I'll call him by *your* name, if I need to call him anything."

I studied his eyes up close, leaned forward, and nipped his lower lip. "Agreed."

He drew back, surprised as I smiled at him. Then he huffed an odd laugh before shaking his head. He settled down, watching me as I unlaced and removed my boots, finally kicking off my pants from around my calves. He did not protest as I lay down next to him again.

Slowly, our hearts slowed, and our bodies cooled; we were lost in our own thoughts, our own troubles which now interlinked more than ever. Then Shyntre surprised me when he turned onto his side, propped on an elbow.

He reached for me, his mage's fingers caressing my flank and ribs. He offered his mouth, his prick rising again between his thighs.

He wants another round.

I dove straight onto his side of the bed to take it.

CHAPTER 29

I RETURNED TO THE CLOISTER WITH MY BLUE PENDANT IN A POUCH ON MY BELT and a sore but grateful sex between my legs. My netherlips dribbled Shyntre's cum inside my leathers. My head was warm and fuzzy, body aglow with lingering sensation and fresh memories of a favorite past time which had become something more.

I didn't see the bag until it was cinched beneath my jaw.

Fighting before I could think, I struck out blind and connected. Someone grunted in surprise and scraped the wall as she stumbled, gripping me with one hand to keep me from running. I smashed her forearm with my fist until she let go and ran back toward the exit, tugging at the bag.

"Get her!"

I collided with another Sister, who overbalanced me and swept my legs. She put me on my back upon the bare stone, knocking the wind out of me.

"Don't move," Rausery warned me in a harsh whisper. "Not a word."

The Elder gripped my armor at my pits and plucked me up to set me on my feet. My head spun, and I still couldn't see. It was getting hot in the bag from my own breath.

"She gonna keep being stupid, Elder?"

"She won't, Prime."

Shit. Fadele sounded annoyed. Had I just *hit* her?

"What about the other three?"

She grew closer.

"Waiting outside with Qivni."

The Prime stood right next to me. "Funny how first thing this one did was flee."

Rausery drew breath to speak then a fist slammed into my stomach. I fell to my knees, gasping.

"Prime, no!" Rausery barked. "She wants them whole. Not another hit like that until the Valsharess sees her."

A dismissive snort. "Sure, General. Whatever you say."

She bound my hands behind my back, pulled the straps very tight, and collared me by the back of my armor to force me to my feet for the second time. Then, she pushed me straight ahead and back out the entrance to the Cloister.

FROM THE SURETY OF THE STEPS AROUND ME, I WAS THE ONLY ONE WITH THE bag over my head.

Jaunda, Gaelan, and Jael were present, the latter two wordlessly flanking me for the parts of the walk where I needed guidance up or down a rock gutter. There was also Rausery, Qivni, and the Prime. I was very concerned about D'Shea being absent on our way to the Palace.

We moved at a brisk pace, but I heard no crowds, no guards letting us by, no steps of other Davrin or servants. We entered the Palace unseen and without announcement. I might have recognized more scents, had some idea where we were inside the Palace, without the bag over my head.

Then again, when we reached the quiet room where I was forced to my knees on smooth, bare stone, I could still smell the incense even through the cloth. It was a new one.

"We are pleased you answered so quickly, Sisters," said the Queen.

"Your Will be done, Valsharess."

"Uncover her head. We would see her eyes."

The Prime rumbled, using several, hard tugs to make its removal as uncomfortable as possible.

My eyes blurred at first, adjusting to a strange, yellow and violet light in the room, and I coughed against the scratch of the fragrant smoke that filled my throat.

Gaelan and Jael were on either side of me on their knees, and Lead Jaunda had taken to one knee to my left. Rausery and Qivni stood to my right, behind the Prime and facing me and my Sisters.

I blinked to see Elder D'Shea standing poised and without expression behind the Queen. Nothing told me if I should be glad to see her here ahead of me or not, but there were no visible marks on her.

The Prime can't command her to slit my throat.

Astonishingly, depending on why we were here, this could worm its way down to a lesser worry. At least Auranka and all Priestess were absent from this audience.

"The Sisterhood stopped a Sathoet broken free of his Mother's control," the Queen said. "You stopped a demonblood from calling the Void to spill into the Great Cavern, where enemies of our Goddess would have overwhelmed Us. Sivaraus would have had no defense ready.

"In addition, the Sisterhood uncovered the Elf mimics, the Dissanguine, posing as true Davrin among Our Noble Houses. The Red Sisters helped to capture them, purge them, and correct the delicate pattern of Her Great Web. You, Lead Jaunda, Sisters Gaelan, Sirana, and Jael. You are Forgiven all actions against the Conceiver, the Priesthood and their Sathoet, and the Sanctuary."

"Bless me, my Queen," Jaunda muttered.

Gaelan, Jael, and I were observant young Sisters and mimicked our Lead. By the stance of their boots, this seemed to satisfy our Elders and the Prime. The hem of the Valsharess's royal purple gown brushed the floor.

"We have a different concern now," She continued. "The Elder Mind who has encroached upon Sivaraus over the past five centuries has taken a Red Sister in retribution for Our capture of one of its servants. Though We have learned more about it, We do not know how long the city now has before it decides its next work."

"My Queen, if I may speak."

"Yes, Fadele?"

The Prime paused. Then, "Before we discuss this, we should put down the novice Sirana. The Elder Mind could be listening through her right now."

"You will *not*," the Valsharess said coldly. "This is not a discussion. We have meditated upon the Sisterhood's Penance. Stand and witness as their Prime."

Growling. "Yes, my Queen."

The Valsharess reached out and first placed Her hand upon Jaunda's head, which was barely covered in white fuzz after the blast. My Lead's body remained still; I couldn't hear her heart nor spot a quiver.

It was difficult to say what was happening. Without change in Jaunda's position or breathing, the deep pulse of the underground caused the shadows to flow along with the incense around us. Something intangible built up, swelling until my Lead twitched. Perhaps that signaled her first thought to struggle against the auspicious contact.

Then, Jaunda responded as Shyntre had by reaching up, clutching at the bejeweled hand. Her teeth gritted in a grimace. "M-Majesty —!"

The Queen released her, and she fell over. Astonishingly, she was still conscious.

"Do you understand, Lead Jaunda?" the Valsharess asked.

"Y-Yes, my Queen," she gasped, rolling to brace her forearm, trying to get back up. She trembled from the effort. "I will s-search for his den."

"Good."

Those tawny eyes focused on Gaelan next, who whimpered as the hand came up. Jael scooted closer to me as we watched a repeat of what Jaunda endured, though Gaelan squirmed and made much more noise.

"Hold still, child."

Gaelan's heart pounded loud enough that I feared it would burst; she jerked in a brief seizure, bit her lip, and it began to bleed as she collapsed. Her eyes were closed. The Valsharess turned to Elder D'Shea.

"Was a compulsion necessary, Varessa?" She asked.

D'Shea bowed her head. "At the time, my Queen, yes. Apologies for the obstacle. I cannot see the full span of threads making up The Web. Not as Your Highness does."

"Hm. It shall not matter to her new mission."

"Which is?"

"Hold this thought."

The Queen took Jael next, who visibly fought Her every step of the way.

My fearless, foolish little Sister.

"L-Let ... *go!*" the young Aurenthin cried toward the end, now trying to peel both Her hands away as tears spilled down her cheeks.

When at last She did, Jael fell toward me. I reached out and caught her without thinking, and the Prime snarled as my Sister's head lolled against my shoulder.

"You *will* find and kill him, Aurenthietti," the Queen said.

Shuddering, Jael nodded to acknowledge, moaning softly, and our Lead crawled around Gaelan to gently pull the cait from my arms.

The shadow of an ancient Davrin fell upon me. I looked up.

My turn to receive my Penance.

THIS WAS NEITHER A SPELL OF COMMUNICATION NOR A MINDLINK AS I KNEW them.

It felt more like two private spaces crashing together, whatever once kept them apart now two hollow, shattered spheres. A jumble of belongings spilled and mixed without order outside their usual hiding places.

So many details we might not want a stranger to see, hidden in plain view within the unsorted mess around us. Don't try to count what was there, and one could hope that, perhaps, she wouldn't recognize what she was looking at.

We had begun in a dark cave with a ladder leading up to a barn loft, a startled pincerworm at the top. Then the stone cracked around us, breaking, and letting in a light which stunned me. The elder female gripped me by my neck, dragged me out into that golden light.

The air felt hot as a Dwarven forge, blowing hard enough to howl past my ears. The massive blue sky was marred by brown haze obscuring the horizon, the fine grains of sliding sediment giving beneath our feet. I could tell no direction at all, no familiar boundary. There was no ceiling, no walls or tunnels or cave-ins.

It all went on forever. It terrified me.

"Your Majest — !"

I choked on the air itself as billowing dust and dirt tried to fill my lungs.

"Inside!" She barked.

The "inside" was a shelter made of heavy hide and cloth that appeared out of nowhere. My Queen grabbed the flapping, tanned doorway and yanked it open, shoving me forward. I fell onto a tapestry laid down upon the soft, shifting ground, unnerved to think that I might begin sinking down without the hard core of the world to stop me.

She followed behind me and closed the flap.

The quiet seemed unnatural in here, but I could still hear the endless breath outside, rushing in all directions without any stone to block or contain it. She loomed behind me as I pushed up with my arms, struggled to my feet, though the world itself tilted to throw me off balance.

I faced my Queen, hunched over either in a bow or prepared to strike, and She rushed in like the wind, knocking my arm to the side to expose my front. I found myself wrapped up in Her arms like a spider holding me in place, preparing to weave a cocoon.

Too close. Far too close!

She sampled me somehow, explored me. She may as well have been digging Her fingers in between my netherlips to feel Shyntre's fresh semen. She never blinked. Never smiled.

"Our First Son. He has touched you."

I gasped, my mind now back in Shyntre's bed, when I had parted my thighs for the third time. So eager to receive him, I heard my own voice cry out in the wind: *Goddess, yes!*

"Oh ..." She cooed.

Her arms were around me, like his. Her gaze wandered over me, studying me like the moving surface of a lake. "He has not exposed his Vis to a cait in centuries."

His what?

Her aged hand reached down to slide over my stomach, covering my womb. She said, "He has not sparked a new gift for Us in even longer. He has been spiteful."

I writhed and whimpered at the disturbing familiarity, frozen by the mental image of Her hurting that new essence, of making me bleed out before I had carried it even a quad-span. She seemed to consider doing exactly this; something like Wilsira's hatred and jealousy passed over Her face.

That face, which was somehow much younger in this place.

Yet whatever patterns ultimately guided Her reasoning — if patterns even existed — I could not read them. Her expression was unfamiliar; Her gaze was too vast and weird.

"We have stopped doing this," She murmured intensely, her yellowish eyes fully translucent, staring through me. "He *knows* We have stopped! We cannot begin again ..."

I attempted to squirm free. She held me tighter. Binding. Squeezing the breath out.

"If We release you, there is a chance the Great Work will not absorb Sivaraus. That fate is of *your* making, all of it which is to come. You have given a sleeping god a spear with which to pierce itself awake, in such a way that even the Shadow Guardian will not aid Us. We cannot forgive this, child."

Her aura was alive, vibrating with Her words. Overwhelming, my mind in seizure.

"After all We have done, all We have fought and sacrificed, We *cannot* lose Our people this way."

I shook my head in desperate denial. *Goddess, Goddess …*

The Valsharess was *insane!*

~Let me go!!~

The Queen dropped me, and I tumbled out of Her threads, rolling until I was at the very edge of the tent lying upon the red sand. In an instant, that comforting border vanished along with the privacy, and we stood within the howling wind once again. She came forward and grabbed me by my hair, twisted me around to face a direction, the wind now at our backs.

"Do you see this?" She demanded. "Do you?"

I couldn't open my eyes for fear of them being scoured by the flying sand.

"Look!"

Quivering, I opened them, expecting immediate blindness, but this did not happen. Instead, the clouds of sand parted, and some blue sky returned. I saw the curve of the world. Approaching us, there was a broad spot of colorless grey, its edges invisible to my eyes, fading out into the blue, fading back into the grey in smooth integration. A perfect transition.

"Y-yes," I said. "I see it."

I didn't know what it was.

"There is a Ley Tower upon the Surface," the Valsharess said, Her voice coherent as if we stood in Her audience chamber. "A Priestess of Braqth and her Sathoet disappeared from there. We never found them. We fear they were taken."

I nodded against the grip on my hair. I'd heard this. Shyntre told me.

The lessons in my wizard's library returned in vivid detail. I recalled the wonderment and awe of trying out the new words, of looking at the map from a bird's view. There *had* been a marker for a watchtower, an unnamed Keep, along a band of two Ley Lines. A landmark for a vague, magical intersection deep in the mountains.

It's always the same, remember, Shyntre had said. *Follow the Ley Lines, and you'll find the more powerful magic users on the Surface.*

"Mages of death and decay have encroached upon it in the turns since," my Queen murmured, laying Her voice over his like a silken sheet. "The crossroads are fouled by machinations of the Hells attempting to usurp them. You are a student of Our Son, and one who wishes to see this land above, are you not?"

"Yes," I answered. A whisper.

"You will perform Penance for Us, Sirana, and We have chosen this for you."

She paused. I waited, held in the suspension of Her Will.

"Discover what may be known of the Priestess's disappearance," She began. "Listen to all stories and rumors of half-bloods of Elven origin. If you find any, bring them to Us. Even if you do not, know this: you must destroy the tainted death mage at the Ley Tower above Us before you can return to Sivaraus. You shall stand at Our side in time to face the greatest threat to Our City. The Great Work."

In time for … ?

"H-How do I know how much time — ?"

"Watch for signs in your Reverie," She answered.

"A-And my Sisters — ?"

"They are lost to you. They shall serve their Penance, but only *you* must return. For the sake of Our people, We shall let you live. But you must achieve this task at the Ley Tower then return to Us without delay.

"Do not disappoint Us. We have infinite ways to punish you and all for whom you care, until this world splinters into shards of tortured Dreams. There is no place you can hide from Us, Sirana, and you will not reject what We've laid upon you."

She released my hair, and I flopped forward, my head swimming. Abruptly, the sky turned upside-down and spun beneath me.

For an eternal moment, I was falling into a Void.

Screaming.

Jael held me tight when I came aware, protective but shaking as badly as I was.

"Enough, leave her alone!" she cried.

"Fucking Aurenthin," the Prime hissed, stepping forward with fists up. "Should have beheaded your Matron's Grand Matron when I had the thought!"

The Valsharess made a very sharp gesture, glaring at Her top officer. "It is to be expected, Fadele. The poor have far less to lose in failing to mind their manners. This child has her Penance. She cannot refuse."

Jael tried to say something. And couldn't. She growled in despair and held me, her cheek damp against my temple. I knew it, then.

We each had a Queen's Compulsion set on us.

And *She* has never died to set anyone free.

"Gaelan?" I asked.

"H-Here," she stuttered, up on her knees now and trembling as she crossed her arms in front of her stomach like she was ill.

"Lead Jaunda," said the Queen. "Stand next to your Elder."

The warrior obeyed; she was the steadiest of us, even not having shrugged off her own shakes yet.

"Elder Rausery."

"Yes, Your Highness?"

"Prepare these three Red Sisters for their missions. You shall leave with them within the cycle, escort and be certain they make the transition to the Surface before you return."

The General gaped. "This cycle, my Queen? But … the only one with any training at all is Sirana."

"*This cycle*, General, and your direct tutoring. You, there and back. That is all We will spare. Choose ranking Sisters you've trained to support the Prime and Elder Sorceress while you're gone, as We've done before."

Rausery looked at Qivni first, who nodded slightly as if she expected it, before looking back and bowing. "Yes, Valsharess."

"We have finished here. All except the Prime, Elder D'Shea, and Lead Jaunda, return directly to the Cloister. These three young Sisters are to remain there until the General reports the moment of departure."

418

She glanced at me and added, "If they leave the Cloister at all, We shall scar their wombs and send them with bleeding thighs to the Surface regardless."

I was petrified.

I would obey to the letter.

Chapter 30

My mind and body were numb returning to the barracks while Jael vibrated with tension beside me. Walking in front of us but behind Elder Rausery and Lead Qivni, Gaelan choked on her tears. She tried to be quiet, yet she couldn't hold it back. No one commented, but we all knew.

I just didn't know why.

We reached the first split in the curving, ill-lit hallways and stopped. Rausery looked at us, her eyes dry but understanding. She jerked her head in the direction of our rooms.

"I have some prep work to do," she said. "I'll come get you or send Qiv. Get the shock out while you can. Be calm and ready when I call."

"Y-Yes, Elder."

"Thank you, Elder."

Jael and I hustled Gaelan down the way to her room before we could stumble into any other Sisters who would see her reddened eyes and wet cheeks. We made it, closed and locked the door, and Gaelan set the ward. We held our breaths. Listening. Then my Sister stepped away, bursting out into noisy weeping, and collapsed on her pallet without any strength left.

"Gaelan!"

Helpless what else to say, I went to her, and she accepted help to sit up and lean against both me and the wall. She tried to speak but only stuttered like before, as if the part of her mind that formed words had forgotten how to make them properly.

"What's wrong with her?" Jael asked, deeply unsettled by the emotional display.

"M-m-ah —" Gaelan responded, clutching and pulling at me, hand trembling like she wanted to hit me to force the words out.

A compulsion. The Valshress had said as much; She found it in Her own sentencing and turned around to lay it at Elder D'Shea's feet.

Why? What could you have possibly done to earn that in the seven turns you've been in the Sisterhood? I had done much more for which an elder female might want me silenced, and D'Shea had suffered the same for over two centuries before she was freed at last.

How could she do this?

Gaelan lifted her eyes, locked them with me. Pleading like D'Shea in the Throne Room. I grimaced at the sharp, lancing ache which came just thinking about it, but I hadn't forgotten her promise when the potion brewer had borne the brunt of my pain, helping Shyntre break my ritual bond with Kerse.

Remember me! I've helped you before you knew me ... I'm so sorry for what I did!

What had she done? Why was she there?

Something to do with why she's crying now.

Taking a slow breath, I reached reluctantly for the pendant in my pouch. I drew it out to place around my neck and tuck it out of sight. Gaelan and Jael watched me do this, but I wasn't sure they understood the reason. I said nothing and cupped my older Sister's face in my gloved hands, paused, then removed that physical barrier.

My naked hands held her face gently, and we met eyes again.

At first, nothing happened. I frowned, and Gaelan was confused. I shrugged, wordless, and my older Sister smiled sadly; perhaps she was relieved in a way, as I was.

She leaned to gently kiss my lips, and something shifted in my head. It hurt. I moaned.

Unwary, Gaelan met my eyes. *What's wrong?*

Multiple sharp aches lanced through my skull. Caught up in the mindlink now whether I wished it or not, I forced my way through the pain. I knew, somehow, that she was hurting more than I was, a grief I'd never known. Loss I could pray never to see.

~Remember me.~

In merchant dress, Gaelan stepped into the tiny shed where I lay dying.

"Heal her!" Jilrina commanded. "If my Matron finds out about this, I will see your shop burned to the ground!"

Wordless, Gaelan checked for a pulse in my neck and breathed out when she found one. With a pinch of powder rubbed between her thumb and forefinger, she brushed my clammy forehead and sunken cheeks, speaking a magic word.

I woke up, my body filling with burning, consuming pain. I didn't know who she was, but I was shocked at her cruelty.

"Drink this," Gaelan whispered. "It will make you well."

I didn't move. Didn't believe her.

"Drink it, Sirana, and you will have the chance to break your silence. Only her death will loosen your tongue."

Was that truth? Dare I think … ?

Please. A way out of this. Please.

I guzzled the potion while Gaelan laid a hand on my thin shoulder and murmured the healing potion's command word. "Iriseav'unal."

The pain began again, intensified, but it was different. Hot and vibrant. The healing was swift, too fast to save my womb and barely enough to save my life.

Gaelan stared into my eyes and made a silent suggestion. *After this healing, forget my face, forget my actions, forget my name. But do not forget my words.*

The First Daughter accepted the cover-up of her botched ritual without gratitude. Gaelan was barred from House Thalluen right after. The House Guard Treyl waited outside but had heard nothing of the exchange between females. He was confused why Gaelan was leaving without even looking at him.

He started to follow her, to reach for her.

She spun around and signed, ★*I am banished from here! No more, Treyl. Please.*★

He hesitated but saw the tears in her eyes and nodded reluctantly. The intelligent bua did not need further convincing. He signed to her. ★*I will miss you, Gaelan.*★

Her handsome House Guard remained dutiful at his post outside the First Daughter's altar room while Gaelan walked off their land for the last time. She wept only until she reached the crossroad to catch a cart ride back home.

Later, she found a bittersweet joy in discovering she had caught Treyl's Daughter at last.

THIS WAS ALL SHE WOULD GIVE ME.

Gaelan wouldn't relive the separation from her baby when D'Shea and the Sisterhood arrived at her shop to seize her entire family because of what happened at House Thalluen.

I didn't push her. I wanted out. *Now.*

I blinked, withdrawing as the throbbing ache continued behind my eyes. Gaelan whimpered; her tears finally exhausted. A muscle in her throat jumped, aftershocks of fighting the spell making her tremble.

I fumbled for what to think, how to feel about what she'd shown me. That we'd met before I was recruited for the Sisterhood might have seemed important, but somehow it wasn't right now. It was—

Natia.

Gaelan had always been present when D'Shea asked me for a report on House Thalluen, hearing any firsthand news about her Daughter. Was this our Elder rewarding or punishing her? With the compulsion still in place, it was impossible to say. Although, I knew why Gaelan cried. Her chosen sire was dead, some poor guard killed at my House by my sister, and any hope was gone.

Gaelan would never see her Daughter again.

Too much. My head hurts …

I moved away, climbing to my feet.

"You okay?" Jael asked, looking bewildered between us. "What happened?"

"I need to …" I choked on the words. "I must go to solitary."

Gaelan nodded. At last, she opened her mouth and spoke. "Yes. You should."

I hesitated. Did she know I was — ?

Or was my obvious weakness around Auslan something she recognized from Treyl?

Glancing at the youngest of us, I could tell Jael hadn't guessed, at least. "Can you stay here with her? I'll be back soon."

"*Mrf.* Fine," she said, slumping down readily on Gaelan's other side, moving very close against her.

I smiled a little when neither stiffened at the contact. Jael put up a tough front, but she was wrung out and scared as the both of us.

AUSLAN WAS STILL DOWN HERE ALONE. ACCORDING TO HIM, NO ONE HAD COME to solitary since I'd left; no one had seen him.

He was out of food. A good thing I'd brought a generous amount.

The last surviving Consort nodded in silent gratitude as I tucked more bags of rations and two pairs of clean, black, boot stockings through the bars. He looked down, realized what the latter were, and cracked a smile.

"Thank you, Red Sister."

"Call me that again, and I'll box your ears."

He gulped and tried not to smile. "What shall I call you?"

"Just my name, Auslan."

"As you wish, Sirana."

I watched him pull on a pair of the stockings; they reached his knees. He still wore his waist wrap, but otherwise had only the grey cloak I'd given him to cover up. For as long as he'd been scantily clad, expected to flaunt his body before, he seemed modest now.

I motioned that we sit on the ground and lean close, my voice kept low, testing my first limits of the new geas. "The Valsharess is sending me to the Surface as Penance for losing a Sister to the Ornilleth."

Stunned only that first moment, Auslan acknowledged my news with a nod. The dread and dismay were clear, a normal response. But I didn't see the confusion I'd expected from this sheltered bua who couldn't read.

Fuck my shit …

"Shyntre's taught you," I said, taking the bars into my hands. "You know what this means."

"Davrin mention the Surface now and then."

"But he's been there to see it. Twice."

The Consort didn't respond.

"I don't have much time, Auslan," I said. "We leave within the cycle."

"Who are 'we?' "

"Gaelan, Jael, and me. Elder Rausery is getting ready now, and this is my only down time. Talk to me. Tell me why you aren't more surprised."

His gaze rested on me, but not my eyes, tracing me as though some distracting insect was fluttering around my head and shoulders. He smiled with a warmth I couldn't know existed, until now.

"I can see my brother's aura within yours, Sirana. He embraced you at last, and you accepted him."

"What the fuck are you talking about?" I demanded, my shoulders hunching as I squeezed the iron in my grip. "You can tell we fucked?"

He nodded, unperturbed. "I imagine the Valsharess could see this as well. Shyntre made the choice I saw in my dream. And now, so must She. As the Game has been between them for a long time."

I shook my head, ignoring what I'd heard my Queen say about him. It was too frightening, still. "Shyntre is Elder D'Shea's son. He's barely more than two hundred! Even the Headmaster acknowledged that."

Auslan shrugged and didn't respond.

"What was your dream?" I asked instead. "What happened? What did you see or hear?"

He shook his head. Mute.

"Yes, Auslan. Tell me. Now."

The damned trophy smiled again. At least he didn't laugh. What was I going to do to him at this point? My head still ached from linking with Gaelan, and I was too afraid to wear the pendant when I came down here; it was back in my pouch.

"At least describe where you stood," I said. "What was around you?"

"Why?"

"Was it like a dry lake of red sediment," I blurted, "impossibly big, with an enormous, blue space above holding the Sun?"

He jumped in surprise. Blinked those wide eyes.

Arrrgh, fuuuck it all …

"How long have you seen this in Reverie, Sirana?"

"Only after I found *you!*" I barked, frustration roiling inside. "Never before then. And there's no better punishment any Matron could have come up with for poaching a Consort who wasn't mine! Here it is, turns later, I have these bad Reveries, I *still* caught by you, and now the Queen's noticed me to send me away this cycle!"

Auslan watched me in silence, careful to look neutral. "She knows you carry?"

"Yes!"

"But you are not to be imprisoned in the Sanctuary to give birth first?"

My rant stopped as if I'd tripped and plunged into cold water. I stared at him.

"What is so urgent on the Surface that there is no time for you to carry and deliver down here?" he asked, looking hopeful. "Are you meant to return at all?"

My throat closed painfully on my answer. I couldn't tell him if I wanted to. He watched whatever he saw in my aura, frowned in concern, and did not ask again.

I kneeled there, silenced again, infuriated, and helpless to know I had to leave my first sire down here and not know what became of him. I couldn't tell him where I was going, when or if I'd return. The Valsharess hadn't said if I was expected to return pregnant, or if I would miscarry in the attempt, if doing so was part of my Penance, or if I might only return *after* the birth.

Giving birth on the Surface. What would I do?

The Queen had Commanded only that I must return to face the threat at Her side. The Ornilleth who would learn about us.

And come for Sivaraus.

Watch for signs in your Reverie ...

Nowhere I could hide from Her.

I released the bars, reached for his hands. Auslan offered them to me, and I took them. I attempted a desperate whisper, close enough to the truth in that moment. "Stay alive, and I will come back to you. My Elder can find another place for you. She told me."

Auslan smiled wryly, acknowledging the quaint wish. For one who appeared as a floating fantasy, my first sire was grounded in his present reality. He wasn't ungrateful for my having made the promise, though; he nodded to accept it.

"I can do nothing else but wait. And I shall, Sirana."

That had to be enough. I glanced down at my gloved hands encompassing his naked ones; that *wasn't* good enough.

I let go, slipped off my gloves to leave them in my lap, and reached out again, touched the smooth skin and soft fingers. I pulled them closer to the bars and caught his scent beneath my nose, rubbing my thumbs along the backs of his hands before sliding up to touch his wrists and his forearms.

I smiled as he shivered, his eyes closing, naked pleasure overcoming the worry and wariness. I lingered, memorizing that face. "Do you remember much of the healing ritual? Or were you in a trance?"

He opened his eyes, warm and limpid. "I remember every moment."

My face heated up. *Great.*

"I don't," I murmured, "but I remember some."

He nodded, lowering his eyes. "You may recall more when you have healed."

"You did that."

"I mended a broken body and offered you another," he said soberly. "The rest of the healing is yours, Sirana, and will be within reach."

"Well." I hesitated. "Maybe then I'll hope for some nicer dreams."

He smiled more than I expected. "Perhaps they will be."

I turned my ear toward the hall then, worried I'd heard the scrape of boots near the exit. "I should go. Don't reject my Elder when she comes. She will protect you."

Another nod.

"Kiss me, Auslan."

He obeyed. Doing this through the bars wasn't quite as enjoyable as rolling unfettered in a soft bed, but we took what we could get.

Even a little tongue.

"You can't leave the Cloister, Jael," Gaelan grumbled irritably on her own pallet, "but you can go sleep anywhere in it."

"I'm sleeping here. I'm not getting rest anywhere else, and I fucking need it."

"Then stop pacing. Lie down before I toss a web pellet at you to keep you still."

Jael flashed her a rude gesture, finished stripping down, and came toward me. She slid between me and the wall, lying on her back and covering her eyes with her forearm. To my surprise, she said nothing more and seemed ready to try and be still.

Neither had asked me about being down in solitary. I let the quiet stretch a little longer, and when Jael said nothing in response, I shrugged and tried to sleep.

At some point in our Reverie, I awoke long enough to be aware of Gaelan joining us. It was a tight fit, Jael behind me and Gaelan in front.

As the latter snuggled her naked bottom against my pubic fur, I slipped my arm around her and held her, aware for the first time that my hand covered her womb. She relaxed quickly, and we drifted back asleep.

I woke up again sweating and trapped between my Sisters, Jael clinging to my back with her breasts pressed to me, her legs entwined with mine, and I still spooned Gaelan. My back was stiff, and my hips and shoulders hurt. A lot.

"Oh, fuck. Ow. Alright, you two, up, awake! Fuck, ow. Time to get washed and eat."

They both groaned. Determinedly, I peeled myself up and out like deboning a fish, stretching to ease the ache and stepping to nudge each in her buttock with my bare toes.

"Come on. The General could call at any time."

Be calm and ready, she had said. So, we tried not to think but to act.

WE NEEDED ELDER RAUSERY'S EXPERTISE WITH THE SPEED OF THE PREPARATION, the crash introduction to unique tools and supplies we would take. There was no debate about the choices.

Gaelan was given a black uniform the same as Jael and me; the red one would make us too noticeable to the Surface dwellers "among the green" and "during the day." So strange to realize Rausery would be wearing a different uniform as well, more gray, muted brown, and mottled, customized from her turns of experience and multiple trips topside.

The Elder General also found a moment to take me aside and offer me a tough, waterproof pouch. I accepted it but waited for more information.

Rausery smirked. "From Shyntre. For you, he said. Not to be divided."

Frowning, I looked inside. Thirty or so tiny pellets, each about the size of my fingernail. "He told you what these are, I hope?"

"Decades ago. He's made them before, but these are fresh. Very handy for a half-turn trek in unfamiliar territory when you can't replenish supplies or carry thirty vials on your belt."

"Oh?"

"Think of it like a dried potion bound into an edible mudball. Tastes about as good." She smirked. "You put one beneath your tongue and let it dissolve."

"What do they do?"

"Different sort of healing potion. These aren't effective on acute injuries; they work too slow. But if you feel fevered or have an open wound turning bad, these help that. You don't need more than one a day while you're feeling ill, and often one is all it takes." She grinned. "At least you know you won't bite the stone because of a festered rodent bite, eh?"

Or due to an early-pregnancy weakness I don't know about yet.

I stared at the little brown things, and Rausery waited for a response. I was speechless.

"He wants you to come back, you know," she said quietly. "He couldn't leave the Tower same as you couldn't leave the Cloister. He's trying to help."

More heat bloomed in my chest. "I-I know, Elder. I do. Thank you. I wish I could —"

Rausery grinned. "I gave him your gratitude in advance."

I kept my eyes down while my whirling thoughts settled, using the time it took to find a new place on my belt for the small, dark pouch. "Will Gaelan and Jael get any of these?"

Rausery shrugged her broad shoulders. "Only if you share. That's up to you, or you can keep them all for when you really need them."

I pursed my lips, nodding. I would have to think about it.

"Go see D'Shea, now. She asked to speak with you before we left."

"Yes, Elder."

The Elder Sorceress was as efficient as her peer. D'Shea called me back to her quarters for privacy and got straight to her point when we got there.

"Hold out your hand, palm up."

I did as she said, although part of me was wary whether she was about to try something last moment to defy the Valsharess and select a different fate for me.

Elder D'Shea placed a larger, softer pouch in my palm with a quiet whisper that I didn't understand. The drawstring loosened by itself, and the mouth of the pouch lay open.

Something inside moved.

"Uh —"

"Be still."

Tentatively, three black spiders crawled out and made themselves comfortable on my black bracers, invisible in candlelight except when a leg twitched. I stared at them, feeling no threat at all.

When D'Shea didn't speak first, I asked, "Are these the spiders that killed Wilsira?"

"Yes," my Elder said, crossing her arms and maintaining control of her emotion. "They are enchanted to protect you, so with you they shall go. They know who their new mistress is."

I swallowed, considering the idea of having living creatures on my belt. Tiny beings which depended on me not to forget their welfare, which I had to tend and keep alive.

The parallel to a possible future wasn't lost on me.

"How do I care for them?" I asked.

"They are not web spinners but hunter-stalkers. They will eat in the pouch if you find insects for them every few cycles, or you can let them out to hunt for themselves. They won't go far from you, and you will be warned if someone sneaks up on you."

She paused. "This is a permanent transfer, Sirana. They shall defend you until they die and will always seek to return to you if they live. Tended properly, they may live for another turn."

I stared. Guardians to watch me while I rested? Again, speechless.

"They can be crushed like any spider," the Sorceress continued, "but they have a great jumping distance for their size and are quick, their venom enhanced. You saw its effects. A mage concentrating on magic might sense them but not passively. These spiders are aware enough to know their purpose, but that is all."

I watched the crouching creatures again. "How do I direct them?"

"They respond to your aura already, and I think your mental gift is sufficient, though you may have to practice. Try a mental push. Simple commands, no more."

I still wasn't wearing my pendant, though I was taking it with me. I hadn't told her about the head pain coming back, much worse than before, but she saw my reluctance regardless. Maybe she remembered something from just before Wilsira was bitten, the last time I tried with her.

Eyes narrowing, she shrugged as if to toss a doubt away. "You can always manually place them where they need to be."

I nodded. "What if they make a mistake, or I do, and bite someone I don't want them to?"

The Sorceress had expected that. "I'll provide you the antivenom, but the tool to deliver it is delicate. If you break it, it will be useless. Instead, I would caution against making mistakes at all."

"Yes, Elder." I paused before accepting. "Thank you."

"I have one more resource I would offer you as well, Sirana."

I waited, watching as she tensely uncrossed her arms, stepping to a cubby in her wall. It took multiple steps for her to undo all the wards and remove a plain, locked chest.

Even more heavily guarded than her hefty Feldeu.

The Sorceress opened it with deliberation, took a slow breath as if she was somehow afraid of what she was about to show me. She plucked out a vial sealed in wax, with a trailing black cord tied into a distinctive arrangement of knots. It did not look like any other vial on my belt.

"Everything has happened very quickly. We have not had opportunity to talk all your options, but ... if you had a choice, whether to continue on your mission in your condition, what would you choose this cycle? And what might you choose as the pressures change?"

"I don't ... understand, Elder."

D'Shea spent the time to secure her box again, joining me with the waxed and knotted bottle. "I am being realistic, Sirana. Depending on who you meet upon the Surface, which enemies you may face, you might find yourself in a position where your best option to live is to induce a miscarriage at a time chosen *by you*. If you choose not to take it, that will be yours to own, but I offer you the option. Better to have it and not need it than the other way around, wouldn't you agree?"

"Mages of death and decay have encroached upon it in the turns since," my Queen murmured. *"The crossroads are fouled by machinations of the Hells attempting to usurp them."*

Death mages, the apparent opposite of my Consort's fertile talents, and the Hells, whatever that was. I knew precious little about either of them; I depended on what Rausery could tell me during our acclimation to the Surface.

I accepted the tiny bottle, choosing a place on my full belt close to the poisons. I *did* feel better having the option. *Only if necessary to return to Sivaraus.*

I must. In this, I had no choice.

"Thank you, Elder." I glanced at the potion box again. "Shyntre said he was never allowed to learn how to make a preventative draught. I imagine he could not make an abortive one, either."

D'Shea arched an eyebrow. "Correct. No male wizard is, except the Headmaster."

"How many sorceresses?"

"A few specialists. I'm surprised you haven't heard of them as a Noble."

She paused to read my face, and I let her. I hadn't heard anything.

"Hm. Matrons and First Daughters alone may test their ability to catch with any bua they choose without being forced to make *that* one their living Heir. A few merchants are granted status by the Queen to fulfill this need, if properly documented and witnessed. It's highly controlled."

My mouth sagged. "Why ... do you have these, then?"

The last Sorceress of her House lowered her chin, holding my eyes in an intense stare. "Prevention is better, Sirana. Always. In the few times it has failed since my son was born, a Sister in need makes her own choice. As you have. Remember that."

I swallowed, my stomach turning cold. D'Shea could be executed for this. I didn't even have to ask; the warning was there in her eyes.

"I ... understand, Elder."

She gestured smartly toward the door. "You are dismissed from my service, Sirana. Take up with Rausery, and I shall await your return. Go. I have plenty to do now while she is gone. Do not delay the inevitable."

"Yes, Elder."

CHAPTER 31

WE RODE MOUNTS TO REACH ONE OF THE HIDDEN JUMP CIRCLES FAR OUT FROM Sivaraus. The lizards allowed more options for crossing the difficult terrains, so long as we clung or otherwise secured ourselves to their backs, they would pass through the circle with us to approach the Surface.

They wouldn't be continuing there, nor would they be returning to our stables.

Rausery kept our tongues silent and the pace punishing as we moved through the Deepearth wilderness, skirting the known territories when we could. We reached the circle without undue attention, and our Elder removed a sizeable ruby from her belt. Presumably, it contained the spellcraft to power such a large amount of mass through folded space: four Davrin and four mounts, with our gear.

I wondered idly if Shyntre had created it. No doubt Rausery would only require a smaller gem on her way back.

That same feeling assailed me in the larger jump circle as it did the smaller ones: the wash of nausea and of the bottom dropping out of my stomach before I knew I stood in a place I'd never been.

The first thing to strike was the sense of distance. We were not within the same press of stone, containing the same thrum near where I'd been born. The air was cooler, the moisture denser in the unmoving air, and the lichen and other underground growth all new varieties. New scents.

I could not sense the deep pulse of my home anymore.

Sometimes the passageways became small enough that we rode single file, lucky to be able to do that. The stone and the Radiants covering it showed me heat dissipating faster than it absorbed more from the core of the world. It would not be long before I might consider it cold, and I was very glad to have my cloak. What water sources we found were chilled as well.

Idle chatter was not allowed on the four-cycle trek at the forced pace, and we didn't stay in any one place long enough to be found. We listened, watched our backs and above us especially. I observed Rausery in all aspects, trying to glean as much as I could for the trek back, Gaelan and Jael attempting the same.

With our Elder's experience and escort, we had very few encounters on our way up. Those we did have were dealt with quickly.

Our anxiety increased as we neared the natural gateway out of the underground, when Rausery signed that we were within a half-cycle of reaching it. It did not help that the pulse of home had been undetectable for a while or that it had become chilled enough that the thought of removing clothing even to wash was something to make us hesitate.

My Sister and I did not recognize the lichen or the mushrooms by this point. There was a "lightness" about the rock — not in appearance but in density — that implied the dripstone, flowstone, and other soft minerals quickly worn away were the norm here.

This created fantastic caverns of sculptures that made our jaws drop open as we listened to more running water trickling and dribbling in continuous echo. How raw it was, unlike far below where even in the wilderness were frequent signs of denizens of the Deepearth.

A No-One land.

No intelligent creatures lived here with the tools to form it, yet we were so close to the Surface now.

Did this mean the Surface dwellers did not consider it worth exploring? Or were they afraid? What motivated them to come down here, given Jaunda had encountered them on her last trek?

Pay attention! Rausery flung at me, making sure Gaelan and Jael watched as well. *The last steps are the most dangerous.*

Yes, so she'd said.

According to Rausery and the few others who kept track, we would be on the tail-end of the "winter" season right now, and many creatures would still be in their dens waiting for the season to finish changing.

Our Elder chose our point to abandon our mounts. We removed all tack so that they might find their own way unhindered and continued by foot with heavy packs on our backs. We paid full attention to those very last steps.

The three of us jumped the first time we heard the deep whistling and moaning above. It sounded like a Dragon sleeping and breathing in large, extended draws, yet was too sustained to be true breath.

It was *loud*.

Rausery grimaced at our nervous stances and signed yet another lesson summary.

Wind moving through the tunnels. Don't wait for it to stop. Remember, your eyes and ears will be constantly assailed. Never still on the Surface, rarely quiet, and you will find no silence of the kind you may crave. Your options are noise or less noise, light or dimmer light. Learn to distinguish louder sound, do not waste time detecting it first.

We signed our understanding.

We crept carefully through the rough tunnels, Rausery sniffing for "bear," or anything close to our size in the form of oil and musk. We found only the smaller, four-legged and furry creatures trying to hide from the weather.

These creatures were numbed by the excessive sound; it took more noise for them to hear us, and sometimes we had to do it deliberately before they skittered away.

The first clear sound I heard of the Surface before seeing it was a constant *pat-pat* like the drop of water landing onto dry stone but multiplied more than a thousand times. It simulated the low, Abyssal drone I'd heard in the Sanctuary but without the bass threat.

This sound seemed immensely large, but …

Neutral.

Constant, but fading into ambient noise in its time.

Right now, it was all I could hear.

Rausery didn't speak or sign as she led us up some steep inclines closer to the noise. I followed behind her, then Gaelan, then Jael. I kept expecting to see light at the end of the tunnel, impossibly bright and cutting into the smallest part of the underground like a blade.

Eventually I realized that we had climbed up higher than the emergence point and were climbing back down. The purpose showed immediately: we would not be giving another creature the "high ground" advantage.

This part of the tunnel was not natural, but rather the only part magically hewn to accept an unnatural upward bend. Not formed by Dwarven tools or creatures' claws; I could believe it might have been one of our mages.

No wonder Jaunda was able to spy on those Surfacers getting closer to her gear
...

No bright light shone down below as we approached the open gateway, but my eyes detected light nonetheless. It grew stronger but was still grey and diffuse, a soft and strange kind of light that helped my sensitive eyes see every crease and curve in the stone.

Not a torch, and it *couldn't* be Sunlight.

Or the Surface is nothing like my dreams.

The wind entered the tunnel in gusts, blowing up and rustling our cloaks, carrying many foreign scents to us all at once. I smelled water, sodden dirt, and stone, but others I wasn't sure I could even describe them.

One smelled of acrid, vast distance; the other, growing things, but unlike anything in the fields of our plantations.

The air opened like the lid being lifted off a stone chest. The constant patter grew ever larger in my imagination, extending to a bending horizon because I couldn't picture where it stopped.

My heart skipped its beat, and I sensed reaction in my Sisters behind me as well.

Rausery kept moving, albeit cautiously, signaling us back to wait while she approached and inspected the exit. She touched the stone lightly as she looked up and around in every direction before looking.

Then she stepped onto the Surface.

We tensed to lose sight of her, but she quickly stepped back in. Many droplets of water had coated her hood and cloak in that brief time.

A waterfall … ?

She smiled at us, signaling us to approach.

I'd prepared myself for pain the first time looking upon the Surface world, but that had been anticipating the Sun.

The Sky above was grey and lumpy. I could see neither stars nor either of the Moons, though their light still filtered through, enough that I was not using my Dark Sight to see that the sky contained a layer of clouds releasing innumerable drops of water.

At last, I understood that I'd been listening to "rain," and that we had reached our goal during the Night.

The Sun hasn't traveled around from the other side of the world yet.

The rain was loudest as we stood in the mouth of the cave; my ears wanted to differentiate every drop, but they were too many. In relation to the land, we were high up in a rise of stone I knew to be a mountain, overlooking the forest I'd been told to expect.

All those trees were dark but clear in their enormous shape and numerous branches, both needled and bare. They were what I'd smelled as the growing things, a spice that promised the potential for nourishment, although it was not a spice I yet knew.

The individual trees stretched on until I did lose sight of them and could no longer make out the detail. I marveled.

It's true. As Shyntre said, we are high enough to see the Surface curve away.

I understood only then how exposed I felt beneath that enormous Sky. The urge to shrink back into the comfort of the cave was intense. I clenched one fist, rejecting it, and looked at Rausery.

She was watching us, her arms crossed. Simply waiting.

My eyes turned back out toward the expanse of new land. My ears were stuffed with sound, my nose and mouth full of new tastes and scents upon an unfettered wind, pushing mist toward us like at the base of a waterfall. Cool air on my cheeks, far more air movement than I'd known possible, to further understand that it would never stop entirely.

My skin would always be aware.

I lifted my hands to slowly tug off one glove, glancing at Rausery. She didn't move; there was no expression in her dark eyes. I exposed my hand and stepped forward as she had, lifting it palm-up to let some of the water land there.

It was cold.

As my cupped palm collected enough drops, I brought the Sky-water to my lips without it ever having touched stone. Clean, and this was where I tasted the vastness which I had been smelling.

The droplets had cut through the Sky, gathered up the very essence of the Air, and brought it down to the earth. I couldn't describe the distance I tasted any better than that.

I stepped out a little farther and felt those drops land loudly on my hood, pat after pat. Lifting my gaze up, the air and cold rain touched my face. It was shocking, but in a good way. I'd never felt the like, fascinated, even knowing it would work against me to become soaked through and chilled.

I stepped back into the shelter of the portal before I could become too wet. My Sisters were signing to Rausery, and I'd missed the start.

★ — do we do first?★

Our Elder and guide smiled a familiar smile. I dared believe she anticipated some of her favorite things in the world.

Seeing it gave me confidence.

★We wait for the rain to move on and for the Sun to reappear. Then, you will see.★

I emerge from the Deepearth for the first time, blinded by searing light. Vast lands beyond my comprehension await me.

I must face them pregnant and alone.

Read Surfacing: Sister Seekers Book 4 now!

Thank you for reading about Sirana and the Davrin Elves of the deep! Help others to find the dark fantasy they want and leave a review for Book 3 on Goodreads, Bookbub, or your favorite retail site!

Sister Seekers is an adult epic fantasy with an ever-broadening scope. Found family is a core theme throughout. Perfect for fans of entwined plots, challenging themes, immersive worldbuilding, and elements of erotic horror. Sexuality and inner conflict play into character growth with nuance, intrigue, action, and magic.

[Follow Etaski and Subscribe to her newsletter at her website]

Do you enjoy fantasy maps, timelines, and glossaries? Do you love to read extra tidbits about the characters and places in the story?

[Be sure to visit Etaski's series lore at World Anvil!]

Read the next book in the Sister Seekers: Surfacing

My Sisters and I have been compelled to take missions in this uncharted wilderness. By order of our Queen and the abyssal power which backs Her, we cannot refuse. For the slimmest chance of success, we must move beyond each other's reach with little knowledge to aid us. The Valsharess predicted we would never see each other again.

When a sisterhood has no demons but each other, what are we to this new land once we've been split apart?

Etaski's fantasy world breaks wide open in *Surfacing*, as the Sister Seekers epic rises to the next level. Beneath the unforgiving sun, webs dissolve into dreams, and scattered shards of dark history wait to be picked up and pieced together.

ACKNOWLEDGMENTS

My immense gratitude for the generous feedback, sharp eyes, and egg-plants for this Third Act!

Eris Adderly, Gerrit, Ile Depak, Leonard, Axelotl, NecrosisBob, Gazukull, and, always, Hubs!

A Very Special Thank You to these supporting patrons. Your generosity allows me to continue.

Sir Cumference, Baelus, Dark Pulse, DocKangey, RainbowNight, Stacy & Roy Meyer, Richard Laney, Emil; Brianna R., Mehrphy; John K.; Katie Lily; Cittran; Does; Dreya K.; Jager; Josanna; Rachel C.; Lexanii; John S.; Jonathan H.; Paul M.; Devodebo; Phillip G.; Nigel; Julie S.; Jack K.; Charles H.; David; Matthew S.; Jonathan M; Alienated, & 3Phayz.

ABOUT THE AUTHOR

Etaski has entertained herself with fantasy stories since the first day she sat on a school bus looking out the window. When hand-written letters were disappearing, she wrote no less than five pages to be worth the postage. Her early stories were written by hand, and she had a writer's callus and three embarrassing novels before graduating high school.

She studied a broad range of topics; science, archaeology and history, as well as theater. Frank discussion of sexuality was rare growing up, so she wrote fantasies, theories and observations within stories, inviting the reader either to contemplate deeper or just be entertained.

History rarely speaks on sexuality, yet biology demonstrates how it sways basic choices. Drama reveals our strongest bonds but may still fade to black. In the Sister Seekers, the sex and the story are inseparable, and their discoveries will change the story of Miurag without cutting away.

Etaski's Website: etaski.com
Etaski's Book Page: etaski.com/sister-seekers
Etaski's Series Lore: miurag.etaski.com
Etaski on Patreon: www.patreon.com/etaski
Etaski on GoodReads: www.goodreads.com/etaski
Etaski on BookBub: www.bookbub.com/authors/a-s-etaski
Etaski on Facebook: www.facebook.com/asetaski
Etaski on Mastodon: mastodon.online/@etaski